OSAMA

Also by Chris Ryan

Non-fiction
The One That Got Away
Chris Ryan's SAS Fitness Book
Chris Ryan's Ultimate Survival Guide
Fight to Win

Fiction
Stand By, Stand By
Zero Option
The Kremlin Device
Tenth Man Down
Hit List
The Watchman
Land of Fire
Greed
The Increment
Blackout
Ultimate Weapon
Strike Back
Firefight
Who Dares Wins
The Kill Zone
Killing for the Company

Chris Ryan Extreme: Hard Target
Mission 1: Redeemer
Mission 2: The Rock
Mission 3: Die Trying
Mission 4: Fallout

Chris Ryan Extreme: Night Strike
Mission 1: Avenger
Mission 2: Armed and Dangerous
Mission 3: The Enemy
Mission 4: Lone Wolf

Chris Ryan Extreme: Most Wanted
Mission 1: Protector
Mission 2: The Specialist
Mission 3: Hard to Kill
Mission 4: The Feared

CHRIS RYAN

OSAMA

CORONET

First published in Great Britain in 2012 by Coronet
An imprint of Hodder & Stoughton
An Hachette UK company

First published in paperback in 2013

1

Copyright © Chris Ryan 2012

A CIP catalogue record for this title is available from the British Library

ISBN 9781444706468
Export ISBN 9781444741421

Printed and bound by Clays Ltd, St Ives plc

Hodder & Stoughton policy is to use papers that are natural, renewable and recyclable products and made from wood grown in sustainable forests. The logging and manufacturing processes are expected to conform to the environmental regulations of the country of origin.

Hodder & Stoughton Ltd
338 Euston Road
London NW1 3BH

www.hodder.co.uk

'When the decision to assassinate has been reached, the tactics of the operation must be planned, based upon an estimate of the situation similar to that used in military operations.'
From declassified CIA manual 'A Study of Assassination'

'We will kill bin Laden. We will crush Al-Qaeda.'
Barack Obama, 7 October 2008

ONE

The White House Situation Room, Washington DC, USA. 1 May 2011, 1430 hours EST.
So this is what people look like, thinks Todd Greene, when they are about to witness a death.

The official photographer to the President of the United States takes his third picture in as many minutes. It is of a plain, narrow room with a long mahogany table, crammed full of laptops and polystyrene coffee cups. Thirteen men and two women are fixated by a screen on the wall at one end of the room. Some stand, their hands covering their worried mouths, their foreheads creased. Others sit: the President in the corner, his white shirt dotted with sweat stains, the Vice President to his right and his chief military adviser, General Herb Sagan, to his left. Unlike those of the President, the VP and most of the others in the room, Sagan's clothes are immaculate. He wears a blue uniform, its lapel emblazoned with line upon line of medal flashes and decorations that Todd does not recognize. He thinks Sagan has the face of a man whose career will be defined by what happens in the next sixty minutes, 3000 miles away in a small town in Pakistan named Abbottabad.

The screen itself shows a dark image. It is the inside of a stealth-configured H-60 Black Hawk, specially designed to reduce radar splash, a dish-shaped cover over the rotors and with an infra-red suppression finish. This is top-secret stealth capability, Sagan has briefed everyone in the room. It will allow the aircraft to enter

Pakistani airspace undetected. The juddering visual feed is from the helmet camera of a US Navy SEAL. For now, the sound is turned down low. There's nothing to hear, other than the dull grind of the chopper circling in dark Afghan skies.

The VP speaks. 'That guy on screen. What the hell does he have written on his armband?'

Sagan blinks at the politician he so clearly loathes. 'His blood group, Mr Vice President, sir.'

The VP nods, embarrassed. 'I see,' he mutters.

Sagan interrupts. 'Mr President, respectfully, DEVGRU are ready to enter Pakistani airspace. They need your authorization to continue . . .'

The President looks around the room. Nervous eyes look back at him.

His own eyes fall to documents on the table. Todd knows what they are: aerial maps of a compound in Abbottabad, taken from high altitude by a stealth drone. One of these grey, bat-winged spy planes is hovering over that faraway town right now, controlled from an operations base in the Nevada Desert. And next to the aerial maps is a photograph of a high-walled compound, taken three months ago by a plainclothes CIA operative. A hazy grey image of a man whose daily habit is to walk up and down outside the house within the compound walls. Despite everything – their surveillance from the air and from the ground, and their covert attempts to gather DNA samples from the occupants of the compound – it has been impossible to make a positive identification of the man. The agents involved simply refer to him as 'the Pacer'.

But the Pacer's strolling days are numbered.

'You just need to give me the go order, sir . . .' Sagan is polite, but tense. Perhaps even a little exasperated.

'The back-up team?' the President asks.

'Three Chinooks,' Sagan confirms. 'Twenty-four men. They're on-line by the Indus River, Mr President, ten minutes' flight time from target Geronimo. That's in addition to the attack team in the Black Hawks.'

'We have surveillance on the compound? We're sure of no unusual activity?'

'Affirmative, Mr President.'

'And our British cousins?'

'Securing the Doctor and his family, Mr President. The Pakistanis won't know what we've been doing in Abbottabad so long as we keep the Doctor out of the hands of the authorities. The British have instructions to maintain the cordon and stay out of the compound.'

He looks back up to the screen. Through the helmet-cam footage, Todd sees the face of one of the SEALs staring back, almost as though he is listening and waiting to hear the President speak. Half his face is in shadow. Moonlight, flooding in from one side of the Black Hawk, lights up the other half, revealing goggles propped up on the helmet and a boom mike beside his mouth.

The President gives a slow but distinct nod.

Sagan wastes no time. He lifts his lapel and addresses an unseen colleague via the microphone pinned to his uniform.

'This is Sagan. I have a go order from the President. Start the clock on Operation Geronimo. Repeat, start the clock on Operation Geronimo. Confirmation code Charlie Alpha Niner.'

He turns back to his commander in chief.

'We'll know within the hour, Mr President,' he says.

Abbottabad, Pakistan. 0030 hours.

'I'm telling you, brudder: if he doesn't stop squealing, I'm gonna frickin' do him.'

Joe Mansfield looked over his shoulder. In the shadows five metres behind him, tied to a rickety wooden chair and with several layers of packing tape stuck over his mouth and eyes, was a thin, terrified Pakistani man. He was the owner of this small

3

house. Nobody important. Just in the wrong place at the wrong time. His body was shaking and the sound escaping his taped mouth was high-pitched. He shifted in his chair and its legs made a scraping sound against the wooden floor. Standing between Joe and the prisoner was Joe's best mate Ricky Singh. Ricky had murder in his eyes.

'Take it easy, big guy,' Joe said. 'No rounds if we don't have to.'

Ricky was a couple of inches shorter than Joe, but broader about the shoulders and torso. Second-generation Indian, with an accent that was more Leicester than Lahore, he was the only currently serving member of the Regiment who could blend into the background in Pakistan without darkening his skin. Useful back in the Stan, where they'd spent the past three months erasing insurgents from the badlands where the green army wouldn't set foot; and it made him a shoo-in for a job like this. His hair was shoulder-length, and like Joe – like all SF personnel currently operating in this part of the world – he wore a full beard. Ricky called everyone in the Regiment 'brudder', like he had the biggest family in the world.

'I've got my blade,' he muttered. But he walked back to the OP. Their captive fell silent – maybe he realized his noises were making Ricky feel like doing something about them – while Joe continued to scan the area outside.

They were holed up on the first floor of a very basic building. The room – which they had reached by means of a rickety wooden staircase that emerged from a ground floor that housed nothing but an unflushed toilet and an old bicycle – was about six metres by four, and almost bare. There was one window, slung open. As soon as darkness had fallen, Joe and Ricky had fixed up a three-metre length of net curtain from the bottom of the window to the ceiling, at an angle of forty-five degrees. This would hide movement inside the room from anyone looking in. Joe had cut a rectangular hole, the size of a letterbox, in the centre of the netting, and erected a tripod behind it. He had three sets of optics to fit on the tripod: a pair of high-powered Canon binoculars, a Spyglass thermal-imaging device and a night sight.

The rest of the room was a lot less hi-tech. The ceiling, bowed and cracked, looked as if it might collapse at any moment. There was a mattress in one corner, covered by a single, dirty sheet and the two sets of robes Joe and Ricky had been wearing over their gear. A ceramic hookah stood next to it. On the opposite wall, hanging at a slight angle, was a yellowed, grease-spotted piece of parchment with some Arabic script – something from the Koran, probably. Beneath it was a small cooking area with a tiny stove. The place stank in the heat – a musty smell of decay mixed with the spicy aroma of whatever the occupant had last eaten, its remnants still in a battered saucepan on the stove. The air buzzed with the sound of a single fly, as it had done all day. All in all, it was a dump. But a dump that had one advantage, even though its owner didn't realize it. Outside the window was a single-tracked road. Beyond that, the five-metre-high walls of an enclosed compound.

And in the compound, if the Yanks were right, the slippery fucker who'd evaded capture ever since 9/11. In the endless briefings that had preceded this op, the CIA operatives had insisted on calling him 'Geronimo', or 'the Pacer', or even by one of his Arabic nicknames, if they were feeling cocksure and sarcastic: 'the Director', 'the Lion', 'the Sheikh al-Mujahid'.

The rest of the world, of course, knew him by his real name.

Joe, Ricky and the rest of their eight-man unit had been in Abbottabad for twenty-one hours, but they'd been studying the imagery of the town and its surrounding areas for a week before that at their base in Bagram, over the border in Afghanistan. Twenty-four hours previously, a Chinook had lifted them over the mountains and in-country, along with a battered white utility van with Pakistani plates and a tape deck full of shite

Arabic music. Their operational movements were covert even to the regular members of the Regiment. Joe, Ricky and the others were part of a specialist cell from the newly formed E Squadron – the highest-vetted and best trained the SAS had to offer, and even among E Squadron the expertise of these eight men in the field of covert surveillance had no equal.

The American SF flight crew that had put them on the ground in Pakistan at 0100 hours didn't know what they were up to either. Fuck-ups aside, nobody would ever know they were here. No acknowledgements. No back-slaps. That suited them just fine. The Yanks needed men on the ground to pull this thing off, and they needed the best, even if they did intend to write them out of history at the end of the day. And of course, as far as Joe was concerned, there was more to it than that. There always was. If they were compromised and the op went to shit before it had even begun, it could be spun as a British cluster-fuck, not an American one.

Ricky had driven the van cross-country to Abbottabad, every inch the Pakistani peasant, down to the stench of farm animals on his rough clothes. The rest of them had been secreted in the back, hidden behind a false panel that guys from the REME had welded on in case of a stop and search. But nobody stopped and nobody searched. By 0300 they had hit the north–south N35 Mankerai Road, just another vehicle entering the surprisingly busy little town.

There had been no need for them to speak when the van came to a halt, the engine cut out and Ricky tapped three times on the back of the cab to indicate that they'd reached their destination. They'd emerged silently into a dark, breeze-block garage alongside a shit-encrusted farm vehicle, before leaving in pairs at irregular intervals to get themselves into position.

The first two to leave, their weapons hidden under their robes, had been Raz and JJ. After Ricky, JJ was Joe's closest Regiment mucker – a sarky, tough little Glaswegian whose house in the wilds of the countryside round Berwick-upon-Tweed had been the location of Joe's holidays with his family for the past five years. JJ and Raz had drawn the short straw, but you wouldn't have known it from their steely demeanours. By now they'd have spent almost twenty-four hours on the far edge of a field abutting the compound, dug into an irrigation ditch, covered with mud, shit and foliage. Watching and waiting, they were invisible even to any locals who might wander within a couple of metres of their stinking hideout. Stevie and Rhys had been next, hiding out in a disused outbuilding at the western end of the single-track road on which the compound stood. Joe and Ricky had followed, waking up their reluctant host with the suppressed butt of an M4 and a roll of packing tape. That left Diz and Jacko to go and babysit 'the Doctor' and his family.

In Joe's opinion, the Doctor was the weak link in the chain. The photograph of him that Joe had studied was burned into his brain: a thin man with a goatee beard, a protruding Adam's apple and round, steel-rimmed glasses. The Doctor was a long-time resident of Abbottabad who had been dishing out free vaccinations to the population over the past several months. The jabs were just a cover. Every time the Doctor administered a vaccination, he took a swab of the patient's cheek. Routine, he'd told them – failing to mention that each of these hundreds of swabs eventually made their way to some lab in North America where the DNA on it was analysed. Nobody seriously expected Geronimo himself to take advantage of the medicine on offer; but if he had family members around him, there was a chance of some of their DNA making it onto one of the swabs and giving the CIA confirmation of their suspicions.

The confirmation had never turned up. Maybe this meant that the occupants of the compound were too cute for the CIA's ruse. But there was a small possibility that the Doctor was not all he seemed to be, and that possibility had increased over the past hour. Jacko's voice over the comms had been tense.

'I'm with the missus. She expected him back at 1100 hours. He's a no-show.'

'You sure she doesn't know where he is?'

'Roger that.' Of course Jacko was sure. He'd used all his powers of persuasion to find out.

Their instructions were clear. If tonight's operation was successful – and even if it wasn't – they were to evacuate the Doctor and his family. But if there was any evidence of him trying to send word to the compound of what was going down, their orders were more straightforward: take the fucker out.

Evacuate or execute. Difficult to do either, if nobody knew where the hell he was.

Silence. Joe checked his watch. 0037. Ricky was standing three metres to his left. His M4 was slung across his front and Joe was almost certain he saw his mate's left hand tremble.

No, that couldn't be right.

'We should have frickin' heard by now,' Ricky said.

Joe returned his attention to the optics. He felt sweat trickle down his back, and his mouth was dry. He scanned the five-metre-high wall that surrounded the compound at a distance of ten metres from the house. Running alongside the wall was a single-track road, stony and baked hard. There was only one entrance to the compound: a pair of heavy metal gates in that wall, twenty-five metres south-west of Joe's position. From this location, he could see anyone approaching the compound's entrance, from either east or west.

But so far there was nobody.

And no word from base that the operation had begun. Maybe it was a no-go. Wouldn't be the first time they'd . . .

A crackling sound in his earpiece. He found himself holding his breath.

Nothing. For a few seconds, he thought it was just interference. Then, a voice.

'Sierra Foxtrot Five, this is Zero. Operation Geronimo is go. Repeat, Operation Geronimo is go.'

Joe and Ricky exchanged a look, before Joe twice tapped the pressel on the comms unit strapped to his ops vest, wordlessly acknowledging this latest communication.

They knew what it meant.

The still night air was about to be broken.

War on terror?

Damn right.

1433 hours EST.

'We've breached Pakistani airspace, Mr President. ETA twenty-seven minutes.'

The President looks across the table. For a moment, Todd thinks he's looking at him, but then he realizes he's turned his attention to the small, jowly man in an elegant brown suit who is sitting just behind Todd and to his left. He has blond hair that is neatly parted to one side, and horn-rimmed glasses. Whereas most of the other men in the room have either loosened or removed their ties, this man still wears a neatly tied dicky bow. Todd knows that his name is Mason Delaney, but doesn't know his title, or even if he has one. He's high up in the complicated hierarchy of the CIA, however, and he's sitting behind the photographer because he doesn't want his face to be recorded on any official photograph. During his time in this job, Todd has learned that there are certain men and woman who do not consider photographers to be their friends, even though the looks Delaney has given him before now are enough to make Todd believe the rumours that he prefers the company of young men.

For the first time since they all filed into this room, the President manages something like a smile.

'Feeling confident, Mason?' he asks.

'I feel eighty-seven per cent confident, Mr President.' Delaney's voice is high-pitched and nasal. Almost girly. Todd notices Sagan's face darken as he speaks. This military man clearly has very little time for such an effete individual, and when Delaney catches Sagan's expression he widens his eyes provocatively. 'What is *your* estimate of success, Herb?'

Sagan's annoyance visibly increases. But this operation is Mason Delaney's baby, and everybody in the room knows it. He takes a deep breath and appears to calm himself.

'ETA twenty-six minutes, Mr President,' he says. 'Twenty-six minutes and counting.'

Abbottabad. 0053 hours.

Joe had eyes on the two metal security gates that formed the compound's only entrance. Distance, twenty-five metres to the south-west, across the single-track road.

'Anything?' Ricky sounded as tense as Joe felt.

'Fuck all,' he murmured. Through the grainy-green view of his night sight, he had seen the occasional flashing eyes of a wild dog, or the bright light of a commercial flight drifting overhead. In his mind he pictured the bat-winged shape of the RQ170 stealth drone he knew was circling up there too, its camera trained directly on the 3500 square metres of the compound. An impressive piece of kit, sure, but not a substitute for men on the ground alert to the arrival of a lookout with an anxious expression, or the frown of a guard in a state of heightened awareness. Joe saw neither. He didn't doubt that the compound was guarded, but the guards were well hidden behind its high walls. At the moment, the exterior was deserted.

Jesus, it was hot. Joe's skin was soaked. There wasn't even the hint of a breeze, but the sound of traffic from the centre of Abbottabad, just under a kilometre away, still drifted towards them. Like everyone else, Joe had always assumed that their target would be holed up in some remote village on the Afghanistan–Pakistan border, or living in a cave with a heavily armed entourage. He'd even heard rumours that the guy was in

Africa, living under the protection of some scumbag warlord. The fact that he was here, in pissing distance of the Pakistan Military Academy and right under the nose of the Pakistani government, had been as much of a surprise to him as he knew it would be to the world at large when it learned that the Americans had finally caught up with him.

If the Americans finally caught up with him. The rabbit wasn't in the bag yet.

'You think he's in there?' Ricky breathed in the darkness.

Joe kept the night sight to his eyes. It could only take a second for somebody to slip in and out of that place, and he didn't intend to miss that if it happened. A bead of sweat dripped down into one eye. He blinked hard, but kept his position. 'The Yanks must be pretty sure.' He half smiled. 'Be a laugh if they send in a squadron to find some farmer banging his wife, though . . .'

He was interrupted by more squeaking from the man bound to the chair. Joe felt himself start. When he looked over his shoulder, his mate was already storming over to their prisoner.

'Ricky . . .'

Ricky was drawing his knife.

'Fucking hell, mate! What's the matter with you?'

No answer. Ricky picked up the roll of packing tape that was lying by the chair, and wrapped even more of it round the man's head, so that now it covered his nose as well as his eyes and mouth. The noise stopped, but now the man clearly couldn't breathe. His body started shaking more violently. Ricky gave it ten seconds, then carefully punctured the tape covering the nostrils with the point of his blade. Just enough for the guy to get some air in his lungs. The loose tape under his nostrils flapped in and out like a fish's gills.

As Ricky walked back to the OP, he didn't meet Joe's eyes. Joe didn't push it.

A minute passed in tense silence.

'Hotter than a hooker's noo-noo,' Ricky muttered finally. 'Flight crews need to be careful.'

He was right. High temperatures like this could thin the air and reduce the lifting capability of a chopper's rotors. No point worrying about that, though. Let the Yanks do their job while Joe and Ricky did theirs: keep the cordon, and if anyone tried to come in or out, deal with them.

Movement.

Joe held up one hand to indicate that he'd seen something. Two figures had just wandered into Joe's field of view. The sound of giggling reached his ears and through the open window he saw a young woman in Western clothes running ahead of a young man. She allowed herself to be caught and pressed up against the high wall of the compound. The giggling became muffled and the man's hands started to wander.

'What is it?' Ricky asked, his voice almost silent.

'Couple of kids. We're on for a live show if Romeo gets his way.'

Joe checked the time: 0059.

'You OK, mucker?' Joe asked quietly, not taking his eyes away from the optics.

'Fine and frickin' dand—'

He stopped mid-sentence and looked towards the window. So did Joe. They could suddenly hear the sound of a couple of choppers.

They were approaching fast. Joe could tell by the way the volume of the rotors increased quickly. He moved his eyes from the night sight and squinted through the net curtain and into the dark sky. At first there was nothing to see – the flight crews would be seeing their way with the aid of night-vision units, all lights on their aircraft extinguished. Twenty seconds later, however, the roar of their engines reached a peak, and Joe could see two great, black silhouettes, one of them hovering twenty metres above the compound, the second thirty metres above that, and maybe ten metres beyond it. In the corner of his vision, he saw the young Pakistani woman wriggle away from her suitor and look up. It crossed Joe's mind that she could be in a lot of trouble if her indiscretions were made public.

Joe bent down at the night sight again and redirected it towards the nearer helicopter. Suddenly the black shadow was converted to green-tinted detail. Joe could instantly tell that he was looking at a modified chopper, one that few people would ever get the chance to see. The familiar shape of the Black Hawk was subtly different. The tail was smoother and more rounded. The nose was sleeker. Joe could tell at a glance that it had been engineered for stealth capability, which meant that the Pakistani authorities wouldn't even suspect its presence here in their back yard.

The door on one side of the Black Hawk was open, and Joe counted six men at the aperture, not including the Minigun operator who had his weapon trained on the compound. He knew there would be another six preparing to drop down from the other side door. He could make out the head cams and goggles fitted to their helmets, the boom mikes to the side of their mouths, the assault rifles strapped to their bodies. Something fell from the chopper – long and snake-like. Joe had travelled in, and fast-roped out of, enough helicopters to realize something was wrong.

'We got a problem,' he said.

Instantly, Ricky was beside him, peering through the netting. 'What's happening?' he demanded tersely.

'Bird's skittering . . .'

As he spoke, the chopper spun through ninety degrees, wobbling. The pilot was obviously struggling to control it in the heat-thinned air, and the fast-rope was spinning with the momentum of the helicopter. Now the Black Hawk was listing alarmingly. It spun back ninety degrees to its original angle, and although he couldn't hear the voices of the SEALs inside over the screaming of the engines, he could see they were shouting at each other as they started to lose height. A couple of seconds later the chopper had lurched ten metres down. Its main body was now hidden from Joe behind the high wall of the compound, but he could just see the tail peeping up above the rim of the wall.

'What's happening?' Ricky shouted.

Joe was about to answer when he heard the noise: an ominous, sharp, crunching sound as the Black Hawk's modified tail caught the top of the wall and a shower of sparks, glowing brightly in his night-vision scope, needled his eyeballs.

'Black Hawk down,' he muttered.

'That's getting to be a frickin' habit . . .'

Joe turned his sight to the second chopper. It too was descending and wobbling as it disappeared behind the compound's wall. Hardly reassuring. The SEALs were supposed to fast-rope into the compound, leaving the choppers to fly away out of earshot so as not to attract unnecessary attention until they were needed to extract. Now they'd both set down inside the compound, and half of Abbottabad must have heard them.

The op was turning pear-shaped before it had even started.

Joe kept eyes on. Stuck in here, he felt about as much use as Anne Frank's drum kit. 'We're going to get a fucking audience any minute,' he muttered. As he spoke, though, he heard a solid clicking sound behind him. He looked round. 'What you doing, big guy?' he asked, his voice dangerously level.

For a moment Ricky didn't answer. He was too busy checking the magazine in his suppressed Sig before replacing it high on his chest rig. 'I'm going in,' he said.

Joe straightened up. 'We're not going anywhere, mucker. We keep the cordon, no matter what happens.'

'Fuck the cordon. They've crashed. They need help.'

'There's two choppers full of SEALs, Ricky. They can take care of themselves.' As he spoke, he edged towards the door, ready to block Ricky's exit.

14

'Get out of the way, brudder.' Ricky's voice was level, but very quiet.

The air vibrated with the roar of the choppers on the ground nearby. The fly that had been buzzing around the stove landed on Ricky's cheek. He didn't seem to notice.

'SOPs, mucker,' Joe breathed. 'The Yanks don't want us in that compound.'

Joe was in front of the door now. Ricky stopped advancing. Standoff.

Ricky scowled. 'Fine,' he said. He turned on his heel, walked back over to the observation post and laid his M4 back on the ground.

Joe joined him. He leaned down over the tripod and looked through the night sight again.

And that was when he saw him.

A man was running along the front wall of the compound. He was keeping close to it and was almost directly in front of the OP, about fifteen metres from their position, across the single-track road. The young couple, who were looking alarmed, were in front of him. He just skirted them, without appearing to acknowledge them, and continued along the wall, clearly uninterested in what they were up to. He was evidently intent on getting to the compound entrance, just twenty metres away.

Joe's eyes were sharp, but it was difficult to make out his features exactly. He was dressed like a local, though – white *dishdash*, sandals – and he had round spectacles and a goatee.

'Shit,' Joe hissed.

'What?'

But Joe was already speaking into his comms. 'Jacko,' he barked. 'Is the Doctor home yet?'

'Negative,' Jacko replied tersely, his voice masked with distortion. 'Why?'

'I think we've found him,' Joe replied. He was already moving towards the door.

'You sure it's him?' Ricky demanded. 'Where did he come from?'

Joe *wasn't* sure. Maybe if he hadn't been keeping Ricky on the straight and fucking narrow, he'd have seen the man arrive, got a better look. But whether it was the Doctor or not, if he was approaching the main entrance of the compound with the aim of reinforcing its occupants or helping them in any way, he had to be stopped.

They were at the top of the rickety set of wooden stairs, the stench of the ground-floor toilet wafting up towards them and no trace of their previous argument in their voices. They needed to get to ground level, because to fire from their OP would immediately give away its location. Seconds later they were hurtling towards the front door. Opening it, Joe stepped out into the darkness beyond, his M4 fully engaged. Ricky was with him.

Joe took in the situation at a glance. The Doctor – if it *was* the Doctor – was fifteen metres away, at Joe's two o'clock. The courting couple had separated. The boy was edging away eastwards along the perimeter wall. Distance, twenty metres, eleven o'clock. He'd left the girl crouching on the ground, yelling her head off at the sight of two men with weapons. They were both in the wrong place at the wrong time: Joe and Ricky couldn't let Romeo go off and alert anyone to their presence. Same went for Juliet.

'Take them out,' he instructed Ricky, and turned his attention back to the new arrival.

The guy was seventeen metres away now. Eighteen.

A single head shot would put him down, but Joe made the split-second decision to aim for the body. If this *was* the Doctor, they needed to identify him, and it was hard to identify a body with only half a head.

He fired. The suppressed M4 made a dull knocking noise and the man went down.

To his left he heard the discharge of Ricky's weapon as he fired on Romeo.

Joe kept his own target in his sight, checking for movement. After five seconds, though, the girl was still screaming. He looked to the left. Ricky had his weapon pointed at Juliet, who was still crouched on the ground ten metres away, to their twelve o'clock. The red dot of his laser marker danced on her throat.

But Ricky didn't fire. His hand was shaking again.

'Fuck's sake!' Joe hissed. He turned his own weapon in the girl's direction. The red dot from his gun joined Ricky's.

One round. A flash of blood and the girl fell backwards.

There was no time for Joe to lay into Ricky for his moment of indecision. An explosion from inside the compound ripped through the air. Both men pressed themselves against the exterior wall of the house. Joe engaged his comms. 'Zero,' he shouted, 'this is Sierra Foxtrot Five. What the hell's going on in there?'

A crackle of interference, then a voice. 'Entry team breaching the internal walls to reach target Geronimo. Hold the cordon. Repeat, hold the cordon.'

'Roger that.'

Joe immediately consulted his mental map of the compound. It was triangular in shape. The main building, situated opposite the triangle's apex, was connected to the main entrance gates by a pair of high interior walls that formed a thirty-metre-long, open-topped passageway. The Black Hawk had crashed in the western segment of the compound, where, intelligence reports suggested, the occupants burned their rubbish. The explosion must have been the SEALs breaking their way through the walls of the roofless corridor that led from the entrance gates – the same gates Joe's target had been trying to reach. The man had fallen into a ditch along the bottom of the compound wall eighteen metres from Joe's position and to his two o'clock. Joe needed to get over there, identify him and finish him off if necessary.

'Cover me,' he said.

Ricky nodded, dropped to one knee and pressed the butt of his M4 into his shoulder, ready to provide covering fire should Joe need it.

Joe ran. The distance between the house and the enemy wall was ten metres, but he had to run double that on the diagonal in a south-westerly direction to reach the man. He'd gone down barely a couple of metres from the security gates. He was clutching with one hand the wound Joe had inflicted on the side of his right leg. It was pissing blood through his fingers, and the man was shaking violently. Joe flicked on the Maglite attached to the body of his M4. It lit up the alarmed, sweating face of the wounded man, whose *dishdash* was soaked with blood.

Joe saw immediately that he was *not* the Doctor. He was about twenty years too young.

He was also feeling for a weapon with his spare hand.

He didn't get very far.

The barrel of Joe's cylindrical silencer was no more than six inches from the target's head when he fired. The round made as much noise entering the man's skull as it did leaving the weapon. Blood spattered over the pale rendered wall of the compound as the shooter slumped back into the ditch, his face no longer a face. But Joe's attention was already elsewhere. There was a second explosion from inside the compound – louder than the first, or maybe Joe was just nearer. He turned to look at the main gates. He was standing just two metres from them. They were metal, about five metres high – the same height as the wall – and each a couple of metres wide. A thick roll of barbed wire covered the top. They hummed and vibrated on account of the mechanism inside.

And they were opening.

A figure emerged – just a shadow in the darkness.

SEAL or enemy? Impossible to tell, but if it was the second, they couldn't be allowed to breach the cordon and fetch reinforcements.

Joe held his fire for a briefest of moments. The figure hurried out into the moonlight. It was a man. Tall. Thin. He wore a dirty white smock and his bearded face was full of wild, sweaty panic. He was clearly not an American, and he was clearly trying to escape. Which meant he was dead.

Joe fired once more. The suppressed round, hardly audible above the sound of the raid, entered the man's right eye, blasting a chunk from that side of his head. He dropped immediately. As his body fell against it, the gate boomed like an oil drum and creaked open a few more inches.

Joe sensed movement over his shoulder. He turned quickly. A figure was approaching, halfway between his position and the observation house. He was only a fraction of a second short of dropping him when he realized it was Ricky. Joe cursed. What the *fuck* was wrong with him? Couldn't he follow the simplest SOP – stay where he was and cover his mate?

Ricky had his personal weapon engaged and was alternating the direction of its aim – first one way along the track, then the other – with every step he took.

Joe no longer heard the roar of the choppers in the compound. He just saw Ricky, and now that he was only five metres away, he could see the sweat on his brow.

Ricky said nothing. He strode past Joe, stepped over the dead body and disappeared into the darkness beyond the partially open gate. Three seconds later the corpse slid into the compound as Ricky dragged him back inside. What the hell was he doing?

Joe felt the acrid taste of bile rising in the back of his throat. Ricky was about to fuck things up good and proper. He cursed under his breath and scanned the area. There was no sign of any movement along the road. Inside the compound, the air was filled with the roar of the choppers.

He had to make a decision. Ricky was alone in there. If one thing had been drilled into him from the very first minute of his

19

very first selection weekend, it was this: never try to do anything by yourself. Either he was with his mate, or he was against him. Put like that, the decision was made for him.

Joe stepped over the threshold and pulled the gates shut. They closed with a rattling clang, then he became aware of the sounds of battle: the choppers turning and burning and the occasional burst of precise, targeted gunfire.

His first thought was for Ricky. Joe could make out his silent silhouette five metres ahead, weapon in the firing position as he hugged the left-hand wall. They were standing in the shadows, but he could just make out Ricky's eyes as his mate looked at him over his shoulder.

They were in a corridor open to the sky, some three metres wide and lined by two five-metre-tall walls. Twenty metres ahead, Joe could see where the SEALs had blasted through these walls: there was a cloud of smoke and dust, illuminated by a beam from the right that he assumed emanated from the downed Black Hawk. Silhouetted figures passed from right to left, obscured by the dust. He counted six men. Seven. He saw the outline of a sniffer dog, then another two human forms. Nobody was heading towards them. They were moving swiftly into position from the LZ to the compound's accommodation area.

The thunder of the Black Hawks' rotors took on a different quality – a slightly higher pitch. The undamaged chopper was rising. Then it appeared above the right-hand wall, huge and threatening, and continued to rise until it was about fifteen metres in the air. Looking up, Joe could see that the Yanks had decided, now that everything had gone noisy, to use the helicopter as a weapons platform. He could see a door-gunner aiming a Minigun down into the compound, plus three other soldiers with their assault rifles pointing downwards. The guys in the Black Hawk showed no sign of being able to see him or Ricky. If he could just persuade his mate to get back to the entrance . . .

The dust was settling up ahead. Peering in the darkness, Joe could make out two piles of rubble, each a good couple of metres high, by the blast site. There were no longer any SEALs moving towards the house. He could hear evidence of their activity, though. There were screams: not the constant, blood-curdling screams of a massacre, but the occasional shouts of women and children, obviously very frightened. And, punctuating the screams, the dull knock of suppressed weapons. Joe counted them. One. Two. Three. The clinical sound of individuals being deliberately picked off. There were more people screaming than being shot, which meant the SEALs were being selective. They knew who they were after. But even though the Yanks might not be greasing everyone, Joe knew exactly what he would do in their shoes if he unexpectedly came across two men as heavily armed as him and Ricky.

'We're surplus to fucking requirements, mucker,' Joe whispered. 'Let's get the hell out . . .'

Ricky's only response was to go on another five metres. He was halfway towards the rubble now, and still advancing. Joe ran after him.

A shout from the other side of the wall. An American voice, clearly a SEAL commander, instructing two of his men: 'Guard the main entrance. No one enters, no one leaves.'

Joe froze.

He looked back towards the gate. Fifteen metres. To get there, re-open the gates and extract? Fifteen seconds. Too long. But the piles of rubble were only five metres away. The light shining from the choppers through the gap in the wall meant the vision of anyone passing through there would be compromised.

He could sense Ricky making the same calculations.

They sprinted towards the rubble. A rectangular block of concrete – about two metres long by a metre high and with a crack running its entire height – was resting at forty-five degrees against what remained of the left-hand wall, with other chunks of debris littered around it. Joe wormed his way into the gap, fully aware that Ricky, with his back against a metre-high boulder of concrete alongside the wall on the right, was less well hidden.

They'd found cover just in time.

Two SEALs ran from the courtyard into the corridor, heading for the security gates. Joe didn't move. His mouth was filled with the dry taste of dust, and the sharp edge of the concrete was digging into his right arm. Through a foot-wide crack in the otherwise undamaged part of the wall, he could see into the central courtyard. It was about twenty metres by twenty. The main house – two storeys with a two-metre-high privacy wall around the first-floor balcony – showed no signs of occupation. The lights were off, the windows shut.

Joe counted six SEALs in the courtyard, the nearest of them about twelve metres away, kneeling down in the firing position, their weapons trained on the house. They all had thick beards like his, and were wearing JPCs in the latest Crye Precision multicam. This was the same get-up Joe and Ricky would have been wearing if they hadn't been in civvies, with the exception of the small Velcro patch on the Americans' body armour bearing the stars and stripes insignia.

Lying on the ground, no more than four metres from Joe's position, was a dead body, clearly an enemy combatant. He was wearing underpants and a vest, and had taken a round to the chest – the vest was dark and saturated. The corpse's head was twisted so that it was looking almost directly at Joe.

A flash of phosphorescent light filled one of the windows, followed by a sharp crack.

Another scream, almost lost under the thunder of the choppers.

The retort of a rifle. It sounded like it came from the first floor of the house.

And, stuck in that cramped, uncomfortable space, barely

daring to breathe and cursing his friend for getting them into this situation, Joe Mansfield couldn't help wondering if that was the gunshot the world had been waiting for.

The White House Situation Room. 1510 hours EST.
'What the hell's happening?'

The National Security Adviser is the first to ask the question Todd sees on everyone's face. The room has been silent for ten minutes, its occupants' eyes fixed on the screen.

Only there's nothing to see. Just darkness. The occasional shadow. Every minute or so, the picture crackles – a reminder that these images are being transmitted halfway around the world. It's quiet as well as dark. The occasional shout, a barked instruction, the sharp rapping of a firearm. There's no way the watchers can know whether this is American fire or enemy fire.

Todd senses movement behind him. He looks over his shoulder and sees Mason Delaney pull a silk handkerchief from his top pocket. He dabs a bead of perspiration from the area of his forehead just under his parting, before neatly replacing the handkerchief. When he sees that Todd has been watching him, he gives the photographer a little smile. 'We should sell this footage on a DVD in Wal-Mart, Mr President,' he announces in his piping voice. 'Pay off the deficit.' Delaney smiles. Nobody else does.

There's movement. The head-cam footage on the screen judders as the soldier whose view is being transmitted to the White House runs along a short, dark corridor, two other SEALs in front of him. The corridor ends in a flight of stairs, which they start to mount. They are halfway up when Sagan stands. He has one hand to his ear and an expression of concentration – or is it alarm? Todd wonders – as he listens to his information feed.

Suddenly all eyes are no longer on the screen, but on Sagan.

Sagan's eyes widen. A smile spreads across his face. 'Geronimo EKIA . . . enemy killed in action . . .' He turns to look at his commander in chief. 'We got him, Mr President. We got the son of a bitch.'

A few seconds of silence. The President closes his eyes. His face visibly relaxes as he kicks back in his chair and punches his palm in a gesture of triumph. It's as if the whole room has exhaled after minutes of holding its collective breath.

A quiet buzz of excited conversation. The President shakes hands with his deputy, before inclining his head appreciatively at Mason Delaney at the other end of the table. When Todd looks back at Delaney, he is put in mind of a cat preening himself. The CIA man's lips glisten with barely suppressed delight and he straightens the bow tie that doesn't need straightening.

The President then turns to congratulate his chief military adviser. But Sagan doesn't appear interested in congratulations. As he sits down at the table again, he urgently directs the President's attention to the footage with a sharp jab of his forefinger.

There is a hallway at the top of the stairs. A number of people are there, kneeling, their backs against a dirty wall and with an armed SEAL standing over them. It's impossible to say how many, because they only appear on the screen for a fraction of a second. Five? Maybe six? They are all women and children, their hands secured behind their backs with cable ties and their mouths covered with packing tape. Their lives are being spared, but not their dignity.

The head cam turns away as its wearer jogs along another corridor, stopping after five metres at an open door to his right.

'This could be ugly, Mr President . . .' murmurs Sagan. But he doesn't suggest that anybody looks away.

The head cam looks into the room. For ten seconds the soldier wearing it is as still as the politicians observing him, as they all stare at the scene it reveals.

It is a bedroom – shabby, untidy. There are two beds – a small double, and what looks like a single camp bed to one side. On the opposite wall there is a window with frayed blue curtains, and along the right-hand side of the room a wardrobe that is little more than a rail holding a collection of white robes. The floor is covered with a patterned rug. The whole place has an air of neglect, as though it is an unloved room in the cheapest and most neglected of temporary accommodation.

But nobody is really looking at the wardrobe or the curtains or the rug. They are looking at the body lying on the double bed.

The face is instantly recognizable, despite the devastating gun wound the man's head has sustained. The gaunt cheeks, the beard flecked with grey and, now, red. His left eye is closed. His right eye is no longer there. It's just a bleeding, gaping abscess, around which a flash of skull is visible. The untidy sheets of the bed itself are saturated with blood in the area around the head. There is spatter elsewhere, and a streak of scarlet on the garish rug.

The women in the Situation Room, and some of the men, avert their eyes. At the same time, the head cam turns to the right. The corner of the room becomes visible. There are two Navy SEALs. They have boom mikes at the edge of their mouths, goggles perched on the top of their helmets and head cams attached to the fronts. They hold their weapons with the light confidence of professionals. But the figure at which they are aiming them is not a threat. It's a little girl. She is wearing a nightgown and is crouched in the corner, her head in her hands, weeping.

'Surely they're not going to—?' says a female voice in the Situation Room.

But Sagan interrupts her. 'His daughter,' he states, having been briefed by his information feed.

Several of the people sitting round the table recoil as one of the SEALs steps towards the girl. He doesn't hurt her, but neither is he gentle. He pulls the kid to her feet and for the first time the occupants of the room see her face. The image might be blurred and scratchy, but the look of terror it conveys is almost as distressing as the grisly vision of the girl's dead father.

'Get the kid out of here,' instructs the second SEAL. His companion drags the girl towards the door. As she passes her father, though, she wriggles free and runs to him, ignoring the bloodied rug she's treading on, and flinging herself at his corpse. She manages to hold on to his thin leg for a fraction of a second before the soldiers pull her away. The head cam steps back and the body disappears from view, to be replaced by the landing once again. The SEALs bind the girl's wrists behind her back and throw her in the direction of the other women and children. She wails as she stumbles to the ground, and shouts something in Arabic. But her distress doesn't seem to affect the soldiers. 'Get him bagged up,' one of them instructs.

'I don't think we need to see any more,' interrupts the President. Sagan nods and presses a switch in front of him. The images disappear from the screen. Silence falls in the room.

Todd raises his camera.

Snap.

Abbottabad, 0130 hours local time.
Joe's heart hammered in his ribcage as he kept watch on the courtyard from the darkness of the pile of rubble. How the hell had they got themselves into this situation? What was going on with Ricky? How was Joe going to get them both out unseen?

Five minutes passed.

There were still six SEALs in the courtyard, kneeling in the firing position, clearly waiting to bring down anybody attempting to flee the building. They didn't flinch when the front door of the house opened and a line of people emerged. They were women and children. Joe counted seven, all of them cuffed and blindfolded. Two SEALs followed, and they directed the captives to the right-hand side of the house before making them lie on the ground face down.

More movement at the doorway. Another two SEALs emerged. They were carrying a body bag, one man at either end. Joe had seen enough body bags in his time for it to be an unremarkable sight. Somehow, though, he couldn't keep his eyes off this one. He knew he was watching the SEALs extract the corpse of the most wanted man in the world.

The two SEALs were about five metres out of the house when he saw yet more movement at the doorway. Another two appeared, carrying a second body bag. Both pairs of soldiers were moving with grim purpose across the courtyard. They stepped over the underwear-clad corpse four metres from Joe's position, each body bag scraping over the dead man's bloodied vest as the SEALs carried them past the pile of rubble – less than a metre from Joe's position – through the demolished walls of the open-topped corridor and into the rubbish-burning area that doubled as an LZ.

The movement of the body bags was like a signal. US troops spilled out of the house. Two men were carrying crates – Joe assumed that these contained materials they were confiscating from the compound – and they were preceded by a tracker dog whose silhouette Joe had already seen. Joe recognized it immediately as a Malinois, a variety of Belgian shepherd – intelligent and highly aggressive – that the Regiment's own dog handlers used as both sniffer and attack dogs. It was wearing a harness that suggested the troops had been intending to winch it down to the ground from the chopper, and had a small IR camera, the size and shape of a Smarties tube, fixed to its side. It scampered ahead of them, clearly unfazed by the noise and stopping only when it came to the dead body near Joe, which it sniffed, paying particular attention to the area around the bullet wound.

The dog looked up. With a sensation like cold ice sliding down his spine, Joe realized the animal was looking in his direction. It tilted its head and scampered over the body. Two seconds later it was inches from Joe's hiding place, its wet nose worming its way into the crack in the wall. He could smell the rank stench of its breath.

The dog sniffed.

A low growl escaped its throat.

Joe's hand moved slowly to the holster on his chest rig, his fingertips feeling for the Sig.

A harsh voice. American. 'Cairo! Cairo!'

Joe saw a hand grab the dog's collar and pull it away. Its handler came into view. The SEAL looked young, most likely no more than twenty. He had a lean face and pronounced cheekbones, but there was a small scar on his upper lip, which looked slightly out of shape – a harelip that had been fixed surgically, Joe reckoned. The soldier pulled Cairo out of Joe's field of view, which meant he could see the whole courtyard again.

The six SEALs were standing but kept their weapons trained on the house while another eight soldiers started to extract, as did the two who were guarding the main security gate. Thirty seconds later the final six hurried from the courtyard. Joe could hear the undamaged Black Hawk returning to the ground, ready to lift them out.

Joe was drenched in sweat, and not just because of the heat. He remained absolutely still for thirty seconds after the last SEAL had passed by him. Only then did he creep out of his OP. Ricky was still hidden, fully obscured by the darkness, his back up against the concrete slab behind which he had secreted himself. Joe edged towards the opposite side of the corridor, and peered round the damaged wall. He squinted as the choppers' lights blinded him, but he was able to make out the second of the two body bags being loaded into the unharmed Black Hawk. Three SEALs were running from the compromised chopper to the intact one; ten seconds later the LZ was deserted and the frequency of the helicopter's engines became a little higher as it prepared to take off.

Joe's stomach knotted. They were abandoning the second

chopper. He knew what that meant. To leave a military asset on enemy territory was a no-no at the best of times. And when the asset in question was a stealth chopper, and the enemy was Al-Qaeda . . .

'It's going to blow, brudder.'

Ricky was standing half a metre behind him.

Joe grabbed his arm. 'Fucking run . . .'

The two men were ten metres from the main gates through which they'd entered the compound when the undamaged chopper rose above the walls again; and they were only two metres away from the gates, alongside the body of the man Joe had killed outside the compound and which Ricky had dragged inside, when the explosions came: a succession of short, sharp detonations, followed by a single, much larger one that made the walls shake and threw Joe to the ground. He jumped up immediately to see Ricky already throwing himself at the gates, knocking up the latch with his M4 just as a shower of dust and shrapnel started to rain down all around them. They hurled themselves out of the compound as a twisted chunk of what was once a helicopter slammed into the meat of the fresh corpse; then both men covered their heads and ran across the narrow dirt road, out of range of the debris that was still showering down.

'What the hell?' Joe almost screamed.

But Ricky was looking back towards the compound. A bright orange glow was emanating from inside the walls where the downed chopper was burning. The second Black Hawk was already thirty metres in the air, and swerving in their direction. It thundered overhead and headed north-west, into the distance.

Ricky was refusing to catch Joe's eye. 'Let's get back,' he said tersely.

Without a word, they ran thirty metres back east along the road to their original OP, where the owner of the house was still tied up on the first floor, trying to breathe slowly as his body shook with fear. It didn't take more than a minute for them to gather their things – the tripod and the optics – and don their robes once more. Ricky was heading for the door again; Joe had stopped stock still.

The two friends stared at each other.

'What?' Ricky demanded.

Joe didn't answer. He strode over to their captive and ripped the tape from his nose, though he left him blindfolded, silenced and bound. Only then did he follow Ricky to the doorway.

'You're out of control, mucker.'

Five seconds of silence.

'What's that supposed to mean?' Ricky retorted, his chin jutting aggressively. 'You gonna go squealing to the frickin' ruperts?' But his friend knew how insulting that suggestion was: Joe sneered at him.

'Let's get out of here,' Joe said. He pushed past Ricky and started running down the stairs. By the time they hit the street again, the Black Hawk had long disappeared into the night sky, but now there was the sound of alarmed citizens shouting from an easterly direction – from the centre of Abbottabad. Joe was confident he and Ricky looked enough like locals, especially in the darkness, not to attract any attention, especially when there was so much else for the townsfolk to ogle back at the compound. But that was no reason to lower his guard: he kept one hand firmly on the handle of his Sig as they made their way back into the town, keeping in the shadows, to RV with the rest of the unit.

And Joe's mind was turning over. What had Ricky been trying to prove? It happened sometimes that a guy lost his nerve and tried to make up for it by putting himself in danger. But Ricky didn't seem the type.

Something else was troubling Joe too. Something he had seen. Why had the SEALs removed two bodies from the compound?

Target Geronimo was one thing – he understood that they couldn't just leave his corpse where it lay – but what reason could they have to remove another stiff? It occurred to him that maybe they had nailed a kid and needed to remove the body to avoid a PR disaster, but in his heart he knew that the body in the bag had been too large for a child. Maybe it was a significant AQ commander? But who? Who else was sufficiently important that the Americans would want him removed along with the Pacer?

Joe tried to clear his head. No doubt he'd find out in time, but for now he had other things to worry about. There was still work to do and this was dangerous territory. Osama bin Laden might be dead, but the blood was still pumping through Joe's veins. He had to remain focused if he wanted it to stay that way.

TWO

Pembrokeshire, Wales, UK. The following morning, 0830 hours.

Mrs Bethan Jones had only been out of bed for an hour, but at her time of life an hour could feel like a day. The very business of dressing herself and making her way downstairs was enough to exhaust her. She had lost count of the number of well-meaning doctors who had tried to persuade her to move out of her remote, cavernous, draughty house and into a retirement home. Or: 'Isn't there a relative who might help you out, Mrs Jones? A friend?' But there were no relatives, apart from a distant cousin of her late husband, Gethin, who'd had her eyes on the house ever since he'd died nigh on twenty years ago now. No friends either, not any more – unless you counted her pale gold cat, Dandelion. And Bethan Jones would rather die than spend the rest of her days dribbling in a home. Anybody who suggested it was given short shrift.

Dandelion was curled up over her feet. Bethan was glad of the extra warmth. Her feet were ulcerated, and she found it too painful even to put on a pair of slippers. She'd been warned by the health visitor who made the journey out here every two weeks – even though it was several miles out of her catchment area – that she really ought not let Dandelion anywhere near the suppurating sores on her feet. The moulted cat hairs had a habit of getting stuck to the skin, causing infection. But there was no way Bethan would ever banish her cat. If Dandelion was comfortable where he was, that was good enough for her.

Although it was a large house, Bethan as good as lived in this one room. Twice a day she would totter out to the kitchen to fill Dandelion's bowl with food and her own glass with an inch of Bell's and water that was practically her only sustenance; come nightfall, she would strap herself into her stairlift and go up to bed. But the rest of the time was spent in here. It was the biggest room in the old house, about eight metres square, with a large, stone fireplace that hadn't seen a fire since the day before Gethin passed on. Instead, an electric heater sat in the fireplace, both bars on.

Bethan's eyes flickered over to the window. The panes were misted with grime and the frames rotting on account of the salty wind. It was raining outside, but that was no surprise. It had rained all winter and showed no signs of stopping now that spring had arrived. She pulled her floral housecoat more tightly around her and turned her attention back to the television. It was on full volume – Bethan was more than a little deaf. It was also positioned just two metres from the sofa as her eyesight really wasn't what it used to be.

For the third time that morning, she listened to the news bulletin – to the only story that the shiny breakfast TV reporters had any interest in today. 'Osama bin Laden, the Al-Qaeda leader and mastermind behind the September 11th attacks, is dead. He was shot in the early hours of this morning by US special forces, who raided his compound in the Pakistani town of Abbottabad. His body has already been buried at sea, in accordance with Muslim practice . . .'

Bethan peered more closely at the television. A familiar picture of bin Laden, one finger raised up in the air, filled the screen. She felt a sour look cross her face. 'Such a wicked man, Dandelion,' she said out loud. On the bookshelf behind the television there was a photo of Gethin, staring out fiercely, with his splendid lamb-chop sideburns. 'He always said so,' she continued talking to her cat. '"You mark my words, Bethan lass," he used to say. "Those Arabs, they'll be more trouble than the blacks before long. Rivers of blood, lass, rivers of blood . . ." He knew what he was talking about, did my Gethin.'

She had been sitting in exactly this seat ten years previously, watching the 9/11 attacks unfold on TV, and she had recalled Gethin's foresight on that day too. Dandelion had been a kitten then, not the elderly clump of fur he had now become. The cat miaowed lazily as the TV cut to footage of the US President announcing bin Laden's death to the world, but suddenly Bethan's attention was diverted. Dandelion had cut short his miaow and jumped up onto her lap, and she could see something else on the television screen. Her own reflection stared dimly back at her in the glass, but she could also see the reflection of a second person. A tall man, standing behind the sofa. Thin. Dark skin. Dark hair. A slight stoop to his lanky shoulders.

Bethan started and fumbled for the remote control, causing Dandelion to jump down to the floor as she located the mute button. Silence filled the room – a silence that was almost as oppressive as the noise it had replaced – and Bethan realized that she was flushed, that her heart was beating hard.

'I do hope I didn't alarm you, Mrs Jones,' said a quiet voice behind her.

It was an effort for Bethan to turn round, and she winced trying to do so. Immediately she felt light fingers on her shoulders.

'Please, Mrs Jones,' said the voice. 'Don't move on my account. I only popped in to say goodbye.'

'Oh, Mr Ashe, I'm afraid I didn't hear you . . .'

'I did knock, Mrs Jones.' The figure was walking round the side of the sofa.

'Oh, I'm sure you did, Mr Ashe, I'm sure you did. My hearing's not quite what it was, you know, and I was just catching up with the news . . .'

34

Mr Ashe smiled. Only now did Bethan see that he was carrying a mug.

'I've brought you a cup of hot Ribena, Mrs Jones. There was no milk for tea.'

'Oh, bless you, Mr Ashe,' she said as he placed the cup on a small table by the sofa intended for just that purpose. She patted the seat next to her, indicating that he should sit down, which he did. Dandelion immediately jumped onto Mr Ashe's lap, where he curled up contentedly and purred as his ears were scratched by his long, well-manicured fingers.

'They've caught that dreadful man.'

'So I understand, Mrs Jones.'

'I'm sorry, Mr Ashe? I'm a little hard of hearing, as you know.'

'I under—'

'Really, I don't know how it's taken them so long.'

'So long, Mrs Jones?'

'To catch him, Mr Ashe.'

Mr Ashe gave a little shrug, as if to indicate that this was, for him too, a profound mystery. For the next two minutes they sat in silence, watching the mute pictures on the screen: the bland white compound in Pakistan, now surrounded by a collection of armed police, reporters and ordinary onlookers. Flashing sirens. Curious locals.

A thought suddenly struck Mrs Jones. 'You're not from . . . ?'

'Saudi Arabia,' said Mr Ashe gently.

Bethan nodded, pretending this meant something to her, but in truth one of these countries was the same as another to her. 'Of course,' she said. 'Saudi Arabia, yes. Of course, I'm not saying all of you are . . . But I don't care what anybody says, Mr Ashe, the world's a better place without him.'

'Safer,' Mr Ashe agreed. 'I wouldn't wish to bring up children in a world where—'

'I was never blessed, Mr Ashe.' She adopted a look of mild tragedy as she glanced at Gethin's photograph again.

A silence, broken by Mr Ashe clearing his throat politely. Bethan blinked. 'Saying goodbye?' she asked, as it dawned on her what he had said several minutes ago. 'But you've only been here for two days, Mr Ashe. You know how I enjoy your company.' And it was true.

Mr Ashe gave her a regretful little look. 'My time is not my own,' he said. He reached inside his jacket and pulled out a thick wad of notes, bound with a red elastic band. 'My rent,' he said, handing it over, 'for the next six months. Would you like me to put it in the sideboard for you?'

'Thank you, Mr Ashe,' Bethan replied. 'Really, I don't know what I'd do . . .' But she failed to finish what she was saying, silenced by a dismissive wave of his hand as he stood up again – Dandelion jumped to the floor – and walked to the far side of the room, where there stood a large mahogany cabinet. He opened a drawer, slipped the notes inside, and walked back over to the sofa, where Bethan was lifting her Ribena to her lips with hands that trembled gently with old age.

'Is there anything I can do for you before I leave, Mrs Jones? Any little jobs around the house? I can't be sure quite when I'll return . . .'

'Oh, no, Mr Ashe. Really, you've done quite enough . . . You might pop some new batteries in the control for my stairlift . . . I wouldn't want them to run out while you're away. Do you know where they are?'

Mr Ashe smiled and bowed his head before striding out of the room. Such a pleasant man. So helpful. Bethan didn't really hold with foreigners. Couldn't trust them, her Gethin used to say, and he should know after all the trouble they'd given him during the war. But Mr Ashe wasn't like most of them. She had taken to him the moment they met. He was so much nicer than any of her previous lodgers. More like a helpful neighbour for whom nothing was too much trouble. So much so that Bethan actively looked forward to him staying. She felt somehow more secure with a gentleman like that in the house. But he was seldom here, even though he paid for his rent many months in advance, and that saddened her. She cast a slightly guilty look up at Gethin at this thought – how he would have disapproved . . .

'All done, Mrs Jones.' Mr Ashe reappeared by the side of the sofa, from which he picked a single one of Dandelion's pale hairs. 'Would you like me to turn the volume up again for you?'

'Thank you, Mr Ashe,' Bethan said. 'My hearing isn't what it used to be . . .'

And as the volume returned and Mr Ashe took his leave, she took another sip of Ribena, closed her exhausted eyes and allowed the sound of the TV to wash over her as Dandelion snuggled up around her feet once again.

Mr Ashe closed the door of the front room softly behind him. The hallway smelled as neglected as it looked: musty and damp. There were cobwebs thickening over the yellowed plaster cornices, and by the heavy oak door a pile of wellington boots and an antique stand containing old walking sticks. Mr Ashe was quite sure they had not been taken outside for years. On the opposite side of the hallway was a door leading into a dining room that was never used. The flagstones on the hallway floor sucked the warmth from his feet as he walked to the wide wooden staircase. Mrs Jones's stairlift was at the bottom, looking out of place beside the burnished, rather ornate banister. There was no way the old lady could make it upstairs without it, however. Mr Ashe laid the remote control on the seat and made his way upstairs.

Seventeen steps. He had counted them the very first time he came here.

Mr Ashe's room was immediately to the left at the top of the stairs. The door, as always, was shut. He let himself in. It was a large bedroom – the largest in the house, Mrs Jones had told him when she showed him the room, but having examined all the others he knew that was a lie. Or rather a mistake, for he suspected Mrs Jones was past remembering such details. There was a lumpy double bed against the far wall with a patchwork quilt, and an enormous mahogany wardrobe in another. Behind the bed was a window that looked out onto the neglected back garden and, perhaps 200 metres beyond that, the brim of the cliff on which this old house stood, overlooking a grey sea that was only just visible through the rain. Three pictures hung lopsidedly on the wall: two of them were inexpertly painted oils of the imposing house, each from a different perspective, framed in cheap plastic with thick layers of dust and grime along the tops; the third, right next to the window, showed a sailing ship battling through stormy seas.

The floor was littered with big cardboard boxes – about fifteen of them – and taking up the centre of the room was a circular table about two metres in diameter and covered with a crumpled yellow tablecloth. Piled high on this were stacks of papers, files and photographs; books; a chunky Dell computer and what looked like an early mobile phone – boxy and with a six-inch antenna – but which was actually an Iridium satellite phone: Mr Ashe's sole link with the outside world in this remote region where internet connectivity and mobile-phone reception were nothing more than rumours.

Closing the bedroom door behind him, he carefully laid on the table the cat's hair he had pulled from the sofa, before walking over to the wardrobe. His few clothes were hanging next to some long-forgotten garments of Mrs Jones's. He selected a heavy green Barbour raincoat and loosened the hood from its pouch, before returning to the table. Lying on top of the Dell was a book. It was about two-thirds the size of an ordinary paperback, but a good two inches thick, and wrapped in a sturdy leather binding with a push-button fastener. Embossed in gold on the front were the words 'Holy Koran', in both English and Arabic. Mr Ashe picked up the book and slipped it into the inside pocket of his coat.

Then, rummaging around in one of the cardboard boxes, he found a small tube of superglue. He recovered Dandelion's hair, left the room and locked the door: the key he used was newer and shinier than the one Mrs Jones had given him, because the very first thing he had done on moving into his new lodgings had been to change the lock after the old woman had gone to bed. She'd never mentioned that her key no longer worked, but that didn't mean, of course, that she had never tried to get in, or would never try in the future. Half blind and confused, it was unlikely that she would ever understand the significance of anything behind the locked door, but Mr Ashe still didn't want any prying eyes. He squeezed two tiny blobs of superglue, one onto the top of the door, one onto the frame, then carefully fixed the cat's hair to them. It would only take a minute to dry, and nobody would notice it was there if they weren't looking for it. He went downstairs again.

The voice coming from the television was slightly muffled here in the hallway, but it was loud enough for him to make out. 'More details are emerging of the daring raid in Pakistan by US Navy SEALs that has killed Osama bin Laden . . .'

Mr Ashe could not help a brief smile. He pulled the hood of the coat over his head, patted his pocket to check that his Koran was still there, and stepped outside. He made it a rule to drive here as little as possible, and Mrs Jones, of course, had no car. So he walked briskly into the rain, not stopping to look back at the solitary shape of the house standing on that deserted clifftop. His face was dripping wet in seconds; within a minute, the rain had soaked the leather of his inadequate brown shoes. When he had walked the thirty-metre length of the driveway and exited through a pair of rattling iron gates, he turned right onto the road that would lead him, if he continued for another four miles, to the nearest railway station, Thornbridge. Perhaps one of the infrequent country buses would pass him before then, but if not he was prepared to walk.

A crack of thunder ripped the sky overhead. Mrs Jones's house disappeared in the distance. Mr Ashe continued to walk, his shoulders still slightly stooped, his brow furrowed, the lower part of his trousers already sodden, his mind deep in thought.

THREE

'I got to hand it to you, Mason. The President's grinning like a goddamn lunatic – I think he'd do just about anything if you asked him.'

Mason Delaney felt his lips twitching with pleasure as he rested his hands on his neat little paunch. 'Well, there's a thought, Jed,' he replied, his voice as quiet as it always was when he was receiving a compliment and pretending to be modest. His eyes sparkled behind his horn-rimmed glasses. 'You make me sound like the new Monica Lewinsky!'

Delaney giggled. Jed Wallace, the President's Chief of Staff, smiled patiently. It was an expression that didn't suit his hawk-like face. His auburn hair was cropped military fashion and Delaney had no doubt this was a conscious style statement. Wallace ran the show in the West Wing, and he did it with military precision. 'Seriously, Mason, you made a powerful friend yesterday, and one who expects to be around for a while. His approval ratings are through the roof. You just bought him another four years in office.'

'I live to serve, Jed. I live to serve.' Delaney inhaled deeply and, with a pleasant smile, looked around his office. The May sunshine was streaming in through the window, casting its light over his desk and the coffee table in front of the comfortable sofa on which the two men were sitting. He had made this office very much his own, transformed it from the bland, beige box it had once been into a place which, he felt, more accurately represented his character. An antique chaise longue stood along the opposite wall, and on the walls were prints of his favourite Michelangelo sketches. He adored the way the artist caught the male form. Really, he felt he could gaze at them all day.

'Shall we take a look?' Wallace interrupted him politely after a full minute of silence.

Delaney snapped out of his reverie. 'I beg your pardon, Jed?'

'The images. Shall we . . . ?'

'Had enough coffee?' Delaney indicated the china coffee pot and the two full cups on the table.

'Sure.'

'Cookies?'

'No cookies, Mason. Thank you.'

'I only ask, Jed, because I think you might lose your appetite when you see them. If you'd rather not put yourself through it . . .'

'I've finished my coffee, Mason.' Wallace pushed the cup away from him to underline this.

Delaney gave him a bland smile before standing up and shuffling over to his desk, where he picked up a manilla A4 envelope and brought it back to the sofa. He sat down, fixed Wallace with a stare that he knew would make the Chief of Staff uncomfortable, then removed a sheaf of photographs from the envelope.

The photographs were in colour, but they were grainy and occasionally out of focus. The first showed an unmade bed and a large bloodstain on the rug in front of it. The second showed the same thing but from a different angle.

'Mason, none of these show the—'

'Always wanting to fast forward,' interrupted Delaney, 'to the money shot.'

'It's what I'm here to talk about, Mason.'

'Then let's talk, Jed.' Delaney held out a third photo with his arm outstretched so that they could both admire it, much as

Delaney had been admiring the Michelangelos a moment before. It was a close-up of a mangled and bloodied man's face. Even Mason Delaney, who had no use for or knowledge of guns, could clearly identify the entrance wound, just above the right eye: a small dot of dark red, surrounded by an orange sun that had spread across the side of his face, taking out the eye and the upper part of the cheek. The rest of the face, including the grey beard, was spattered with blood. The mouth was open, and the man looked as though he had been gunned down just as he was screaming in terror.

Delaney dropped the photograph onto Wallace's lap before reclining on the sofa with his hands clasped behind his head. The Chief of Staff looked nauseous. 'Of course,' Delaney said, 'you might be of the opinion that the great American public ought to be shown this. On the other hand' – he coughed gently – 'you might decide that publishing such a sight would be a tad inflammatory.'

Jed Wallace appeared unable to take his eyes off the photograph.

Delaney continued to talk, a little quieter again, but his voice still as nasal as ever. 'What is it that that Sagan doesn't like about me, Jed? Is it the way I look? The way I sound? Is it that I wear a Turnbull & Asser dicky bow and not a pair of fucking epaulettes? What peg has the little shit got me hung on, huh?'

'Really, Jed, I don't know what you're—'

'Sagan wants the President to publish, no?'

Wallace looked up from the grim image. 'How did you know that, Mason?'

Delaney removed his glasses, breathed on them and meticulously cleaned both lenses with his handkerchief. 'Here's the deal, Jed,' he said, and all of a sudden his voice was not quite so shrill as usual. 'You put that photograph out to the news wires, it'll be on the front cover of every damn newspaper in the world within twenty-four hours, not to mention the computer screen of everyone with an internet connection in about twenty-four seconds. It's grotesque, Jed. Every last Islamist on the planet will think the President's gloating. DEVGRU went to a lot of trouble to drop the bastard's body in the Indian Ocean to stop his grave becoming a shrine. If you give that picture to the world, you'll be creating a million shrines.' Delaney blinked heavily three times. 'I don't think you should do it, Jed.' He stretched out, lifted his coffee and took a long sip, raising his eyebrows at Wallace over the brim of the cup.

The Chief of Staff turned the photographs over on his lap. 'It's the President's decision, Mason,' he said.

'But of course it is, Jed. Of course it is. And I hope the President knows I'm here to watch his back.' He folded his hands over his paunch again.

Wallace stood up. 'I have to get back to DC. Could I . . . ?' He pointed at the envelope that was still on Delaney's lap.

'Of course.' Delaney stood up and watched as Wallace stowed the photographs first in the envelope and then in his briefcase. 'And Jed?'

'Yes?'

'Enjoy it.'

A pause.

'Enjoy what?'

Delaney gave him a surprised look. 'The victory, Jed. America hasn't been the good guy for a long time, remember? Maybe the President can be persuaded to flex his muscles a bit more now he's had a taste of success. Bin Laden's not our only high-value target, you know? And as my physician never tires of reminding me, prevention is better than cure.'

Wallace looked as though he was in two minds whether to respond. 'Look, Mason,' he said finally. 'I know you think this administration is a bit wet, but times have changed. America can't afford to boss the world around in the same way any more—'

'You start taking any flak,' Delaney interrupted, as though Wallace had said nothing, 'I'll give you what you need. We got DNA samples, we got eyewitness accounts . . . damn, we've even got bin Laden's daughter who was in the same room as him.'

A knock on the door. 'Come!' Delaney called.

The door opened and a young man appeared. He was extremely handsome, with lustrous black hair and well-defined cheekbones. Preppy – like he should be wandering the lawns of Princeton. He stood in the doorway without saying anything, but the anxiety on his face was evident as his eyes flickered between the two men in the office.

'Scott,' Delaney greeted him, blatantly – and lasciviously – eyeing the young man up and down.

'Mr Delaney . . . we, er . . .' Scott Stroman's voice cracked. He cleared his throat again. 'Mr Delaney, I need a word.'

'Mr Wallace was just on his way out, Scott.' Delaney held out a chubby hand, which the Chief of Staff shook. 'So long, Jed,' he said.

Wallace nodded and, without another word, left the room.

Stroman stepped inside, closed the door behind him, then stood with his back to it.

'We've got a problem, Mr Delaney.'

Delaney wandered over towards his desk. 'Go ahead.'

No answer. Delaney stopped and looked back at his young colleague. 'Go ahead, Scott.'

But Stroman shook his head. 'I think you need to come and see for yourself, sir,' he replied, in what was little more than a whisper.

Delaney could see that he meant it. The two men left the room, Delaney locking the door behind him.

The corridors of CIA headquarters were alive with people. They all knew Mason Delaney – he was as much a part of the place as the enormous presidential seal on the floor of the main entrance – and they all knew that today was his day. He lost count of the number of congratulations he received. He did notice too that his colleagues, for once, did not appear to be suppressing knowing smiles at the sight of his pretty male assistant. But as they descended into the basement, the number of passers-by diminished until finally they were walking by themselves along a deserted narrow corridor with pale grey walls. And at the very end of the corridor was a door with a numerical keypad next to it. Scott punched in a number and there was a faint click. He opened the door and they both entered.

It was a small room – no more than five metres by five – and it appeared even more cramped on account of the large quantity of audiovisual equipment it contained, including four daisy-chained screens and two sets of reference speakers. Scott sat at the comfortable chair in front of the screens and pressed a green button. The same silent moving image appeared on all four screens. At first it was dark, blurred and indistinct.

'What is this?' Delaney asked, a hint of impatience in his voice.

'Camera footage from the Black Hawk leaving Abbottabad, sir,' Stroman replied.

And as he spoke, the image started to make sense. Delaney could see the ground receding, and in the top-left corner of the screen he could make out the dark shape of the compromised chopper. The Black Hawk rose higher. Now they could see the high compound walls, and the uncovered corridor that led from the main security gates.

And movement.

'Who's that, Scott?' Delaney asked, his voice dangerously level.

Stroman shot him a glance that said 'This is what I wanted you to see,' and pressed a red button. The image froze. The young man spun a dial and zoomed in on that part of the picture which showed two shadowy figures. Delaney fancied he made out an assault rifle strapped to the body of one of these individuals.

Without waiting for an instruction from his boss, Stroman started the film again. The Black Hawk rose sufficiently for the perimeter of the whole compound to be visible. A shudder, and an explosion of orange light, as the compromised chopper exploded down on the ground. The compound receded from view as the chopper banked; when it straightened up again, Delaney could see that it was outside the perimeter of the compound.

Stroman hit the stop button again. He pointed to the bottom right-hand corner of one of the screens. Two figures again, both crouching and watching the departing chopper. Both holding their faces directly up to the camera. Stroman zoomed in again. The level of magnification caused the faces to appear a little pixellated, but it was still possible to determine their features with some accuracy: the long hair and dark skin of one of them, the full black beards of both; as well as the weapons they were carrying.

'Facial recognition?' Delaney asked.

'I've already run it, sir.' Stroman pressed another button on the console. The image on two of the screens was replaced by a portrait of an Asian-looking man with shoulder-length hair and a thin scar along the left side of his nose where the dark skin was slightly lighter. The remaining two screens showed a different man: Caucasian, no beard in this picture but thick eyebrows that met in the middle, unruly hair and dark bags under the eyes which looked like no amount of sleep would chase away.

'Introduce me to these handsome young men, Scott,' Delaney breathed.

Stroman pointed first at one, then the other. 'Richard Singh, Joe Mansfield. British SAS. Records show they were part of the unit holding the cordon.'

'Have any of our guys reported making contact with them?'

'No, sir.'

'And you've been in touch with Hereford HQ?'

'Of course, sir. They deny there was any breach of SOPs.'

Delaney closed his eyes, removed his glasses and pinched the bridge of his nose. 'So, tell me, Scott. Tell me this. If they were supposed to be holding the cordon, and there was no breach of SOPs, what in the name of *fuck* were they doing running out of the compound in the wake of the raid?'

Stroman looked at his knees. 'I don't know, Mr Delaney, sir. I just don't know.'

A thick, uncomfortable silence fell as the two men stared up at the faces on the screens.

'Do we know where they are now?' Delaney asked.

Stroman nodded. 'Yes, sir,' he said. 'Of course we do.'

FOUR

Bagram Air Base, Afghanistan. 1700 hours local time.

The Chinook that put Joe's team back on the ground didn't close down. It was needed elsewhere. Joe barked at the Doctor's wife and their three daughters to get off the transport. The old woman gave him a look of loathing – she hadn't liked the abrupt way Joe and his mates had manhandled her family out of Abbottabad without looking for her husband. Joe reckoned he could live with that. He worked for the British Army, not Thomas fucking Cook. He pointed towards the tailgate to indicate she should take her daughters and get out.

The rotors were kicking up a massive wall of brown dust as the unit lugged their gear off the plane. One of the kids was crying because the sand was in her eyes. He saw Ricky help the little girl out of range of the downdraft. His mate hadn't said a single unnecessary word to him since they'd left the vicinity of the compound. The way Joe was feeling, that suited him just fine.

The tailgate closed; the chopper lifted; the dust swirled around a larger area for a few seconds. Only as the dust settled did the peaks of the Hindu Kush that filled the horizon come into view. Joe had stopped being impressed by the sight. The snow-capped mountains were just another obstacle in this dog turd of a country. Closer to hand, the LZ was surrounded by a sea of cargo containers – impossible to say how many, but in the hundreds. Some of them were covered with camo-nets; others were

49

just scratched and exposed. Bagram – all six and a half square miles of it – was an important staging post for the Americans. A large proportion of the goods necessary to keep the US's show on the road in Afghanistan passed through here.

Military vehicles – Humvees, mostly – were driving all over the place, as well as large SUVs that wouldn't have looked out of place on the New Jersey Turnpike. Joe knew that the drivers of half these SUVs were only moving around because the air con in their vehicles was better than that in their bunkhouses. The Chinook flew out of earshot; the grind of its motors was immediately replaced by the ear-splitting din of an F-16, flying low, probably on its way to put the shits up the locals – a not-too-subtle warning of what they could expect if they messed with the stars and stripes.

Nobody approached to help the unit with their gear, and the unit wouldn't have wanted anyone to. They worked alone. Everybody knew that. Joe and his mate JJ – whose brown beard was longer than the rest of the unit's because he'd worn it for years – lifted a crate of weaponry in the direction of a large hangar situated 100 metres from the LZ, just beyond a two-metre-high HESCO wall over the top of which an array of satellite receivers and other signalling apparatus was visible. A couple of Paras stood guard at a gap in the wall, next to a green and white sign stating: 'No Unauthorized Entry'. There were thousands of signs, plastering every inch of Bagram. Even the thunderboxes had a notice telling you not to piss on the seat.

One of the Paras was lazily scraping the Afghan dust from the inside of his nostril with a rolled-up piece of Kleenex. Both had expectant looks on their faces. Word of bin Laden's death had obviously got out, and anyone who knew that Joe's unit had been on ops in Pakistan at the same time would have put two and two together.

Joe looked over his shoulder. Ricky and the rest of the unit were walking towards the hangar, their bodies appearing to waver in the heat haze. Beyond them, three guys whom Joe recognized as American DOD personnel had surrounded the Doctor's family, and five black SUVs were driving up towards them. Fuck knows what was going to happen to them. A new name and a safe house in a faceless North American suburb, he supposed.

'Been busy, lads?' one of the Paras asked.

'Aye,' JJ replied. 'Shagged out, me. Never knew your sister was such a goer.'

The Para grinned. 'She told me you had a dick like a maggot, JJ.'

JJ gave a look of mock acceptance. 'Aye, it's true,' he said. 'Maybe that's why she got her rocks off with the rest of the unit as well. I'm telling you – she was walking like Charlie Chaplin by the end, and Joe here has been grinning like the Cheshire fucking cat ever since . . .'

'Yeah, looks like it.' The Para nodded at Joe. Joe glowered back.

The hangar housed the Regiment's operations base at Bagram. A third guard standing outside and armed with an M16 slid open the huge metal doors that remained closed as a matter of course, to reveal the cavernous space bustling with activity. The hangar itself was about eighty by forty metres. There were windows along both sides, but these had been covered up against curious eyes with sheets of plastic tarpaulin. The space was lit by twelve portable floodlights aimed up at the flat metal ceiling to stop them dazzling the people inside, of whom there were thirty or so. The combination of the metal walls and the powerful lights could easily turn the hangar, big as it was, into an oven in this climate and so, evenly spaced along both walls, were six air-conditioning units. Out of sight, on the other side of the far wall, Joe knew there was a large petrol-operated generator, which added to the general noise.

The hangar was divided into four quadrants. Closest to Joe and on his left was a bank of computer screens. A mess of wires on the floor trailed through the wall towards the signalling area and the Genny, and a handful of the guys, as well as two female 'terps, were leaning over the screens examining maps and other imagery. Joe counted seven men and one woman he didn't recognize. They were standing in a group by themselves and watched Joe and the others with interest as they entered. To the right was a weapons store: crates of hardware piled high, manned by a grizzled member of L Detachment. He nodded at Joe and JJ to indicate that they should dump their own crate just next to him.

In the far-left quadrant was an R & R zone: a television mounted on the wall, a few old sofas and a kettle for anybody wanting to make a brew. This area was deserted. No rest. No recuperation. Not out here. The fourth quadrant in the far right-hand corner of the hangar was blocked off by a series of large screens. This was the briefing area – the place where Joe and the unit had first been informed about the nature of their operation. Now a tall, gangly rupert with a lean face and a two-day-old beard was walking out of it. Major Dom Fletcher, OC E Squadron, looked and sounded like the prince of public-school twats. To hear him talk, nobody would guess he'd come up through the ranks, or that his rough London accent and squaddie turn of phrase had miraculously disappeared the day he got his commission. Overnight, Dom had become Dominic. But the guys had learned the hard way not to test his patience, and just called him 'boss'. Fletcher wasn't beyond issuing an RTU for anyone who took the piss. He nodded in Joe and JJ's direction, jabbed his thumb towards the briefing area and turned on his heel to walk back into it.

'You know,' said JJ, 'what I really love about this place is the warm welcomes. I could murder a Mr Kipling . . .'

Joe glanced behind him. Ricky was walking alone, about ten metres back. His eyes were fixed on the floor.

The briefing area was nothing to look at. Twenty or thirty

plastic stackable brown chairs in rows; a long table at the front; a whiteboard with clips on the top to hold mapping sheets. Fletcher stood next to it, his arms folded, his face unreadable. Within thirty seconds all eight members of the unit were there.

'Sit down,' Fletcher said. It wasn't a polite offer. Joe took a seat in the back row, the others all sat forward of him.

Fletcher spoke sufficiently loudly that they could hear him over the noise of the hangar, but not so loudly that anybody outside of the briefing room could eavesdrop. 'You've all seen the news?'

'We stopped off at a Travelodge just outside Abbottabad,' JJ cut in. 'Jerked off over Kirsty Young on the telly while she told us all about it.'

'JJ, shut up. Target Geronimo was KIA and extracted at 0110 local time. The Americans dumped him in the Indian Ocean just before dawn. "Burial at sea" is the phrase they're using. The President made the announcement this morning. We've got CIA swarming round the base with fucking hard-ons. They'll assist with the debriefs later. My guess is they'll want to know why you came home without the Doctor in tow. Which is a pretty good fucking question.'

'The Doctor wasn't there,' Jacko growled.

'Right,' Fletcher said. 'Now remind me, are you a specialist unit under the command of E Squadron, or a bunch of *fucking Girl Guides?*'

A pause. Fletcher looked at each member of the unit in turn. A question was coming. Joe could sense it.

'Anyone care to tell me why the CO took a call from our American cousins asking if we were aware of anyone breaching SOPs during the raid?'

Silence. Joe found himself staring not at Fletcher, but at the back of Ricky's head. Once more the OC directed his gaze at each of them. Was it Joe's imagination, or did he linger on him slightly longer than the others?

Thirty seconds passed. They seemed a lot longer. Finally Fletcher inclined his head, plainly aware that nobody was going to give him an answer.

'Stand down,' he said. 'Get yourself cleaned up. Eat. Full debrief at 2030.' He looked in turn at each member of the unit once again. 'Now', he said quietly, 'would be a good time for you all to decide what you're going tell me. And more to the point, what you're going to tell the Yanks.' The OC walked from the briefing area and out of sight before any of them could even stand up.

JJ was sitting in the front row. He turned round to look at the others. 'What the fuck was all that about?'

Nobody replied. They started to file out of the briefing area; all except Joe and Ricky, who remained in their seats.

For a moment Ricky didn't look back. 'Thanks, brudder,' he said quietly.

'We need to sort our story out,' Joe said under his breath. 'Right now.'

Ricky looked around and nodded.

'Not here,' Joe said. 'Let's take a walk.'

They left the Regiment hangar and headed towards the centre of the base. It was teeming with American troops, hanging out in pairs or threes, all wearing their standard uniform of camo, aviator shades and Berettas hanging from their belts in non-standard-issue leather holsters. To a man they had crewcuts, some of them with elaborate razor-cut patterns on the sides of their heads. Then there were the air base staff – contractors, mostly, wearing blue overalls, baseball caps, cigarettes glued to their lower lips and facial hair that marked them out as non-military personnel. Very few locals. There were plenty working on the site, Joe knew, but they were mostly doing just that: scrubbing toilets, cleaning floors. He couldn't count the number of times he'd overheard the words 'bin Laden'. There was a mood of self-congratulation around the place.

They'd been walking in silence for ten minutes – past the packed Burger King and Subway concessions that would have made the whole place feel like a Midwestern mall if it hadn't been for the twenty-ton MRAPs filled with troops coming back from, or going out on, patrol – when they came to another hangar. This one had its doors flung wide open, and it contained a US Air Force Boeing E-3 Sentry. The engines were turning over, and perhaps fifteen engineers swarmed around the aircraft. The noise was sufficiently loud to drown out Joe's and Ricky's voices. They headed round to the side of the hangar.

Joe spoke first. 'We saw the enemy target heading to the security gates. I nailed him, you nailed Romeo and Juliet. When the gates opened, you approached and took out the dude trying to leave. We extracted to the opposite side of the path and held our positions till the Yanks left. We singing from the same hymn sheet?'

Ricky nodded.

'Look, mucker.' Joe looked round, checking that nobody could overhear them. 'You've got to sort yourself out. You haven't been . . .'

'What?'

'You haven't been yourself. Not for a long time. Maybe it's getting to you.'

'Maybe what's getting to me?' Ricky stuck out his chin, oozing defensiveness.

'This.' Joe gestured all around him. 'Nobody would blame you. It's intense. I'm telling you, mucker, they're going to be spending more on shrinks for the craphats than they are on prosthetics for the amputees.' He paused. 'And not just the craphats.'

'What you trying to say, Joe?'

Joe noticed that Ricky was clenching his teeth. He could sense his mate's tension. The noise of the E-3's engines suddenly grew quieter. Neither man spoke.

Until finally, Ricky said: 'I'm Hank frickin' Marvin. Let's get some scran.' He turned to his friend. 'I'm fine, brudder. Really. I fucked up back there. Hands up. It won't happen again.'

Joe nodded. If Ricky said he was fine, that was good enough for him. 'OK, mucker. If you say so.'

Ricky grinned suddenly. 'So did you see the big BL? I couldn't see fuck all from where I was . . .'

'Nah,' Joe said, shaking his head. He might be giving Ricky the benefit of the doubt, but something told him his mate didn't need anything else to fuck with his head. 'Thought for a minute that Malinois was going to come and sniff my bollocks, though. Could have been interesting.'

'You should have let him,' Ricky said. 'Better-looking than some of the dogs in Hereford.'

The two men headed off to find some food.

0350 hours.

Joe lay in his low cot, still fully dressed in camo trousers and black T-shirt, but with his boots and ops waistcoat dumped on the floor beside him. It was dark inside the thin-walled Portakabin mounted on two skins of roughly rendered breeze blocks that served as digs for him, Ricky and JJ. The first thing they'd done when they'd moved in here was board up the windows against the possibility of mortar attack. Joe was knackered, but sleep wouldn't come. It wasn't the noise from outside. It wasn't even the heavy breathing and occasional snores from Ricky and JJ. It was his head, reliving the debrief with the Yanks where he and Ricky had stuck to their story even though they could tell someone was smelling a rat.

He found himself remembering the cold, glazed look on Ricky's face in the compound. Joe had lost count of the number of kids he'd seen take on that same thousand-yard stare after a particularly traumatic op, then learned that they'd handed in their badge and headed back to their parent unit in the hope of a quieter life. But these days there were no quiet lives in the military. Even the greenest of green-army soldiers found themselves stuck in a shit-filled Afghan ditch on six-month rotation with some Taliban fucker trying to put holes in them three times a day, or separate their legs from their torso. And as for Regiment ops, they'd grown increasingly dangerous at the same rate.

The first time he'd gone out on the ground on this tour, he'd come across what looked like a father kneeling at the roadside and weeping over his dead son. The kid was naked, his belly sliced open and his skin bloody and stained. Joe had approached, and only when he was five metres away did he realize there was more to the scene than he had noticed at first. There was a wire leading from the kid's stomach wound to a switch in the weeping man's hand. Only he wasn't weeping any more. He had started muttering to himself. Joe had only needed a single shot to the head to take him out. And once he was kneeling by the two dead bodies, he followed the wire that led from the switch. He'd had to insert his hands into the still-warm innards of the boy's stomach to pull out an old Russian mortar round that was hidden inside.

The memory of that child with the split-open stomach had haunted him of late. Maybe life in the Regiment was getting to him too.

His watch glowed a pale green in the dark: 0400. He hadn't slept for days. Not properly. It was one of the things the medics had told them to look out for – but none of the guys took that shit seriously.

He swung his legs over the side of his cot and fumbled in the darkness for the bottle of water he knew was there somewhere. His fingers brushed against it and it toppled over. He heard the contents sloshing out and felt a sudden wave of anger. He thumped the side of the bed in frustration, and by the time he'd picked up the bottle again, it was only a third full. He downed what was left, threw the bottle back on the floor and stood up.

No point lying here in the darkness. He pulled on his boots and headed out of the Portakabin into the camp outside.

The bunkhouse Joe shared with Ricky and JJ was one of twenty located behind the Regiment hangar and surrounded by yet more HESCO walls. He weaved his way among them until he found himself along the back end of the hangar itself, where the generator was sited, turning over noisily and stinking of petrol. Light was escaping from a back window where the tarpaulin had failed to cover the glass completely, and he knew that the hangar would be full of activity, even though it was only the small hours. He didn't feel like company, so he kept to the shadows as he skirted round the edge of the hangar, not really knowing what he was doing or where he was going. Wandering without purpose.

It was a noise overhead that made him stop and press his back against the wall of the hangar.

He recognized immediately the distinctive sound of a Black Hawk, and it sent a series of images flashing through his head: the two body bags; the shower of shrapnel from the exploding chopper . . .

He snapped himself out of it and turned his attention back to the Black Hawk. It was flying low over the base – thirty metres max – and was heading in from the south over towards the LZ in front of the Regiment hangar. The outline of the helicopter immediately told him it was one of the stealth models he'd seen in Pakistan. No one had access to these machines but Delta and the SEALs. One or the other was about to touch down.

Joe kept close to the edge of the hangar, stopping at one of the front corners. Light was spilling from the front – the main door was open – and peering round he could see the elongated shadow of someone standing at the entrance.

The modified Black Hawk hovered above the LZ and starting losing height. The shadow moved forward and Joe saw the thin, tall form of Dom Fletcher walking towards the HESCO that separated the hangar from the landing zone. Someone inside the hangar slid the door shut and the sudden absence of light messed momentarily with Joe's night vision. By the time he'd got it back a few seconds later, Fletcher had disappeared.

Joe crossed the ten metres between the corner of the hangar and the opening in the HESCO wall. He could hear voices on the other side.

'Yank friends of yours, boss?'

'Shut the fuck up and keep your positions.' Fletcher sounded distracted.

A pause.

'Wanker,' the first voice said. The OC had clearly left.

A second voice just grunted in agreement.

'Fucking Yanks,' the first voice continued. 'Why's Fletcher licking this lot's arses, anyway?'

Joe moved, away from the opening and along the HESCO wall, coming to a halt after about fifteen metres. He didn't want the OC to see him loitering there. Fletcher had already given him, Ricky and the others the third degree during their debrief, massaging the egos of the two American spooks who'd been in on the meet, and Joe had had it with his mock-Sandhurst bullshit. So he kept still in the shadows, waiting for a good moment to head back to his cot.

Twenty seconds passed. Fletcher appeared, striding back through the opening and towards the hangar. A line of soldiers followed, walking less quickly than the OC, some of them in pairs, others in single file. He counted them: twelve, not including Fletcher. When the OC slung open the door of the hangar again, the glow from inside lit them up. All the new arrivals except one had big, bushy beards. They were distinctively American. Some wore jeans, others 511 pants. They were all carrying helmets, plate hangers and rifles – M4s with torches and laser sights mounted. Joe instantly recognized the slow, confident swagger of special forces personnel, and as one of these newcomers looked over his shoulder to say something to a mate, he recognized something else as well.

His face.

The guy might have been fifteen metres away, but Joe's eyes were sharp and he'd been trained to record the tiniest detail almost without knowing he was doing it. The soldier was the only one without a beard, and his upper lip jumped out at Joe: the tiny scar – the harelip, surgically repaired.

Instantly, Joe was back in Abbottabad, hidden among the rubble, staring at the face of the SEAL manhandling Cairo away from the scene.

A second later the guy had turned his head again and was walking into the hangar. And after ten seconds the whole unit was inside, and somebody was sliding the metal door shut.

Darkness. Silence. The Black Hawk had powered down and it felt as though the whole camp had suddenly plunged itself into a moment of uncharacteristic stillness. Joe crept back to his bunkhouse. He didn't expect to sleep.

0600 hours.

Ricky was scowling. JJ too. Joe didn't blame them. The sun wasn't even up when the summons had come: Fletcher needed them in the briefing area. Sharpish.

'What the fuck does he want?' JJ muttered, scratching at his beard. Joe's own face was itching too. It might be early, but the temperature was already hot and he still hadn't showered since they'd returned from Abbottabad. He knew he must stink, but everyone stank out here. He half wondered if he should tell the others that at least one of the guys who'd conducted the raid on Abbottabad had just popped in for a cosy little chat with Fletcher. Maybe if he'd been alone with Ricky, he would have. But he kept quiet as they headed to their RV.

Fletcher didn't look like a man who'd been up in the small hours. His eyes were bright, his uniform fresh and now he was clean-shaven. When they entered, he was examining imagery at the computer screens, accompanied by three men Joe didn't recognize. One of them was wearing standard Yankee multi-cam; the other two were in suits and did not have a military bearing. The moment Fletcher saw them, he jabbed his thumb in the direction of the briefing area before turning back to his screens. Joe and Ricky exchanged a look and followed his instruction.

Raz, who had partnered JJ back in Abbottabad, was already in the briefing room. He was sitting in the back row of seats, looking thoroughly pissed off. He was not the only man there. Standing silently against the walls were the twelve American SF men that Joe had seen arriving just a couple of hours ago. Joe got a better look at them. They were all wearing black and white shamags around their necks, and their shades were either propped up on their foreheads or hanging round their necks on black cord. Seven of them wore beards that were even more unkempt than Joe's; none of them wore smiles. They all had skin that was baked leathery brown and, with the exception of three of them, had multicam baseball caps fitted backwards over their heads. The standard uniform of the American SF soldier. Joe picked out the man with the scarred lip. He wore neither a baseball cap nor a beard. He looked Latino, with slicked-back hair and pock-marked skin. He was staring straight ahead and, like all the others, he didn't even acknowledge the arrival of the SAS men.

'Sit down!'

Joe looked over his shoulder to see Fletcher enter, along with the three strangers. Joe and his mates took seats next to Raz. None of the Americans moved; not until the three strangers had reached the front of the briefing area and the uniformed man had nodded at them. At his signal they silently occupied the front two rows, while Fletcher and the three others remained standing at the front.

It was Fletcher who spoke first. He neither welcomed nor

introduced anyone. Not his style. 'OK gentlemen,' he instructed. 'Here's what you need to know. Intelligence wires are buzzing. I don't have to tell you why. We've got every AQ cell from Kabul to Kidderminster planning a revenge attack.'

'Surprise surprise,' Raz muttered.

'Village of Nawaz, thirty-five klicks south-east of here. Our American friends' – he indicated his three companions – 'have been monitoring ICOM chatter radiating from a known Taliban communications centre based in an old school building. It seems to suggest that—'

The uniformed Yank stood forward. 'Why don't I take it from there?' he said in a lazy drawl.

Fletcher nodded, but Joe noticed a slight tightness around his eyes.

'The name Anwar Zahari won't mean anything to any of you gentlemen,' the Yank said. 'No reason why it should. He's a Taliban grunt, but he's a very skilled explosives engineer. Last known location was an AQ sanctuary in Eritrea. We weren't aware of his presence in this part of the world until just a few hours ago when his name started coming over the ICOM. If he's in the area and active, he's only doing one thing. We need to stop him from doing it. From what we can establish, he's only going to be in Nawaz for a few hours. We can't wait till nightfall.

'Intel suggests all the roads in are being watched, so you'll have to approach cross-country by foot. We have two Black Hawks online for Bagram. They'll be on the ground in thirty minutes. I want two teams: one to enter Nawaz from the west, one from the east. You'll have drone support, but don't rely on it. It's a heavily populated area, and we need to keep civilian casualties to a minimum.'

'So why the drone support?' JJ butted in.

'Tell you what, soldier, why don't you let your superiors do what they're good at, and you can do what the fuck we tell you? Hernandez' – he indicated one of the US soldiers, and Joe saw that it was his man with the scarred lip – 'will lead team Alpha from the west, McGregor' – he pointed at one of the men with baseball caps, the back of whose neck was so tanned it was almost black – 'team Bravo from the east. ISAF directives, this is a joint operation. Each team will take two Regiment scouts.'

The American turned to Fletcher, who was ready with his instructions: 'Joe, Ricky, team Alpha. JJ, Raz, team Bravo.'

'You have' – the American checked his watch – 'twenty-five minutes to familiarize yourself with the imagery. Departure 0645. We have support groups preparing your gear. Let's move, gentlemen. We've caught the big fish; now let's hose up the tiddlers. You find our man, and remember he's notched up a fair few American names on his bedpost. You have my express permission to fuck him up pretty good.'

He looked directly at Hernandez and nodded. The Americans stood up as a single man as their commander left the room.

FIVE

The sun, low in the sky, streamed into the dirty interior of the Black Hawk. A thick, oily stench of aviation fuel clung to everything and the surfaces were covered in sand. Joe couldn't remember the last time he'd eaten a mouthful of food that didn't contain grit, or wiped his arse without it feeling like he was sandpapering it.

Joe sat next to Ricky on the dull, hard, black seats that lined the chopper. No attempts to disguise themselves as locals today. Kevlar helmets cut away around the ears. Body armour and multicam. Ops vests stashed with extra ammo and grenades. If – when – they caught up with the bomb-maker, they'd need to go in hard and fast. A Camelbak full of fresh water was strapped to each man's back, with a little plastic tube emerging around his neck. Rehydration was almost as important as ammo in theatres like this. Stopping to drink from a bottle could mean wasting time they didn't have.

Every man wore the Skye Precision gear common to the Regiment, the SEALs and Delta, the only differences being that the Yanks had their kneepads sewn into their trousers, whereas Joe and Ricky had had to fix theirs around the outside. The Yanks had Velcro patches with the stars and stripes fixed to their body armour; Joe and Ricky had Union Jacks with a difference. In common with some of the other old sweats in the Regiment, their badges were embroidered with Arabic lettering which translated, very precisely, as 'Fuck Al-Qaeda'. The Yanks were all bigger than both Joe and Ricky, and they carried a bit more shite on them: there were more knives tucked into their rigs, and Joe saw that Hernandez had a pair of surgical scissors to snip Plasticuffs with.

He felt eyes on him. Why was Hernandez looking at him like that? He shook off the paranoia. He'd seen enough men go off on missions to realize that different people prepared themselves in different ways. There was seldom a party atmosphere while you were waiting to be inserted. When the loadie shouted 'Five minutes in!' above the noisy grind of the aircraft, and held up five fingers in the direction of the Americans but ignored Joe and Ricky, he told himself it was a US chopper and a US flight crew. Of course they were going to pay more attention to their countrymen than to the Brits. Joe had been on enough joint ops to realize it was always that way.

He closed his eyes and cleared his head. He wished he'd slept last night.

They started losing height, suddenly and sharply. Standard flight practice: keep high, out of the range of the type of rockets the Taliban were expected to have, then swoop down at a steep gradient when you're almost at your insertion point. They didn't touch down immediately, but skirted just a couple of metres above the desert. Joe knew why this was – their final insertion point was camouflaged by undulating ground and this man-oeuvre would decrease the chance of their being spotted by Taliban scouts. But it was dangerous. The pilots' vision would be compromised by dust from the downdraft, and the aircraft could easily lose that couple of metres of height. This was something only a special forces flight crew would attempt.

Final checks: weapons locked and loaded, ops vests tightly strapped. The Black Hawk finally touched down, and within seconds the eight men were exiting from the side, forming a semicircle around the back of the chopper and kneeling down in the firing position. Once more, Joe found himself surrounded by a cloud of dust which only started to settle as the chopper lifted up into the air.

The blur of brown-out all around faded and their location eased into view. They were in a patch of bare desert. The area around Bagram was a featureless dustbowl, a harsh environment even for the locals, and the earth was baked hard even this early on in the year, but with a fine, silty covering of dust that accepted footprints. Here and there, some hardy foliage was trying to force its way out of the cracks in the ground. To Joe's left, two metres away, was the long, craggy branch of a mulberry tree. But there were no other trees in the vicinity. Either it had been blown here in a winter storm, dragged here by a wild animal, or a person had placed it here: a reminder that even deserted places were never deserted for long. The mountain ranges of the Afghanistan–Pakistan border were at Joe's six o'clock. Ahead of him, the terrain sloped uphill. Gradient, one in five, peaking in the brow of the hill about half a klick on and 100 metres high, curling round to the south. To the north: horizon.

Joe's earpiece crackled into life. Hernandez's voice was clearer through the comms than in person, even though he was only five metres to Joe's right. 'Team Alpha in position,' he said. Only when he had relayed this information back to their ops centre at Bagram did he raise his arm again and jab his forefinger north in the direction of the brow of the hill.

Joe and Ricky stood up. Their role was well defined. You could have all the intel in the world, but until real men with real eyes had scoped the place out, you never quite knew what was waiting. They bent low as they ran uphill, knowing that the Americans had them covered. They ran fifteen metres apart – that way, if they did get into contact, they weren't bunched up as a single target – and it took approximately three minutes to cover the ground.

Fifteen metres from the top of the hill they hit the dirt. Joe looked to his right and caught Ricky's eye. They both nodded at the same time and started to crawl, edging closer to the brow and keeping low. Stand here on the summit and you'd be observable for miles around.

The terrain beyond the downhill slope of the hill was an open plain. A deep wadi – one of the dried-up river beds that characterized this part of the world – ran from the bottom of the hill, across the wide expanse of open ground and into the heart of Nawaz, two kilometres away. The town itself was a sprawling hotchpotch of compounds around the edges and low concrete buildings surrounding a tall, thin minaret in the centre, all wavering in the heat haze. A road ran into it from the north-east, and even with his naked eye Joe could make out the metallic glint of three vehicles heading into the town. Their plan was to approach Nawaz using this wadi with high, craggy sides as cover, knowing that it would take them within 100 metres of their target's suspected hideout.

Joe edged forward another couple of metres, keeping his body pressed flat against the ground, and moving slowly. His pixellated digicam would help him blend into the scenery from a distance; but it was movement, more than anything else, that caused people to be seen. Before leaving camp, he had carefully removed his wristwatch. Rule number one of daytime surveillance: remove anything reflective.

Now he carefully took a small, handheld scope from his ops vest. It was coated with non-reflective black paint to prevent sunlight glinting off it; the lens was hooded for the same reason. Joe draped a camo-net over the end of the lens to make triple sure that the sun didn't reflect off it, then put it to his eye and started to scan.

It was immediately obvious that they would not be able to approach Nawaz from this direction.

There was no sign of activity within the wadi itself, but the open ground surrounding it was crawling with militia. Joe counted six motorbikes – the Taliban grunt's vehicle of choice – as well as four open-topped Land Rovers each carrying a minimum of three armed men. They were all moving, none of them following any particular pattern – just exerting their presence.

An insect landed on Joe's left eyelid. He didn't move to swat it. And when he spoke into his comms, he barely moved his lips. 'We've got company.'

A pause. Twenty seconds. Then a crackle in the earpiece. 'Roger that,' came the voice of Hernandez. 'Get back down here, both of you.'

Joe and Ricky edged backwards, then slid ten metres down the hill on their backs before standing and running back to the unit. They were still in a circular formation, each of them kneeling and with their guns pointing out into the desert. Joe approached Hernandez directly. 'It's a no-go,' he said. 'The wadi that leads into the town is fine, but the open ground around it is crawling. They'll spot us when we go over the hill, no question.'

The American considered it for a moment. 'OK, listen up. We're going to re-route. Cut round, enter the town from the south.' A bead of sweat was running down his face. It collected on his upper lip just where the scar was. 'We move in pairs—'

'Hang on,' Ricky interrupted.

Hernandez stopped talking and looked at Ricky as though he'd only just noticed he was there. 'You got a problem with that?'

'You've seen the mapping, brudder. The area south of Nawaz is shitful of legacy mines and IEDs. That's why we're supposed to be heading in from the west . . .'

Hernandez took a step closer. 'Well, here's the thing, *brother*. You want to go back up there, get your head full of holes, you be my guest.'

'I'm not walking into a fucking minefield.'

'You'll walk where I damn well tell you to walk.'

An ominous pause. In an uncomfortable instant, Joe realized there were three Colts pointing at him and Ricky.

It was Hernandez who broke the silence. 'As you've studied the maps so damn carefully,' he said, 'you'll know that bomb disposal teams have marked safe passage through the area. You'll see the chalk lines on the fucking ground. Even you Brits aren't so dumb you can't follow the white line.'

Joe breathed deeply. It was true that he'd seen pathways through the minefield marked on the mapping. 'He's right, Ricky,' he murmured.

'What is it, friend?' Hernandez interrupted. 'Lost your nerve?'

'Fuck you.' Ricky looked in contempt at the others. 'You can tell your homeys to point their rifles at the bad guys, Hernandez,' he hissed, before turning back to Joe. 'Come on,' he said. 'If we're going, let's go.'

0742 hours.

The desert was already a furnace, and Joe's clothes clung to him. He took a pull of warm water from his Camelbak and surveyed his position. To his nine o'clock was the incline of the hill, a little gentler now that he and Ricky had covered 500 metres east from their insertion point. At their three o'clock, open, empty ground and the mountains in the distance. At six o'clock, two of the Yanks 400 metres back, indistinct in the heat haze. And at twelve o'clock, a fucking wasteland.

There were three derelict breeze-block buildings approximately 500 metres ahead. They delineated the edge of the town – about 200 metres beyond them were more buildings, though it was clear that this area was seldom visited. There was no sign of any human activity; just a thin, lame cat that limped towards them from the direction of the breeze-block huts, and stopped, 100 metres from their position, when it saw Joe and Ricky. It stood still for five seconds, before limping away in the opposite direction.

'How many lives do you reckon Tiddles has used up?' Ricky murmured.

More than nine, Joe thought to himself. The 500 metres of ground between them and the breeze-block hut was like a junk yard. The burned-out shells of cars littered the whole place. With his scope, Joe could make out the ravaged corpse of some unidentifiable animal, the size of a large dog, but headless. And, a few metres to its left, what looked like the remnants of a kite, knotted and tangled round a twisted chunk of metal, drooping in the windless air.

Five metres from where they were standing, the hard-baked earth was stained white. A straight line – it was only a couple of inches wide – extended twenty metres in the direction of the shacks, before veering left at forty-five degrees and straightening up again after another five metres.

'Follow the yellow brick road?' Ricky said.

'I don't like it,' Joe replied, his voice low. 'Maybe we should skirt round the whole area.'

Ricky shook his head. 'We don't know how far the frickin' things extend. The Russkis mined this place to hell, you know. If the Yanks' minesweepers have done the hard work, we should follow their line.'

Ricky was right. Thank fuck it hadn't rained for six weeks, and the chalk line was still mostly intact, although it was scuffed out in places. The chalk lines marking safe passage through a minefield weren't just good for soldiers. Local people and enemy militia used them too.

'I'll go first,' Joe said.

'Hey, brudder . . .'

'Forget it, Ricky. We're good now, OK?'

Ricky grinned. 'OK.' If he suspected that Joe didn't want him taking the lead for any other reason, he didn't show it.

'Keep a twenty-five-metre distance,' Joe said. Ricky didn't have to ask why: that was the buffer he had to keep to stay out

70

of the kill zone, should Joe end up stepping on a pressure plate.

'Roger that, brudder. See you on the other side.'

They clapped palms, then Joe stepped onto the white line.

He wouldn't have walked more carefully if he'd been treading a high wire. He took each footstep very slowly, placing his toes down first and feeling for anything unusual before allowing himself to release his whole weight on to his foot and take the next step. The dry earth crunched slightly beneath him, sounding almost as though there was a dusting of snow. No fucking chance. It was already pushing forty degrees and the sky was an intense blue. Sweat continued to ooze from Joe's pores, and he had only gone ten metres before he had to stop and wipe the salt from his eyes so that he could see the way ahead.

Fifteen metres.

Twenty.

He reached the apex of the line where it angled off, forcing him to change direction. He allowed himself another sip of water to ease the burning dryness in his mouth and throat. All his attention was on the line ahead and it was only out of the corner of his eye that he saw Ricky starting out on it.

The shell of a Toyota on its side – it still had a few tiny patches of peeling red paint here and there – lay ten metres to his right. Joe's skin prickled as he passed the shattered glass that lay all around, and spotted the rough hessian bag twisted around the remains of the front seat that had perhaps once belonged to the driver. He looked up to see that he hadn't covered more than a tenth of the distance to the breeze-block huts.

Another slug of water.

Another step forward.

He looked over his shoulder. Ricky was about thirty metres back. A safe distance. Beyond him, Joe realized he could no longer see the Americans. In a corner of his mind he wondered why they weren't still advancing, but he didn't have the head-space to worry about it for long.

He took another step.

And another.

Movement up ahead. It was the cat, hobbling across the chalk line. For a moment, Joe considered shooting it – if it trod on a pressure plate, they'd all be fucked – but the animal, almost as if it knew what Joe was thinking, changed direction and scampered off in the direction of the breeze blocks.

Joe's blood was thumping through his veins. His right foot crunched down onto the chalk line.

Then his left foot.

Then his right again.

He almost missed it. Had the feral cat still been diverting his attention, he would have done. It was a footprint to his left, about twenty centimetres from the chalk line and facing towards it. And a second footprint, half a metre – a stride's length – beyond that.

Joe stopped.

He stared at the ground.

Something wasn't right.

He crouched down and touched the footprint. The indentations of the sole had made a regular, symmetrical pattern in the dust, not unlike his own prints. He recognized it as a military boot.

But if it was a military boot, why had it not been walking along the chalk line?

All of a sudden, Joe felt as though somebody had slowed time down to a crawl. He looked over his shoulder to see Ricky, still thirty metres back. His mate had his head inclined, clearly wondering why Joe was crouched down on the ground.

And he was taking a step forward.

'*Don't move!*'

Joe shouted so loud, his voice cracked. Ricky looked puzzled, but he continued to put his foot down.

'Ricky! Don't fucking move!'

But it was too late.

As Ricky's boot touched the earth, he clearly realized something was different. He looked down, but only for the fraction of a second that remained of his life.

Joe had a snapshot vision of a huge geyser of dust and rock spurting ten metres up into the air, accompanied by the ear-splitting retort of at least five charges exploding in quick succession. A tremor rippled across the ground, so violent that it knocked Joe onto his side. He rolled to his front, his eyes clenched shut, before throwing his forearms over the back of his neck and waiting for the debris to fall.

It was like a hailstorm. Rubble hammered down on the back of his helmet; stones pelted his back and his legs. He found himself tensing his body, ready for a piece of shrapnel to fall and tear into his tissue, for his ribs to crack, his legs to be mashed. His ears rang with the explosion, and with the sound of debris hitting the ground all around him, like rain on a metal roof.

And then, ten seconds after the initial detonation, a sudden and profound silence.

He looked up. At first he could see nothing but the cloud of light brown dust all around. Still settling, it reduced his visibility to less than a metre. But after twenty seconds his view cleared.

There was no sign of Ricky. Not of his body at least. Joe could see nothing but his helmet. It was lying at his ten o'clock, approximately eight metres from his position. The strap was broken and the helmet was half filled with rubble.

Joe closed his eyes. Opened them again. They smarted from the dust, and his brain felt just as clouded. He tried to clear his mind. He had probably only missed by inches the same pressure plate Ricky had trodden on.

He looked to his right, squinting through the heat haze and the dust cloud. Was he imagining it, or could he see, twenty metres away and almost parallel to the path he had been

73

following, a line of displaced earth? Was that the original chalk line? Had they been following a dummy line, laid by whoever had left the footprint in the dust?

Joe was too shocked even to curse. He was taking in short, jagged inhalations of breath, trying to master the fear rising in his gut. He had to get off this chalk line. It was booby-trapped, that much was obvious. But now he had no way of knowing where to step. He looked back the way he'd come. Fifty metres, he reckoned, to get to the point where it would be safe.

Fifty metres, and there could be triggers, wires or pressure plates anywhere.

He started to crawl. Slowly. Gingerly. Every few centimetres he gently brushed the earth with his fingertips. He didn't even know what he was looking for. He'd recognize the small, circular pressure plate of an old anti-personnel mine, but the art and science of IEDs had come on since the Russians left their calling cards all round the country. There were countless ways to hide a detonator. They could even be remote, and if some Taliban cunt saw an enemy soldier crawling in the vicinity . . .

Five metres gone.

Ten metres.

He stopped. He looked at his right hand. It was shaking. He clenched it, and immediately remembered how Ricky had done the same thing. He gulped in more air, trying to steady himself. Up ahead, he scanned for the Americans. No sign.

Fifteen metres.

Twenty.

There was something blocking his way, two metres ahead, about the size of a bowling ball. He had thought it was a rock, but now he was up close he realized it was something else: an indistinguishable chunk of human flesh, swaddled in scorched clothing. He moved it out of the way. Ricky's warm, sticky blood glued itself to Joe's palm.

He continued to crawl.

Thirty metres.

Thirty-five.

How long had he been edging through the dirt? Ten minutes? A little more? He had to fight the urge not to stand up and run. Go slowly, he told himself. Go carefully.

He'd crawled forty metres when his fingers, still brushing away at the dusty ground, touched something hot. His hand flew away from it and his heart started to race even faster. At the same time he could hear shouting in the distance behind him. English, but harshly accented.

'Hey, Amer-ee-can motherfucker! You go bang bang, Amer-ee-can motherfucker!'

He looked back. A group of kids – maybe ten of them, none older than thirteen, he estimated – had congregated by the breeze blocks. Where had they come from? The village was two klicks away, but there was nothing to stop them alerting the adult militia on the other side of the hill. One of them was waving a rifle in the air; his neighbour was pointing at Joe, clearly urging his friend to take a shot. The others were all jeering and laughing, obviously wanting Joe to give them a show by pressing on the wrong piece of ground.

He turned his attention back to the metal, blowing on it to get rid of the sand. But his breath did not uncover the pressure plate of an anti-personnel mine. It was one end of the bulbous, gun-metal-grey body of a shell of some description, embedded in the earth so that only a couple of inches were showing. And there was no way of telling the mechanism by which it was to be detonated.

Joe lightly traced a circle round the shell, his thick, calloused fingers sensitive like feathers. He needed every ounce of self-control to stop his hand trembling, but it didn't take him more than a few seconds to find the trip wires.

There were four of them, attached to the shell and running at ninety degrees to each other. Joe realized he'd been crawling parallel to one of them, no more than ten centimetres to its left. And if he was going to cross the trip wire, he would have to get up from his crawling position and step over it.

Easier said than done.

He became aware of two sounds at once. The first was the hum of a helicopter up ahead. He couldn't see it yet, but he knew it was arriving. The Yanks must have called in a pick-up. Where the hell *were* they? Why weren't they giving him fire support?

The second sound was gunfire.

It came from the crowd of kids, and it had the unmistakable bark of a Kalashnikov.

Joe cursed under his breath and rolled onto his back. He could only see one kid with a gun. He had raised it in the air above his head to fire a burst. No doubt he'd seen adult insurgents do the same thing any number of times in his young life. Now, though, he was lowering it and, egged on by his mates, preparing to fire in Joe's direction.

Joe estimated the distance at between 400 and 500 metres. He was at the edge of the Kalashnikov's effective range, but he wouldn't bet his boots on the kid missing him . . .

The rounds from the second burst landed over an area of about ten square metres, twenty metres from Joe's position. Unable to control the recoil of the rifle, the kid had staggered backwards and turned to grin at his mates. More shouting from their direction; the boy raised the Kalashnikov again.

Joe had to do something. He hadn't signed up to nail kids, but these were insurgents in the making. He pulled a white-phosphorus grenade from his ops vest. He squeezed the detonation lever and pulled the pin with his teeth. Then he tensed his stomach muscles, forced himself into a half-sitting position, and hurled the grenade with all his strength. A thick curtain of white smoke would give him chance to swastika it out of there.

But the explosion that followed was ten times louder than he expected. The ground shook; the air rang; the earth between Joe and the kids erupted, and the bang echoed across the desert, shredding Joe's nerves. There was a cloud of smoke all right, but a whole lot more than he'd have expected from a white-phos grenade. He could only assume that the canister had hit another pressure plate.

'Run,' he hissed at himself. 'Fucking run!'

Pushing himself to his feet, he stepped over the trip wire. Distance to the drop-off point, half a klick. If he wanted to extract with that chopper, he needed to get there fast.

He sprinted. He knew he was risking his life, that he still had ten to fifteen metres of the minefield to clear, but he couldn't let the Yanks extract without him. People other than the kids would have heard the explosions; people better armed and with greater skill; people Joe didn't want to get into contact with all by himself, especially now that the smoke from the grenade was dissipating. Each time his foot hit the ground, he expected to feel the telltale spring of a pressure plate, to hear the blast that was going to kill him.

But it didn't come.

He cleared the minefield in five seconds. Behind him, the noise of more gunfire, but he knew he was fully out of range now. All he could do was leg it back to the chopper.

Even weighed down by his gear, he'd never run so fast. No point shouting at the others that he was coming, he realized – they'd never hear him over the noise of the chopper, and his energy was better expended on moving quickly.

He bolted round the curve at the base of the hill. A hundred metres. Two hundred. The chopper came into sight. It was kicking up the dust, and even in the daylight he could see a faint glow where the particles of sand were sparking against the rotors. The Americans were there, but they were little more than shadows in the cloud that surrounded the aircraft. It was 250 metres away. A hundred and fifty. The figures had disappeared inside the Black Hawk.

He could see the outline of the tail rising. Overhead, a second Black Hawk screamed across the sky: Team Bravo, extracting.

Fifty metres. A change in the quality of the noise coming from the chopper's engines. Higher-pitched. It was preparing to lift.

Joe stopped just short of the dust cloud, twenty metres from the aircraft, and skirted round so that he was facing its front. He grabbed his firefly beacon from his vest and turned it on. To start with there was no visible light, but he ripped off its infra-red filter so that now a strong white light flashed from the beacon. All he could do now was hold it up above his head and pray that the pilot could see it through the dust.

But the dust cloud was getting bigger. Two seconds later it had engulfed Joe. He could see nothing but the silhouette of the Black Hawk every second as the firefly lit it up. He could see it rising. Five metres in the air. Ten metres.

And then, the sound of the rotors powering down. The dust subsided a little. The chopper returned to the ground.

Joe sprinted round to the side of the aircraft, where he could just make out the sight of the American loadie, headphones on, urgently ushering him in. He jumped inside and could feel the Black Hawk rising almost immediately.

Joe's face was a filthy mixture of sweat and dirt, but it was not so black as his mood. He strode directly up to Hernandez, who was sitting impassively with his back against the wall of the chopper, surrounded by his men. He grabbed the SEAL by the front of his body armour and yanked him to his feet.

'Where the fuck *were* you?' he roared, his voice dry, hoarse and full of fury, before swinging the unit leader round and hurling him to the floor. He started to bear down on the guy, but instantly he felt hands pulling him back. A solid blow behind his knee forced him to the ground; next thing he knew, Hernandez was standing above him, weapon at the ready, his scarred and pockmarked face a picture of distaste.

'We heard two explosions, pal. We thought you were both KIA.'

'And you didn't come to check?'

Silence.

The Black Hawk swerved in the air. Hernandez had no reply. He just jutted his weapon in the direction of the opposite side of the aircraft. Joe knew what to do. He took his place, and as the chopper returned to Bagram he felt the heat of the Americans' unfriendly glares on him, and the gaping absence of the friend he'd left in pieces on the ground.

0923 hours.

The Regiment hangar was a blur of activity. American military commanders were in and out, trying to get the low-down on what had happened out there. None of them were getting anything but the shortest shrift from Fletcher, who, for all his faults, was doing the only thing the guys would have expected of him: making sure that Ricky's next of kin knew he wasn't coming home. That they couldn't even find any bits to stick in a box so the family had something to plant was information that could wait for now. Let it sink in that the poor bastard was dead first.

Joe sat in the R & R quadrant of the hangar, away from it all. His helmet was by his side, next to a full bottle of sterilized water that he hadn't touched even though his throat was desert-dry; his filthy face was in his hands. Five minutes ago he had been vaguely aware of some broad-shouldered American rupert with a lapel full of badges on his khaki uniform and couple of intelligence officers by his side. They were looking in his direction and talking to Fletcher. The OC had obviously told them where to get off, because they hadn't bugged him; but they hadn't left either, and were now hanging around by the main doors.

The TV on the wall behind him was murmuring quietly. BBC News 24 drifted in and out of Joe's consciousness.

'*The White House press secretary has backtracked on claims that*

Osama bin Laden was armed when he was shot dead by American special forces . . .'

This information barely registered. Joe was reliving for the hundredth time the explosion that killed Ricky.

'The White House has attributed mistakes and contradictions to "the fog of war" . . .'

He was only alive himself by chance . . .

'Osama bin Laden's twelve-year-old daughter has told Pakistani investigators that her father was captured alive and shot dead in front of family members . . .'

Family members. The words caused a leaden feeling in his stomach.

'Will someone turn this fucking television off?' Joe heard his own voice, but it didn't seem to come from him. There was a click, however, and the commentary fell silent. Joe looked up to see Fletcher standing over him.

'You should get some water down you.'

'What are you?' Joe retorted. 'Florence fucking Nightingale?'

'I'm your OC, and if you talk to me like that again I'll fuck you up and have you on the next boat back to Hereford.'

Joe looked away.

An awkward pause.

'Ricky was a good lad,' Fletcher said, his voice subdued. 'I'm sorry you had to see him go.'

Joe closed his eyes. The OC was right. Ricky was a good lad. A good lad who shouldn't even have been on ops, and Joe had known it.

'You want to tell me what happened out there?'

'We re-routed through a minefield. American sweepers had got there first. Someone had fucked with their chalk lines. Laid new ones. Led us straight to the IEDs.'

'The Yanks say you insisted on taking that route.'

Joe gave him a contemptuous look. 'They're talking out of their arses.'

'How did you get out?'

Joe looked to the other end of the hangar. The three Americans were still loitering by the door, casting glances in his direction and clearly speaking about him.

'No thanks to the Yanks,' he said. 'Cunts tried to extract as soon as Ricky went up. Left me to it.'

Fletcher wasn't one to hide the displeasure in his face, and he failed to do so now.

'Joint debrief,' he stated. 'We'll get to the bottom of this.'

Joe shook his head. 'Forget it.'

'No can do, Joe. You know that . . .'

'I said, forget it.'

'And I said, no can do. I'm ordering you to—'

'I want out, boss.'

A pause.

'What?'

'You heard me.'

'What do you think this is? A fucking poker game?'

Yeah, Joe thought to himself. And the Yanks have all the aces.

'Get yourself cleaned up,' said Fletcher. 'I want you back here in an hour.'

Joe was barely listening. Two brushes with death in as many days. His best mate blown to pieces in an Afghan minefield.

'I quit,' he said.

'Bullshit. Our numbers are too low for you to start throwing your toys out of your pram, Joe.'

'I said, I quit.'

'Then I'll recommend that the adjutant defers you. Six months. And another six months after that. If you want to go AWOL, that's your choice. Now clean yourself up and get your arse back in here.'

Such powerful anger rose in Joe's gut that for a minute he thought he might give Fletcher his own reason to head home: a broken limb, or worse. It descended on him like a fog, and the effort it took to stop himself exploding in a barrage of violence against his own OC was so profound that it seemed to make his whole body shake.

He stood up, his eyes burning.

'Get out of my way,' he whispered. His voice trembled.

Fletcher didn't move. 'You need to calm down, Mansfield.' His voice was as low as Joe's. He was clearly aware – as was Joe himself – that their argument was being observed.

The OC couldn't have said anything worse. Joe pushed past him and, ignoring the sharp looks from the twenty-odd support personnel in the hangar, he stormed towards the exit.

And there he stopped.

The broad-shouldered American commander was standing in his way. He was fully bald, highly tanned and wore a superior expression that only made the rage inside Joe burn more fiercely. 'Say, Sergeant Mansfield, maybe it's time for you and me to have a little summit.'

'Maybe it's time,' Joe breathed, 'for you to get out of my way.'

Joe noticed a couple of Yanks immediately drawing close to their boss, flanking him on either side. Joe sized up the fucking cavalry. They were a metre behind their boss and were both thickset, with crewcuts and aviator shades on their foreheads.

'Same goes for Dumb and Dumber,' Joe added.

The American commander's face gave no sign of irritation or offence. His voice, though, was threatening. 'Let's get this straight, soldier. This is an American air base . . .'

The Yanks flanking him started grinning in a stupid, arrogant way, clearly enjoying the show. The two intelligence officers Joe had seen on his way in had also joined the little party. Standing a couple of metres apart from Joe, they glanced at each other in amusement.

'. . . and on an American air base you—'

The commander didn't finish his sentence.

There was nothing subtle about Joe's attack. He just raised his knee hard into the American's bollocks. The Yank doubled over in pain, at which point Joe shoved the heel of his right hand into his nose. The big man fell backwards. Blood spattered from his nose over the clothes of the two intelligence guys. His body clattered against the door of the hangar. It rattled and echoed, and anyone who hadn't had their eyes on Joe sure as hell did now.

Joe looked at his palm. It was smeared with blood. For an instant, the gruesome image of the chunk of Ricky's flesh he'd pushed out of the way in the minefield flashed into his mind. And then another vision: the dead body in the courtyard of the compound in Abbottabad, staring blindly at Joe as he hid in his OP of rubble.

And then hands – strong, forceful hands – pulling him back, away from the confrontation. The two Yanks shouting at him, telling him to cool it. One of them had allowed his shades to fall onto his face. Joe caught sight of himself and was shocked by the look on his face.

He struggled. He was screaming something, but he didn't even know what. He realized that one of the men holding him back was JJ, whose expression was more alarmed than anything else. He wrestled himself free of his mate and the other two Regiment guys who were trying to hold him back just as the American, his face bloody and standing at a safe distance of about three metres, roared some kind of instruction that Joe barely heard.

More men. Yanks. Five of them swarmed round him and hustled him to the floor. He felt a crack in the bottom of his ribcage as one of them kicked him hard; the heel of a second boot was raised, ready to stamp into his face . . .

But then JJ and the others were there, pulling the Americans away. He saw his mate raising a fist, clearly ready to do one of the Yanks some damage, but a voice stopped him from doing it.

'*Enough!*'

Fletcher's voice rang across the hangar. Looking up, Joe saw him bearing down on the Americans, his eyes furious.

'Get the hell out of my hangar!' Fletcher was shouting. '*Get the hell out!*'

Commotion. Bustle. Joe felt himself being pulled up to his feet. He saw that the Americans had left, but now he was faced with the full fury of his OC. 'What's fucking *wrong* with you, Mansfield?' Everyone else in the hangar had fallen silent.

'I told you: I quit.'

'And *I* told you it's not an option.'

'Then there's going to be a load more Yanks with broken noses over the next few days.'

A pause.

'Fine,' said Fletcher. 'You want to spend your days stacking shelves in Tesco's and reading bedtime stories, be my fucking guest.'

Joe felt his cheek twitch, but he didn't say anything.

Fletcher had turned his back on him and started pacing. Joe could see his shoulders rising as he took deep breaths to calm himself. When he turned and spoke again, his eyes still flashed, but his voice had calmed down a bit.

'You're on the next flight out of here,' he said. 'But it's temporary. You even *think* about shaving that beard off, I'll throw you to the fucking dogs. Do whatever you need to do to get your head sorted out.'

'There's nothing wrong with my head,' Joe murmured, but he knew he didn't sound convincing.

Only now did Fletcher turn round to look at him. 'That wasn't a piece of friendly advice, Mansfield. That was an order. Follow it. Get back to your bunk while I sort this shit out, unless you want me to book a room at one of the Yanks' facilities. I'm sure they'd love to entertain you for a couple of hours.' He headed towards the exit, but stopped when he was almost at the doors, turned and called back: 'Think about the rest of us when you're down the Dog and fucking Duck, won't you?'

The OC stormed out. Joe could feel the eyes of everybody in the hangar staring at him. He could also feel his hand shaking again. About ten metres to his left, he saw JJ approaching warily. He didn't want to talk. Not to JJ, or anyone. He followed the OC's lead and strode out of the hangar.

Thirty seconds later he found himself half walking, half running through the maze of bunkhouses, not knowing where he was heading for, his mind spinning.

And thirty seconds after that, he realized he was sitting on the ground, his head bowed and buried in his hands. He didn't remember dropping down there, but that hardly mattered. It was all he could do to concentrate on breathing slowly and deeply. On getting air into his parched and dust-filled lungs.

SIX

Bristol, UK. The following day, 0900 hours.
'Bastard Coke's gone flat.'

'I can't believe you want to drink Coke first thing in the morning, man,' said a drowsy voice, barely awake. 'That's sick, you know? Sick, man.'

'Who left the top off? Was it you, Rak? It was you! I can't believe you left the bastard top off.' Narinder Kalil, whose yellow teeth made him look like his mother had lactated Coke, slammed the two-litre bottle down on the grubby carpet by his camp bed, emerged fully dressed out of his sleeping bag, sat up and looked around the room.

It was gloomy in the first-floor bedroom. The thick curtains were drawn, and only a little light peeped through from a tiny triangle where the corners met the rail. It shone a beam onto the table in the middle of the room and last night's KFC Bargain Bucket – Narinder, Rakesh and Adi could put one of those away in a matter of minutes. Next to it was Adi's pot of aqueous cream that he rubbed into the eczema on his neck half a dozen times an hour, and enough orange Semtex to turn not only this one but all the terraced houses in the street into a pile of rubble. Narinder stood up and glanced hopefully into the KFC bucket. Nothing but a mess of chicken bones, soiled napkins and empty ketchup sachets. He'd finished the Cheerios yesterday morning, and nobody had been to the shops since. 'I'm going for a cigarette,' he announced. No reply from Rak or Adi. 'Bastard lazy, you two,' he muttered as he walked to the door. And then, a little more loudly: 'Don't touch the shit, OK? *OK?*'

Snores. Narinder shook his head in disgust and left the room.

The three of them had been living in this house for just two days, and had met for the first time the day before that. None of them knew who owned the place, only that the key Narinder had received at his gran's house had fitted the lock, and that the sea of pizza delivery slips behind the door suggested nobody had been here for some weeks. It had the air of rented accommodation: threadbare carpets, no furniture except the old brown sofa downstairs and the table and three camp beds in their room, a cooker that didn't work and a kettle that tripped the fusebox for the whole house if you tried to make a cup of tea.

The door of the only other bedroom upstairs was locked. They'd tried to look through the keyhole, but someone had stuck a piece of tape over the other side, and something told them it wouldn't be a good idea to puncture it with a pencil – which had been Rakesh's first suggestion. Now Narinder padded downstairs in bare feet, opened the front door and sat down on the step before rolling a cigarette and lighting up. Of the three of them, he was the only one who smoked, but he hadn't left the bedroom out of consideration. He'd left it because although he didn't think a flick of cigarette ash could detonate the plastic explosive, he wasn't sure and this was not, he decided, a good area for experimentation.

The house was in Easton, one of Bristol's dingier inner districts. Narinder, who had lived in the city for all of his twenty-three years, had never been here. At first he'd worried that keeping the bedroom curtains closed day and night would attract attention, but you didn't have to spend more than a few hours in Crown Street to realize that at least half the windows in the road were permanently covered. The house opposite was derelict, with boarded-up windows and a steel security door. The squatters had still got in, however. Narinder had realized this on the first night, when he'd seen light seeping from cracks in the boards, and he couldn't help wondering why the house he and his companions were in hadn't been taken over. Maybe the squatters knew something about the person who owned it. Certainly nobody had given Narinder any aggro. Apart from an old lady who walked past three times a day with a shopping trolley, everyone else he had seen had been black or Asian. That suited him fine. It meant he, Rak and Adi were just three more faces. Nobody even questioned their presence.

It took him no more than a minute to suck down his first roll-up, stub it out under his Reeboks and roll a second. It was just as he was licking the Rizla that he noticed he was being watched.

He started, and jumped up to his feet. A tall man with a slight stoop was standing three metres away, where the pavement met the litter-strewn front yard. He wore a waxed green raincoat – the sort of garment, Narinder thought, that an English country gentleman might put on for a day's shooting. But this was no English gent. He had dark skin and thin, floppy black hair. He was staring at Narinder with an expression that was impossible to read.

'Who the bastard hell are you?' Narinder demanded, silently cursing himself for taking a step backwards.

A frown of disapproval flickered across the stranger's face. Narinder found himself stammering. 'I mean . . . who . . . who are . . . ?'

'You must be Narinder,' said the stranger. He opened the gate and started walking towards the door. 'You've made yourself at home, I hope?'

Narinder nodded.

'I'm pleased.'

He stopped. Narinder didn't move.

'Well?' said the stranger. He was standing just half a metre away. 'Are you going to let me in, Narinder? It's a crisp morning, and I'd rather not spend it standing outside.'

Narinder shook his head. 'No,' he said. 'I ain't supposed to let anyone . . .'

The stranger smiled. 'Your grandmother is in good health?'

Narinder's eyes widened as he recognized the pass phrase by which he would know the man they were waiting for. He nodded, as though the newcomer was really interested in the well-being of his relations, hastily shoved his unlit roll-up behind his ear, and kicked the door open with his heel before standing aside to let him enter. Once he was inside, Narinder walked in too and closed the door behind him. He followed the man along the hallway, suddenly full of questions. 'What's your name, mister? This your place, is it? I don't want to make a fuss or nothing, but you could have left us some bog roll. We had to use the *Daily Mirror* first day we got here.' They were walking up the stairs now, Narinder three steps behind the man. 'They're still asleep, Rakesh and Adi. Bastard lazy, them two. Dunno where you found them, mister. What you say your name was again?'

They had reached the landing now. The older man stopped and turned. He had a patient look on his face. 'My name is Mr Ashe,' he said quietly. 'Narinder, have you and the others started work?'

'Course. We've been here three days.'

'So you have.' He glanced towards the door of the locked bedroom. 'You'll excuse me, I hope? I'll be pleased to meet the others when they've caught up on their well-deserved sleep.' He turned and, pulling a key from the pocket of his coat, approached the door. 'You're happy with their abilities? Rakesh and Adi, I mean.'

Narinder was surprised by the question. 'I guess,' he said. He gave a grin that Mr Ashe couldn't see with his back to him. 'Y'know, bastard lazy and everything . . .'

'If you have any concerns, you'll come to me? I need good people like you that I can trust, Narinder.'

'Er, yeah. Course.' He stood on the landing while Mr Ashe let himself into the room and closed the door.

The house was silent again. Somewhere outside, in the distance, Narinder heard a police siren, but it faded away after five seconds. He took a step towards Mr Ashe's door, raised one fist as though to knock, then thought better of it and returned to the bedroom he shared with the others. It was still dark in there, and they were still asleep. He flicked on the light – a pendant with a spherical paper shade that was covered in cobwebs and as yellow as his teeth. 'Wake up,' he said. 'Mr Ashe is here. Told him you was bastard lazy. You're lucky he sent me to wake you up.' He walked round the table, first to Rak's bed, then to Adi's, kicking each one of them in turn. 'You think these things are going to make themselves while you're sleeping, do you? We got to get to work.'

'Who's Mr Ashe, man?' Rakesh stood up. Like Narinder he was still wearing last night's clothes, and he too cast a hopeful glance into the KFC bucket. 'He give you the password?'

'What you think I am? Stupid?'

'Yeah,' Rakesh said, as if it was an obvious answer to an obvious question.

'You want to watch it, mate. Hey, Adi, man, you got to do that in front of us?'

Adi had approached the table, opened his aqueous cream and was slathering it onto his neck. 'Did you ask him?' he said quietly.

'Ask him what?'

Adi wiped the surplus cream from his fingers onto his faded black jeans. 'You know. Did you ask him?'

Narinder did know, of course. The three of them had talked of little else. They had watched the news of the Lion's death on the television like everybody else. Unlike most people, however, they had not rejoiced.

Osama bin Laden – the Lion, the Sheikh al-Mujahid, the Director – had been in hiding for as long as these three young men had known who he was. And yet Narinder felt a strong bond with him, and he was sure Rakesh and Adi did too. It was a bond that had been forged when, in his early teens, he had looked up to the older kids at the mosque who talked openly about the evils of the Great Satan America, and Little Satan Britain. Who had hinted of their allegiance to, and recruitment by, Islamist cells. And of course there was one Islamist movement that they all wanted to be associated with. When Narinder was nineteen, and doing Islamic Studies at Thames Valley University, he was given the chance to travel to Pakistan. Nobody mentioned the name 'Al-Qaeda' until he was actually there, one of twenty men of a similar age, spending a summer at a training camp thirty miles south-west of Quetta where they learned how to strip down an AK-47, how to make a serviceable detonator, and how to hate – really hate – the West. If the War on Terror truly was a war, he learned, then it needed soldiers on both sides. When Narinder returned to the UK he didn't look or sound any different, but he certainly felt it. On the outside, an unremarkable young man of British-Asian descent. On the inside, a soldier waiting for the chance to fight.

But what now? That was the question these three young Al-Qaeda recruits had been asking each other. The Lion was gone. What did it mean for Al-Qaeda? What did it mean for them? Had they backed the wrong horse? When the young men at the mosque who were affiliated to other groups – the Muslim Brotherhood or the Young Muslim Organization – gave them superior looks the day after the news broke, were they right to do so? Narinder, Rakesh and Adi knew they were waiting here for somebody who was much higher in the Al-Qaeda hierarchy than they were. Surely this Mr Ashe would be able to tell them what the future held.

'No, I didn't ask him,' Narinder muttered. 'He only just got here. Guy don't want us—'

'Ask me what?'

Narinder, Rakesh and Adi looked suddenly round. None of them had heard the door open, nor seen Mr Ashe standing there. He was no longer wearing his raincoat, but an elegant grey suit.

They blinked stupidly at him.

'We was just, you know, thinking, Mr Ashe,' said Narinder. 'With the Director being, you know—'

'Our struggle,' Mr Ashe interrupted, 'continues.'

He looked at each of them in turn. His face, Narinder thought to himself, was much softer than those of the fiery-eyed teachers he'd had in Pakistan. But he had authority. No doubt about that.

Mr Ashe stepped into the room. His gaze fell on the contents of the table, and he nodded appreciatively for a moment. 'When this' – he stretched out his arm to indicate the Semtex – 'comes to fruition, they will understand that they cannot defeat us simply by killing one man.' He smiled at them and pulled out a book from the pocket of his jacket. It was smaller than an ordinary book, bound in leather and fastened with a strap. Narinder caught sight of the words 'Holy Koran' written on the front cover in gold lettering. 'We shall pray together,' said Mr Ashe.

Narinder glanced at the other two. The truth was that they were more interested in action than prayer. Back in the training camp, he had knelt towards Mecca because he'd been told to; his trips to the mosque were more social than religious. But he sensed that they were as unwilling as he was to disobey this strange, quiet man. And so all three knelt with him as he read in Arabic from his Koran, before intoning a familiar prayer. And once he had left the room, each went silently about his business, carefully cutting the slabs of Semtex as they had been taught into smaller, flatter rectangles, ready to accept a charge, ready to pack them into whatever housing they were eventually given.

It was an hour later when Narinder suddenly scraped back his chair and got to his feet. Rakesh and Adi both looked up at him.

'I need a slash, all right?' he said.

He left the room.

The toilet was separate from the bathroom, and situated next to the locked bedroom. A piece of worn, grey vinyl flooring, curled at the edges, was covered with sticky yellow piss stains around the pan. Rakesh, Narinder had observed, was bastard filthy and couldn't aim properly. He loosened himself from his fly and was about to empty his bladder when he heard something unusual. It came from his left, from the other side of the wall that separated the toilet from the locked bedroom. Narinder edged towards it, put his ear to the wall and held his breath so that he could hear better. It was white noise, like an untuned old-fashioned TV set. It meant nothing to Narinder, who just shrugged, stepped back to the toilet and pissed noisily into the water. Once he'd flushed, he waited for the cistern to refill before listening against the wall again. The noise was still there.

Back out on the landing he stopped outside Mr Ashe's door. He could hear the white noise more clearly from here. Again he wanted to knock, but there was something about Mr Ashe that made him feel nervous. His instructors at the camp in Pakistan had been brutal, and Narinder had been scared of them, but Mr Ashe didn't need to threaten any of them with violence for them to do what he said.

And so Narinder almost surprised himself when he found himself rapping his knuckles against the door.

'Do come in.'

Narinder opened up, and stepped inside.

He hadn't really known what to expect, it was true, but the room that had been locked these past three days was disappointingly bland. The curtains were closed and the light switched off. There was a camp bed, just like the ones the three of them had been sleeping on. Mr Ashe was sitting at what looked like an IKEA table. A laptop was open in front of him, and his face was bathed in the glow from its screen. Next to it was a handheld digital radio – it was this that was making the white noise – and his copy of the Koran, open about halfway through, and face downwards.

'I'm glad you knocked, Narinder.' Mr Ashe smiled, and Narinder flashed his yellow teeth at him in return.

'Wicked,' Narinder said, but his mouth was suddenly dry.

'Please tell the others to stop work. You are needed elsewhere.'

'What?' Narinder shook his head in confusion. 'But . . .'

'Please, Narinder. I'll explain everything when we're all together.' He gave him a meaningful look. 'I can rely on you to organize the others?'

'Yeah,' he nodded. 'Yeah, course. I'll just . . .' He jabbed his thumb over his shoulder and stepped backwards out of the room, closing the door as he went. He sniffed, then turned and re-entered the bedroom he shared with the others. They didn't even look up as he walked in – they were too busy cutting out their rectangles of explosive. 'OK, you two. On your feet.'

Rakesh and Adi looked at him with scorn.

'Whatever,' Narinder shrugged. 'If you don't want to do what Mr Ashe says, that's your bastard decision.'

It was enough. The other two stood up with obvious reluctance. 'What we doing?' Rakesh asked.

Narinder gave him what he hoped was an enigmatic smile. 'Ah, you'll find out, man,' he said. 'Mr Ashe, he'll tell you what you need to know when you need to know it.'

Before they could ask any more questions, Narinder left the room and stood in the hallway, waiting for the others to join him.

Mr Ashe watched Narinder leave the room, and he continued to stare at the closed door for a full ten seconds after he was alone. Only then did he turn his attention back to the laptop.

He was looking at a black and white image, rather grainy, of an ordinary street. Anybody would be able to tell from a glance

94

that it was in the UK – there was a pillar box on the right, and the blur of a BT van driving out of the shot. Mr Ashe, however, knew a bit more than that. He knew, for example, the name of the road – Lancing Way – and that the street was located in the border town of Hereford. In the bottom-right corner of the screen was a time code. It read '10:58', and indicated that this was the final frame in a stop-motion video lasting ten minutes and fifty-eight seconds. He pressed the laptop's mouse button with his right thumb and, keeping it down, swiped the trackpad with a long-nailed forefinger. The video restarted and Mr Ashe watched it all through again.

Time code 00:00: nothing but Lancing Way. No cars parked on either side, the pavements lined with temporary barriers indicating that roadworks were to take place soon.

01:20: a man walks towards the camera with a black Labrador on a lead.

05:26: a harassed mother ushers two children along the pavement in the opposite direction.

08:41: a black Land Rover Discovery trundles slowly along the street towards the camera. It stops about fifty metres away in the middle of the road. The driver climbs out and opens the rear passenger door. A second man appears. He is wearing jeans and a hooded grey top, and has a black North Face bag slung over his right shoulder. He is half a head taller than the driver and has an unkempt black beard. Even with this low-quality footage, Mr Ashe can make out the dark rings around his eyes, and he observes the heavy slump in the man's gait as he squeezes between two of the roadworks barriers separating the road from the pavement. The driver watches him go. When it becomes clear that he's not going to get any acknowledgement from his passenger, he shrugs, climbs back into the Discovery and drives off out of view.

08:44: the bearded passenger stops outside one of the houses. It has a neatly trimmed hedge at the front. He stares at the house for a minute before walking up to the front door and ringing the bell. Almost a minute passes.

08:45: the door opens. Mr Ashe cannot see who is there, but he can sense the awkwardness as he or she stands back to let this bearded man enter. The door closes, and now the only thing moving on the screen is the time code, ticking down to the end of the video.

A knock on the door. 'Do come in,' he said for the second time.

It was Narinder.

'They're ready, Mr Ashe.'

Mr Ashe smiled. 'Do come in, all of you,' he said. With a last glance at the screen, he shut the lid of the laptop, then looked up at his three young recruits. They seemed nervous, but eager to do well.

Just the men for the job.

SEVEN

Hereford, UK. 1008 hours.

The duty driver who drove Joe to Hereford had offered him a seat in the front. Joe had preferred to sit alone in the back of the black Discovery. That way it was easier not to talk.

Bagram one day. Brize Norton the next. It was enough to fuck with anyone's head. The sun had been rising over the English countryside as they came in to land. After nearly six months of seeing nothing but the yellows and browns of the desert, the green fields were almost blindingly intense. Joe supposed he should welcome them. For some reason, he didn't. Now, though, clouds had rolled in and there was a chill in the air. A typical English May morning.

He was standing on the ordinary pavement of this ordinary street. An empty street. No Humvees or MRAPS, nor even any Astras or Fiestas, their absence explained by a sign pinned to a lamppost: '4–6 May, roadworks, no parking'. Joe stood on the pavement for a full minute, listening to the silence. It was something he had barely heard for months. In the Stan there was always the noise of a vehicle, or an artillery shell, or some squaddie shouting at his mates. He became aware of a tawny cat sitting on the pavement five metres away, staring at him with pale yellow eyes, and he remembered the lame cat that had limped over the minefield the previous day. 'Fuck's sake,' he muttered as he pushed that picture from his mind, hitched his bag further up his shoulder and stepped in the direction of his own front door.

Number 38 Lancing Way was a tiny two-bedroom terraced house, just big enough for Joe, his girlfriend Caitlin and their boy, Conor. Caitlin and Joe had met in Northern Ireland back in 1995, when he was a newbie to the Regiment and she was a local girl serving beers at Daft Eddy's on Strangford Lough. What they'd both assumed would be a no-strings-attached Sunday-afternoon shag had turned into something more permanent, and Joe had got to know pretty well the route from the Regiment base at Aldergrove to the flat Caitlin shared with two other girls in central Belfast. He'd never told her that he'd run police checks on all three of them before seeing her for a second time. What she didn't know couldn't piss her off.

When Joe was recalled to Hereford in the summer of '97, he'd come clean to Caitlin that he wasn't really working for British Telecom. She told him she'd politely pretended that she had believed his little deception, and agreed to come with him. They'd shacked up in army accommodation, and while Joe was hoovering up war criminals in the Balkans, or pulling Royal Irish Rangers out of enemy strongholds in Sierra Leone, Caitlin had seemed happy to play house. When she fell pregnant in '00 – a surprise to both of them – she'd insisted that an army house was no longer good enough. Which was why Joe now found himself here, walking past the neatly maintained front garden, all shrubs and white gravel, and rapping a dirty fist on the red front door.

He saw her approach through the two glass panels: the silhouette of her curly red hair, the gentle slope of her slim shoulders. He saw the way that she hesitated for a few seconds before opening up, doing something to her hair as she prepared to welcome home the man she hadn't seen for six months.

The door opened. Caitlin's pretty face was midway between pleasure and nervousness.

'Hi,' she whispered.

She wasn't one for make-up. Her clear, delicately freckled

skin had a beautiful, natural glow to it. Today, though, Joe noticed she was wearing lip gloss and mascara. She had on slim jeans and a halterneck top that clung slightly to her small breasts – the kind of clothes she normally wore on a night out, not at ten o'clock on a Wednesday morning. Some of the lads used to tell Joe that she looked like something out of the Corrs; no doubt they said other things behind his back.

'Hi,' he replied.

Caitlin stepped back so he could cross the threshold. Only when he had shut the door behind him did she wrap her arms around his neck and give him a brief, awkward hug, before standing back again and brushing her fingertips against the wall. 'I redecorated,' she said.

Joe blinked. The walls were powder blue, though what colour they'd been before, he had no idea. 'Right,' he replied.

'Conor's in his room. I said he didn't have to go to school . . .'

Joe glanced up the stairs. His boy was only nine years old. Or was it ten? He realized, in a moment of guilt, that he'd had a birthday in April that Joe hadn't even acknowledged. Conor was a good kid, at least that's what his teachers said. Privately, Joe wished he would spend a little less time with his nose in a book, or at a screen playing games. When Joe was Conor's age, he'd spent every spare hour out of doors, getting muddy, playing imaginary versions of the war games that would become his life. Conor just didn't seem interested in stuff like that.

'He's been looking forward to seeing you,' Caitlin said.

Joe dropped his bag on the hallway floor. When he looked at Caitlin again, he saw that her eyes were brimming with tears. 'What's the matter?' he asked.

Caitlin wiped the tears from her eyes. She looked angry with herself for crying. 'Nothing,' she said.

'Christ, Caitlin, it's been a long couple of—'

'Two months,' she interrupted, her voice cracking. 'Two months, Joe.'

'Since what?'

'Since I *heard* from you.'

Silence.

'Right.'

'Conor's been asking every day when he's going to see his dad. When he didn't get a birthday letter from you, he asked me if you were . . .' The tears had reappeared; she wiped them away again, this time smearing mascara over her stricken face. 'Sorry . . . I'm sorry . . . I wasn't going to . . .'

'I'm going to get cleaned up,' Joe said. He pushed past her, but then felt her hand grab his wrist.

'I've missed you so much, Joe,' she whispered. 'We both have.' She hugged him again, this time resting her head against his chest. Joe breathed in her perfume and allowed the warmth from her body to saturate his. In his six months away he had forgotten how good it felt.

'I really need to wash,' he said. Caitlin separated herself from him and squeezed his hand. He headed up the stairs.

Conor's room was at the top of the staircase on the right. The door, which had a tattered Spider-Man poster pinned to it, was closed. Joe put his ear to it and heard the beeping of his son's DS. He tried to force his face into a look of pleasure. It didn't come naturally. He was about to put his hand to the doorknob when he sensed that he was being watched. Looking over his shoulder, he saw Caitlin at the bottom of the stairs, staring up with swollen eyes. Joe lowered his hand, turned away and walked across the tiny landing into the double bedroom.

Thick carpet. Flowery curtains. Neat bedspread. It couldn't have been more different from the Portakabin he'd been sharing with Ricky and JJ in Bagram, and Joe didn't even feel he belonged in this room. Like he dirtied it. He immediately returned to the landing, and from there went into the bathroom. He stripped naked, dumping his clothes on the ceramic tiles. Caitlin had laid out wash things for him: toothbrush, razor, shaving gel. She was a lot less keen on his beard than the ruperts were. Joe didn't bother with the gel. He started hacking at his matted beard with the razor. Clumps of hair fell into the apricot-coloured basin; the blade became dull after about fifteen swipes. He changed it, and continued to swipe at his face until he felt the blunt steel against his skin.

It took five minutes and three changes of blade to remove the beard. By the time he'd thrown the razor into the hair-filled basin, his face was bleeding in several places. Joe didn't care. He stepped over the edge of the bath, pulled the opaque, floral shower curtain closed and turned on the water, maximum temperature. It was scalding, but Joe didn't flinch as he held his face up to the shower head and allowed it to burn and soak him. He didn't move for a minute. When he finally looked down, he saw that he was standing in an inch of dirty water, and still his skin wasn't clean. He checked the thermostat, wanting to turn the heat higher. When a sharp twist confirmed that the water was as hot as it could be, he slammed his fist in anger against the wall tiles next to him. How the hell could he wash off six months of shit and death without . . . ?

Now the water was freezing. His eyes were closed. He opened them to see that he was sitting in the bath, the shower pouring from a height over his head. The water that had collected in the bath was clean now, save for a layer of gritty silt sitting along the enamel. He had no memory of how he'd got down here, or how long he had been sitting.

But it wasn't that which scared him the most. What scared him were the shadows behind the shower curtain.

Two people. One standing further back than the other.

Joe slowed down his breathing to stop the panic rising in his chest, and moved his right hand to where the shower curtain was stuck to the inside of the bath. He carefully scrunched it in his palm and, with a sudden yank, ripped down the whole curtain, jumping to his feet at the same time.

A scream. Caitlin had her hand to her mouth, and little Conor, his russet hair scruffy and his face pale, edged backwards in alarm. Joe stared at them, naked and confused, as Caitlin ushered their son out of the bathroom before turning off the shower.

Silence. Joe looked around the room, but couldn't bring himself to catch Caitlin's eye.

'You've been in here over an hour, honey,' she said. Her voice was full of concern.

Joe looked down at his naked body, at the scars on his chest and the blisters on his feet. 'I was dirty.'

Caitlin looked like she wanted to say something else but was too nervous to do so. Joe stepped out of the bath. There was a white towel hanging on the back of the door. He wrapped it round his waist and walked into their bedroom, where he sat on the edge of the bed, staring at the striped wallpaper, and at a small picture Conor had drawn about a year ago, mounted in a cheap glass frame. It was a childishly drawn picture of Joe, dressed in what Conor called his 'army clothes' and wearing a Tommy Atkins hat with a strap under the chin that made him look like something out of the First World War. Not a laser marker or a flashbang in sight.

After waiting outside for a minute or so, Caitlin entered the room. She stood with her back to the closed door, as if wary of intruding.

'Why did you pull the shower curtain off like that?' she asked.

Joe sniffed. 'I thought you were . . .'

'What?'

Yeah, Joe thought to himself. What? 'Nothing,' he said.

'Come on, honey, what did you . . . ?'

'Leave it, all right?'

Silence.

'I heard about Ricky,' she said.

No surprise there. Nothing travelled faster than gossip among the Regiment wives and girlfriends. Caitlin sounded frail as she said it. She'd been fond of Ricky. He used to tease her, and her face would light up every time he did it.

'I was with him.'

Immediately she was by his side, one arm around his shoulders.

'How did it happen?' she whispered.

'You don't want to know.'

'I just . . .'

'Look, forget it. He's not fucking here. He died. Just like every other fucker that goes out there.'

Silence. Caitlin kept her arm around his shoulder for a few more seconds, then awkwardly withdrew it. 'Sorry,' she said.

Joe nodded.

'I spoke to your adjutant,' Caitlin whispered. 'He said you were . . . he said maybe . . . they were sending a doctor to talk to you . . . this afternoon . . .'

'Tell them not to bother.' Ricky was the one who'd needed a fucking doctor.

'But Joe, if something's wrong . . .'

She raised her hand to his face and gently forced him to look at her. All he saw were mascara-smudged eyes.

'I'm sorry I gave you a hard time, Joe. I'm *so* sorry. I just—'

'I need to sleep,' Joe interrupted. He stood up suddenly, walked around the bed and closed the curtains. They had thick blackout linings, and blocked most of the light from the room.

'I'll leave you then,' Caitlin said, standing up.

'Right,' said Joe.

He knew he was being a bastard, but somehow he couldn't stop it. And by the time he was under the duvet, she had left the room.

It was a sleep of sorts, but troubled, broken and disturbed by dreams that were both vivid and sickening. Joe saw himself in Abbottabad. From his hiding place under the rubble, he watched first one body bag emerge from the house, and then the second.

They were halfway across the courtyard when the first bag mysteriously split open. A body sat up: a thin man with a grey beard, wearing a bloodstained smock. He had a gruesome gun wound to the head that had turned one eye socket into a crater of bloody pap. But the good eye was blinking and looking directly at Joe. The mouth was moving. Joe couldn't understand the sinister Arabic intonation. He didn't *want* to understand it. He tried to block his ears, but it only made the noise louder. He felt for his pistol. The only way to stop it was to shoot the bastard again. Joe steadied his shaking hand and took aim . . . he was ready to fire . . .

Only he wasn't looking at a corpse any more. He was looking at Ricky, sitting up from the body bag and giving Joe a perplexed look.

And then he was sitting up in bed, sweating, trembling. The bedside clock showed 11.58.

Joe swore at himself, before lying down again and closing his eyes, determined to rest.

But his dreams took him somewhere else. He was on all fours, pressed against the dusty desert earth with the sun beating down on his back. He heard a child's voice: 'Amer-ee-can motherfucker . . . Amer-ee-can motherfucker . . .' He looked over his shoulder to see who was speaking. It wasn't a kid. It was the same figure from his previous dream, with the same crater-like wound in his eye socket.

And then another explosion.

And another . . .

And another . . .

Joe was back in his bedroom at home. 13.02. The sheets were soaked. His breath came in short gasps. But the explosions – they weren't in his head any more. They were real.

He jumped out of bed. A pair of jeans and a fresh shirt had been laid out for him while he slept. He pulled on the jeans as the explosions continued. He stormed out of the bedroom and onto the landing. Gunfire, short bursts from an automatic weapon. And it was coming from the direction of his son's bedroom.

Joe didn't hesitate. He burst through the door, which swung on its hinges and bashed against the wall.

Conor's room hadn't changed since he'd been away. The cabin bed was still neatly made; the encyclopedias he loved were lined up on his bookcase. Conor himself was sitting on a spotty beanbag in the middle of the room. He was facing a small television, with an Xbox controller in his hand. Joe looked to the screen. His son was playing one of the war games that were so popular with the younger men back in the Stan. From the point of view of a player with an assault rifle, Joe could see a realistic desert landscape, with an animated Chinook hovering in the distance. Two Taliban fighters, their heads wrapped in keffi-yehs, approached. Conor was ignoring the game now, looking up at his father with frightened eyes. The animated Taliban drew knives. Now they were at the front of the screen. An instant later there was the sickening sound of metal puncturing flesh and a rattling death groan from the device.

Joe felt an unstoppable rage. He stepped into the centre of the room, grabbed the controller from Conor's tiny hands and yanked the cords that connected them to the console. The Xbox flew forward, but the game played on. The virtual soldier was on the ground, virtual blood spilling onto the virtual sand. Joe stormed up to the TV and before he knew it he had yanked the screen off its little stand and sent it crashing to the ground.

At last there was silence.

Joe looked down at the smashed television, and then at Conor, whose lip was wobbling as he tried to hold back his tears. He tried to think of something to say. But he couldn't. The explosions and gunfire were still in his head, like distant echoes, distracting his attention.

Footsteps up the stairs. Caitlin appeared in the doorway, taking in the scene with a single glance. She had swapped the halter-neck for an altogether less glamorous black T-shirt. The three of them remained very still, in a triangle of silence, Conor and Caitlin staring at Joe like he was a stranger.

Ten seconds passed before Joe stormed out of the room, pushing past Caitlin and heading downstairs. 'He shouldn't be playing that shit all day anyway,' he muttered. 'Can't he play fucking football?'

He could hear their voices through the thin ceiling as he walked into the front room, though he couldn't make out what they were saying. He was angry with himself. What the hell had he been thinking? He stood at the bay window, looking out at the street. Some kid was sitting on the front garden wall of the house opposite. Almost as a reflex action, Joe found himself recording his features: dark skin; greasy black hair; yellow, rotten teeth; late teens, early twenties. He was twirling an empty bottle of Coke in his right hand. For an instant he thought the kid was looking straight through the window at him.

'Tell me what's wrong?'

Caitlin had entered the room without Joe hearing.

'You wouldn't understand,' he said.

'Try me.'

Silence.

Caitlin approached him. Her face had softened, and for the first time in days he felt his defences lower. 'I heard the noises from that fucking game,' he said. 'I thought they were real.'

He stared at Caitlin, as though daring her to laugh. 'You're home now,' she whispered. 'With us.'

From the corner of his eye he saw movement on the street. Another kid had approached his mate with the rotten teeth. They shared a few words and walked off down the street.

'Go and talk to him,' she said. 'Properly, Joe. He's been aching to see you.'

Conor was still in his room, but had moved from the beanbag

to the raised bed, where he had wrapped himself in his duvet and had a sketch pad open in front of him, and next to that the small grey elephant that had been his since he was a baby. Joe could never work out how one minute he could be playing war games, the next running his finger over the worn fabric of a soft toy. He had his mother's colouring: copper hair and pale freckles on his nose and cheeks. In fact, he was as unlike Joe in looks as he was in personality. Joe approached the bed and glanced down. Conor's gaze was fixed on the drawing he was making, two figures, scrappy and childlike. He refused to look up at his dad.

'Hey, champ,' Joe said quietly.

'Hey.' Conor didn't look up as he spoke.

'School OK?'

Conor shrugged, treating the question with the lack of interest it deserved.

'What you drawing?'

'Nothing.' He looked embarrassed.

'Mind if I keep that?' It sounded to Joe like the sort of thing a good dad should say.

Conor shook his head and ripped the sheet from his pad, before handing it to his father.

'Got a bit carried away there, I guess,' Joe said, pocketing the picture without really looking at it.

Conor looked like he was pretending it didn't matter, but Joe could see salt marks on his cheeks where the tears had dried. He put one hand on his boy's bony shoulder; when, after ten seconds, it became clear that neither of them knew what else to say, he turned and headed for the door.

'Why were you sitting in the shower like that, Dad?' He sounded frightened.

'Don't worry about it, champ,' Joe replied. He winked at Conor, wanting to change the subject quickly but not knowing how. Conor smiled thinly back. 'Hey,' said Joe, 'it's great to see you.'

'You too.'

An awkward silence. 'I'm going to talk to your mum, OK?'

'OK.'

Joe left the room, closed the door and stood with his back to it.

Why were you sitting in the shower like that, Dad?

'Don't worry about it,' he breathed to himself.

He went downstairs.

On the mantelpiece in the front room was a tinny little carriage clock. It chimed 4 p.m. As the fourth chime disappeared, the only sound in the room was the continued ticking of the clock. Joe shifted uncomfortably on the chintzy sofa that faced the window looking out onto the street. There was a matching armchair in the bay; sitting in the armchair, holding a red clipboard and a pencil, was a pretty young woman whose hair was tied back with a ribbon and who was patiently waiting for Joe to answer her.

Thirty seconds passed. The young woman repeated her question. Her voice dripped sympathy and it set Joe's teeth on edge. He didn't *want* sympathy.

'How have you been sleeping?'

'Like a baby.'

'I see a lot of soldiers who have trouble with it.'

'You ever tried sleeping in a war zone, Dr McGill?'

'Are you telling me you haven't been sleeping?'

'I'm telling you I could do without the stupid questions.'

Dr McGill ticked a box on the paper clipped to her board.

'Do you suffer from blackouts?'

'Blackouts?'

'Short periods when you can't account for your movements. Temporary amnesia . . .'

'I know what a blackout is.'

'So do you?'

'No.'

'Your wife—'

'Partner.'

'Your *partner* told me she found you this morning sitting in the—'

'I'm not suffering from blackouts, Dr McGill.'

The doctor inclined her head. 'Anxiety attacks? Breathlessness? Hallucinations? Paranoia?' she asked.

'Is this going to take much longer?'

'That depends on you.'

'No, no, no and no.'

She didn't look like she believed him. Maybe it was the way he refused to catch her eye.

'I have to ask you this question, Joe,' she continued. 'Have you, at any point in the past six months, had any thoughts of hurting yourself in any way? Or worse?'

Joe couldn't help himself looking scornful. Images flashed in his mind of operations out on the ground in Afghanistan. He saw himself creeping by moonlight through villages known to be overrun with insurgents; he saw himself cutting the throat of a seventeen-year-old Taliban recruit who he knew had laid an IED that had killed three British soldiers; he saw himself stuck inside the compound at Abbottabad, praying that the Americans wouldn't see him. Thoughts of hurting himself? His every thought over those six months had been about keeping himself safe. Hurting other people, maybe – but this earnest young doctor hadn't asked about that.

'No,' he said. That, at least, he could answer honestly.

'Are you sure? I understand that these things can be difficult to talk about.'

'Look, love,' Joe replied. 'If I'd wanted to get myself hurt, I'd have had plenty of opportunity, believe me. Why don't you fill in the rest of your boxes and get the hell—?'

He stopped.

Through the bay window, he could see something. The kid with the rotten teeth. He was sitting on the wall opposite again. His bottle of Coke was full now, and as he took a swig he kept his eyes on Joe's house.

Joe stood up. 'Wait there,' he murmured.

He found Caitlin standing in the hallway, looking anxious. She opened her mouth to speak as Joe came out of the front room, but he hushed her sharply and edged towards the front door. There was a spyhole in the door – Caitlin had insisted on having it for when Joe was on tour. He peered through it. The street appeared distorted, like he was looking out from inside a goldfish bowl. He couldn't spot the kid, but there was a flicker of movement on the edge of his vision.

'Joe, what . . . ?'

'Stay where you are.' Joe ran back to the kitchen, where he rummaged quickly in the drawer by the oven for a blade. He found a five-inch chopping knife and ran with it to the front door. He opened up and strode outside, the knife hidden behind his back.

But the kid had gone.

He looked up and down the road. Nothing.

Caitlin was standing by the front door now, and he could see the doctor a couple of metres behind her. Neither woman spoke but Joe could almost hear their thoughts as their eyes flickered between his face and the knife in his hand. 'I thought I saw someone,' he said, and when that didn't appear satisfactorily to explain his actions to Caitlin or Dr McGill, he pushed past them and into the living room, where he dropped back down onto the sofa and distractedly examined the blade. He could hear the women talking in the hallway, but their voices were just a blur.

Two minutes passed. Caitlin and Dr McGill returned.

'You need to understand, Joe,' the doctor said, sitting down beside him and giving him a kind look that made him want to throttle her, 'that sometimes, when people have experienced extreme stress, they can be traumatized in ways that they find difficult to control.' She sounded like she was talking to a child. 'I'm prescribing you some tablets. They might help you. Some people experience side effects . . . they can make you feel worse before you feel better . . . but it's very important that you take them every day.' She started writing out a prescription. 'And I'm going to recommend that you see someone. Talking therapies can be very useful in situations like this.'

She held out the prescription, but Joe didn't take it, so she placed it on the sofa next to him.

'You'll get that prescription as soon as you can? Today, if possible?'

No answer.

'I'll explain everything to your wi— your partner.'

No answer.

'It's very important that you take this medication, Joe.'

No answer.

'I'll show myself out.'

'You do that.'

More voices in the corridor. The sound of the front door opening and closing. Joe saw the doctor walking briskly past the front window. And then Caitlin was there again, standing over him with a worried frown.

Joe took the prescription, but didn't even look at it before ripping it in two, scrunching up the pieces and throwing them into the centre of the room.

'Joe . . .' Caitlin started to say, but she fell silent as he stood up.

'I'm going out,' he said.

There were the pubs of Hereford, and then there were the places people went to drink. The Three Barrels was one of the latter. Frosted-glass windows. Sticky tables. Sticky floor. Slippery customers. A faint, lingering smell from the urinals. An old TV set hanging in one corner, the volume muted, which nobody watched.

Joe had been dry for six months. There was plenty of hooch knocking around Bagram, of course, and it would have to be a fucking stupid officer who didn't let his men relax after several days of repeated contact. But for the Regiment lads it had been a no-no, and that was nothing to do with the ruperts. When your fitness and a clear head are all that's between you and an enemy round, you do everything you can to take care of them.

Now Joe drank like he was watering the desert. Pints of strong, cold lager – Kronenberg – he wasn't even counting how many, though he had the impression that the Aussie barmaid, with her nose stud, low-cut top and the edge of a tattoo peeking above her cleavage, was. The winos came and went; it grew dark outside. Joe maintained his position at the bar, carefully avoiding eye contact with anyone, doing everything he could to drink himself into forgetfulness. It didn't seem to be working. When the TV screen showed what he immediately recognized as the compound in Abbottabad, swarming with journalists, he turned and looked the other way before downing what was left of his pint and ordering another.

He only left because the barmaid told him three times that she was closing up. He certainly had no idea what time it was, or how long he'd been in there; it was only as he staggered to the door, finally drunk, that he realized he was the last punter. Out on the pavement he swayed as he looked up and down the street, trying to get his bearings. A line of people snaked out of the door of a kebab shop on the other side of the road. The yellow and red signs became momentarily blurred, tracing neon lines in the air as he moved his head from left to right; the headlights of cars travelling in either direction, one every three or four seconds, did the same. Ten metres to his left he saw a little mob of six townies starting the opening salvoes of what would clearly end up as a fist fight; he saw a couple snogging in the bus stop opposite; he saw people walking up and down both sides of this busy Hereford street, even though it was late.

He saw a kid with dark skin and yellow teeth leaning against the window of the kebab shop, a bottle of Coke in his right hand.

The alcohol in his system made everything spin. He staggered back against the door of the Three Barrels, his head suddenly filled with the shouts of the little mob. He tried to shake off a wave of nausea.

Then he looked up again. The kid with the Coke bottle was gone.

The mob's disagreement had shifted to the area of the pavement bang in front of Joe. He burst through them – they fell silent for a couple of seconds – then strode into the road. He heard the screeching of brakes and saw the line of people outside the kebab shop turn to look at him. He stepped among them, moving along the line, checking their faces, grabbing those who had their backs to him by the shoulders and yanking them round. Angry mutters quickly became more forceful. A squat guy with balding scalp and a rugby player's physique pushed Joe in the chest. 'Get out of it, sunshine. You're fucking steaming . . .' Joe fell backwards, regained his balance and scanned the line once more. No, the kid with the Coke wasn't there, and as he looked beyond the queue and over his shoulder, there was no sign of him.

Maybe he'd been seeing things. A pint or two of Kronenberg too many.

Sixty seconds later he was away from the main road, walking on autopilot through the network of streets that formed the route from the Three Barrels back home. The names were familiar: Ashbourne Crescent, Meadow Way, School Close. In the corner of his mind he thought it should be comforting that he was here, and not patrolling some shithole of an Afghan village. Somehow, though, it wasn't. The street lamps dazzled him and he couldn't walk in a straight line. He saw two young women cross the road to avoid passing him. One of them wore a T-shirt with 'Arctic Monkeys' emblazoned over her breasts, the other was holding a rat-like chihuahua on a lead.

Antrobus Road. Fielding Avenue. Grosvenor Place.

And finally, Lancing Way. No parked vehicles. No pedestrians. The no-parking barriers edging the pavement glowing fluorescent orange in the lamplight. Joe weaved drunkenly across the pavement and clattered noisily into one of them.

He swore, then looked up and saw a car in the road.

It was forty metres away, about ten beyond his own front door. Its headlights were on full beam, but it wasn't moving. He squinted. It was a 4 x 4 – a Range Rover maybe? He could make out rails on the front . . .

Joe stopped. He didn't know why. He found himself estimating how quickly he could get to his house. Ten seconds, at a sprint.

Palpitations. Something was making him nervous. A sixth sense, finely honed after years on the front line.

Only this wasn't the front line. This was Lancing Way. Home.

This was paranoia. He remembered the doctor's questions.

'Fucking bullshit,' he muttered under his breath. He needed to get back to the house. Sleep off the booze. Start his whole fucking disastrous homecoming all over again.

He looked down the road. The car was moving towards him. Slowly, he thought, though it was difficult to judge speed in the darkness. He shoved his hands into the pockets of his leather jacket and upped his pace. It was with a kind of defiance that he ignored the approaching car. So what if it was moving slowly? Probably just some John kerb-crawling for a hooker. He was in the wrong street . . .

Or maybe it wasn't. He could hear the revs of the car's engine as it increased in speed. Suddenly. Violently.

The car was twenty metres away when, still accelerating, it veered across the road towards Joe. It was ten metres away when it mounted the kerb. There was a massive clattering sound as it

114

ploughed into the barriers, slicing through them with two wheels on the pavement and two on the road.

The headlights blinded him. Everything started to spin again. He dived to the side of the pavement, where his face scraped against a rough brick front-garden wall and his left shoulder thumped down heavily on the pavement. The stench of burning rubber hit his senses, and he was aware that the car had come to a halt just three metres forward of where he had fallen. Joe pushed himself up to his feet as it started reversing away from him, back the way it had come. Still blinded by the headlights, he sprinted towards the car. The distance between them closed to two metres. One.

The car stopped abruptly. Joe was alongside the driver's door now, and the lights were no longer shining in his eyes. Although he was still dazzled, he managed to feel his way to the door handle and yank it.

Locked.

More revs from the engine. Joe raised one leather-clad elbow and smashed it hard against the driver's window. The glass splintered, cobweb-like, but didn't shatter. It needed another blow, but the car was moving forward. His vision was clearing now, and he could see through the rear passenger window.

A face was looking out at him. He recognized it, even though he didn't notice the yellow tinge of the teeth.

And then the car was back on the road, accelerating away, the engine screaming. Five metres. Ten. Joe sprinted into the middle of the road and squinted after it, trying to make out the plates. But his vision was blurred and he couldn't read them.

The car turned right into Grosvenor Place, out of sight; the noise of its engine disappeared.

Silence.

Joe felt his left cheek. It was wet with blood. His shoulder throbbed. On the other side of Lancing Way, the door to number 17 opened. A fat man Joe half recognized appeared, wearing a dressing gown and lit up by the hallway light behind him. 'What the bloody hell's going on?' he shouted. 'It's half past bloody twelve at night! What you doing standing in the middle of the road? I'm calling the bloody police . . .'

Joe didn't answer. He just put his head down and hurried back to the pavement. Thirty seconds later he was walking up to his own front door, inserting the key in the lock and stepping inside.

The house was quiet.

The lights were off.

Joe was dripping sweat, and breathless.

Whatever had happened out there, it had sobered him up. He locked the door behind him and, instead of climbing the stairs to bed, he hurried into the kitchen, where he found the same knife he'd taken earlier on, and which Caitlin had now returned to its usual place. Back in the front room, he pulled open the curtains of the window that looked out on the street.

No movement.

It did nothing to ease his state of mind. He wiped away the patch of condensation made by his breath.

'Joe?' Caitlin's voice was timid. 'Are you coming to bed, honey?'

'Get upstairs.' He threw her a dark look over his shoulder.

'Oh my God, Joe – what's happened to your face? What's going on?'

'Get Conor. Take him into our room. Lock the door. The windows too.'

Silence.

'*Do it!*'

'Joe, sweetheart, you've been drinking. I can smell it . . . Joe, you heard what the doctor said . . .'

He turned on her, his face ablaze, the knife still in his hand. And the look she gave him, lit only by the shard of yellow light that came in from the street lamp outside, was no longer irritated, or anxious. It was scared.

'Get upstairs,' he said, his teeth gritted.

She nodded and stepped back slowly, her fingers spread out, pacifying him. Joe turned and looked out of the window again; seconds later he heard Caitlin thundering upstairs, and the ker-fuffle as she woke Conor up and took him into their room.

And then silence again.

Just Joe's heavy breathing, the ticking of the clock and the thumping of his heart.

He stood by the window, motionless, his eyes alert for any sign of movement. The clock chimed: 1 a.m. He felt tired, but he forced himself not to give in to it.

Maybe he *was* sick. Maybe he *was* paranoid.

But one thing was sure. For the second time in forty-eight hours, he'd almost died. And a single question that he couldn't answer was rebounding in his head.

Why?

EIGHT

Joe had thought that things might look better in the morning. He was wrong. As the sky grew lighter and condensation dripped down the inside of the window, people started to appear. A man walking his dog. A Lycra–clad cyclist hunched over her handle-bars. The same two girls he'd passed last night, staggering home, the worse for wear. Every movement made him tense. The axe-split of a headache he was suffering wasn't just the booze. Joe didn't let go of the knife.

The clock chimed six times. He didn't move. Seven. There were sounds from upstairs. Floorboards creaked. Footsteps descended. He sensed Caitlin staring at him from the door.

'Pack a bag,' he said.

'Joe . . .'

'Pack a bag.'

He didn't know at what point during his vigil he had come to the decision, but now that it was light he had made up his mind: they weren't staying here. Maybe someone had tried to kill him last night; maybe it had just been a bunch of pissed-up, joyriding dickheads unable to keep control of their vehicle and the kid with the Coke bottle was just a kid with a Coke bottle. Either way, getting out of Hereford felt like the right move.

'Where are we going?' Caitlin asked.

'JJ's.'

'Does he know?'

For Joe and his family, JJ's meant holidays. Whenever Joe's

mate had any down time – which was hardly ever – he spent his time at the secluded old farmhouse, ten klicks from Berwick-upon-Tweed, that his grandparents had owned. There, he kept his eye in by shooting every last game bird he could find with an old two-bore shotgun. 'No difference,' he'd said to Joe just three weeks previously, 'between a bird and a bad guy.'

'Joe, does JJ know we're . . . ?'

'No!'

'But—'

'JJ's got other things on his mind, trust me.'

Caitlin didn't much like it up in Berwick, but Joe loved the remote bleakness of the place. And with JJ stuck out in Bagram, he knew the house would be empty. More importantly, he'd be off the radar.

'Maybe we should just stay here . . . The Regiment want you to go in and—'

'*Fuck* the Regiment.'

Caitlin jumped. She had that look again. Anxious. A little scared – maybe of him? Perhaps he should tell her what had happened last night.

Or perhaps not. She already thought he was losing it.

Joe took a deep breath to calm himself, then approached her and brushed one hand against her soft cheek. 'We need some time out,' he said. 'Just the three of us. I need to wind down, babe. Get away from it all.'

It was the right thing to say. Joe knew it would be. Caitlin's eyes softened; she bit her lower lip and nodded at him. Fifteen minutes later she had three bags packed and was back in the front room, standing just behind Conor with her hands on his shoulders.

The boy looked tired. Dark rings. Pale skin. He was wearing a light blue anorak and clutching his DS. 'What happened to your face?' he asked.

'Don't worry about it, champ.'

'Just asking.'

'We should get moving,' said Joe.

'What about school?' asked Conor.

'Look, just forget about school, OK?' Joe snapped. Conor flinched and withdrew a little into his mother's embrace. Joe pushed past them. 'Let's go,' he said.

It was a silent trip north. Conor slept in the back of their silver Mondeo estate; Caitlin removed her shoes and hugged her knees in the passenger seat; Joe put talk radio on to fill the silence. Some arsehole of a shock jock was presiding over a banal phone-in. Joe barely heard what they were saying until two hours into the journey when, snapping out of his driving trance on the M6, he realized the conversation had inevitably moved on to bin Laden. An 'expert' – he sounded Middle Eastern – was giving his opinion: '. . . and it's quite simply wrong of the American government to suggest that Osama bin Laden's body was disposed of according to Islamic practices . . .' Joe slammed the button to turn the radio off, drawing another of Caitlin's anxious glances. He could tell she wanted to talk to him about what they'd just been listening to. She wasn't stupid. She knew that ops like the raid in Abbottabad were Joe's bread and butter. But she also knew it was a waste of breath asking him about what he did when he was on Regiment time.

Joe glanced in the rear-view mirror. His face was still dirty and scabbed, but he wasn't looking at that. He saw a red Citroën Picasso behind him, and an XK8 behind that. He hadn't noticed either car before, but he still pulled out into the centre lane and lowered his speed suddenly, forcing them to overtake on the inside before he dropped back into the slow lane behind them. If Caitlin noticed what he was doing she gave no indication of it – she had removed a bottle of nail-polish remover from her bag, along with a wad of cotton wool. She dabbed her nails in silence, while Joe kept his eye on the two cars. The Picasso pulled off at the next junction; the XK8 zoomed off into the distance.

Conor woke at midday. Joe kept driving as Caitlin passed their son sandwiches she'd made before they left. Neither she nor Joe had an appetite for them. He kept his eyes on the road. She kept hers on her nails. From the back came the beep-beeping of Conor's DS.

They stopped around 3 p.m. to buy food in a dingy super-market – the closest to their destination, but still thirty klicks south-west of JJ's. Caitlin didn't comment on the booze Joe piled into the trolley: a case of Tennent's, two bottles of Famous Grouse and half a dozen bottles of cheap wine. She concen-trated on adding microwave meals – JJ was no Jamie Oliver and his kitchen looked like it. Twenty minutes later they were back in the car. And an hour later they were at their destination.

JJ's house stood alone at the foot of a hill that was covered with grazing sheep. When he was younger, Conor always used to say that it looked as though it had a face, and he was right. The narrow windows and cracked pebbledash render made it look mournful. It wasn't helped by the rain that had started the moment they had caught sight of it. An old iron fence, about a metre high, marked the boundary of the property, but it was so covered with bindweed that the metal was barely visible. The grass to the front of the house was a couple of feet high. Their vehicle made a clear track through it as Joe pulled up by the front door, whose green paint was peeling to reveal the white undercoat beneath. The house looked a little shabbier every time they came here.

There was an old coal shed along the right-hand side of the house and it was here, hidden behind a loose brick, that JJ always kept a key. Joe found it immediately and let them in.

'I'm freezing,' Conor complained as the door swung shut behind them and they stood in a hallway that was somehow darker than it should have been given it was still light outside. The terracotta tiles on the floor seemed to leach any warmth out of the air, and the woodchip walls had yellow patches of damp rising up from the skirting. Against the right-hand wall stood an old mahogany grandfather clock, its hands stuck at seventeen minutes past twelve. The air was thick with the musty smell of neglect.

Caitlin flicked a light switch. Nothing happened. A minute later Joe had his head stuck inside a corner cupboard in the kitchen, poking around at the fuse board. He flicked a trip switch and heard the beep of the microwave as the kitchen lights turned on.

'I'll sort the beds out,' Caitlin said as Joe emerged. 'Come on, Conor, you can help me . . .'

'I want to stay with Dad.'

Conor was lingering in the doorway. His face was still pale, but the rings around his eyes had faded. Caitlin looked askance at Joe, who nodded. 'Come on, champ,' he said. 'Let's make a brew.'

Caitlin left them alone while Joe wiped the dust off an old kettle with his sleeve and filled it with water, before turning to look at his son. Conor had moved into the centre of the room, next to the long pine table. He looked troubled.

'How's your mum been, champ?' Joe asked. 'You been looking after her like I told you to?'

Conor nodded gravely. 'But sometimes I hear her crying. I don't think she likes you being a soldier any more.'

There was an awkward silence. Why was it that Joe could hold his own in the testosterone-fuelled hangars of Bagram, but when he was alone with his own son, he could never find the right words to say?

'Your mum's fine,' he muttered.

'She's not fine.' Conor spoke so forcefully, and in such an adult tone, that Joe was taken aback. A memory flashed before his eyes. He saw himself as a kid, standing up to his own dick-head of a father, pretending not to be scared of his strong, tattooed arm. Whenever Joe's dad came back from a stretch away, he'd been at Her Majesty's pleasure, not at Her service. But that meant nothing to Conor. Joe wondered if he was pretending not to be scared now.

'Are you always going to be a soldier, Dad?'

Joe frowned.

'What did happen to your face?'

Joe touched the scraped, sore skin. 'Fell over.' He could tell Conor knew it was a lie. Joe crossed the length of the kitchen to the window that looked out to the front. Their car was the only sign of human life that he could see. For some reason, that made him relax. 'You remember learning to ride your bike out there?' he asked.

Conor was standing next to him now, looking out too. He wormed his little hand into Joe's, and they stood there in silence for a moment.

'You don't ride your bike much now, huh?'

'I prefer my computer,' Conor said. 'And I don't like it when Mum cries.'

'Nor do I, champ,' Joe said. And he meant it. 'Let's make sure she's got nothing to cry about, hey?'

For the first time since Joe got back, he saw a smile spread across his son's face. 'Do you want to see my new DS game?' Conor asked.

'Sure,' Joe said, and Conor scampered off to find it.

Joe looked out the window again. He felt a million miles from anywhere. A million miles from danger. It was a feeling he hadn't had for a very long time. The Regiment would be wondering where he was. The adjutant was probably banging on his door at home right now. He didn't give a shit. Tomorrow he'd get a message to JJ. Let him know he was here. He was sure his mate wouldn't mind if they stayed here for a bit. Long enough for Joe to get a few things straight in his head.

God knows he needed to.

*   *   *

'I thought I'd see if Charlie was around.'

It was the following morning, and Joe felt refreshed. His sleep had been far from dreamless, but it had at least been uninterrupted. Now he was sitting in the kitchen with Caitlin, drinking coffee and watching Conor through the window. Their son was tramping out a pattern in the long, dewy grass.

'Charlie?'

'His friend. From last year.'

Joe vaguely remembered. There was a kid about Conor's age living in the nearest village. They'd met on the beach last summer. The mother was blonde, overweight and bubbly. The father was a twat. Dressed head to foot in army surplus gear that covered his paunch, he thought he was David fucking Stirling, not some shitkicker from Berwick with a beer belly and a shelf full of Bear Grylls DVDs. It was true that Conor and Charlie had hit it off, but now something made Joe reluctant to be in contact with anyone else.

'It's better if he stays with us,' he said.

'He can't stomp around the house by himself all day, Joe. He needs someone his own age.'

'It's safer if—'

'What are you *talking* about, *safer*?' Caitlin took a deep breath, as though calming herself down. 'Nobody knows we're here, sweetheart. Even JJ doesn't know we're here. And anyway . . .' She glanced down sheepishly. 'It would be nice for you and me to spend a bit of time together.'

Joe nodded. 'Right,' he said.

Conor had other ideas. At midday, once Caitlin had spoken to Charlie's mum and arranged for Conor to spend the night with them, he looked crestfallen. 'What if we can't think of anything to say?' he asked.

'You'll be fine, sweetheart. He'll be fine, won't he?'

Joe nodded. He'd be fine.

At 4 p.m. he was packing Conor into the car. 'You take him,' Caitlin had whispered in his ear. 'But hurry back.'

Conor hugged his mum tight, clearly holding back some tears. Joe looked away. He didn't want anyone to see his frown. Why couldn't his son be a bit tougher?

It was a short, silent journey to Charlie's. Joe felt himself growing tense as soon as JJ's house disappeared from the rear-view mirror. And as he rounded the base of the hill that hid the house from sight, he found his senses were as alert as if he was driving out on ops. He scanned the fields on either side. A tractor trundled over the horizon two klicks to the south-west. A silver Clio sped up behind him and overtook dangerously just before a hairpin bend – female driver, two kids in the back. A white Transit van passed from the other direction, registration number VS02 RTD. Driver bearded, baseball cap shading his face. Rear doors, Joe saw when it was behind him, blacked out . . .

Ten minutes later he was entering the small village of Lymeford. A road sign announced that it welcomed careful drivers, but Joe was tipping eighty: the Mondeo's brakes screeched as he slowed down and passed the Crown and Sceptre, where he and JJ had sunk more than a few pints in years gone by. There was a quaint little pond where a couple of kids were feeding the ducks. Here he turned left, into a close of modern red-brick houses, then pulled up outside one that had a black Cherokee Jeep parked outside, with a Help for Heroes sticker on the rear window.

'OK, champ?' he asked.

Conor nodded mutely.

Charlie's mum – Caitlin had reminded him that her name was Elaine – greeted them at the front door with a wide, bubbly smile and a hug for Conor that wasn't really reciprocated. 'It's so lovely to see you again . . . Charlie's been dying to have you round . . .'

Charlie, who was waiting for them in the front room, didn't look like that was true. He'd grown in the last year, both upwards and outwards. Conor looked tiny next to him, and when Elaine encouraged them to go upstairs to play, neither boy looked very enthusiastic.

'Bless,' Elaine observed. 'Would you like a cup of tea, Joe?'

'The man doesn't want tea,' came a voice from the next room. Two seconds later Charlie's dad, Reg, appeared carrying two cans of Carling. He wore camouflage trousers that were several sizes too small for his considerable waist, and a Parachute Regiment T-shirt. 'How do, mate.' He nodded gruffly and handed Joe the warm beer. 'What happened to your face, eh? Bit of bother with Terry Taliban?'

Joe had a vague memory of telling Reg that he was off to the Stan, though of course he hadn't mentioned the Regiment.

'Something like that, Reg,' he said, taking a sip of beer.

'Sit down, then.' Reg plonked himself in an armchair that was already indented with the shape of his arse. Next to it there was an occasional table on which lay a copy of *Jane's Defence Weekly*.

'I should go . . .'

'So we've given those fuckin' Al-Wotsit bastards a good seeing-to, eh?' Reg spoke proudly, as if he'd nailed the Pacer himself. Then he belched.

'Right,' Joe muttered. Elaine had already rolled her eyes and left the room.

Reg leaned forward. 'You want to know what I think, though?' Joe didn't, but knew he was about to find out. 'That bin Laden – something fishy about him. Our Charlie, always on the fuckin' computer, he is. Always on that fuckin' . . .' He clicked his fingers three times and shouted, 'Elaine! What's that You-Wotsit he's always on?'

'YouTube,' came the reply.

'Always on it, lookin' at dancing cats and shit like that.' He lowered his voice. 'Probably lookin' at all sorts of mucky stuff an' all. Anyhow . . .' he tapped himself proudly on the chest '. . . I've been looking on it myself. Wouldn't believe the stuff I've found, you wouldn't.'

'Right.'

Reg leaned forward. 'You know 9/11?'

'Yeah,' said Joe. 'I know.'

'Well, did you know that there was a third building went down that day? Just near the Twin Towers, it was. And did you know it was reported on the news *before* it happened?'

Reg sat back and took a triumphant swig of his beer.

Joe put his down on the mantelpiece. 'Look, mate,' he said. 'Really, I've got to—'

'So if it were on the news *before* it happened, how come they knew about it?' He leaned forward again, as though he was about to reveal a great secret. 'Mark my words: that Bin Laden, he was a double agent' – he almost spat it out – 'working for the Americans . . .'

'Reg, I'm sorry, mate. I've really got to be off.'

'None as blind as them that can't see,' said Reg, 'but you answer me this: what was he doing living where he was, eh? Right under everyone's noses? You think the Americans didn't know?'

Fortunately, Joe didn't have to say what he thought, because just then Elaine walked back into the room. She put an affectionate hand on Joe's shoulder.

'Never mind Reg, love,' she said quietly. 'He's always looking for someone to listen to his loony ideas.' Reg shrugged, and belched again. 'Now don't you worry about Conor. They'll have a lovely time. I've got fish fingers for their tea, and I'll make sure they're not too late . . . Oh, and I'll bring him back round first thing after breakfast. We pass your place on our way to school. Now then, Reg, say bye-bye to Joe.'

Reg just raised his beer in Joe's direction.

Joe couldn't get away quickly enough. Guys like Reg were fucking everywhere, keeping the army surplus stores in business and boring everyone shitless about their knowledge of modern combat from the comfort of their armchair. Put a fat fuck like him within sniffing distance of a contact situation and he'd be browning his boxers before you could say RPG. But he was harmless enough, and Elaine would look after Conor.

He looked through the windscreen. Conor was at a window on the first floor. His pale face looked almost ghostly. Joe gave him the thumbs up, and the boy smiled unconvincingly back.

Joe checked the time: 1710 hours. With a nagging sense of guilt he reversed the car, drove away from the house and headed back to JJ's.

It was growing dark when he got there. The sheep had moved from the hillside and a flock of noisy geese, silhouetted against the sky, were flying north-westerly in an arrowhead formation as he stepped out of the car. Their croaking echoed across the landscape. Once they had gone, everything was silent.

Joe looked at the house. There were no lights on.

Why the hell not?

Something was wrong.

He checked the long grass at the front of the house. He counted three sets of tyre tracks: arrival of the Mondeo yesterday, departure to Charlie's, arrival just now. He located the indentation of Conor's footprints from this morning. And nothing else.

But still, no lights.

He circled the house. The back garden was just as overgrown as the front. There was a modern, two-storey annexe here. On the ground floor was a kind of boot room, with a spiral iron staircase that led up to the landing on the first floor of the main house. But the rear door to the annexe was locked. Windows closed. No light. No sign of access.

A gust of wind picked up, carrying with it the bleating of a distant sheep.

Nobody knows you're here, Joe told himself. He walked round the other side of the house, past the coal shed. The rickety wooden door was closed, the loose chain tied round its bolt in a figure of eight, just as he had left it. When he reached the front door again, the evening had grown a shade darker. And still there were no lights from the house.

He opened the door and slipped inside.

He was about to call Caitlin's name, but something stopped him. The chill darkness of the hallway, perhaps. Or the silence, broken only by the ticking of the grandfather clock that Joe had wound that morning.

The kitchen: empty and dark, the remnants of their lunch still unwashed by the sink. The sitting room on the other side of the hallway: ditto. Joe headed silently up the stairs. The steps were nearly two metres wide, with a winding, burnished-wood banister. Joe walked lightly along the left-hand edge of the treads, to minimize the creaking. The staircase turned back on itself. The banister continued horizontally for two metres along the landing, overlooking the staircase.

At the top of the steps, he stopped and listened.

Silence.

He was on the verge of calling Caitlin's name again. And again, something stopped him.

The landing was ten metres long and covered with a musty grey carpet. To his left, there was a closed door that led back to the annexe, with its spiral staircase down to the ground floor. At one end of the landing was a door leading to the bathroom. This too was shut. The room Conor slept in was at the far end on the right. His door was fully open but no light was on inside. Opposite this was the room he shared with Caitlin. The door was a couple of inches ajar, and from it emerged a faint, flickering glow.

A glow he hadn't seen from the window that looked out onto the front.

He approached with care, treading lightly, the tip of his shoe checking for any looseness in the floor that might make a noise

129

before the heel went down. It took him twenty seconds to approach like this. When he was just inches from the doorway, he stopped and breathed deeply.

Then he kicked the door open.

The flickering glow, he saw instantly, came from a single tea light burning on the chest of drawers by the door. Against the left wall was a wardrobe with two long mirrors on the double doors. Opposite it, just to the right of the window, where the curtains were closed, was an old four-poster bed without any drapes.

And on the bed was Caitlin.

'Jesus!' She had sat up suddenly when Joe kicked the door in. 'Joe, what's the . . . ?'

Caitlin closed her eyes, inhaled deeply, then forced a smile to her face. She wasn't wearing much. A satin vest that did nothing to hide the curve of her breasts; skimpy underwear.

Joe stood stupidly in the doorway. Caitlin approached him, took his hand and led him over to the bed.

'I've missed you,' she whispered as he sat on the edge of the bed. She clambered up behind him and started massaging his shoulders. 'Baby, you're so tense. Take your shirt off.'

Joe removed his shirt; behind him, he could sense Caitlin taking off her vest. When she started massaging again, he could feel her breasts brushing against his back.

'Lie down,' she whispered.

He obeyed.

Conor placed his knife and fork together on his empty plate, the way his mum had told him. He didn't really like fish fingers, but he'd eaten them anyway, as well as the potato waffles, both smeared with ketchup.

'Looks like blood, doesn't it?' Charlie had said as he squirted his own plate. Conor had kept his eyes fixed on his food. Charlie's dad, who was passing through the kitchen on the way to the fridge, had said, 'Too thick for blood, sunshine,' before his mum had asked them to change the subject. After that they'd eaten in silence. They weren't really getting on, and Conor didn't want to be there.

'Half an hour's telly before bed, boys,' Charlie's mum said as she gathered up their plates. They walked through into the front room, where his dad was sitting with a can of beer in his hand reading his magazine. He gave Conor the creeps, and he sat as far away as he could, at the other end of the sofa.

They watched *Doctor Who* on DVD. Conor found it scary, but Charlie was rapt and he didn't want to look like a wimp. He was glad when Charlie's mum came in and said, 'Seven-thirty, boys. Time for bed.'

Conor slept on a blow-up mattress on Charlie's floor. Or rather, he didn't sleep. He lay there in the darkness, listening to Charlie's slow breathing and the sound of the TV downstairs. Thinking of his mum, and how she put on a brave face when it was just the two of them, even though he knew how much she hated it when Dad was away. And thinking about Dad too. How he had been sitting in the bath with the water pouring over him. How he had ripped his Xbox away from the screen when he'd been playing *Call of Duty* – something he was only doing because he thought playing a game like that might make his dad think more of him.

Thinking how Dad was just different this time.

He didn't know how late it was when he started crying. All he knew was that once he started, he couldn't stop.

Joe and Caitlin lay together, naked. Spent.

'What's that?' Joe breathed.

'It's nothing, baby. Just the old house creaking.'

The curtains were open now, and their bodies were lit more by the moonlight that flooded in through the window than by the tea light. Caitlin had her head on his chest and one hand on his stomach, which she stroked reassuringly. She was warm, and there was something about her touch that made Joe feel more relaxed than he had for months. She was right. No need to be scared of things going bump in the night.

'I'm sorry,' he said after a long pause. 'This wasn't the homecoming I had in my head. I've been—'

'Shhh . . .' Caitlin soothed him. 'I do understand, baby. I know the old Joe's in there somewhere. I wish I could just make it better.'

'I'll make it up to you. And to Conor. I promise.' I'll be a dad, he thought to himself. I've had enough of being a soldier.

'You don't have to promise anything, baby.' Her voice cracked slightly. 'It's enough that you're back with us.'

Silence. He stared at the ceiling, listening to the soft sound of her breathing. Neither of them felt the need to speak. Joe pretended to himself that he was not keeping an ear out for another creak from elsewhere in the house.

A minute passed. Something caught Joe's eye.

It was almost nothing. A dot of light, reflecting from the wardrobe mirrors and zigzagging like a firefly across the ceiling before vanishing. Joe sat up immediately, bringing Caitlin with him.

'Joe, what is it?'

'Quiet!' he hissed. 'Lie down . . .'

'Joe, *please* . . .' She was sitting on the edge of the bed, naked, her arms crossed over her breasts as though she was trying to protect herself from something.

'Lie down.'

But Joe was looking out through the edge of the dirty window, casting around for movement. Clouds were scudding across the sky; the long grass out front was rippling in a light breeze. But apart from that, nothing.

Joe quickly pulled on his jeans, blocking out the sound of Caitlin's voice, which was tearful once more. 'Joe . . . it's all in your head . . .'

But it wasn't in his head. He'd seen something.

He looked around for anything that would serve as a weapon. Finding nothing, he removed his sturdy leather belt from his jeans and held each end tightly. At least you could strangle someone with it – just.

'Stay there,' he said.

The tea light was guttering. Joe snuffed it with his thumb and forefinger before stepping back out into the hallway. He remembered that JJ kept his shotgun and cartridges in a locked cabinet in the basement. If he could get there . . .

He edged down the landing. But he'd only gone a couple of metres when he stopped and stood very still. There was no doubt about it. He could feel a breeze in his face. He peered into the darkness. The door leading to the spiral staircase and the annexe was open.

'*Caitlin!*' he roared. '*Caitlin, get dressed!*'

Many things happened at once. Two figures appeared, one at the end of the corridor, emerging from the open door, a second from Conor's bedroom two metres away at Joe's eight o'clock. But it wasn't the presence of these figures that momentarily paralysed him with terror. It was what they were wearing: white, all-in-one outfits.

A dazzling light. The man at the end of the corridor was holding a pencil-thin torch. He switched it on, shining the bright halogen beam in Joe's face. Half-blinded, Joe turned to attack the man who had emerged from Conor's bedroom. He had a torch too, and so did a third man behind him. Joe hurled himself at them, and they crumpled down onto the floor. Joe only had to touch the guy's clothing to realize what these men – he assumed they were men – were wearing: reinforced-paper SOCO suits. They covered everything: shoes, bodies, heads. They wore tight yellow rubber gloves, sealed to the SOCO suits with layers of packing tape. Their faces were covered with what felt, as he clawed his hand into the assailant's face, like tinted cellophane.

A scream. It was Caitlin. 'He's got a gun! *Joe! He's got a gun!*'

Rage surged through him. He didn't bother with the belt, but brought his fist down on the nearest man's face. He could instantly feel the wetness of his blood slipping around between the cellophane and the man's nose. He rolled off the intruder, ready to jump to his feet and strangle the cunt that was threatening Caitlin. But now the one he'd seen coming in from the annexe door was standing right over him, shining the torch in his face. Joe started to push it away.

But then he saw that the intruder was carrying something else: a Taser rod, about forty centimetres long. A high-voltage strike from that would put him down immediately. He tried to parry it. But too late.

Joe's whole body juddered for about three seconds as the electricity surged through him. When it stopped, he felt as though the blood in his veins was made of lead, and the room was spinning. All he could do was concentrate on staying conscious. Not easy. He had palpitations in his neck. Nausea . . .

And something else was happening.

One of the intruders – he couldn't tell which – had pulled down his jeans and taken hold of his penis. Joe felt the sharp pain of a needle being inserted into the urethra, followed by a dreadful sensation that felt as though molten lead was seeping into his abdomen. Still dazzled by the halogen light, he couldn't see what was happening, but he knew he'd been injected. He tried to push himself up again, but his muscles would barely obey the commands his brain was giving them. The molten-lead sensation spread down his limbs. He dropped the leather belt and collapsed, his body limp, the back of his head motionless against the floor.

He couldn't move. *Jesus, he couldn't move . . .*

Caitlin wasn't screaming any more, but whimpering. Fast, terrified sobs. All three intruders had moved into the room now, and Joe heard them say something, though he couldn't make out what. Caitlin said 'No,' but then there was a scuffling sound. Joe tried to call out, but all that came was a dry, dusty gasp. His eyes rolled as he desperately tried to move his head at least. Nothing doing. Whatever they'd injected had caused muscle failure. Suxamethonium chloride, was Joe's guess. Very difficult to trace in the bloodstream, especially when injected in that part of his anatomy. The panic inside him was like a bullet ricocheting in a small room. What were they doing? Why hadn't they just killed him?

What was about to happen?

Movement on the edge of his vision. He managed to roll his eyes forward sufficiently to see Caitlin, still naked, being dragged from the room by two of the intruders. Were they going to rape her? He didn't think so. The SOCO suits were on for a reason. It wasn't a comforting thought.

With a cry, Caitlin broke away from them and threw herself at Joe, sobbing uncontrollably. But she only managed to hold on to his immobile body for two or three brief seconds, before the intruders pulled her up again and bundled her into the bathroom. They switched on the light, which cast a confusion of shadows onto the grey hallway carpet, but Joe could not see inside.

He wanted to roar with anger and frustration. More than that, he wanted to move. He couldn't. He couldn't even twitch. He could only lie there, a prisoner in his own body. Listening. Caitlin was screaming again. '*What are you doing? Oh God, what're you doing?*' There was a clattering sound. Some kind of movement in the bathroom that Joe couldn't work out.

A thump. Caitlin's screams grew louder. More desperate, if that were possible.

And then two of the intruders were standing above him. They had dropped their torches, and the cellophane in front of their faces was misted from their heavy breathing. They bent over, each grabbing one of his arms and, with obvious effort, pulled the deadweight of his body up from the ground, before dragging him into the bathroom.

What he saw in there horrified him.

The intruders had ripped the shower curtain from its rail and used it to wrap around the naked Caitlin, who was now lying in the bath, her feet at the tap end. She was shaking violently and trying to speak, but the only sound that came from her mouth was of retching. She vomited. It smeared over the front of the shower curtain, lumpy and yellow. One of the intruders was standing over her, but the moment the other two dropped Joe onto his knees, so that his top half drooped over the edge of the bath, this man disappeared.

Now the only sound in the bathroom was Caitlin's sobbing, which echoed off the mildewed tiles. Joe couldn't see her face. His head was pointing the other way, so all he could see was the shower curtain wrapped round the dark triangle of her pubic hair – soaked with urine – and her naked legs, her feet twisted awkwardly, and a bulbous, distorted reflection of the room in the bath taps, showing the two men standing over him.

It took no more than a minute for the third man to return. Joe didn't know what he was carrying until the other two pulled him back up from the bath again. The man spoke, but his voice was still muffled by the SOCO suit, so Joe couldn't discern his accent. 'Do the fingernails,' he instructed.

'Joe,' Caitlin whispered, her voice oozing dread, 'what's happening?'

But all Joe knew was that his hand was being lifted towards Caitlin's face by one of the intruders, who bent his fingernails forward and scraped them two inches down Caitlin's left cheek.

And suddenly Joe understood.

They were making him scratch Caitlin's face to put her DNA under his fingernails, to make it look as though there had been a struggle between them. And they were wearing the suits to stop their own DNA from contaminating the crime scene.

Because that was what they were creating. A crime scene.

A murder scene.

Conor's door opened. He immediately gulped down his tears because he didn't want anyone to think he was a baby. But it was too late. Charlie's mum was leaning over him. He could smell her perfume. 'What's the matter, my little love?' she asked in a concerned whisper, stroking his hair.

'Nothing,' said Conor, but his voice wobbled as he said it, and he couldn't stop himself crying again.

'Homesick?'

Conor nodded.

'Why don't we call your mum?' she suggested. 'Would you like that?'

He nodded again. He would ask Mum to come and get him. He didn't want to stay here any more.

Joe's brain was shrieking at him. If he could just move . . . If he could just do something . . . But it wasn't possible. His horrified thoughts were trapped inside a useless body. He was powerless.

A new sound. The ringing of Caitlin's mobile phone from the bedroom. The intruders stood perfectly still, obviously listening to the ring, and the faint buzzing as the phone vibrated.

It fell silent.

'Do it,' came the order from behind a SOCO suit. 'Now.'

With every ounce of his being, Joe tried to lash out. But all he showed for it was a hoarse whisper from the back of his throat. 'No . . .'

Now he saw what the man had fetched from downstairs: a kitchen knife with a slightly buckled blade of about three inches long. One of his assailants was forcing it into his hand, wrapping his fingers around the handle.

It was only as one of them lifted him under his armpits and another clenched his knife hand firmly that Caitlin appeared to understand what was happening. In an instant she stopped shaking, as though her body was frozen. 'Joe,' she whispered. 'Don't let them . . . please don't let them . . .'

But there was nothing Joe could do. His eyes were fixed on Caitlin's face. He thought he had witnessed true terror before. He realized now that he had not.

Charlie's mum put her phone back down. 'Oh dear,' she said kindly. 'She's not answering.'

They were sitting in the front room now, Conor in his pyjamas, still sobbing. Charlie's dad was in his usual place, a can of beer in his hand and a glazed look on his face.

'Why don't you have another go at going to sleep?' said Charlie's mum. 'It'll soon be morning, eh?'

But the suggestion only made Conor cry even more. He had given up trying to be brave. 'I want to go home,' he said. 'I want to see my mum . . .'

'Ah, take the lad home,' muttered Charlie's dad. 'We won't get any peace until you do.'

Charlie's mum gave her husband a dark look, but then started stroking his hair again. 'Would you like that, love? Would you like me to take you home?'

Conor nodded.

The shower curtain was not easily punctured.

At first the point of the knife just made an indentation both in the curtain and in the soft flesh of Caitlin's belly. It needed a sharp yank forward to pierce the plastic, but once it came into contact with Caitlin's skin, it slid in with gruesome ease.

'*No!*' Joe roared. But the roar was only in his head.

Caitlin gasped. Immediately blood gushed from the wound. Most of it remained trapped between her skin and the clear plastic curtain, but some of it seeped through the hole and onto the handle of the knife, Joe's hand and the paper suit of the man controlling him.

Joe's mind started to spin. He heard Caitlin's sharp, pained intakes of breath. He felt his hand being pushed downwards, slicing through her belly in the direction of her womb. A distended bubble of intestine slid softly, monstrously, from the gash as his hand was pulled back and reinserted, not into her belly this time, but into the area around her left breast. This was clearly more painful. She shouted out, but her cry faded after only a second as the strength sapped from her.

There was so much blood, most of it still caught between the shower curtain and her skin. Joe tried once more to fight against his paralysis, to take control of his body. It was useless. His assailants were moving him further up the bath now, forcing his knife hand towards the vicinity of Caitlin's throat.

Their eyes locked. Joe had seen enough people die to realize that life was ebbing from her.

She spoke. A single word. 'Conor . . .'

And there would have been no time for Joe to reply, even if he'd been able to. All his effort was focused on trying to stop the intruder from moving the knife forward. For an instant, when the tip of the blade was just three inches from Caitlin's throat, he thought that maybe . . . *maybe* . . . a little strength was returning to his useless muscles.

But it was much too little, and much too late.

The incision of Caitlin's throat was physically the easiest. There was no shower curtain to get through – just the unblemished skin of her smooth neck. And below the skin, the tight lengths of sinew that required a little more pressure from the intruder, but not much.

Caitlin's eyes rolled. A disgusting mixture of blood and saliva foamed from her mouth and over the vomit that was now oozing down the side of the bath. Her whole neck was scarlet. As the knife was pulled out, she tried to breathe in. But her windpipe was punctured, and all Joe saw was a little of the blood around the wound being sucked back in, before oozing out again.

'Enough,' said one of the men behind him.

Joe felt himself being dropped, the knife still in his hand. His head hit the side of the bath before he crumpled to the floor. All he could see now was the pedestal of the basin, the toilet next to it and three pairs of SOCO-suit-clad feet walking out of the bathroom and into the hallway.

He could hear a sinister gurgling sound from the bath.

It lasted no more than ten seconds. And then there was silence.

A small spider crawled out from behind the basin's pedestal. It scurried in the direction of the bath and out of Joe's field of view.

His left leg twitched. Movement. He tried to manoeuvre it consciously. Still nothing.

Something was happening on the landing. He didn't know, and couldn't see, what. And he almost didn't care. The horror of the past few minutes was burning his mind. He kept seeing the knife entering Caitlin's body, kept seeing the blood piss from her wounds. Kept hearing her last, strangled, desperate word.

'Conor . . .'

He felt his body jerk. The leaden numbness of his muscles was dissolving. Was the injection wearing off? He tried to move again. His knife hand shifted an inch. But no more.

And then they were picking him up again. They dragged him backwards out of the bathroom so that he could see Caitlin's body again as he exited. Her face was a fixed mask of terror, the skin a shocking, pallid white – a sharp, monstrous contrast with the devastating wound in her neck and the scarlet smears trapped within her shower-curtain shroud. He tried to say her name – like that was going to do any good now – but he was still no more the master of his voice than of his body.

Within seconds she was out of sight and Joe was lying on his back at the far end of the hallway, by the banister overlooking the staircase but up against the opposite wall. His body was twitching again, as though an electric shock was passing through it every ten seconds. He could move his left foot, but that was all.

He managed to roll his eyes to the right. One of the intruders had his back to him and was doing something to the banister. After fifteen seconds he stepped away. Joe saw that he had tied a length of rope to the rail. It was about two metres long and the other end, which the intruder held in his gloved hands, was tied in a loop.

A noose.

Another of the men came into view. He grabbed the banister and shook it. It rattled a little.

'Will it take his bastard weight?' his muffled voice asked.

'Let's find out,' came the reply. The two men turned to face him.

Joe's body jerked. He managed to move his right arm at the elbow. It lifted forty-five degrees, then flopped down to the floor again.

The drug was wearing off . . . His strength was definitely returning. But not fast enough. The intruder with the noose was bending down. Joe's body twitched. He could hear the man's heavy breath from behind his mask, and just make out his eyes behind the misted plastic.

The rope was barely twelve inches from his head . . .

A noise.

It came from outside: the sound of a vehicle pulling up. The ghost of a headlight beam shone through the bathroom window and along the hallway. The engine cut out. The two intruders that he could see straightened up. The one holding the noose dropped it.

'Leave him. Take the rope.' The instruction was curt, and responded to only by a nod. The intruders left quickly but

141

silently. By the time – ten seconds later – Joe heard three sharp raps on the front door, they had already reached the spiral staircase, having shut behind them the door that led to it.

He tried to shout: to scream to whoever was at the front door to get to the back of the house. Nothing but a feeble croak emerged. Another three raps. He concentrated all his energy on trying to move, but all he could do was roll uselessly onto his front.

He heard the front door open.

'Hello?' called an uncertain voice. 'Hello? I did knock!'

Joe would never have thought his stomach could get even more knotted. He recognized Elaine's voice well enough, and he knew what it meant.

He knew Conor was downstairs.

He tried to call out again, to scream at them not to come up. Still the words wouldn't come. With a massive effort he pulled his knees up under his body. Elaine was still shouting. 'Hello? Hello? It's only me . . . Elaine . . .' He could hear her moving into the kitchen; he could also hear footsteps up the stairs. Small, tentative footsteps.

A child's footsteps.

Joe was kneeling now. He stared at his blood-covered hands, and at the knife he was still holding. With a terrible, painful struggle he managed to look over his shoulder at the open door of the bathroom. Then he turned back, and saw an unmistakable sight through the railings of the banister: Conor's scruffy, russet hair, his earnest young face, his shoulders, his blue dressing gown.

'Go!' was all Joe could say.

Conor was six or seven steps from the top of the staircase. He turned to his right and looked through the railings. His eyes widened in shock.

'Is anybody here?' Elaine's voice, back in the hallway, sounded worried. And then: 'Conor? Conor, is everything OK?'

Conor was shaking his head. He was staring now at the bloody knife in Joe's hand.

'Where's Mum,' he whispered.

'Go!' Joe croaked again.

But now Conor was running up to the top of the stairs and past his dad. Joe forced himself to look back again. He saw Conor disappear first into his own bedroom, then into his parents'. And only when he was satisfied that his mum was in neither room did he approach the bathroom door.

It was almost as if he knew there were unspeakable horrors behind it. He opened the door slowly, as if scared to see what nightmares the room contained. He looked so small, framed in that doorway, wearing just his night things. But his shadow was long, and stretched half the length of the landing.

Joe couldn't bear to watch. He turned back. At some point during the past twenty seconds, the knife had fallen from his fingers. He managed to lift his arms, to bury his face in his hands.

If he could have joined in with the animal scream of his ten-year-old son, he would have done. But he couldn't. He could only listen to Conor's howling, feeling that his heart was being ripped from his chest, and wondering if it would ever end.

NINE

Joe remembered the way Elaine's screaming had joined Conor's: she standing at the top of the stairs, he in the bathroom, begging his mother not to die.

He remembered trying to stand up, but not yet being back in full control of his body.

He remembered Elaine shouting at Conor to come with her, and how his son, as he passed him on the landing, threw himself at Joe, beating him with his tiny fists, a puny flurry of rage that Joe wouldn't have resisted even if he'd been able to.

He remembered the minutes passing like hours as the strength seeped back into his body.

He knew he was alone in the house with Caitlin's corpse, that Conor and Elaine had fled. He knew it would be just minutes before the police arrived. They wouldn't see what they were supposed to have seen – a sight that told a story of Joe having murdered his wife before hanging himself. But they would see enough. And when he heard the sirens – faint at first, but quickly growing louder as the cars approached – he knew what he had to do: forget all thoughts of running to Caitlin's side, or trying to see his son, or attempting to explain the truth of what had happened.

Forget about everything, except getting out of there. The police would have his name. They'd know who he was. They wouldn't be sending some two-bit bobby and a community service officer. They'd be sending an ARU, fully prepared to drop him if necessary.

Somehow he found himself standing up, holding on to the banister like he was learning to walk again. He remembered edging towards the top of the stairs, the sirens blaring now, their blue strobes flooding in through the bathroom window, lighting up the hallway. The sound of the door being kicked in. The red dots of laser scopes flashing up the staircase. He could hear his own voice, a shadow of itself, shouting as loud as it could: 'Unarmed! I have no weapon!'

And he remembered his legs giving way, and the brutal, soul-shaking thump as his body collapsed down the stairs and everything around him went black.

When he reawoke – it couldn't have been more than a few minutes later – he was surrounded by SOCOs, trying to force him, feet first, into a paper body bag to preserve any incriminating DNA on his clothes and skin. Every muscle in his body shrieked with pain, but that hadn't stopped him lashing out with heavy fists. It had taken at least six officers to pin him down, bind his hands behind his back and continue the process of wrapping him in the DNA suit, before forcing him outside where the night was lit up by flashing blue lights. He remembered shouting – *screaming* – his innocence, yelling about assassins and bin Laden; roaring at them to let him see Caitlin, to let him see his son . . .

But nobody even answered him.

Then he was in a local police station, held down by the same six officers in a small cell where he was formally cautioned, while a shocked-looking young forensics woman wearing a white coat and pale blue latex gloves took swab samples from inside his mouth, his fingernails, his foreskin. He didn't stop shouting . . . his throat was raw, like he'd swallowed a razor . . . his mind was burning up . . . the room was spinning . . . he was screaming Caitlin's name . . .

When he heard the forensics woman call for a semen detection kit, it made him roar louder than before . . . made him raise his knees and kick two of the officers holding him down in the face. Now he was banging his own head against the hard floor – if he did violence on himself, perhaps he could stop the agony . . .

Lights and faces danced before his eyes.

He heard the call for a sedative shot and he shouted even more – not words, but strangled animal noises.

For the second time that night he felt a needle slip through his skin . . .

And then darkness once more.

He had no way of knowing how long he was out. When he drifted slowly back into consciousness, he was in a vehicle. It was dark. He was lying on his front on a cold, hard, metallic floor and his hands were tied behind his back. He was wearing only jeans. Bare feet. Bare torso. It was noisy. The floor was vibrating with the movement of the vehicle. The drugs had fully worn off now, but every cell in his body was bulging with pain. His skull throbbed, but that was nothing compared with the agony that exploded in his head when he remembered what had happened. It didn't matter if he opened his eyes or closed them. All he saw was Caitlin: stricken, brutalized, begging him to help her.

Dead by his hand.

Joe started to dry retch. It would have been better if they'd succeeded in faking his suicide. Then, at least, Conor would be safe. He knew now that somebody was trying to eliminate him. They'd do anything to achieve it. If they could do such a thing to Caitlin, they wouldn't think twice about targeting his son. He retched again.

Minutes later he pushed himself painfully up to his knees. He figured he was in the back of a secure vehicle about the size of a Transit, maybe a little bigger. On one side there was a small slit in the chassis, the size of a letterbox, with three vertical bars.

Getting groggily to his feet, he managed to peer through this peephole. He was on a motorway. Checking the rate at which they passed the cat's eyes on the hard shoulder, he estimated the speed at 70 mph. The landscape beyond the motorway was enveloped in blackness. He moved to the rear of the van, turned to face the front and felt behind him for any bolts with his bound hands. There was a bar across both doors, like on a fire exit, but it wouldn't budge. He was locked in from outside. Broken and shuddering, Joe slid once more to the floor in the back of what he guessed was a police van.

He couldn't read his watch because his wrists were tied behind his back, and there was no way of guessing the time, but it was perhaps two hours after he awoke that the van stopped to refuel. Joe positioned himself by the peephole again. The owner of a Porsche Cayenne was staring in his direction as he refuelled. The guy was lit up – as was the whole service station forecourt – by a blue strobe. Joe realized he must have a police escort. Nobody was taking any chances.

After five minutes they set off again. Joe remained on his feet, looking out of the letterbox, trying to see landmarks he recognized. The angle of his vision made it impossible to read the road signs as they passed, and they had travelled for at least another three hours before he was able to get a bearing: they were crossing the River Thames over the QEII bridge. He counted the lights of four vessels on the river, three heading west, one east. After another half an hour, they turned off what was clearly the M25 and from the motion of the van he calculated that they were heading towards London. It was all the information he needed to work out where they were going.

Remand prison. High security. South-east London. It could only be HMP Barfield.

He'd been there once before, a decade ago. The squadron had been on standby in Hereford when word had come through from the Home Office that the Barfield screws were predicting a riot. They were clearly expecting something big to go off, because the police had requested Regiment support. Sixteen men had travelled down from Hereford to Greenwich and remained in a state of readiness for twenty-four hours. Nothing had happened. Maybe the inmates had got wind that they might have more than a few plods to deal with. Good thing too. Joe and the guys were only ever called into situations that needed the precise and ruthless application of violence. Send a squadron into a Cat A institution – home to some nasty fuckers who made Ronnie and Reggie look like eccentric uncles – and you could be sure of one thing: prison numbers would fall.

The lights above Barfield's high wire perimeter glowed brightly in the early morning darkness as they approached the entrance. Joe heard a babble of male voices outside, then felt the van move forward again, through the entrance and into an empty reception yard. He tried to estimate the distance they travelled from the gates before stopping. Fifty metres, perhaps. A long way to run, especially with his arms bound behind his back and bare feet. Maybe if he had the element of surprise? Unlikely. He could see flashing lights illuminating the yard. There was a reception party.

He didn't see the face of the man who opened the back of the vehicle. All he saw were the four armed police, with flak jackets, visored helmets and MP5s, two kneeling five metres back from the van, two standing ten metres behind that. Between the two standing officers was a uniformed screw, tall and thin, carrying a clipboard. 'Get him in!' he shouted, his voice echoing in the night. As Joe stood at the vehicle's exit, squinting against the sudden influx of light from a powerful beam behind the screw, he clocked a look of disgust on the man's face.

Two more men appeared from the wings. They also wore prison officers' uniforms, but were burlier than the guy with the clipboard. They pulled Joe roughly from the van, each man taking one of his elbows. Instinctively, Joe wrestled away from them. He was rewarded with a solid truncheon blow in the stomach that knocked the wind from his lungs and bent him double as he was dragged across the yard – his bare heels scraping painfully against the rough tarmac – and into a single-storey brick building, the armed police following some five metres behind.

This first building was little more than a waiting room: five lines of brown plastic chairs and an old vending machine in one corner. There was a door on the far wall, and Joe's two guards pushed him through it.

In a weird way, the room he found himself in reminded him of the armoury back at Hereford. It wasn't big – maybe eight metres by five – and there was a long counter with an open doorway into another room behind. There was a desktop computer on the counter, next to which Joe saw what looked like a webcam, and a small flatbed scanner. On the wall behind the counter was a laminated poster entitled 'Coping with Prison'. At the far end of the room there was a third doorway, this one closed by a heavy metal door studded with bolts and with two keyholes. Apart from Joe and his two guards, the only other person in the room stood behind the counter. He wore a ginger moustache and the bored expression of a clock-watching official. He said three words: 'Belt, shoelaces, watch.' Then he looked over the counter and saw Joe's bare feet and lack of belt. 'Watch,' he corrected himself.

Joe gave him a dark look and didn't move. His hands were still tied behind his back. How the fuck was he supposed to do anything?

The thin screw with the clipboard entered. He took one look at the situation, then nodded at the man behind the counter, who produced a pair of wire cutters and handed them over. 'We know who you are,' the thin screw said to Joe in a reedy cockney accent. 'Let's not do anything stupid, eh?'

'I want to see my son.'

'Tough shit.'

With one squeeze of the cutters, Joe's hands were free.

Distance to the exit, five metres. Two guards, thin screw, ginger moustache: he could put these four guys down with his bare hands, but he didn't know what was waiting for him outside. He didn't move.

'Watch.'

Joe removed his watch, but kept his eyes on the jobsworth with the moustache. When he placed it on the counter, he saw the man's face change. Joe looked down at his own hands. His right hand – his knife hand – was blood red, from the fingertips to an inch above the wrist. There was spatter all the way up his arm.

'Empty your pockets,' the man said, his lip curled with disgust.

Joe's eyes flickered to the left. The two guards were standing three metres away, one with his arms folded, the other tapping his truncheon lightly against his right leg. To his right, the thin screw was scribbling something on the clipboard – Joe could hear the sound of his pencil on the paper.

'Pockets!' Joe could smell the tobacco on the breath of the man behind the counter. He noticed a signet ring on the little finger of his right hand, and dirt under the fingernails. 'Come on, I haven't got all fucking night!'

Joe pulled a five-pound note and a handful of change from the front pocket of his jeans. From the back pocket he removed a folded piece of paper. For a moment he didn't know what it was, but then he remembered. Conor's picture, the one his lad had given him in his bedroom back home.

'You're not having this,' Joe muttered, making to put it back in his jeans.

The thug with the truncheon didn't hesitate. The second blow was even more violent than the first, and Joe felt the paper being ripped from his hands even as he bent double with pain. It took five seconds to grab his breath. When he straightened up, he saw that the man with the moustache had unfolded the paper. With a malicious glint in his watery eyes, he tore it in two, then in two again.

Something snapped in Joe. He hurled himself at the counter, grabbing the officer by his greasy ginger hair and slamming his head down so that it smashed against the counter. The guy cried out. When he stood up again, blood was flowing from his nostrils and he had his hand pressed to his face. Vaguely aware that the thin screw with the clipboard had run from the room at the first sign of trouble, Joe turned to the two guards. They were edging away from him, the thug with the truncheon holding it forward threateningly like a sword. Joe was ready to jump them, but at that moment the armed police officers burst in. Total confusion. Four of them, MP5s dug into their shoulders, shouting at the tops of their voices: '*Hit the ground, hit the fucking ground!*' Joe dropped to his knees, his hands raised, fully expecting the brutal kicks that his two guards now delivered to the side of his stomach with their heavy black boots. The thin screw reappeared behind the armed police, watched for thirty agonizing seconds, before saying 'Stop!'

The two prison guards straightened up, leaving Joe in a pile on the floor.

The silence that followed was broken only by the pained swearing of the guy with the ginger moustache. As he tried to stem the flow of blood from his nose, he staggered backwards through the door behind the counter and out of sight. The thin screw gave a nod to one of the ARU. They lowered their weapons and withdrew to the entrance.

'Stand up.'

Joe stood.

'Look, pal,' the screw said. 'In twenty minutes' time you'll either be in a cell or in the hospital wing. The duty nurse is six foot three and called Albert. Lovely bloke. Family man. It's a very funny thing, but last time he had a wife-beater in there, another inmate managed to stab the little shit with a dirty needle while Albert's back was turned. Cunt got a nice case of Hep C off of it. Now I might be wrong, but I reckon someone who just killed his missus could find Albert's got his back turned on him, too . . .'

'I didn't kill her,' Joe muttered, his voice hoarse.

'Save it for the beak, pal. Now take the rest of your fucking clothes off before we give Albert something to ignore.'

Joe blinked stupidly up at him. 'What the fuck?'

'Clothes!' barked the screw. 'Off! And don't look at me like that. There's plenty of faggots on the block, but *we've* all got WAGs to suck us off at home. Your arsehole's safe on this side of the door . . .'

Joe stood up slowly. Without taking his gaze from the screw, and aware that everyone in the crowded room – the two guards, the thin screw, the four armed police by the door – were watching him, he stripped, then stood up straight.

'All right, He-Man, turn round.'

Joe turned.

'Squat.'

Joe didn't move.

'*Squat!*'

Joe squatted.

'Cough.'

He did as he was told.

'All right, you're clean. Put your fucking trousers back on. Just so's you know, we've got a nasty habit of asking you to do that whenever we feel like it. Remember that if you get tempted to keister anything . . .'

Joe pulled his jeans back on, then felt himself being yanked towards the counter. The guy with the bloody nose was still missing. Another screw, bald and thickset, had emerged from the room behind the counter. 'Hand,' he said, and pointed to the scanner. Joe stretched out his bloodstained hand. The guy grabbed him by the wrist and looked at his palm. He didn't seem at all bothered by the gore, other than to say: 'Too much blood. Won't work. Give me the other one.'

The next thing Joe knew, his clean hand was palm downwards on the scanner bed, and a fluorescent white strip was moving from top to bottom under the glass. 'What is it?' he demanded.

'Biometric ID,' the screw said proudly as he held up the webcam, looked at the screen and pressed the button. 'Matches your palm print to your face. Course, clever bloke like you won't be thinking of no funny business.' He seemed to find this amusing, and grinned at the others.

The thin screw started talking. 'My name's Sowden,' he said. 'You call me guv and you do what I tell you. Trust me, sunshine, we've heard it all and seen it all. You want a quiet life, put your head down and do as you're told.'

Joe had zoned out. Sowden continued talking – a list of rules and regulations, something about a lawyer and remand custody. His words barely registered.

The bald man handed Joe a bundle of beige clothes, then took a set of keys, walked round to the other side of the counter and opened up the heavy metal door. It was a good eight inches thick with two sets of internal locking bolts each at least three inches in diameter. Joe felt himself being nudged through the door.

He found himself in what felt like a cell – three metres by three, with an identical metal door on the opposite wall. The two prison guards and Sowden joined him, leaving the ARU in the reception area. The door clanged shut behind them. Joe heard the bolts closing. Thirty seconds passed before the second door opened. Another screw was there, his keys attached to his belt by a length of cord. Joe's guards pushed him out into the corridor beyond, and the door was locked behind him.

This corridor had yellow-painted concrete walls and bright

strip lighting. After fifteen metres it led to a second set of double security doors, then to another courtyard, half the size of a football pitch and surrounded by imposing brick buildings four storeys high. Even though it was still night, the sky was bathed in light – Joe had the sense that the whole exterior was lit by floodlights. Every window he could see had bars over it. He counted four prison guards circling the courtyard, each with a German shepherd on a lead. One of the dogs looked in his direction, its ears flattened. Its handler yanked its lead sharply and continued to circle the courtyard.

The building to which the guards led Joe was on the opposite side of the courtyard at his ten o'clock. This time they passed through a single security door, which Sowden carefully locked behind them. They were in a small annexe with a sign on the opposite wall: 'Category A'.

'You said remand,' Joe muttered.

'We've been advised you're a flight risk. You're under observation. Do yourself a favour and keep your head down.' Joe opened his mouth to argue. He didn't get the chance. 'Give me any more trouble, fella, I'll stick you with the fucking Irish. I reckon they'd make short work of a nice army lad like you. Trust me, mate, you're better off with Hunter.'

Joe didn't ask who Hunter was. He figured he'd find out soon enough.

The block Sowden and the two guards led him to consisted of three landings, each with a set of security bars at intervals of fifteen metres and lined with solid metal doors with shuttered peepholes every seven or eight metres on either side. Joe's guards led him to the third door on the right of the ground-floor landing. One of them rapped on the door – three heavy thumps – then unlocked it.

'In,' said Sowden.

Joe entered: he had no other option. The cell door clanged shut behind him. He found himself in almost total darkness.

Silence.

In the corridor outside he heard the rattling of a set of security bars dissolve into nothing.

Silence again.

Joe realized his muscles were tense. He didn't know who this guy Hunter was, or why he was here. But he *did* know that he couldn't afford to display a moment of weakness in front of whatever fucking maniac he was banged up with. He expected Hunter to be in the bottom bunk – that, he knew, was where the dominant cellmate traditionally installed himself. Joe considered pulling him out and forcing him to the top – to show he didn't intend to take any shit – but before he could do anything, there was a voice.

'Ain't *someone* been a bad boy?' A nauseating sound, somewhere between a giggle and a snort.

Joe peered through the darkness, trying at once to see his cellmate and work out what his voice said about him. Hunter sounded older than Joe, probably in his fifties. London accent – east, not south. Probably white. He didn't sound very hard. Quite the opposite. Almost effeminate, and it was clear he was already occupying the top bunk . . .

'*Very* bad boy, to end up with old Hunter.'

Joe managed to pick out some dark shapes in the room. A table along the right-hand wall with a small TV on top. A set of bunk beds along the left. The outline of a window at the far end, about a metre square and with the shadows of six metal bars just visible. A toilet at the near end, with a tiny sink next to it; a wardrobe to his right. The cell smelled of bleach. Joe installed himself on the bottom bunk.

'A bad, bad boy, to end up in here with me,' the voice persisted. It had a sing-song lilt to it, the voice of a man doing what he could to sound like a child. Joe had a flashback of another voice, so far away but with the same rhythmic sing-song: *Amer-ee-can motherfucker. Amer-ee-can motherfucker . . .*

'You speak again,' Joe said, his voice level, 'I'll break every bone in your fucking body.'

His cellmate sniggered, then fell silent. Five minutes later Joe heard the deep breathing of sleep.

As for Joe, it still didn't matter if he kept his eyes open or closed. Either way, he relived the night's events, over and over, like a film loop in his head. Like a knife being stabbed into his own guts, withdrawn and then thrust in again.

Just as he had done to Caitlin.

He could hardly bear to think of it, and yet he couldn't think of anything else.

And, in another corner of his brain, questions. The sortie through the minefield that had killed Ricky: was that just an accident, or had they been manoeuvred into position? But manoeuvred by who? The Americans? Was the car that had tried to run him over anything to do with it? The driver hadn't *looked* American. Middle Eastern, if anything. And the intruders in the SOCO suits, who'd tried to make it look as if he'd killed Caitlin before committing suicide. Who were they? How had they tracked him down? No one knew he was there.

It all led back to that night in Abbottabad. He was sure of it. And if whoever was behind all this had had their way, Conor would be dead too.

The sick, distraught, unreal feeling that was running through his body grew stronger. He didn't give a *fuck* what the Yanks were trying to hide. As far as he was concerned they could have nuked the compound and good fucking riddance.

But who could he tell? Who would listen? He was surrounded by the impenetrable walls of a Cat A prison. There wasn't a single person in the world that he could trust.

A chill fear started to descend on him. He counter-attacked with thoughts of revenge.

Somehow, he told himself, someone was going to pay.

* * *

It was not the grey light of morning seeping through the barred window of the cell that roused Joe from his open-eyed trance, nor was it the rustling and heavy breathing from the top bunk. It was the rattling noise from the corridor outside and the subsequent scrapes and shouts of the prison population waking up. He turned onto his side and faced the wall. A minute later the overhead rustling stopped and he was aware of his cellmate getting ready to climb down. Joe slowly turned. He took in the details of the cell. The textured beige tiles on the floor that wouldn't have looked out of place in the changing rooms of a public swimming pool. The exposed pipes running along the bottom of the wall opposite, their grey paint peeling. The graffiti scribbled on the wall, detailing the names of inmates past and present who were cocksuckers, motherfuckers and cunts.

His cellmate climbed down and stood beside him. He was in his fifties. He wasn't much more than five foot tall, and had a pasty, pallid, jowly face with thin, moist lips that looked like they were permanently on the edge of laughter. He wore brown trousers and an open-necked shirt, presumably the prison uniform. One of the buttons was missing, and the hair on his fat stomach protruded through the gap. His thin, greying hair was combed over to make it look thicker, and he wore unfashionable, black-rimmed glasses, with lenses so thick that they slightly distorted his eyes. A smell wafted off the man: a musty, pungent, unwashed odour. The wall behind him was covered with magazine centrefolds. Not the beaver shots Joe was used to in military installations where the tits-only rule was regularly disobeyed, but brightly coloured pictures of pop-star kids not much older than Conor. Justin Bieber and Miley Cyrus. Joe felt sick. He looked back at the guy. He had two thin scars just below his jugular, raw enough for Joe to deduce that they had been recently sustained.

'They ain't given me a little friend for ages,' said the man.

His eyes lingered on Joe's torso for a few seconds, before

noticing his unfriendly look. But it didn't seem to worry him much. He smiled at Joe and walked over to the toilet at the end of the bed. Joe donned his khaki shirt to the sound of his cellmate pissing thunderously against the steel pan.

'Hunter's the name,' he said over his shoulder. 'Four years. Won't bother you with the details. Sure you'll find out. The ladies here do love a little gossip.' He sniggered again before turning around with his dick still on show, licking his lips slightly, then zipping up his fly and continuing. 'So, what's a nice boy like you doing in a place like this?'

Something exploded inside Joe.

The force with which he grabbed Hunter and thrust him up against the door was enough to make the door itself echo. The smarminess instantly disappeared from Hunter's flabby face. He looked like he might cry. 'You even *speak* to me,' Joe breathed, 'I'll see to it that you get another pair of scars on the other side of your neck, only these ones won't heal up so pretty. Got it?'

Hunter nodded. When Joe let go of him, he didn't move, but stared at him, a frightened rabbit.

There was the sound of the door being unlocked. It opened a couple of inches. Hunter looked like he was about to say something, but then he thought better of it. He disappeared from the cell, leaving the door ajar. Joe kicked it closed, then stood at the sink. He turned on the tap and a trickle of scalding water ran out.

Caitlin's blood had dried to his hands. He had nothing to scrub it off apart from the hot water and his own fingernails. He started slowly, scraping hard at his palm and the back of his hand. But the stain refused to budge. After two minutes he was soaping his skin in a kind of frenzy. Pink water ran into the steel sink – he watched it circling down the plughole – but his skin remained stained pink. He couldn't get it off, and as he rubbed harder he started to feel dizzy.

He was on the floor, his head in his wet hands . . .

'Looks like our new celebrity's feeling sorry for himself.'

Joe looked up sharply. There was a screw standing over him, no older than thirty but with a thick head of white hair and almost as broad-shouldered as he was. He looked at Joe's dripping hand. 'Shower block's the place for that.'

Joe breathed deeply to calm himself. There was no point making an enemy of yet another screw. He stood up. 'Where is it?'

The white-haired screw shook his head. 'Too late. Breakfast.'

'I'm not hungry.'

'Word of advice. You might be on remand but this isn't the fucking Ritz and you don't get to choose what you do or when you do it. Now get to the dining hall before I stick you in the fucking Seg Wing.'

Joe stood up. He wiped his wet hands on his prison clothes. The remaining blood smeared over them, but at least his right hand was relatively clean now. He said nothing, but followed the screw out of his cell.

The dining hall was in the adjacent block. Joe could smell it from the exercise yard – the cabbagy odour of mass-produced food that reminded him of the cookhouse at barracks in Catterick in his Recruit Company days. The hall itself was filled with row upon row of trestle tables and benches – Joe noticed immediately that they were fixed to the floor – with a four-metre-wide gangway up the middle. The room was brightly lit by glaring strip lights hanging from the high ceiling, and it was crowded – he estimated that there were close on seven hundred men in there. At the far end was a serving area where a line of hotplates were manned by six inmates. Joe assumed the door behind the hotplates led to a kitchen, and he stored that information away. Kitchens, he knew, were good sources of hardware. Provisions and waste moved in and out of them. The remnants of a queue – maybe fifteen or twenty people – snaked down the gangway, and Joe counted fifteen screws standing with their backs to the wall at regular intervals around the edge of the hall.

'All yours,' said the white-haired screw, before leaving the dining hall.

Joe felt eyes on him as he walked up the gangway, and it was only then that he twigged what the screw had called him back in the cell: 'our new celebrity'. Had word of what had happened really leaked out so fast? Joe's definite impression was that it had. As he walked towards the serving hatch, he found himself picking out sets of eyes staring at him as he went: a thickset, shaven-headed man with inked-up forearms; a skinny, wea-selly-looking guy with round glasses and a weak chin; a young Asian lad, his face covered with wisps of bumfluff; Hunter, sitting on his own at a table well apart from the others, a dedi-cated screw standing over him as he chewed slowly and watched Joe with bright eyes. There was an immense, echoing hubbub in the dining hall. Maybe it was just Joe's imagination, but the conversation seemed to lull at the tables he passed.

He joined the end of the queue. It had gone down to ten people now. The final three had their backs to the serving area and were watching him approach. They were bulky men, all with jet-black hair and green eyes. They looked like they might be brothers. There was a pause of thirty seconds before one of them spoke. His hair was Brylcreemed back, and he had a pasty, unhealthy face. He stank of cigarettes.

'You our new army boy?' he asked. He had a thick Ulster accent. When Joe didn't reply, he continued: 'Always a pleasure to welcome a brave lad like you.' He didn't sound like Joe's presence gave him any pleasure at all. His two companions gave Joe a menacing stare.

Two years in the Province meant Joe could spot a crew of PIRA hoods from a mile off. Even back in the day, the majority of these lads were more interested in Republicanism as a front for their criminal activities – drugs, long firms, contraband booze and smokes, you name it – than anything else. Their criminality hadn't disappeared with the Troubles, so it was hardly surprising to run into their type in a place like this. And though the politicians liked to pretend that the days of antagonism were at an end, Joe knew that was bullshit: the British Army were the bad guys in vast swathes of Northern Ireland, the SAS even more so. If these lads found out he was Regiment, they'd be almost duty bound to have a crack at him.

'Not looking for any trouble, fellas,' Joe said quietly.

'You hear that, boys?' the other guy sneered. 'He's not looking for any trouble.'

His mates laughed, and the queue shuffled up a couple of places.

'Well, you never know, army boy,' the guy continued. 'Maybe it'll come looking for you.' An unpleasant smile crossed his lips. 'A filthy Brit and a beast in the same cell. It's like Christmas came early.' He turned his back on Joe. 'Course, if you don't want every Tom, Dick and Harry having a pop at you each time you leave your cell, there's ways and means, army boy.'

'What're you talking about?'

'Ah, it's just a matter of keeping in with the right people. People with clout, who can protect you.'

Joe sneered. 'You?' he asked.

'Well now, that's *your* choice, army boy. That's *your* choice.'

Two minutes later a member of the kitchen staff was spooning rubbery scrambled eggs into one of the compartments of a tin tray, baked beans into another. The table Joe sat at was three rows down from the serving area and populated solely by black prisoners: eight of them, four along either side. The guy closest to Joe had elaborate patterns shaved into the side of his head, but his face was a lot less pretty than his haircut. He wore a vest and the muscles in his arms were enormous and well defined. He had black tattoos on his dark skin. As Joe sat down, the man pushed his food tray away and turned to stare at him.

Joe concentrated on his food, but he felt every part of his

body enter a heightened state of alertness. He could sense the potential for violence in the air, and he gripped his plastic fork more firmly than he otherwise might have done. Not much of a weapon, but all he had: if he splintered it, he could wreck an eye at the very least . . .

'Stand up!'

Joe had barely forced down a couple of mouthfuls of his unwanted food when Sowden, the tall, thin screw from the previous night, walked up to him. 'Follow me,' he said.

'Why?'

All the black prisoners were watching the exchange in silence.

'Because I told you to.' And then, perhaps remembering Joe's outburst the night before, he added: 'Your lawyer's here.'

'I don't have a lawyer.'

'You do now.'

Joe wasn't sad to leave the dining hall. It felt like a war waiting to happen in there. Sowden led him into the courtyard for the second time that morning, towards another prison block and into a small room with nothing in it but a table and two chairs. A woman was sitting at the table. She was dressed in a two-piece business suit and had her brown hair arranged in a bun. Not a looker, and her face was pinched, unfriendly and covered in a thick layer of foundation. As the door was locked behind Joe, she nodded at the spare chair on the opposite side of the table, but she failed to catch his eye.

Joe sat. The woman pushed a copy of *The Times* across the table. 'You'd better read that,' she said in a slightly hostile Scottish accent, sounding as though her mind was elsewhere. 'Page five.'

Joe wasn't sure he wanted to, but he navigated past the front page and a picture of Princess Anne on page three. He pretty soon wished he hadn't.

He had no idea where they'd got the pictures from. There was one of Caitlin that he recognized as being the photo her dad kept on his mantelpiece in Epsom. It was about five years old, taken at Christmas. She had a smile on her face and was wearing a scarf Joe had bought for Conor to give her. The mere sight of it made him feel hollow.

Next to the picture of Caitlin was one of him, taken the day he'd been awarded the MC for bravery in Iraq, having pulled a couple of wounded Yanks from the debris of a roadside bomb while under fire from insurgents. There was no image of Conor.

He read the caption above the pictures: '*Partner of Afghanistan hero found murdered*'.

He looked up at the lawyer. She was studying papers in a file on her lap, almost as if he wasn't there.

Looking back at the paper, he continued to read. '*Northern Ireland-born mother of one Caitlin O'Donnell, 36, has been found brutally murdered in a remote cottage near Berwick-upon-Tweed. A police spokesman confirmed early this morning that her partner Sergeant Joseph Mansfield of 2nd Battalion the Parachute Regiment is currently assisting the police with their enquiries. Sergeant Mansfield was recently returned to the UK from Afghanistan, where it is thought he was considered unfit for active service. The Ministry of Defence has declined to comment. Statistics released by the MOD suggest that troops returning from Iraq and Afghanistan are ten times more likely to suffer the effects of post-traumatic stress disorder than those who remain at home . . .*'

Joe threw the paper to one side.

'PTSD?' He remembered Ricky. He tried not to think about his own behaviour, but he knew how easy it would be for the fuckers to slap that label on him.

'Clearly they can't say outright that you did it, for legal reasons,' said the lawyer.

'I didn't do it.'

The lawyer finally looked at him. 'You're on remand, Sergeant Mansfield. Do you understand what that means? You've been arrested on suspicion of murder, which means you're not eligible for bail until you come to trial, which could take anything up to a year. My name's Jacqueline Thomas. I've been assigned to your case and I'm—'

'Where's Conor?'

'I understand he's being looked after by his paternal grandfather. Sergeant Mansfield, I'm going to recommend from the get-go that you don't attempt to—'

'I didn't do it,' Joe said, keeping his voice quiet.

There was a pause. Jacqueline Thomas's eyes flickered towards the door, and Joe could tell she was wondering whether to call in the guard from outside. She obviously decided against it, and continued as though Joe hadn't said anything. 'A plea of diminished responsibility could reduce the charge to manslaughter . . .'

'I didn't do it.'

The lawyer laid her file on the table, removed her glasses and looked him in the eye. 'Fine,' she said in a neutral voice. 'Perhaps you'd like to tell me what happened last night?'

Joe closed his eyes. The horror flashed back into his mind. The knife entering Caitlin's body, the noose, Conor's scream . . . When he opened his eyes five seconds later, he saw that his hand was shaking again. The lawyer made a show of noticing it too. One eyebrow shot up meaningfully. 'Sergeant Mansfield?' she pressed.

He stared at her. Unbidden, another image returned to him. Dom Fletcher, his OC, asking if any of them had breached SOPs. The way his gaze had lingered for a fraction of a second on Joe.

'Who sent you?'

She blinked. 'I told you, I've been assigned to your—'

Joe made an impatient tutting sound. Why the fuck should he trust this woman? Why should he trust *anyone*?

'I want to go back to my cell,' he said.

'You can't do that. You're looking at life without parole, Sergeant Mansfield. As your designated legal counsel I'm obliged to advise you that we request a full psychiatric evaluation, and that we do it immediately . . .'

'*Shut up!*' Joe roared at her. '*Just fucking shut up!*'

He could feel himself losing it, feel his whole body shaking with anger.

He could see Ricky, looking at him across the minefield . . . Caitlin's face as the knife entered . . .

He was on his feet, banging on the door with his fists, vaguely aware that the woman behind him was shouting for help.

The guards were there . . . barking at him . . . restraining him . . .

And ten minutes later Joe was back in his cell, trembling, his breath jerky, cold sweat soaking his body.

Hunter stared at him like he was a lunatic. He was sitting cross-legged on the top bunk. The TV was on. Some fucking Noel Edmonds game show. Behind him, Joe heard the sound of a key in the cell door. He kept his back to the door, breathing deeply, trying to regain control of himself.

'Lock-up till twelve-thirty, fella,' Hunter said nervously. Joe stepped forward and switched off the TV. No complaint. Hunter clearly knew what was good for him. Joe lay on the bottom bunk. Perhaps emboldened by the fact that Joe hadn't threatened violence, he spoke again. 'I can sell you some snout,' he said. His voice had taken on a wheedling tone. 'Pay me back when you get—'

'What's that?'

A huge din had erupted outside. Shouting. Clattering. Joe jumped up and strode towards the window. He opened it – it was grimy and smeared – and looked through the bars onto the exercise yard. Approximately twenty inmates had walked out into it. Without exception they had their hands in their pockets and their heads down. None of them spoke to anyone else, and everyone ignored the din. It came, so far as Joe could tell, from the windows that overlooked the exercise yard, of which there had to be almost fifty. He could see hands emerging from the windows, grabbing the bars and rattling them.

Amid the chaos of shouting, he heard two words repeated: 'beast' and 'nonce'.

'I saw you talking to Finch.' Hunter's voice was slightly strained, as if he wanted to distract Joe from what was going on outside. Joe closed the window – the noise deadened slightly – and turned back to him.

'Who's Finch?' he demanded.

'He's from Northern Ireland.'

Joe remembered the man in the breakfast queue.

'Give you a word of advice for free?' said Hunter.

'What?'

'Finch thinks he's top dog. Least, he wants other people to think that. But he can't touch Hennessey. Don't matter *where* he is . . .'

'Who the fuck's Hennessey?'

'He's in the Seg Wing,' Hunter said. 'Solitary. Often is. Reckon he prefers it that way. Don't stop him running the place.'

'What do you mean?'

'You think the screws are in charge here?' Hunter snorted dismissively. 'That's bullshit. *Hennessey's* in charge. Ain't afraid of nothing or nobody. Up to his eyes in drugs and killings when he was on the outside. Done three murders since he's been banged up. Knows he ain't never getting out.'

'Who did he kill?'

'Scoobies wouldn't give him his own cell up in Hull when he got banged up. Bumped his cellmate off first night he was in. Smashed the bloke's skull against the wall, that's what I heard. Done it another two times before they give him his own room. Fucking stupid, some of these screws, if you ask me. Anyway, what Hennessey says goes. Even the scoobies do what he tells them, and there ain't a single inmate won't follow his orders. Except Finch and his crew, of course. But they'll learn. He's a clever bastard, Hennessey, on top of everything else. Sly. Knows how to make things work for himself.'

Another pause. Hunter started examining his fingernails.

'Does he get visitors?' The more information Joe could get on this Hennessey, the better.

'Why you so interested?'

Joe gave him a dangerous look.

'All right, all right,' Hunter said quickly. 'There's a woman, least that's what I heard. Comes in once a month. Scoobies let them hook up, dunno where.'

'Know her name?'

'No.'

'Anyone else get the same treatment?'

Hunter shook his head. 'Special privileges. Word is, the only thing that's stopping Hennessey's lot rioting is his say-so. Take away his privileges . . .' He made a sign with his hands like a bomb going off. 'Like I say, clever bastard. Knows how to fix things. Course,' he added quietly, 'it's because of Hennessey that I'm not in the Seg Wing with the others.'

'What others?'

'The others that are . . . in here for the same as me.'

'The sex cases?'

Another sniff. 'If that's what you want to call us. Got the scoobies in his pocket, ain't he? Knows he'll never get us all out into the general prison population, so he's doing us one by one. Last fella they done in the showers. Cut him to ribbons, his dick and all. Broke both his arms. Didn't kill him, though. Dunno why. Young lad. Nice fella.' He sniffed again. 'I'm next. They already had a go, didn't they?'

'The train tracks on your neck?'

'You been eyeing me up?'

Joe immediately stepped forward and grabbed the disgusting little nonce by his hair. Hunter squealed like a frightened girl. 'What did they use?' Joe hissed.

'A shiv.'

'What the fuck's a shiv?'

'A weapon,' the nonce babbled. 'Home-made. The block's full of them . . .'

Joe let go of his hair in disgust. 'How did they make it?' he demanded.

'The one that done me? I think it was a toothbrush they used. Two razor blades superglued to the end.' Hunter scrambled up into a kneeling position, then made a swiping gesture with his right hand. His eye burned brightly as he did it, but when his imaginary slice was complete, he shuddered and put his fingers to his neck, as though reliving the pain. 'But they done me with a power cord off the telly once, too. Blades tied to it.' He made a whipping gesture to explain how that worked. A frown crossed his face. 'Reckon they're playing with me. You know, like cats and mice.'

'You got a shiv of your own?'

Hunter shook his head timidly. 'The scoobies don't want me to defend myself,' he said. 'They search me more than the others.' But Joe had immediately noticed the way his eyes darted towards the wall behind him. He looked over his shoulder, to see Justin Bieber and Miley Cyrus grinning back. Joe marched over to the posters and was about to rip them from the wall, when Hunter spoke quietly.

'Don't do that, fella . . .'

Joe's hand stopped inches from the top of Justin Bieber's gay haircut. Hunter looked anxiously over at the locked door, then carefully peeled back the Blu-tack fixing the bottom corner of Miley Cyrus to the wall so that Joe could see the back of the poster. There were two strips of masking tape, each about two inches long, stuck to the shiny paper. Underneath each strip, Joe could see the outline of a razor blade. 'I won't go to the showers,' he admitted. 'I wash in here. Reckon this is where they'll try to do me, when the time comes.'

Hunter lowered the poster and stuck the Blu-tack to the wall again. He waddled back to his ladder and climbed up into the top bunk. His lips spread, fat and toad-like, as he watched Joe return to his own bunk.

'Do the other inmates see newspapers?' Joe said.

'Course. If they pay for them. What d'you want, Page 3?'

Joe didn't answer. All he really wanted was to find out if the rest of the prison population had access to the article about him. It seemed they did.

'There's blow,' said Hunter. He sounded desperate, as if he was trying to get on Joe's good side. 'If you know where to get it . . .'

But Joe didn't want drugs, he didn't want tobacco, and he didn't want anything to do with the man he was sharing a room with. If Hennessey's boys felt the need to do Hunter, they were welcome to him. All Joe wanted was to get out of this stinking, scum-infested shithole. Or, failing that, to protect himself.

He had access to two razor blades and nothing else.

It wasn't much, but it would be enough.

TEN

It had been a good shift, Eva Buckley thought to herself. Tiring, but good.

She'd been on since midnight, working from her desk in Scotland Yard. Things had been quiet. She'd not been called anywhere or hassled by anyone. For a lowly, overworked DI such as herself, that was unusual. But it had meant she could spend the night dealing with the paperwork that had been piling up over the past couple of weeks. And anyway, she found herself less inclined to put herself on the front line these days. Maybe it was the first sign of growing old. Now she was winding down with a latte and a blueberry muffin in Starbucks at Victoria Station. At least that was the idea. But now the latte was cold, the muffin uneaten, and there was no doubt about it: her day had just taken a turn for the worse.

She read the article in *The Times* for the third time, grinding her molars absent-mindedly, as was her habit, and then her eyes returned to the picture of the fresh-faced young soldier – slightly blurred and spotted with age – that she recognized so well. '*Sergeant Joseph Mansfield of 2nd Battalion the Parachute Regiment is currently assisting the police with their enquiries,*' the report said.

'Joe?' she whispered, shaking her head in disbelief.

Eva looked up, seeing but not registering the crowd of Japanese tourists that had just flooded into Starbucks. She was trying to work out when she had last seen him. Ten, eleven years ago? The afternoon of Millennium Eve. It should have been a happier occasion than it was. Her mum and dad, who still lived in Lady Margaret Road, Hounslow, where Eva and Joe had grown up, were having a get-together. All the old faces. Joe had shown up with his Irish girlfriend. She was beautiful and graceful. Everything Eva had hoped she wouldn't be.

Eva looked back down at the paper. If anyone had asked her, she'd have pretended she couldn't remember the girl's name. But she could, of course. How many times had she wondered whether Joe had talked to Caitlin about her? Had he explained that, growing up, he and Eva had been like brother and sister? Had Caitlin ever felt a twinge of jealousy? Had he ever had to explain that he'd never even so much as kissed her on the lips, no matter how much she had wanted him to?

Or had it never come up?

Joe had stayed at the party an hour, then left. Eva had never heard from him again.

She'd thought about him, though. God knows, she'd thought about him. On his birthday – 22 April, she never forgot that. At Christmas. And when she was lonely, and wanted to talk to her childhood friend.

He'd been such a quiet boy, but none of their group took that as a sign of weakness. That was partly because of his dad. Reg Mansfield had a reputation. Now that Eva was in the Job, she knew his type well enough. A bit of door work, always happy to earn a few quid roughing up some poor sod who owed a couple of weeks' rent or hadn't paid their bar bill. Brought his work home with him too. Joe's mum had the bruises on her face to prove it. Sometimes she'd make a go at camouflaging them with a bit of cheap foundation but most of the time she didn't bother. It was no secret in Lady Margaret Road that Roberta Mansfield's biggest concern was where her next bottle of vodka was coming from. You didn't often see her sober, though best not to mention this in front of Joe.

Reg eventually got out of his depth when he found himself

caught up in an armed robbery that went wrong. Eva had never got to the bottom of it, mainly because it was something Joe would never talk about. All she knew was that it had been a raid on a post office during which a police officer who'd been in the wrong place at the wrong time had taken a hit. Two days on life support and a widow's pension for his missus. Joe's dad hadn't fired the trigger, but that didn't stop him from receiving a fifteen-stretch. The Scrubs – frankly the best place for him.

Joe couldn't have been more different from his dad. Eva remembered a time, just a month before that last blag, when they had met at their usual hangout – the old bandstand in the recreation area at the end of Lady Margaret Road. It was winter-time, and Joe's skin was flushed with anger. He was holding the knuckles of his right hand, and Eva saw that they were bleeding. At first he didn't want to tell her what had happened, but after a few minutes of cajoling he gave in. His mum had been hitting the bottle. His dad had been hitting her. Joe had stepped in. It was a brave man that muscled up to Reg Mansfield, but Joe had done it and come out best. Eva remembered how she'd looked at him in a different light that night, how she'd realized that he was a teenager with a man's strength and a man's determination. Realized that even though he'd grown up in a den of thieves, he knew right from wrong.

She stared back at the article.

Joe knew right from wrong.

It was a surprise to everyone, Eva included, when he joined up at the age of sixteen. With his dad banged up and his mum now a slave to the bottle, nobody really believed he could make anything of his life. But Eva could tell, when he came back for his first home leave, that the life he had chosen was the right one for him. The quiet, steely manner had intensified. When their loudmouth friends in the pub bragged and swaggered, Joe kept quiet. He didn't feel the need to big himself up. He didn't feel the need to do anything but watch.

Apart from that one time.

He'd been home for two weeks. Joe, Eva and a few of their mates were drinking in the Hand and Flower, a local pub that turned a blind eye to the fact that they were all under-age. Ashley Bamber had left school to become an apprentice mechanic. He had been sinking pints of lager at twice the rate of any of the other guys, and was growing lairy with it. Joe, as usual, had sat in the corner, quietly watching. Then, just as last orders had been called, Ashley started coming on to Eva. There was nothing friendly and flirty about it: he'd groped her in front of everyone, and said something filthy. For what seemed like the first time that evening, Joe had spoken. 'Time to go home, Ash.'

Ashley had looked at him over his shoulder. 'Knob off, Action Man,' he'd said. 'Just because you've spent the last three months sucking the sergeant major's dick . . .'

They'd left then, all of them, embarrassed and awkward. Outside the Hand and Flower, however, Eva had watched as Joe grabbed Ashley by the arm and led him down the side of the pub and into the deserted beer garden. Two minutes later he returned alone. 'He ever gives you any trouble again, you tell me,' he said.

She never found out what had happened in that beer garden. Joe wouldn't tell her. But Ashley never gave her any bother again, and whenever Joe was back home, he stayed away.

It was thanks to Joe that Eva had joined the force. She'd half thought of joining the army like him, but her courage deserted her and she had decided to dedicate herself to a life of policing, thinking – maybe wrongly – that it was the softer option. She'd seen some things in her time. Rubbed shoulders with some nasty bastards who'd done some nasty things. She knew how they ticked. Knew the kind of men, and sometimes women, that they were.

And she knew Joe. Murder Caitlin? Eva no more believed him capable of that than herself. But then war did things to people, or so she'd heard. Maybe the Joe Mansfield she'd grown up with was not the same one who would now be in remand custody, awaiting trial.

She closed the newspaper and pushed the cold coffee away from her, before leaning her head against the back of the banquette and closing her eyes. She felt sick. Maybe it was because she was tired. Or maybe it was because she didn't know what the hell to do.

Two minutes later she was walking east up Victoria Street. Hundreds of workers from the surrounding area had emerged from their offices in search of an early sandwich. Eva battled against the tide, growing more and more anxious the closer she got to the Yard. By the time she had turned into Broadway and could see the revolving logo fifty metres away, she was out of breath.

Eva worked out of an office on the third floor which she shared with four other colleagues. To her relief it was empty – she hadn't even thought up an excuse for returning after her shift was over. They shared a single terminal of the Police National Computer, and it was to this terminal that she headed. Her fingers hovered above the keyboard as she sat down, but something stopped her from using her personal login. Every piece of activity on the PNC was logged, and searching for information not directly linked to an ongoing investigation was a sacking offence. But Eva had a workaround. One of her colleagues, a sleazy fat bastard by the name of Daniels, had been hitting on her a few months back. She'd found herself trapped in his office while he sang his own praises, clearly thinking that was how to worm his way into her underwear. He hadn't realized he'd left his login details in full view on his desk, or that Eva's memory was far better than his feeble pulling techniques. She'd stashed the login on her phone, never knowing when it would come in useful. Now was the time. She gained access to the database and in less than a minute she had the information she required.

Barfield. That was where they were holding him.

'Fuck me, Eva. Bit keen, isn't it?'

Eva immediately shut down the screen she was looking at and spun round in the chair. A young, friendly DI called Frank was walking over to his desk and removing the leather jacket he always wore to motorcycle into work. She and Frank had gone out a couple of times about a year back, once to a film, once for a meal. He'd taken her home on the bike after the second date and hinted that he might come in for coffee. When Eva had said no, he'd taken it fine. No hard feelings. She hadn't let on that it was the closest she'd ever got to a relationship, and Frank had never mentioned it again. As colleagues, they rubbed along together just fine.

'Just finished now,' said Eva, feeling her cheeks flushing. She stood up. 'I'll, er . . . I'll see you, yeah?'

Frank slung his biker's jacket over the back of his chair, raised one palm in farewell, and Eva hurried out.

Her heart was thumping as she walked the corridors to the exit, avoiding the eyes of all the Yard employees she passed in the hope that nobody would stop and talk to her. Nobody did. And as she sat on the Tube from Victoria to Green Park, then headed west on the Piccadilly Line, she was almost glad that she couldn't get a seat. She felt too anxious, too restless to sit.

Eva was sufficiently clued-up on prison regulations to know that a remand prisoner could receive visitors. Normally it was enough just to phone twenty-four hours in advance and she could get away without showing her face in the office, she reckoned. But as she locked herself into her cramped third-floor flat, all IKEA furniture and framed photos of her mum and dad, she found herself doubting the wisdom of making such a call. She knew Joe would be a high-profile, high-risk prisoner. Maybe the rules were different for him. Maybe she'd be causing him more harm than good if she tried to arrange a visit.

All these thoughts spun around in her head as she sat on her

futon sofa staring at her phone. It was with a head full of confused misgivings that she finally called directories and requested
a number in a quavering voice: 'HMP Barfield,' she said.
'London.'

'HMP Barfield – that's the prison?' asked the operator.

'Yeah. The prison.'

ELEVEN

During the night the agony of Caitlin's death kept coming to Joe in vividly accurate flashbacks. Fear too. It was a dark shadow on the edge of his mind. He was trapped. Set up. And if anyone wanted to have another go at him, it would be easy.

As it grew light, he realized he would soon have to go back to the dining hall. When the door was unlocked at seven-thirty, he decided to head straight there without saying a word to Hunter. But his path was blocked. Sowden, the screw who had received him when he first arrived, was standing in the doorway. 'All right, Mansfield,' he said. 'Hands flat against the wall. You too, Hunter.'

It was a brisk but thorough search. Sowden patted down his arms, his legs, his torso, back and crotch. 'Go,' he said shortly when he was satisfied Joe was clean. 'Your turn, Hunter.'

Joe left them to it and made his way to breakfast.

His senses were heightened, tuned in to any possible sign of danger, like he was in the field. Maybe the eyes that he felt burning into him *weren't* really following his progress towards the serving area. Maybe Finch, still surrounded by his crew at a table halfway along on the left-hand side, *wasn't* staring at him as he passed.

Or maybe they all were.

Joe ate everything he was given, shovelling Alpen and rubbery eggs down his throat like he was filling a magazine with rounds, and gulping down a cup of hot, sweet tea. All around him he heard cons complaining about the food. Try a cold MRE after three days in the snow, he thought to himself. It took him no more than three minutes to get his breakfast down him, after which he headed straight back to his cell, intending to stay there till the next mealtime.

No such luck.

It was 10 a.m. when he heard the sound of truncheons banging against the doors of the corridor. 'Exercise,' Hunter said from the top bunk.

'Fuck that,' Joe replied.

'Won't let you, fella. Everyone's got to go outside. Half an hour. It's the rules.'

Hunter was right. When Joe refused to leave his cell, three screws arrived to persuade him otherwise. He quickly decided it wasn't a battle worth fighting. A minute later he was outside in the yard.

It was a warm spring day. A third of the yard was in shadow as the sun had not fully risen over the prison buildings. Joe scanned the inmates. There were two men walking on their own. They looked anxiously at the other cliques and groups who had congregated in different areas. Were they nervous that they might be targets? If so, they were doing the wrong thing keeping close to the walls. If anyone decided to close in on them, they'd have nowhere to run.

Finch and his crew – Joe counted seven of them now – were standing ten metres away. In the opposite corner four Middle Eastern-looking guys were talking, and there were several groups of black prisoners. And as always, the screws – five of them this time – patrolling the yard, but keeping their distance from any of the prisoners.

Joe started walking, bisecting the yard, which meant passing within three metres of Finch. The crew from Northern Ireland fell silent as he approached. He had cleared them by two metres when he sensed them closing in to follow him. He was practically in the centre of the yard now. Twenty-five metres to the nearest walls, fifteen to the nearest screw, who had obviously seen what was happening but was keeping his distance.

Joe stopped and turned. Finch was standing two metres away, at the head of his crew, who were holding back slightly, looking menacing but in a disorganized, ragtag formation.

'Enjoying the sunshine?' Finch gave him a crooked smile.

'If you've got something to say, Finch, say it. Otherwise take your goons and fuck off.'

Finch raised a sarcastic eyebrow as he looked round at his mates. 'You hear that, lads? Goons, you are.' The goons didn't look very amused. 'You thought about what I said?'

'Not really.'

Finch's face remained expressionless. 'Here's the deal. You do something for me, I do something for you: protection. It's worth more than money in this place, but you've got to earn it.'

From the corner of his eyes, Joe could see Hunter. He had circled round the perimeter of the yard and was now at Joe's two o'clock, staring at them.

'You want to do Hunter, you do him yourself,' Joe replied. 'I don't provide muscle for the nutting squads.'

A look of suspicion crossed Finch's face. 'And where did *you* learn so much about nutting squads, army boy?' He shrugged. 'No, you can be sure one of *us* will look after the paedo. I'll take a knife to him myself if I can. I got someone else in mind.' Finch looked to his right. 'See the Pakis?'

Joe followed Finch's gaze. The four Middle Eastern-looking guys he had already noticed were now sitting cross-legged on the ground. They were deep in conversation, seemingly oblivious to anybody else around them. To Joe's eye, they didn't look Pakistani. Lebanese, maybe, or Syrian.

'Got a thing about the Pakis. I don't think too much of the niggers, neither, but they're busy enough doing our work for us and fucking each other up. Now the *Pakis* – they need *proper* cutting up, maybe more. Reckon you're the man for the job. It's what you army boys like to do, isn't it? Fuck with the towelheads . . .'

Fuck with the towelheads.

He was back in Abbottabad, firing rounds into Romeo and Juliet . . .

Snap out of it, he told himself. *Fucking snap out of it . . .*

'Do your own dirty work,' he said. 'And you can shove your protection up your fat Irish arse.'

There was a silence. Joe was aware of a pigeon flapping down and settling on the ground three metres to his right.

'Bad call,' Finch whispered. '*Bad* call.' He turned round to his cronies. 'Looks like Rambo here's going the way of the nonces,' he announced.

Finch backed away, and was immediately surrounded by his lads. The movement caused the pigeon to flap noisily up into the air and settle again between the bars of a second-floor cell window.

'Be seeing you, army boy,' Finch said, then turned and walked off. His crew joined him one by one, leaving Joe standing alone in the middle of the yard.

Joe stepped away. His hatred of the PIRA was deeply ingrained. He turned his attention instead to his surroundings. It was second nature to him to look for an exit strategy, but nothing presented itself here. The walls were nearly ten metres high and topped with barbed wire, every window was barred, every door bolted. There was a reason why prison escapes were so rare: they were almost impossible. He paced the exercise yard. He circled it twice. Then he saw, fifteen metres ahead, a man blocking his way.

He wasn't tall – perhaps five-eight – but he was stocky with slicked-back grey hair and a neatly trimmed beard. He had a lit cigarette in his right hand, and an old-fashioned wooden crutch under his left.

Joe stuck out his chin. The two of them shared an unfriendly look for a full ten seconds before he sidestepped the lame man and prepared to continue his circuit of the exercise yard.

But there was another obstacle awaiting him.

He could see in an instant what was happening. On the far side of the yard, five metres from the door through which the inmates had entered it, Finch was talking to two of the screws. At Joe's nine o'clock, two of his crew had started arguing, one pushing the other in the chest and attracting the attention of the remaining three screws. It was a clumsy diversion, but it was working: two more of the guys from Northern Ireland were striding in the direction of the lame man, violence in their eyes.

They were three metres from the inmate . . . Joe could see something shining in one of their fists. He acted almost without thinking. With a couple of strides he was between the lame man and the newcomer. The two from Northern Ireland continued to bear down on him, but they soon regretted it: Joe grabbed the fist with the weapon in it and, with a single move, twisted it as he brought his knee up into the pit of the man's stomach. He went down.

Joe turned his attention to the second guy. There was no need. The man with the crutch was not so lame as he appeared. He had lifted it into the air and swiped it solidly round the second assailant's head. The lad fell to the ground. So did the lame man, but not by accident. He knelt down and stabbed his lit cigarette into his attacker's left eye. The lad screamed. Suddenly, screws were all around. It was the lame guy they surrounded, confiscating his crutch, grabbing him under his arm. 'All right, Hennessey,' one of them shouted. 'Back to the fucking Seg Wing . . .'

'We didn't bother to change the sheets, hope you don't mind . . .' said a second screw.

Before Joe knew what was going on, Hennessey was being marched across the courtyard. It didn't seem to bother the guy. He had a fiery glint in his eyes, and it was directed at Joe. He gave a nod of acknowledgement before he disappeared. Joe stepped away from the trouble as a medic rushed in. The whole exercise yard was suddenly awash with conversation as the other inmates started discussing loudly what had happened. All of them except Finch, who stood by the door with his back against the wall, looking at Joe with poisonous hatred.

Eva was used to prisons. She was used to the smell of them, and the noise. She was used to the way the inmates stared at her as she passed.

In Holloway and other women–only clinks, the women would stare at her without even trying to hide their contempt. They could spot a pig a mile off. In male prisons it was different. In these places she was a woman before she was a cop, and the inmates leered at her, checking her up and down, their eyes lingering on her tits and arse without any attempt to hide what they were doing. Her first ever trip into a prison had been behind the thick, ancient walls of Maidstone to interview a convicted rapist in the hope that he might be able to give her a lead on a sex crime she was investigating. They'd been talking for five minutes before she realized he was jerking off under the table.

But she'd never been as a visitor before, and there was something about the visitors' centre at Barfield that put her on edge. Maybe it was just this depressing waiting room, where the plastic chairs were lined around the edge and the walls were covered in posters advertising counselling for families with a parent behind bars, or benefits for mums left on their own. Maybe it was the aggression steaming from the wives and girlfriends waiting to be admitted along with her. Eva counted sixteen of them, all done up to the nines with Wonderbras and lip gloss like they were heading up West, but with eyes that flashed like flick knives any time they caught her looking at them. About half of these women had kids in tow. They were quiet, mostly. Eva wondered whether they were scared of their mums, scared of the prison, or scared of the dads they were here to visit.

Or maybe her nerves stemmed from the prospect of seeing Joe again. In a place like this. At a *time* like this. When he wasn't even expecting her. She realized she was grinding her teeth and made an effort to stop.

There were also three men waiting to visit. One of them was an elderly black man – the father of an inmate, Eva assumed. The second was a lad of about seventeen wearing the standard uniform of a London rude boy – hooded top, baggy jeans, trainers, bling, cigarette behind his ear. He was chewing gum and pretending he was the only person in the room. Eva would have put money on there being a few lumps of hash wrapped in clingfilm in the bag at his feet. The third man seemed a little out of place somehow. He had dark skin – Asian maybe, or Middle Eastern – and wore a smart suit that looked elegant on his slim frame. He had a large, hooked nose, slightly stooped shoulders and looked quite serene as he waited for the screws – two male, one female – to call them forward.

It was 2 p.m. exactly when they called the visitors to the reception desk at one end of the room, next to which there was a magnetic security arch leading further into the prison. There was a bit of jostling as the wives and girlfriends competed to be first in the queue. Eva found herself one place behind the Asian man but in front of the two others. The queue moved very slowly. The female screw patted each woman down and asked them to empty their pockets while the male officers stashed any bags or possessions into lockers behind the counter. More than once Eva heard the woman explaining the regulations in bored tones to visitors. 'You can take a maximum of five pounds in change past security. Anything else you leave here. Come on, you know the drill . . .'

It took twenty minutes for the other women to disappear through the security arch and for the Asian man in front of Eva to reach the counter. She'd already removed her bracelet and earrings and put them in her handbag, and counted out five pounds exactly to take through with her. Now, though, she was thinking of just walking out. She should have written to him instead. *Asked* if she could come and see him. Not just turned up.

'What's this?'

One of the male screws had been patting the Asian man down and was removing something from the pocket of his suit.

'It is a book,' said the man politely, as if he were not answering a stupid question.

'You can take a maximum of f—' The screw started to repeat the mantra.

'It's only a book,' the man protested mildly. 'I am accustomed to carrying it with me at all times.'

But the screw wasn't having it. He flung the book onto the counter. Eva saw the words 'Holy Koran' in gold letters on the leather cover.

'Hand!'

'I beg your pardon?'

'I need to scan your hand. All male visitors.' As he spoke, the screw held up a webcam and took a picture of the Asian man, before indicating the scanner on the counter. The Asian man looked uncomfortable, as though he was about to protest further. But then he thought better of it, gave the screw a nod of thanks and disappeared through the security arch, by which time the female screw was patting Eva down and finding nothing but the five pound coins in her back pocket.

Beyond the security arch she found the other visitors waiting in a small holding room, a third the size of the one they'd just left. It stank like the perfume hall in Debenhams. Eva stood slightly apart from the others, next to the Asian man who was blinking calmly into space. The remaining two visitors and the three screws arrived a couple of minutes later. The female screw locked the door behind them before opening one on the opposite side of the room. The visitors were led across a deserted exercise yard and into a brown-brick building on the other side.

The visiting hall looked more like a day-care centre than a prison. It was large – probably thirty metres long by twenty wide – with strip lights hanging from the ceiling. Every couple of metres there were sets of four chairs, all fixed to the carpet-tiled floor; three of each set were yellow and one red. In the middle of one long wall was a serving hatch – as Eva entered the hall the metal grate was being raised to reveal a couple of dinner-lady types in plastic hairnets, two stainless-steel tea urns and, behind them, boxes of Kit-Kats, Mars Bars and crisps. There were another four screws in here, already patrolling the room. The door at the far end, which was clearly where the inmates would enter from, was locked.

'All right, everyone,' barked one of the screws. 'Find your-selves a seat – prisoners on the red, visitors on the yellow.' The wives and girlfriends hustled forward. Clearly the seats nearest the serving hatch were the most sought after and were filled in seconds. Eva took the one nearest the entrance, naively thinking that she could make a sharp exit if she wanted to – until she saw the female screw locking the door behind her. Then the woman nodded at one of her colleagues who had approached the entrance at the other end.

The door opened. Men entered.

Eva realized her palms were sweating as she watched them come in. These lags' faces looked eager. Some of them were even smiling as they hurried into the room. She looked at them all in turn, as they peeled off from the other prisoners and headed to hug their women or their kids. At another time and place the sight of these incarcerated men softening at the sight of their children might have caught Eva's heart. Not today. Today she hunted for the features she knew so well.

And she couldn't see them.

All the inmates had entered. Joe wasn't among them.

Maybe she'd missed him. She stood up from her yellow chair and scanned the room again. There was the old black man, sitting and talking quietly with a guy in his thirties who shared his features. Next to him, the Asian man was talking with two others who wore plain prison clothes but had their heads covered according to the rules of their religion. She was so distracted that she didn't see a final figure appear in the doorway. When she did notice him, she had the feeling he'd been staring at her for several seconds.

Her eyes widened. She swallowed hard. He looked terrible.

His face was covered in scabs, as though he'd been in some kind of accident, and he had a couple of days' dark stubble. He was leaner about the face than Eva remembered, but it was his eyes that shocked her the most. They were haunted. Unfriendly. Mistrustful. He didn't smile as he looked at her. In fact, his face barely registered any expression. And he didn't move.

Eva felt Joe might have just stood staring at her for the duration of the visit, but the screw instructed him to walk into the room.

He walked slowly, his face still set. A kid ran in front of him but he barely seemed to notice. When he reached the little group of four chairs at which Eva was standing, he stopped. Still he didn't talk.

'Inmates on the red!' shouted a screw from across the room. Joe sat down. Eva sat opposite him.

'Hi,' she said. Her voice cracked, so she swallowed, smiled and tried again. 'Hi.'

No reply.

'It's Eva,' she said.

Joe looked around and beckoned to the female screw who was patrolling about five metres away. 'I want to go back to my cell,' he said.

'Visiting time one hour. You go back then. No exceptions.'

The room was a hum of quiet conversation. About ten people were queuing up at the hatch.

'I could get you a coffee,' Eva suggested, 'or some chocolate . . .'

'Why are you here?'

Eva blinked in surprise. 'Joe . . .' she whispered.

'Who sent you?'

'Nobody sent me. Joe, it's *me* . . .'

She saw his eyes narrow as he looked briefly around the room.

'I saw . . .' Her voice cracked again. 'I saw it in the paper . . .'

'I didn't kill her.' He said it quietly. Not much more than a whisper. For an instant his gruff, unfriendly voice sounded just like the kid she'd grown up with.

'I know you didn't. I just thought . . . I could help?'

Silence.

'You want some ch—?'

'No.'

A screw walked past. They sat in silence until he was out of earshot.

'What happened?' Eva said. 'Who *did* this?'

He leaned forward. Eva did the same. For a moment she was back in Lady Margaret Road with him.

'You expect me to believe that you just *happened* to get a sudden itch to see me after ten years? You think my brains have dribbled out my fucking ears?'

'Joe . . .'

'I don't know who's got to you, Eva. The Firm? Someone else? But whoever sent you, you can tell them this from me. I don't *care* what happened in the compound. But I *do* care what happened to Ricky and Caitlin. You tell them that. You tell them, if they think they can set me up for this, they got another think coming. And when I'm out, I'm going to track them down and do something that *is* worth sending me down for . . .'

'Joe, I don't know what you're *talking* about. *What* compound? You're not making *sense*.' She looked around the room.

'Are they . . . taking *care* of you here? You know you're only on remand? They shouldn't be treating you like you're convicted.' She paused, while Joe made a hissing sound from behind his teeth. 'Have you seen a lawyer?' And then, more quietly: 'A doctor?'

Joe stood up. Immediately two screws bore down on him. 'Red chair,' one of them called across from ten metres away, and everyone in the room turned to look at him. With a dark expression on his face, Joe sat down again. He didn't look at Eva, but stared into the middle distance.

They sat like that, in silence, for five minutes. Eva found that she was holding back tears.

'You're different,' she said finally.

No reply.

'Do you remember the last time we met at the bandstand?' she whispered.

It had been a cloudy Saturday afternoon, two days before what Joe had called 'selection week', whatever that was. Joe had told her that he was applying to join a different regiment. A 'special' regiment, he had said. Eva hadn't known what he was talking about, though she had a good idea now. It would mean a lot of travel. Staying away for months at a time, or leaving the UK at short notice. She'd made him promise to keep in touch, but he hadn't. Not really. Their paths had diverged. An uncomfortable thought crossed Eva's mind. Maybe she didn't know Joe as well as she thought. Maybe the things he'd seen, the things he'd done, had changed him.

She wondered how many people he had killed in the line of duty. And she wondered if once you'd killed one person, it was easier to kill the rest.

'I'll get us some coffee,' she said weakly, and she stood up immediately because she knew Joe wouldn't give her any response.

The queue was still long, which was a relief. It gave her time out. When she returned to the seating area ten minutes later, Joe hadn't moved. He was staring into space. He didn't take the coffee, nor did he speak as Eva drank hers.

'I shouldn't have come,' she said when she had drained the dregs from her plastic cup. 'I'm sorr—'

'You ever been in the jungle, Eva?' He still didn't look at her, but he seemed to know that she had shaken her head. 'Last time I was there, I spent five days lying on the jungle floor. Hard rations. Mosquitoes, snakes, fuck knows what else. Had to piss and shit where I was. Didn't move more than half a metre in any direction.'

He turned to look at her, his eyes flat.

'You *tell* them that.'

'Tell *who*?'

'You tell them I can do my time better than any man alive. And when I'm done, when I'm out of here, I'm going to find out who they are and—'

'*Joe . . .*' Eva knew that the tears were flooding her eyes now. He sounded paranoid. And what was it she'd read in the newspaper? About soldiers coming back with their heads messed up. Maybe he really *had* lost it.

Maybe he really *had* killed her.

'Joe,' she whispered. 'I don't know what you're talking about. Really I don't.'

But the conversation was over. Eva was left counting down the minutes until visiting was over. She made an awkward goodbye: 'I still live in the same place . . . Dawson Street . . . if you need anything.' Joe didn't respond. The inmates and visitors divided into two groups. One standing by the door that led further into the bowels of the prison, the other by the exit that would take them back to the freedom of the outside world. And as the lags waved at their kids and wives and girlfriends across the open room, Joe stood by the door with his back to them.

Ten minutes later Eva was walking away from Barfield. The world was misty with tears. As she waited at a zebra crossing, she became aware of a man standing next to her. She recognized his suit, his stooped shoulders and his hooked nose, and she sensed that he was looking at her with interest. But Eva just kept her head down and crossed the road as soon as the little green man told her she could. It had been a traumatic afternoon, and she really wasn't in the mood for talking with strangers.

'Who's your girlfriend, army boy?'

Finch was two steps behind Joe and talking in a quiet, taunting voice. 'Wouldn't mind getting *her* sweet lips round my chubby.'

Before Joe knew it, he had grabbed Finch by the neck and forced him up against the corridor wall. Instantly they were surrounded by a semicircle of inmates.

'Go on then, army boy,' he rasped. 'Take your best shot, why don't you? Might be your last chance.'

Joe squeezed his fist. He could feel Finch's stubble against the palm of his hand, and the pulse of his jugular. There was a thickening of the neck as the blood constricted. Finch tried to kick him in the shins, but Joe barely felt it. He threw the bastard down. 'I wouldn't waste it on a piece of shit like you, Finch.'

Finch just grinned at him.

'Be seeing you, army boy,' he said. 'Sooner than you'd think, eh?'

He dusted himself down and pushed through the semicircle of onlookers, who dissolved among the other inmates walking the corridor.

TWELVE

Douglas McGuire looked more like a con than a screw. Cropped hair, tattooed forearms. A stench of Golden Virginia roll-ups followed the prison officer everywhere. But there the similarity ended. McGuire had never met an inmate he trusted. These two – Hunter and Mansfield, the nonce and the soldier who'd done his missus – were no exception.

'Strip.'

McGuire stood by the door while Sowden gave the instruction. It was 6 p.m. Dinner time. Out in the corridor there was the bustle of inmates making their way to the dining hall. Sowden was showing McGuire the ropes. Or as he had put it, 'clue you up to how we do things around here'. It was only his first day in Barfield.

'You gone deaf, Action Man? I said, strip.'

The soldier looked unwilling. But he did as he was told and started slowly unbuttoning his top.

'No need to grin, Hunter,' said Sowden. 'You're next.' He looked back at McGuire. 'So, what made you transfer from Whitemoor?' he asked.

Like McGuire was going to tell anybody *that*. Like he was going to talk in front of a couple of inmates about the piece of scum he'd found smearing a shiv – made from a shard of mirror, the thick end wrapped in black electrical tape to form a handle – with his own shit, in the hope that his victim would get infected with AIDS. Like he was going to mention that one of his bitches who served up in the canteen had melted down a Mars Bar and spattered the burning caramel over his face.

'Change of scene,' he said. 'Missus wanted to move to the smoke.'

'Don't know why you'd want to come and work in this dump.' Sowden stopped. The soldier had removed his trousers without saying a word. He was now naked in front of them.

'What do you think we are?' Sowden whispered in near disbelief. 'Fucking idiots?'

McGuire wasn't surprised to see what this surly con had been hiding beneath his trousers. A length of electrical flex was wound several times around his shin. The screw could see at once that it had been ripped from the small television on the table. A good weapon, in the right hands.

'Take it off, Mansfield, and give it to me,' Sowden instructed. The soldier gave him a baleful stare, but still he didn't open his mouth as he bent down, unwound the flex and plonked it into the screw's waiting hands.

Sowden looked over his shoulder at McGuire again. 'They'll try anything,' he said. His nose wrinkled as he turned back to the soldier. 'Jesus,' he said. 'You stink. You need to get your arse down to the shower block, Mansfield. And speaking of arses – crouch and cough.'

McGuire didn't like the look the prisoner gave them as he crouched down, fully naked, opened his lips just a fraction and cleared his throat.

'Stand up and pass me your clothes.'

Mansfield did as he was told and Sowden started going through them minutely, checking all the pockets and seams for anything he might have hidden there. 'I'll give you the pleasure of doing Hunter,' he muttered as he worked. 'All right,' he said. 'You're clean. Get dressed and get the fuck out of here.'

McGuire opened the door and watched Mansfield leave. There was something about him that he *really* didn't like. *Really* didn't trust. He prided himself on being able to spot the rotten apples. That soldier was a bad 'un through and through.

Left alone with Hunter, McGuire felt ill. The dumpy little nonce stripped off in front of him, rolls of pasty fat wobbling as he crouched and coughed. He sent him to the dining hall as quickly as possible. McGuire didn't suppose he was long for this world. Most sex cases like him were segregated from the rest of the prison population, for obvious reasons. Someone had decided that this guy should have a bit of freedom. And that could only end one way.

Besides, he wanted a few minutes alone in this room.

The bedclothes on the bottom bunk were neatly squared away, unlike Hunter's bunk at the top, which was a mess of blankets. McGuire stripped them both back and stared at the mattresses below. He didn't know quite what he was expecting, but whatever it was, he didn't see it. He cursed, turned and walked towards the door.

But then he stopped. Something had caught his eye. A small thing, but it screamed at him.

There were two posters on the wall. They showed pictures of two young pop stars, a boy and a girl, whom McGuire couldn't have identified himself, but he wasn't really looking at the images. He was looking at the bottom right-hand corner of the nearest poster. The Blu-tack had come away from the wall.

He stepped towards it and lifted up the loose corner.

His tiny eyes narrowed.

Stuck to the back of the poster were two pieces of masking tape. One of them was sticking a razor blade to the paper. The second had been peeled back. Whatever had once been there was there no longer.

'Bastard,' McGuire said under his breath. That flex round his ankle had been a decoy. The cunt had a blade on him.

The new prison officer left the cell and stormed down the corridor towards the dining hall.

*   *   *

The razor blade Joe had secreted under his tongue nicked the soft flesh inside his mouth. He could taste his own blood, but kept his lips tightly closed as he entered the dining hall.

He sensed the mood immediately. Atmospherics. Like going into an enemy village when the enemy know you're coming. The buzz of conversation was quieter, the dull tapping of plastic cutlery against steel trays louder. More than usual, Joe saw inmates cast furtive glances in his direction as he walked slowly up the gangway towards the serving area. Even a couple of the screws standing along the side walls looked anxious.

Joe had covered a third of the gangway when he spotted Finch. He was sitting ten metres ahead and to his right, at the table closest to the serving area and with his back to it. His eyes were fixed on Joe, and he was chewing very slowly.

Joe walked on, the blade still needling at the underside of his tongue.

He recognized two members of Finch's crew sitting to the left of the gangway, also with their backs to the serving area.

Also watching him.

His every sense was heightened as he walked. He felt he could hear every chink of cutlery.

Now he was next to Finch. The guy was two metres to his right and had laid his fork across his half-eaten tray of food. He followed Joe with his gaze as he passed, but he didn't stand up.

Two metres from the serving area, Joe stopped. He could feel something dripping from the left corner of his mouth.

Three cons were waiting behind the hotplate, dressed in grease-spotted aprons and white paper hats. They were staring at the crimson trickle on his chin.

Joe saw himself distorted in the tea urn – like in a funfair.

And there were four men behind him.

They were not Finch's. He recognized the Middle Eastern men who had been sitting cross-legged in the exercise yard that morning. He couldn't tell how close they were because the distance was warped by the urn. Five metres? Less?

But they were definitely gaining on him quickly.

Joe spun round. So many things happened at once.

McGuire had appeared at the far end of the gangway. He was shouting something, but Joe didn't register what it was. He was too busy with the Middle Eastern guys. The closest of them was three metres away, the other three a metre behind that. They were all carrying something. Two of them had bootlaces. One had the plastic tube of a ballpoint pen, its end sanded sharp. The leader had a broken bathroom tile, fashioned into a jagged blade. He was holding it like a dagger.

The whole room had fallen silent. There wasn't a single inmate in the dining hall who didn't have his eyes on the violence they knew was about to happen. But Joe's focus wasn't on the audience. It was on the enemy, two metres away.

He opened his mouth, pulled out the razor blade and spat a gobful of blood into the face of the fucker with the bathroom tile. He knocked the tile away with his left hand, and slashed with the razor in his right. It was exquisitely sharp, and cut a gash into the left side of his assailant's throat as if the flesh wasn't there. Blood spurted from the wound. There was pressure behind it – so much that the dark liquid sprayed over one of Finch's men's food – until the guy fell to his knees, a horrific gurgling coming from the back of his mouth. It was the only noise in the suddenly silenced room. Joe felt several hundred eyes on him – not least those of Finch and his crew. Even the screws had momentarily frozen, clearly shocked by the sudden violence. But Joe's own attention was already on his other attackers. They had stopped in their tracks as their leader went down, but their eyes still shone and Joe could tell they didn't intend to back off. He stepped over the puddle that was leaching from the dying man and grabbed the one carrying the sharpened plastic tube. He sliced his hand, causing him automatically to drop the makeshift weapon.

Suddenly the silence erupted into a storm of chaos. Finch and one other man Joe hadn't seen before jumped from their seats and started laying into the two remaining attackers. Within seconds they had brought them to the floor and were kicking and pummelling them. The gangway filled with inmates, some pressing towards them to see what was happening, others struggling to get away as if they were afraid to be linked with, or affected by, the violence. The hall was filled with roars of encouragement, or shrieks at other inmates to get out of the way. Joe was deaf to it all. He muscled his man to the floor half a metre from the twitching body of his comrade, grabbed his hair with his left hand and positioned the bloody razor blade millimetres from his pumping jugular.

'OK, you piece of shit,' he hissed. 'Time for some fucking answers.'

The back of the guy's head was soaked with the blood oozing from his friend, but he looked neither disgusted nor frightened. He simply grinned.

'Who put you up to it?' Joe slammed the guy's head against the floor. 'Who *fucking* put you up to it?'

The man spat in his face. 'I'll die before I tell you.'

Joe thumped the fucker's head down again, and this time there was a cracking sound. 'How much pain can you manage, you piece of shit?'

'Pain is nothing to me,' the man whispered. 'I will be welcomed into Paradise . . .'

The shouting all around was getting louder. A bell started ringing and Joe heard the sound of whistles being blown. Rage surged through him. Suddenly he didn't even care about questioning this man: he just wanted to hurt the cunt. He slashed the blade across the right side of his face, ripping a deep seam in his cheek. The pain made the guy take a sharp breath in, and as a curtain of blood drew itself across the lower part of his face, Joe heard himself spitting words at him. 'Be my fucking guest. And say hi to your bum-chum Osama while you're at it. He's had a few days there – he can show you the ropes . . .'

The man's eyes grew brighter. 'Sheikh al-Mujahid?' He made a dismissive, hissing sound. 'He's not dead . . .'

Joe blinked. Again the noise all around seemed to dissolve, even though he knew the chaos was increasing. 'What do you mean?' he whispered. And then, when the man didn't reply, he roared: '*What the fuck do you mean!*'

Joe felt hands grab him from behind as the noise of the dining hall burst into his head again. The screws had him, they were shouting, and now they were pounding him with their truncheons . . . a blow to his stomach winded him . . . a second one, and then a third to the hand gripping the razor. He dropped his only weapon and covered his head as the screws started beating his already bruised and damaged body in an orgy of unrestrained brute force.

The next few minutes were a blur. His mouth still bled profusely, sharp pain splintered through him. He felt himself being pulled up to his feet and realized his clothes were sopping with the blood of the man whose throat he'd just cut. McGuire and Sowden were on the ground next to the Middle Eastern guy, covered in his blood and attempting to give him CPR, but Joe knew they were trying to resuscitate a stiff. The crowd parted as he was pulled along the gangway, surrounded by six screws screaming at everybody to get back.

He'd just killed a man, in front of hundreds of witnesses. It wouldn't matter that it was done in self-defence. In everyone else's eyes he was not only a murderer, but a double murderer. He might be incarcerated in the most secure prison in the country, but it hadn't stopped his enemy getting to him.

And there were only so many attacks he could survive.

The cell Joe had shared with Hunter had been a dump, but the Segregation Wing made it look luxurious. Joe didn't care. One cell was the same as another, and it was better to be alone than with scum like Hunter. The moment they threw him into this tiny, stinking space, where the toilet was ten times more rancid and the single mattress covered in disgusting stains, he collapsed to the floor, his back to the wall. He felt like he was saturated in blood. His own. His enemies'. Caitlin's. He could taste it. See it. It was everywhere.

Time passed. Joe didn't know how long. Hours. The door opened and a screw he didn't even look at placed a tray of food inside. Breakfast. It went untouched.

All he could think about was what the Middle Eastern guy in the dining hall had said: '*Sheikh al-Mujahid? He's not dead . . .*'

Would some banged-up minor terror suspect really know something like that? Or was this just another mad theory? '*Mark my words . . . a double agent working for the Americans . . .*'

Joe shook his head. He'd *seen* the SEALs go in. He'd *seen* them remove the body bag containing their target.

While it was true that the Yanks had been in bed with the Mujahideen back in the seventies – hell, even the SAS had trained up the AQ-in-making – the idea that they were working hand in hand with the leader of their sworn enemies was ridiculous.

Wasn't it?

And it had been Arabs who had just tried to kill him. What was it – revenge? Or had it just leaked out that he was army and they wanted to have a crack at him, like Finch and the rest of the fucking Micks?

The thoughts were so all-consuming that he barely noticed the door of his cell open for the second time. He looked up. His food tray was still there on the floor. The door was only slightly ajar. Nobody else was in the cell.

Joe scrambled to his feet, eyes screwed up, fists clenched, ready to defend himself.

The door opened a little wider.

Joe saw the narrow end of an old-fashioned wooden crutch appear in the gap, followed by a limping foot.

Hennessey stared at him. There was a silence. Long. Threatening.

'How did you get in here?' Joe demanded.

Hennessey didn't immediately reply. He limped into the centre of the cell and started rolling a cigarette with a heavily tattooed hand as he leaned on his crutch.

'I'll be straight with you, son,' Hennessey said. His voice was a cold, wheezy whisper, south London through and through. 'I don't have much time for wife-beaters. If you hadn't done me a service in the yard, we'd be having a different chat right now.'

He lit the cigarette and inhaled.

Joe remembered Hunter's words: '*You think the screws are in charge here? That's bullshit.* Hennessey's *in charge . . .*'

And as he had just acknowledged, Hennessey owed him one.

'I have to get out,' he said.

Hennessey finished his cigarette with a second long drag and dropped the butt to the floor. 'Missing Hunter, are you?'

'Not the Seg Wing. The prison.'

'You and every other fucker in this place,' Hennessey said dryly.

'I mean it.'

A humourless smile played across Hennessey's lips. 'Well, let's see now,' he said. 'How to break our new boy out of here? Double murder, is it? Usual procedure is to make a shiv and cut your wrists. That way they take you out in a box. Leaves a little mess for the screws to clean up, but you won't have to worry about that.' He waved one arm about the room. 'My advice, lad, is get used to your new home, and make sure you stay in with the right people.'

'Not good enough, Hennessey.'

'Is that right, son? Ah well, we all have to live with these little disappointments.'

Hennessey wasn't giving much away. What had Hunter said about him? A clever bastard. Joe sensed he was right. But what

199

did he, Joe, have on Hennessey? What weapons were left in his arsenal?

'Word is you've got half the screws in your pocket,' he said. 'How d'you do it? Blackmail? Threaten their families?'

'Ways and means, son. Ways and means.' He sounded – and looked – wary. 'Let's just say I call in a favour now and then, and leave it at that.'

'Like the tart they smuggle in to service you every month? That's quite a favour. Someone must really like you.'

'What is it, son?' Hennessey's voice was very quiet now, but with an edge that hadn't been there before. 'On heat, are you? She's coming in at five tonight, you know, but I'm afraid she'll have her hands full. If you want someone to help you lose your load, I could always have a word with Hunter—'

'Be a shame, wouldn't it,' Joe cut in, keeping his voice casual, 'if word got round that the screws cut you slack in return for you grassing up the other inmates?'

A pause. Hennessey blinked at him, then suddenly gave a short, humourless bark of a laugh. 'That a threat, son?'

'More than that, Hennessey. I'm army, remember. I've got contacts. Trust me, there's plenty of bent coppers in my little black book who'd deposit a few quid in one of your family's bank accounts if I asked them. I guess some of the animals in this place might get funny ideas if they thought you were on a police payroll . . .'

Hennessey stared impassively at him, trying to judge if Joe was serious or not. 'You'll have to do better than that,' he said finally, before giving Joe a contemptuous look, turning his back on him and hobbling towards the door.

The window of opportunity was closing. 'You think you're the big man, Hennessey?' he called after him. 'You think you scare me like you scare the other shitheads in this place? Trust me, *son*, I can fucking break you. The best way for you to stay king of the hill is to get me the hell out of here.'

Hennessey halted. For ten seconds he stood still, his back to Joe. When he finally turned, his expression was cold. He stumped back towards Joe, stopping when they were just a metre apart. 'And how do you work *that* out?' he barely whispered, derision dripping from his voice.

Joe moved quickly. He grabbed the food tray by the door – its contents went flying – then smashed the plastic over his knee so that it broke, with lethally jagged corners on each half. He swiped the crutch from under Hennessey's arm. It didn't appear to make the prisoner any less steady until Joe used it to push him violently up against the wall, before pressing a sharp corner of the shattered tray against his jugular. 'Listen to me, you piece of shit. You think I don't have friends who wouldn't think twice about taking a smack at your whore if I asked them to? You think they wouldn't break her legs just for fun?' It wasn't true, but Hennessey didn't know that.

'You think I care?' Hennessey whispered. 'She's just a pair of lips to me . . .'

'Of course you don't care. But just think about it. Big bad Hennessey, stuck in the Seg Wing and not even able to stop his bit of skirt getting done over on the outside, even when he's in the police's pockets. Not to mention that, as long as I'm here, I'll break a different bone in your fucking body every time I see you. You'll need more than a wooden crutch.'

To emphasize his point he pressed the plastic harder into Hennessey's throat – the guy broke into a sweat – before throwing it, along with the crutch, to the floor. He knew better than to turn his back on a man like this, so he stepped away while Hennessey caught his breath and bent down to pick up the crutch.

'You're a brave man, army boy,' Hennessey said hoarsely, rubbing at his throat with one hand, 'talking to me like that.'

Joe ignored him. 'Course,' he added, 'pull some strings for me and it wouldn't do your reputation much harm.'

'What wouldn't?'

'You really are as stupid as you look. Think about it. The inmate who does Hennessey a favour gets out. They'll know your name on every landing in the country after that. They'll be falling over themselves to help you out.'

Hennessey fixed him with a dead-eyed stare. He made no attempt to hide his loathing of Joe, but he was clearly deciding what call to make.

Joe feigned indifference.

'You're in the Seg Wing of a Cat A prison,' Hennessey said finally. 'People don't just walk out of this place.'

'Except your bird.'

Hennessey's eyes tightened. 'What do you mean?'

'How does she get in? I'm guessing she doesn't just bang on the front gates.'

The inmate inclined his head, but didn't answer.

Joe took a step towards him, and was pleased to notice Hennessey flinch. 'You think I'm playing twenty fucking questions, Hennessey?' he hissed. 'You think I'm playing around? I'll ask you one more time. *How does she get in?*'

He was watching Hennessey carefully. Examining his expression. He saw the way the eyes narrowed, just a millimetre. Hennessey had made a decision.

'There's a delivery of medical supplies. Once a month. The screws make a point of not checking too closely what's in the back of the van when it arrives.'

'And when it leaves?'

'That too.'

Joe started pacing. 'Where do you meet her?' he demanded. 'Does she come to you?'

'No,' Hennessey replied. The wariness had returned to his voice. It was as if they were tiptoeing around each other. 'I go to her when they've finished unloading . . .'

'How long for?'

Hennessey's eyes narrowed.

'*How long for?*'

'Half an hour.'

'Where does the van park?'

'Delivery bay, behind the kitchens.'

'Who takes you there?'

'One of the screws,' Hennessey said evasively. And then he added quickly – a bit too quickly? – 'Hobson, ginger moustache . . .'

Joe remembered the screw he'd attacked the night he arrived. He'd hardly be queuing up to do Joe a favour. But that didn't matter. Not if Joe worked it properly.

'There's a route from the back of the Seg Wing,' Hennessey said. Joe noted that he was volunteering information without being pressed. 'Winds round past the bins to the delivery bay. No cameras. That's the way Hobson takes me.'

'What time does the delivery arrive?'

'Five p.m. Sometimes a bit later. Never earlier.'

Joe absorbed that information for a few seconds. 'OK. Here's what's going to happen. Hobson's going to take me instead of you. You can tell him that if he doesn't play ball, I'll grass him up. If I'm still in this cell at five-thirty, you'll both wish you never even heard my name.'

There was a hostile silence. Hennessey stuck his chin out at Joe. 'I'm beginning to wish that already,' he said. 'Five o'clock. Be ready.' He started limping out of the room.

Joe wasn't fooled. He knew Hennessey had given in too easily, that he couldn't be trusted. Joe wanted him to think that he, Hennessey, had the upper hand, that Joe was so desperate to escape that he'd do anything, *believe* anything. He strode after him, grabbed him by the back of the shirt and spun him round. 'Listen to me,' he hissed. 'Hunter told me you've got a habit of knocking off your cellmates because you know you're never seeing the outside again. If I'm still in here at five-thirty, I'll know *I'm* never seeing the outside either. I guess then it'll come down to which one of us can fuck the other up best. Is that a game you really want to play? *Is it?*'

He let go of Hennessey, who said nothing. He just smoothed down his shirt, gave Joe a look of utter contempt, then limped out of the cell.

Joe heard the key turn in the lock. His mouth, he realized, was unbearably dry, the nape of his neck soaked with sweat.

He'd played his only card. All he could do now was wait.

THIRTEEN

It was impossible to keep track of time in that cramped, windowless cell. All Joe knew was that one mealtime and several hours had passed. That meant it had to be approaching 5 p.m. Hennessey hadn't returned. They only person he'd seen was the screw who'd dumped his meal tray in the cell and collected it thirty minutes later. No words, no eye contact. If Hennessey had this man in his pocket, there was no way of telling. He half expected a police officer or another lawyer to walk through the door at any moment. Nobody did. They knew, he supposed, that he wasn't going anywhere.

He sat by the door, listening. Occasionally there were voices in the corridor outside, but they were muffled – he couldn't tell who they belonged to or what they were saying – but that didn't stop him trying. Hennessey was his only hope, but also the last person on earth that he could trust. But Joe's eavesdropping yielded nothing.

It was during one of the frequent moments of silence, while he was pacing the room to keep warm, that the door suddenly clicked open. Nobody appeared. He approached it with care, half expecting an attack, which didn't come, and slowly opened it wider.

The corridor was brightly lit with strip lights. The walls were beige – paint applied directly to breeze blocks – and the smell was antiseptic. The corridor extended about twenty metres – to his left there was a locked metal door, to his right the corridor turned a corner. Two men were standing opposite his cell: Hennessey and Hobson, the screw with the ginger moustache whom Joe had lamped during his first minutes at Barfield. His upper lip was swollen, and he had steristrips across the bridge of his nose. Hennessey was leaning heavily on his crutch and rolling a cigarette. Both men looked at Joe with cool hostility.

'Time?' Joe asked.

Hobson stepped forward and held up a pair of handcuffs. 'Put these on,' he instructed.

'No.'

Hobson glanced back to an alert-looking Hennessey. 'If anyone finds me taking a segregated prisoner unrestrained to the loading bay,' Hobson whispered, 'I'm fucked.'

'Then you'd better make sure nobody finds us,' Joe said.

Hobson shook his head in disgust. 'Forget it,' he said. He was looking at Joe, but clearly talking to Hennessey. 'Just forget the whole fucking thing.' He turned and stomped off down the corridor.

'You got kids, Hobson?' Joe called after him.

Hobson stopped, but didn't turn.

'Think they'll fancy visiting their dad in prison? Mine was banged up. I didn't bother with him after he went inside. And helping this piece of crap smuggle some tart onto prison property has to be worth a couple of years, hasn't it?'

Hobson turned, his swollen face carved with even more hatred than before. 'No one will believe you,' he said.

'If you really thought that, you wouldn't have just opened my cell door. But it's your call.' He gave a shrug and stepped backwards towards his cell.

'Do it, Hobson.' The instruction came from Hennessey and Joe immediately noted that there was something calculating in his expression. Was he just eager to get Joe out of his hair? Joe didn't think so.

Hobson was pacing back to them. He was sweating. 'If I can't cuff you . . .'

'Hand them over,' Joe said. He took the cuffs from Hobson and placed them round his wrists without locking them. It wouldn't pass a close inspection, but at a glance he would appear to be restrained. He turned to Hennessey: 'Give Hobson your crutch.'

The skin tightened around Hennessey's eyes and for a moment he looked like he was going to argue. But he clearly thought better of it, and handed his crutch to the screw. He was evidently not nearly so lame as he pretended, because he was able to stand quite well without it. 'When you get to the van,' he said, 'knock five times and she'll let you in.'

Joe nodded. 'Let's go,' he told Hobson.

Hennessey said nothing. He just lit his cigarette, blew smoke into Joe's face, then turned and limped without much difficulty back down the corridor and round the corner. Before he disappeared from sight, however, he looked over his shoulder. He seemed neither nervous nor angry. More pleased with himself. Then he was gone.

He had something planned. Joe was sure of it.

'The medical van's arrived. They're unloading now.' Hobson wouldn't look at Joe as he spoke. 'You need to walk in front of me.' He indicated the opposite direction to the one Hennessey had taken, towards the locked metal door at the end of the corridor.

Joe held his wrists against his stomach to stop the cuffs from slipping, and walked. When he reached the door he stepped aside to let Hobson open it.

The door led onto an alleyway about two metres wide, and the facing wall was at least ten metres high. Joe deduced that this was the exterior wall of the prison. Dried leaves had blown into the alleyway, along with old crisp packets and other bits of rubbish. This was evidently a little-visited part of the prison. It was raining quite heavily, but they were protected from the worst of it by the high wall. It could rain all it wanted as far as Joe was concerned. The more the better. It would keep people inside.

Hobson locked the door behind them, then nodded at Joe to walk down the narrow passageway. He didn't like having the screw behind him, but he understood that it would look suspicious if Hobson didn't have eyes on him at all times. They continued for twenty metres, Joe scanning ahead, though all he could see was a right-hand turn at the end of the alleyway, and all he could hear was the rain.

At the end they turned right. The corridor extended for just a couple of metres, then opened up into a tarmacked yard about fifteen metres square. Five metal catering bins, each a couple of metres high, were lined up on the far side of the yard, outside a set of closed double doors that Joe assumed led to the kitchens. The rain drummed noisily on the metal lids. Parked in the middle of the yard, ten metres away, was a white Transit van. 'MediQuick' was written in blue lettering on the side and the rear doors were open. Hanging back in the protection of the alleyway, Joe could see the legs of three individuals hidden by the open doors of the Transit. Then two inmates emerged from the protection of the doors, each carrying a cardboard box that Joe took to be part of the delivery, their faces sour on account of the driving rain. And following them, after they'd slammed the van's doors shut, he saw Sowden. Unlike the inmates, he wore a black raincoat, with the hood up.

'Stay there,' Hobson said. Joe saw that he had leaned the wooden crutch against the wall before stepping forward a few paces. Sowden clearly saw this, and Joe felt himself tensing up. What the hell was Hobson doing? His question was answered by a brief nod of acknowledgement from Sowden. Clearly the fucker was in on Hennessey's little treat too. Sowden barked an indecipherable instruction at the two prisoners. They carried the boxes through the double doors, followed by the screw, who closed them and – Joe assumed – locked them behind him.

But had Sowden seen him? Joe didn't think so. The courtyard was empty now, and the rain coming down even harder. Joe slipped his hands out of the cuffs and indicated to Hobson that he should retreat into the cover of the alleyway. Hobson obeyed. He looked like shit. Bedraggled hair, rain running down his face.

'Who's the driver?' Joe asked.

'Always the same guy. Stays in the cab.'

'Does he know what's going on? Does he know it's me?'

Hobson nodded. His eyes flickered anxiously to the left, almost as though he was expecting something to happen.

Joe acted on impulse. He grabbed Hobson and thrust him up against the wall, pressing his right forearm into the screw's neck. He didn't say anything for a full twenty seconds, by which time both Hobson's arms had gone into spasm and his rasping breath was noisier than the rain on the metal bins. 'What's Hennessey got waiting for me in there?' he finally demanded.

At first Hobson said nothing. He just tried to shake his head. But another twenty seconds and his eyes were rolling up – he was as close to passing out as it was possible to be – and his wheezing and struggling told Joe he was trying to speak. Joe relaxed his arm, but only slightly. 'What's he got waiting for me?' he repeated.

'There's no girl . . .' Hobson managed to say, but as he spoke, his eyes rolled again. Joe swore as the screw crumpled to the ground – two fingers to the jugular confirmed he was still alive, just unconscious – but Joe had enough information to know that whatever was waiting for him in the back of the Transit, it wasn't some chick expecting to give Hennessey a blow job. He dragged Hobson by his feet back down the alleyway, out of sight. It was impossible to know how long he'd be out for, so he took the precaution of cuffing him to the bracket of a hefty metal drainpipe and removing his keys from his belt.

Even if he awoke, he'd have to scream over the rain to raise the alarm.

Back at the end of the alleyway, Joe took Hennessey's crutch and checked out his path to the van. Apart from the driver, the courtyard was deserted, though he didn't know how long it would remain so. Joe couldn't see the guy, but he knew that he'd be visible in the passenger-side wing mirror as he approached the rear of the van. He looked at the angle of the mirror: about seventy degrees. Joe estimated that the driver's field of view had a radius of approximately five metres. Did it matter if he saw Joe? Perhaps. If someone else was waiting for him in the back of the van, they might be communicating with each other. Much better to keep out of the driver's field of view until he was directly behind the Transit, at which point he would be able to walk directly up to the rear doors, unexpected.

A crack of thunder ripped through the sky. A fresh torrent of rain hammered down. Soaked through, Joe stepped out into the courtyard.

He kept close to the perimeter wall, moving quickly while he had the advantage of an empty yard. It took no more than five seconds to get to the point where he was directly behind the Transit, at a distance of about seven metres. He suppressed a grim smile at a sign on the back of the van which read: 'Remember: if you can't see my mirrors, I can't see you.'

He checked the doors leading into the kitchen. No movement. He checked back in the direction of the alleyway. No movement.

He removed the crutch from under his arm and advanced.

His mind was calculating with every step he took towards the van. Hennessey and Hobson's game was clear: they didn't want him in the prison, and they didn't want him grassing them up. That meant that whoever was waiting for him in the van would have strict instructions: get Joe beyond the prison walls, then make sure he never speaks again. It would cause a fucking stink, and spark a massive investigation, but Hobson and Sowden would be hoping nothing could be pinned on them. Better that than have their cosy relationship with Hennessey revealed. So whoever was waiting there in the van would attack immediately. And his eyes would be used to the gloom inside, putting him – or them – at a distinct advantage. Joe had Hennessey's crutch – a sturdy bit of timber, but hardly his weapon of choice. He did have the element of surprise, though: whoever was there wouldn't expect him to go in fighting.

'Knock five times,' Hennessey had said. Like hell he would. He gripped the crutch firmly, then yanked open one of the rear doors and jumped inside the van.

As Joe expected, it was pretty dark inside, even with the door open. He turned his head to one side to take advantage of his peripheral vision – more attuned to low light – and spun Hennessey's crutch ninety degrees so that it was horizontal in front of him. At once two figures rushed at him. Definitely male. Joe surged forward, throwing all his weight behind the crutch, which thumped brutally against both the silhouetted figures. His attackers dropped, their fall broken and muffled by a bank of cardboard boxes like the ones Joe had seen being removed from the van minutes earlier. One of them cursed in what sounded like Arabic.

Joe's eyes were adjusting to the darkness. He recognized the men ahead of him: the two unharmed Middle Eastern guys from the dining hall. Hunter had been right: Hennessey *was* smart. He'd relied on the two men in this shithole who most wanted to kill him.

Joe didn't give them even a second to recover.

He threw down the crutch, then, with all his strength, smashed his fist into the face of the nearer of the men. He heard the nose crack, but was already delivering the next blow.

And another.

And another.

He kept pounding the man's bleeding face, splintering the already broken nasal bone. As the fucker collapsed, his mate got to his feet again. Joe seized his throat and dragged him down too. Grabbing a clump of his greasy black hair, he slammed his face as hard as he could against the metal floor. The guy went limp.

Silence. Joe stepped back and closed the door.

He was breathless and sweating, but thankful for the rain pounding down on the Transit because it would have masked the sound of the struggle. Although the driver would have heard the rumpus, Joe was sure he would have assumed it was he who'd been overpowered. He stood still for twenty seconds, waiting for his eyes to readjust to the increased darkness. He found himself imagining Hennessey's sordid little encounters in the bleak darkness of this vehicle. He couldn't help thinking they were as much to do with keeping up his reputation as the sex itself.

He edged forward. There was a wall of cardboard boxes in front of him, but with a gap to their right that led to another space behind them, less than a metre wide. Perhaps it was where Hennessey was accustomed to losing his load. His assailants were bony to look at, but heavy to drag. Joe manoeuvred their limp frames to the hiding place behind the boxes with difficulty, before retrieving Hennessey's crutch and joining them. It crossed his mind to try and revive them, to squeeze every last bit of information out of them – not about Hennessey, but about whoever had ordered them to take him out in the first place. He quickly rejected that idea: his focus had to be on escaping. Better these two remained out cold.

The darkness sharpened his senses: the pungent stench of his assailants' body odour, the taste of blood in his mouth where the razor blade had nicked the flesh, the pounding of the rain on the roof. The driver would be waiting for a signal, so he thumped the metal wall dividing the rear section of the van from the cab. Three solid blows.

The engine coughed immediately into life, and the Transit moved forward.

Joe felt the van swing to the right then slow down. He wished he had the geography of the place clear in his mind so he knew when they were approaching the prison exit. But he didn't. The van came to a halt, but the engine continued to turn over. A minute passed. It felt like much longer. What was happening outside? What was the hold-up? Had someone found Hobson? Were they locking the place down?

But then they were moving again. Slowly at first, then accelerating. Too fast, surely, to be within the confines of the prison. He felt a surge of grim satisfaction. Was he out? Had he done it?

Joe moved quickly. One of his attackers was wearing an overcoat – hardly prison issue, he thought. Were they being rewarded for killing him by a well-planned escape of their own? He pulled the coat off, slipped it on, then pushed himself to his feet – he had to fight a sudden, leaden exhaustion that threatened to knock him back down again. He didn't know where he was being driven to, nor did he want to find out. In the gloom, he ripped open one of the cardboard boxes and rummaged inside. Perhaps there would be something useful. His fingertips identified a pencil-length scalpel, tightly sealed inside sterile packaging. A roll of bandage. Some surgical tape. He stuffed all these in the deep pockets of his overcoat, then lurched to the back of the Transit. They were now doing some 40 mph, he reckoned. He could hardly just open the door and jump out. He'd kill himself. He had to wait an excruciating couple of minutes before the van slowed down. It ground to a halt.

Joe seized his opportunity, opened one of the rear doors and debussed.

The rain was still pissing down, and he was instantly blinded by the headlights of the vehicle behind him. It took a moment for him to realize that it was a bus, which had stopped no more than a metre behind the Transit. Joe closed the door gently so as not to alert the driver, covered his eyes with one hand and staggered across the road to the pavement.

The traffic moved on. The Transit disappeared. Joe blinked heavily in the rain and tried to get his bearings.

He was in a high street standing outside a McDonald's. Boots on one side, Coffee Republic on the other. A road sign thirty metres to his right indicated that he was a mile from both Brixton and Wandsworth, and two from Clapham. He turned on his mental GPS and continued to look around. The weather had forced most people off the streets – a blessing, given Joe's appearance – but one woman passed, huddled under an umbrella, dragging an unimpressed cocker spaniel on a lead. She gave him a look of distaste and hurried on. Joe half considered entering the McDonald's and cleaning himself up in the bathroom, but he quickly dropped that idea. There were about twenty people in the restaurant and he couldn't risk one of them recognizing his face from the papers. Instead, he pulled up the collar of his overcoat, lowered his head and started to walk.

He had only two things in mind. First, he needed to get as far off the Transit's route as possible. It wouldn't be long before his disappearance from the prison was noticed, and it wouldn't take a genius to work out how he'd done it – at which point every police officer in the capital would be looking for him.

And second? The world thought he was a murderer. The people he loved were dead, or in danger. And someone was hellbent on killing him. He needed money, shelter, help. He needed someone he could trust.

The rain fell harder, soaking through his coat and running into his eyes. But his mind's eye, for the first time in days, was clear. It focused on the pale, frightened face of a woman who, once upon a time, he had trusted without question.

The trouble was, in a world turned upside down, how did he know he could trust her now?

FOURTEEN

'I still live in the same place . . . Dawson Street . . . if you need anything.' When he had heard these words in prison, Joe hadn't expected to act on them. He'd been wrong.

Number 132 Dawson Street, Hounslow, was a small terraced house: two up, two down. The curtains were shut both downstairs and upstairs, and he could see no chinks of light. He lingered outside for a few minutes. He felt like he had a fucking spotlight following him, like everybody he'd passed on his way here had stared at him, recognized him. Like they could see through his overcoat to the beige prison uniform underneath. And with dried blood on his fingers, he kept his right hand hidden inside the sleeve.

He noted that he was under a Heathrow flight path. Aircraft flew overhead at a rate of one every three or four minutes. He could use that. A black van drove down the street, registration KT04 CDE. If he saw it a second time, he knew he'd have to disappear. If any of the occasional passers-by paid him too much attention, same deal. And his senses were alert for any other sign that this place was being watched. That was the trouble with surveillance: you often didn't know what you were looking for until you saw it.

The rain had stopped, but his clothes were still uncomfortably wet and he had to suppress the occasional shiver as walked fifty metres along Dawson Street before coming to the end of the terrace. The final house had a two-metre-high wooden gate to its side, clearly giving access to the back garden. Joe checked once more that he wasn't being watched. The gate was bolted so he climbed over it and squeezed past two wheelie bins to the back of the house. It was a postage stamp of a garden, mostly taken up with a kid's trampoline. The shared fence was only a metre high. He clambered over it, then crossed the intervening gardens with little difficulty, until, counting carefully, he reached number 132.

A tiny water feature tinkled gently in one corner of the garden. The rest of the space was paved and covered with twenty or thirty plants in pots. He examined the rear of the house. On the left was a door – no catflap, two mortise locks, and a bolt at top and bottom. Impenetrable without proper equipment. He could see through the window next to the door into a small kitchen. To the right were French windows, each with two panels. It was a moonlit night but he couldn't make out much inside, except that it was a sitting room. His eyes scanned the darkness for the glow or blink of a burglar alarm's sensor. There was nothing.

From the pocket of the overcoat he removed the scalpel and the surgical tape. As long as he was silent, he could use these to gain entry.

The glass of the French windows was wet. Joe removed his overcoat and used the sleeve of his prison jacket to dry the lower right-hand pane. Taking the scalpel, he slowly, precisely, scored around the edge of the glass, loosening the putty that held it to the frame and easing it out. It was slow work – it took about ten minutes – and he had to be quiet. If the neighbours heard a constant scratching sound, they'd be out to investigate.

Once he'd removed as much putty as he could, he unrolled the tape and stuck strips across the pane until it was entirely covered. These two jobs done, he returned to the water feature and selected a smooth, grey pebble no bigger than an orange and carried it back to the French windows. He stood very still, brandishing the pebble, waiting for another plane to pass over-head. And when the air was filled with the thunder of jet engines again, he struck.

The pebble made a flat thud as it hit the taped window. There was a slight indentation at the point of impact but the glass itself remained fixed. He struck another three times while there was still enough noise from the aircraft to mask the sound. As it faded away, he stopped and waited another three minutes for a second plane to pass.

It took two more strikes with the pebble for the glass to slip from its frame, but it remained in one unshattered piece on account of the tape. Joe cautiously removed the glass, before crawling through the opening and gently laying it on the carpet inside. He listened hard for any sound of movement in the house. Nothing.

He needed to make sure this was the right place, so he stepped towards the mantelpiece where he could see the silhouettes of three framed pictures. At random, he selected the middle one. It was too dark to make out the details, so he stepped back to the French windows to take advantage of the moon. Now that he could see the photograph properly he inhaled sharply.

It was of him.

He looked so much younger. No frown lines on his forehead, no scars on his face. His skin looked less leathery, his frame less bulky. In his eyes there shone a quiet enthusiasm that he had not felt for years.

Joe was not alone in this picture. She was standing next to him, looking like she always had done in his mind. The girl next door. His best friend for so many years. Only he could see now what he'd never seen then. The way she had brushed up against him, the way she had leaned her head on his shoulder the way friends seldom did. Joe felt a pang of something like guilt, and the sickening image of Caitlin, bleeding and begging and dying, flashed across his eyes. He returned the picture to its place before creeping towards the door of the sitting room, then along the hallway and up the stairs.

He found her sleeping in a bedroom where the curtains were open a few inches. She stirred the moment he opened the door, rolling in her bed and muttering something under her breath. He recognized the voice. It was definitely her. Definitely Eva. Joe stood in the doorway, waiting for her to settle, but she didn't. He could hear her teeth grinding, and remembered the way she used to do that whenever she was on edge. Whatever dream was troubling her continued to do so. It gave Joe no pleasure to realize that he now had to drag her into a waking nightmare. He clutched his scalpel once more and walked the few paces from the door to the bedhead.

His eyes were used to the darkness now, and in any case there was a thin shard of moonlight. He could make out the hair streaked sweatily across her face, and could see her lips moving silently.

And he saw her eyes suddenly open wide to stare up at him.

Her mouth opened to scream.

Joe moved like lightning. He slapped his left hand over her open mouth just in time to turn her scream into a mumble. He held the scalpel three inches from her eyes.

'You see this?' he whispered.

She nodded frantically, her eyes huge with terror.

'It's sharp enough to slit your throat with one cut. And that's what's going to happen if you make a sound, and unless you tell me who sent you to visit me in prison. Understood?'

Eva nodded again.

Slowly Joe loosened the grip on her mouth, but he kept his hand two inches above it and the scalpel just where it was. 'Talk,' he said.

'How did you . . . ?'

'*Who sent you?*'

Her eyes were brimming with tears. That told Joe nothing.

218

People cry when they're falsely accused, but they also cry when they're scared.

'*Nobody* sent me. I *told* you. Joe . . . *how* did you get out?'

'I'm asking the questions, Eva.'

'I know you're not going to hurt me, Joe.' She was whispering. 'And I *know* you didn't hurt Caitlin. Let me sit up. Let me *talk* to you.'

Joe didn't move. There was ten seconds of silence. And then: 'I swear to God, Eva. You make a fucking sound, you'll regret it.'

She swallowed hard, but nodded. Joe moved his hands back and she shuffled up to a sitting position.

'Can we turn the light on?'

'Absolutely not.'

'Why?'

'Because I don't know who's watching.'

'How did you get out?' Eva pressed. 'Did they give you bail?'

'Not exactly.'

'But you're all wet . . . you smell like . . . Joe, I'm scared. What's going on?'

She *was* scared. He could tell. But was she scared of him, or scared of someone else? And Joe had interrogated enough people to realize that if they didn't want to tell you the truth, there was only one way to make them. Eva might not be lying to him. But equally, she might.

Moving fast, he put the scalpel on her beside table, grabbed her body and spun her round onto her front. He pressed her, face down, into the pillow and yanked her right arm up behind her back until he could feel the tendons reach straining point. He kept her in that position for a full ten seconds before speaking.

'Who sent you? You've got five seconds to tell me before I break your arm.'

He yanked her head up by her hair and she gasped.

'One,' said Joe.

She inhaled again: half breath, half sob.

'Two.'

'Oh, God, please . . .'

'Three.'

'Nobody sent me . . .'

'Four.'

'What's *happened* to you, Joe?' Her voice was weak. Almost inaudible. 'It's me. It's *me*!'

He didn't reach five. Suddenly he saw himself, as though from outside his own body, torturing his oldest friend. Was this really him?

'Joe . . . *please* . . .'

Slowly he released the pressure on her arm. She scrambled away from him to the other side of the bed. And the way she looked at him was like a knife twisting inside him. He felt himself screwing up his face as the agony in his mind became acute. Looking away, he caught sight of himself in a full-length mirror on a wardrobe beside the bed. The knife twisted further. He looked fucking demented. No wonder Eva was terrified.

Her breath was coming in short, shaky gasps, like a child unable to stop sobbing.

'How . . . how did you get into my house?'

'We can't stay here,' Joe interrupted. 'They'll know you visited me. It won't take them long to come knocking.'

'Who? Who's "they"?'

It was a good question. Joe couldn't answer it.

'Joe, if you're in trouble, maybe I can help?' Her voice was very small.

'Maybe.' He stood up and walked to the other side of the room, where he peered out into the back garden between the gap in the curtains. A cat was drinking at the edge of the water feature. Other than that, nothing. He turned to look back at her. A thought had crystallized in his mind. What mattered now wasn't whether he trusted Eva. It was whether she trusted him.

'Get dressed,' he said. 'Quickly. Is there any money in the house?'

'Next door . . . in the cash box on the table . . . It's open . . .'

'Do you have a weapon?'

She blinked in the darkness. 'Of course not.'

Joe nodded and quickly left her to get dressed. He found the money – four £50 notes. Next to the box was a copy of *The Times*; it was the same one the lawyer had showed him in prison, open at the article about him.

Something else caught his attention. Through the thin curtains he could see the headlights of a vehicle parked outside. He pulled the curtains a centimetre apart, just enough to scope it out.

A black van. Registration: KT04 CDE.

"They" were here . . .

He sprinted back to Eva's room. 'We've got company,' he said.

'Who?' She was dressed – jeans, jumper – and had just pulled on her trainers. She picked up a small bag from the table beside the bed.

'*Just move!*' Joe hissed.

He grabbed her arm and pulled her down the stairs. No time for stealth – their footsteps seemed to shake the whole house. The van's lights were illuminating the frosted glass in the front door, and he could see silhouettes approaching. 'Who *is* it?' Eva shrieked.

'This time of night, it's not the fucking milkman. Get out the back!'

Eva groaned as she saw the glass missing from her French windows, but she clambered through the hole with Joe following close behind. He helped her over the low fence into the neighbours' property. They sprinted across the half-dozen gardens, giving no thought to secrecy or silence. Joe saw the upstairs lights come on in two of the houses. Clearly they were disturbing people with their noise.

They reached the end of the terrace in a little under a minute. From the last garden they could open the gate over which Joe had had to scramble. The moment they were on the street he grabbed Eva's hand and pulled her in the opposite direction to her own house. He looked over his shoulder. Two figures were running towards them, unrecognizable in the pale yellow lamplight, but Joe instantly spotted the handguns they were clutching. The two men were thirty metres away and closing.

'Run!' Joe hissed.

They turned out of Dawson Street and into Halfway Parade. On the other side of the street, the Hand and Flower, where Joe and Eva used to drink when they were teenagers, was turfing out its customers. The road was busy – buses, minicabs, even a couple of cyclists with flashing head-torches and hi-vis jackets. Twenty metres ahead, two passengers were stepping into a bus. Still clutching Eva's hand, Joe ran towards it, just managing to jump on board before the doors hissed shut. It pulled away almost immediately as Eva, breathless, waved her police ID at the driver.

Joe's attention was elsewhere. He was staring through the window at the two figures that had just arrived alongside the moving bus. They both wore jeans, trainers and hoodies. The face of one of them was obscured, but Joe just caught a glimpse of the other. Dark skin. Yellow teeth. The same kid who had been loitering outside his house in what seemed like another lifetime.

Weapon or no weapon, he wanted to burst out and get his hands on the fucker. Eva would be safe on the bus. Now it was accelerating, and the kid had disappeared. All twenty or so other passengers were staring at the two of them with suspicion.

Joe turned to Eva. 'We can't stay on here,' he breathed. 'Too many people. Where can we talk?'

Her face was deathly white. She looked almost too petrified to respond. 'Next stop,' she whispered.

A minute later they stepped off the bus. Eva walked briskly, with Joe following. She turned left, off the high street and into a long residential road that Joe remembered from his youth. It extended half a mile, becoming gradually more shabby the further they walked. It started to rain again. In the distance Joe saw the twinkling lights of three tower blocks, and it was only then that he realized where Eva was taking him.

The bandstand – that crumbling old relic by the swings and slides in the recreation area, a stone's throw from Lady Margaret Road – was *their* place. It had always been deserted in bad weather, and it was deserted tonight. Joe only gave up his heavy overcoat, putting it around Eva's shoulders, when they reached the recreation area and he had established that nobody would see his prison uniform. Eva gave him a grateful look, but then he noticed her eyes lingering on the blood on his hand and the uniform. She wasn't at ease, and Joe didn't blame her.

Stepping onto that empty bandstand was like stepping back in time. The white paint on the wrought-iron railings was still peeling. There was the familiar smell of rotten wood from the damp decking. The park around them was bleak and neglected, with high-rises twinkling all around. An old tramp was sleeping on a bench by the adjacent playground, using his coat as a tarp against the downpour, but apart from him, there were only Joe and Eva in the vicinity. They sat down side by side with their backs against the railings, looking towards the middle of the bandstand.

They remained silent for a full minute, listening only to each other's exhausted, shaking breath and the patter of rain on the roof of the bandstand. When Joe finally spoke, his voice sounded monotone.

'I was in Pakistan when they went in for Osama bin Laden.'

He could sense Eva holding her breath.

'I saw something I shouldn't have seen. My mate who was with me died the next day. I got sent home and someone tried to do me in a hit and run. I took . . .' He felt a shadow cross his mind. 'I took Caitlin and Conor away, somewhere I thought was safe. They found us, I don't know how. They killed Caitlin and tried to make it look as if I'd committed suicide. But then they were disturbed . . .' He heard his voice waver. '. . . Conor saw his mum's body. He saw the knife in my hands.'

Eva put her hand on his knee.

'What did you see?' she whispered. 'In Pakistan, I mean.'

Joe shook his head. 'I don't know. Only that they removed two bodies from bin Laden's compound.'

'Two? But . . . I saw it on the news. They all said—'

'I know what they *said*.' He sensed Eva tensing up at his aggressive tone, and immediately regretted it. He took a deep breath and continued. 'In Barfield four Arab guys tried to kill me.'

Another silence.

'Joe,' Eva said timidly. 'Are you sure about all this? It sounds like . . .'

Joe snorted. 'Like I'm cracking up? That's what they all think. My OC. Even Caitlin thought I was imagining things.' He turned towards Eva. 'And they're right.' It was the first time he had admitted it, even to himself. Somehow it made him feel lighter. 'I have flashbacks. Blackouts. But they *did* kill Caitlin, Eva. They *did* try to cut me up in Barfield. Someone's turning your house upside down right now, and I'm not making *that* up either . . .'

'Wait,' Eva breathed.

On a reflex, Joe looked over his shoulder to check nobody was approaching. But the rain was falling heavily again. Apart from the sleeping tramp, they were alone.

'The men who attacked you in prison. They were Middle Eastern?'

Joe nodded.

'Were they in the visiting room the day I came?'

224

Joe thought back. He could see two of them in his mind, sitting ten metres to his left. 'Yeah.'

'There was a man,' said Eva. 'He looked, I don't know, Arab or Asian. I know that doesn't *mean* anything, but he *was* in the visiting room with us.'

Joe tried to sharpen his memory. There *must* have been a third man sitting there – the inmates wouldn't have been in the visiting room without a visitor – and the more he concentrated, the more a blurry face came into his mind. If Joe saw him again, perhaps he'd be able to make a positive ID. But without something to jog his memory . . .

'Would you recognize him?' he asked Eva.

She nodded. 'I think so . . .'

They fell silent again, then Joe said quietly: 'You don't have to help me. If anyone suspects you know where I am, they'll—'

'—break into my house at night? I think it's safe to say somebody already suspects.'

Joe nodded. 'I'm sorry.'

Eva stood up, walked to the other side of the bandstand and stared out into the rain. 'Remember last time we were here?' she asked. Joe nodded. He also remembered the photograph he'd found in her sitting room.

'Every male visitor to Barfield has their photograph taken and biometric information recorded,' Eva continued, suddenly brisk.

'Barfield will be crawling with—'

'I don't need to go to Barfield. It'll be on the system, somewhere. I'll just have to locate it.' She looked out at the rain again. 'I could go to the office first thing.'

'I don't like it,' Joe said.

'Better than sitting and shivering in the bandstand. I'll drop into my place first, see what state it's in, get a few things—'

'Absolutely not,' Joe cut in. 'They'll have eyes out for you.' He still didn't know who 'they' were.

'I can look after myself, Joe.'

'You can't go home.'

There was an edgy silence. 'Fine,' Eva said. She looked at her watch. 'It's just gone midnight. I'll wait till six before I go to the office – any earlier and it'll look suspicious.'

Joe closed his eyes. People close to him were suffering. Dying. He didn't want Eva to be next in line. But he didn't have any better ideas.

It was almost as if she knew what he was thinking. 'I'll be careful,' she said. 'How will I contact you?'

Eva gave him some paper and a ballpoint pen from her bag, and he wrote down two random strings of eight letters, numbers and symbols, following them both with the suffix '@hotmail. com', and by each one he wrote an equally unguessable password. Then he copied them exactly onto a second piece of paper, and handed it to Eva. 'I'll create these accounts,' he said. 'The first one's yours, the second's mine. Check it regularly, every hour if you can, but not from your phone and never from the same location. If you don't hear from me, meet back here at 1800 hours.'

Eva neatly folded the piece of paper and placed it in her bag.

A sudden wave of exhaustion crashed over Joe. He sat down again, his head against the edge of the bandstand. 'I need to sleep,' he murmured. He'd had no shuteye since his first night in prison – forty-eight hours ago – and even that had been more a trance than a sleep. He looked down at his prison clothes. 'And I need to clean up, find something else to wear before it gets light. And then . . .'

He paused.

'Then what?'

'They told me Conor was staying with Caitlin's dad in Epsom,' he said quietly. 'I need to know he's safe.'

Eva nodded. It looked like she understood.

Silence. Joe tried to fight his drowsiness.

'These attacks . . . are they . . . revenge?' Eva asked quietly. 'For bin Laden, I mean?'

Sheikh al-Mujahid? He's not dead . . .

'Don't know,' Joe replied. He was slurring from exhaustion. 'I just don't know . . . Doesn't make sense.'

Maybe something showed in his face, because Eva suddenly crouched down beside him. She put her arms round his shoulders and rested her head against his chest, much like she had been doing in the picture he'd seen in her house. 'I'm sorry about your friend. And I'm so, so sorry about Caitlin.'

From anyone else, the words would have been inadequate. From Eva, they were everything.

'Go to sleep,' she said. 'I'll wake you if anybody comes.'

Joe nodded. His fatigue was overpowering everything else. He sensed Eva removing the overcoat and spreading it over him.

His eyelids became heavy.

In seconds he was asleep.

It was midnight.

A dark-haired man with stooped shoulders stood in a quiet suburban street. The rain was still falling, but that made no difference to him as he wore a heavy waxed raincoat. Its pockets were equally weighted on either side: in the left one, a small, leather-bound copy of the Koran. In the right, a Browning semi-automatic pistol and two cable ties.

The house opposite which he stood had, as a focal point of the front garden, a magnificent magnolia tree in the early stages of budding. It also had, the man noticed, a flashing burglar alarm and one window open on the first floor. People only opened windows at night to give themselves ventilation as they slept. It meant someone was home.

He crossed the road, opened the front gate, passed under the magnolia branches, and rang the front door bell. He heard no chime, but a red light by the button indicated that it was working.

Twenty seconds later, through the glass of the front door, he saw a landing light come on and the silhouette of a figure descending the stairs rather slowly, apparently tying a dressing-gown cord as he went. The figure stopped on the other side of the front door. 'Who's that?' The male voice sounded elderly and tired.

'Police,' the man replied. 'I need to speak to you about Conor. I know it's late but this is urgent. We think you might be in some danger.'

A short pause. Then a click as the door opened to reveal a man in his late sixties, a pair of half-moon spectacles propped on his hook-like nose, the remnants of his hair in two dishevelled tufts on either side of his head, and wearing a navy blue kimono-style dressing gown. 'You'd better come—'

The man stopped short, perhaps realizing that his guest was not uniformed, nor did he have the demeanour of a policeman. Then his eyes darted down and he saw the Browning in the man's left hand. On an instinct, he tried to slam the door shut, but the man already had one foot over the threshold – enough to keep it open.

'Be so good, Mr O'Donnell,' said the man, 'as to keep utterly quiet as you step back from the door.'

Mr O'Donnell did as he was told. Within seconds the man was inside and the door was shut.

The first thing he noticed was the smell of flowers. The wide hallway was lined with bouquets of lilies and roses, all of them still in their plastic wrappers, with notes of condolence tucked into the foliage. As the old man staggered back, he knocked over one of the bouquets.

'The boy?'

Mr O'Donnell shook his head, as if to say that he wasn't going to answer, but the newcomer noticed the way his eyes glanced momentarily up the carpeted staircase at the end of the hallway. He flicked the gun in that direction, and O'Donnell backed nervously up the stairs, unable to keep his eyes off the weapon. He stumbled into a sitting position a quarter of the way up the stairs, making a heavy thump that seemed to echo around the whole house.

'Get up, turn around, keep walking,' said the man. O'Donnell had no choice but to agree.

There were three doors on the landing. Two were open. One led into a small bathroom, the other into a bedroom where the light was on and the head end of a double bed was visible. It meant that the third door was the one he wanted. 'Open it,' he told O'Donnell. 'Wake him.'

'Please,' the old man croaked. 'He hasn't spoken since . . . You don't know what he's *been* through.'

But that wasn't true. The intruder knew *just* what he'd been through. He knew the boy would be traumatized. That would make him easier to handle. 'Wake him,' he repeated.

The terrified old man staggered into the bedroom. 'Conor,' he said hoarsely. 'Conor, you must wake up.'

As the intruder followed him into the little bedroom, he switched on the light. The boy was drowsily sitting up in a single bed against the far wall, clutching a small grey soft toy in the shape of an elephant. Next to him stood a white bedside table on which were a glass of water, a framed photograph of a woman and a *Horrid Henry* book. At the other end of the bed was a matching chest of drawers. There was no indication that this was ordinarily a child's bedroom – no toys or pictures, just a figurine of the Virgin Mary on a melamine shelf along the left-hand wall, and a wooden chair with some neatly folded clothes.

It took a few seconds for the boy to realize what was happening, by which time the intruder had raised a gloved finger to his lips. 'Shhh . . .' he hissed gently, before turning back to the old man. 'On your knees,' he whispered.

The old man sank to the ground.

'My name is Mr Ashe,' said the man to the boy. 'You must do exactly what I say. Do you understand?'

Conor nodded mutely.

'Go to your drawer. Remove two pairs of socks and give them to me.'

Like his grandfather, the boy could not take his eyes from the gun. He crawled the length of his bed and fumbled in the top drawer before removing the socks as he had been told. One pair was plain black, the second had a Spider-Man logo. He handed them to Mr Ashe, then quickly retreated to the pillow end of his bed.

Mr Ashe stepped up to O'Donnell. 'Open your mouth,' he instructed, and when the old man had done so, he stuffed the Spider-Man socks inside, pressing down so that they reached the back of his throat, before filling the remaining cavity with the second pair. The old man gagged, and his eyes bulged, but he remained immobile in the kneeling position Mr Ashe had forced him to adopt.

Mr Ashe removed one of the cable ties from his coat and tied the old man's hands behind his back, speaking as he worked in a quiet, unflustered voice.

'I want you to watch your grandfather very carefully,' he said. 'I want you to understand, and to remember, how much this will hurt him.'

The old man made a panicked sound and tried to stand up, but Mr Ashe was too fast for him. He wrapped the second cable tie around his victim's neck and yanked it tight.

The noise was disgusting: a feeble croak accompanied by the unmistakable sound of the old man pissing himself in fear. His neck bulged outwards and became red, blue and blotchy. He fell to his side, flailing like a landed fish, growing weaker and weaker as the seconds passed.

He had, Mr Ashe, estimated, no longer than thirty seconds of consciousness left. It was important to make the most of them.

He stepped round the old man and approached the bed. The boy cringed away from him, backing into the corner, pulling his duvet with him. His lower lip was trembling, and tears had appeared in his eyes.

Mr Ashe held the gun up to the boy's head. He made a sudden small movement with the weapon. The child started and closed his eyes, before opening them again five seconds later, apparently surprised that he was still alive.

'You understand, Conor,' whispered Mr Ashe, 'what will happen if you do not do exactly as I tell you?'

The boy's terrified nod was barely visible. But it was enough. Mr Ashe tucked his weapon back into his coat. 'If you make a sound,' he said, 'I will kill you. If you try to run, I will kill you. If you fail to do what I say, I will kill you. Are you sure you understand, Conor?'

The little boy nodded.

'Good,' said Mr Ashe. 'Then get dressed. Now.'

FIFTEEN

0600 hours.

Eva walked through the main entrance into Scotland Yard.

As a plainclothes officer it was normal for her to be wearing civvies, but ordinarily that meant something smart. This morning, having thrown on jeans and a sweater when she fled her house, and then spent the remainder of the night shivering in the shelter of the bandstand watching Joe muttering feverishly as he slept, she looked a mess. Her clothes were still damp, and she was in no doubt that she smelled none too fresh. She kept a change of clothes in her office, but until she got there, she'd stick out horribly.

These offices never slept. There was always a selection of mostly male officers, thickset and burly, wearing cheap suits, and with physiques that suggested they'd spent a lot more time behind desks writing reports and drinking sweetened coffee than was good for them. But this was the Yard's quietest hour. The main shifts wouldn't change over till 8 a.m. – that was when Eva was officially due in – but the bulk of the night's work was done and the corridors were largely empty. The security guard at the desk gave her a friendly nod, with perhaps a hint of surprise that she'd arrived at this unusual hour looking so bedraggled, but she was a familiar enough face to walk straight past him and along the corridor that led to the lifts.

Eva knew, of course, that there was CCTV all over the Yard, but she'd never registered just how many cameras there were.

She counted three on the short walk to the lifts, and as she ascended to the third floor she pictured herself as a monochrome fish-eye image on a screen somewhere in the bowels of this place. Never before had she felt so *watched* . . . It occurred to her that she had been infected with paranoia, and she put from her mind the obvious truth: that the source of the infection was on the run from the police, wanted for the murder of his girlfriend and, by his own admission, messed up in his head.

The lift doors hissed open. Eva turned left. Her office was twenty metres along this corridor on the right. Once she was in there, she figured, she would not be disturbed for an hour at least.

'Eva?'

The voice, male, had come from behind. Eva stopped and turned slowly. On the other side of the lifts from which she had just emerged was her colleague Frank. She felt sick. They shared an office, but their rotas were normally in sync. She hadn't expected him to be here.

Frank caught up with her. Unlike most of the men who worked out of the Yard, he was lithe and fit. He looked tired, but had a big smile on his face.

'Twenty-four hours, then I'm EasyJetting it out of here.' He started to whistle 'Viva España'.

'What?' Eva asked, confused.

'Annual leave,' he said. 'Flying at midday.' He gave her a broad grin. 'Heard about Daniels?'

She shook her head as they continued to walk down the corridor. Daniels, the sleazy colleague whose PNC login Eva had stolen. 'What about him?'

'Some lag broke out of Barfield. Turns out Daniels made an unauthorized PNC search on this bloke a few days ago. Commissioner's spitting feathers. Looks like a suspension and he's got one of Jacobson's murder investigation teams knocking on his door. Still, couldn't happen to a nicer fella, eh?'

He stopped and looked at Eva as though for the first time, noticing her crumpled casual clothes and that she looked rough. 'You all right?' he asked.

'Why the MIT?' she asked.

'What?'

'You said the murder investigation team were banging on Daniels's door. Why? I thought it was just an escaped convict.'

Frank shrugged. 'Looks like he killed another inmate before he got out. Sounds like a right fucking psycho. Him and Daniels deserve each other. Tell you what – I'll get us some coffee. Black?'

Eva gave him a weak smile. 'Great.'

Frank wandered off and she hurried into her room. She felt sick. Joe had said nothing about another inmate. Nothing about . . .

She drew a deep breath and remembered what he'd supposedly done to Caitlin. The scalpel he'd held in front of her face. The threats he'd made. Had he been lying to her after all? She closed her eyes and saw him, and the look of confused anger on his face when he'd told her all that stuff last night. Bin Laden . . . assassination attempts . . . Did she really believe him, or was she just *trying* to?

'No,' she muttered to herself.

She reminded herself of the figure approaching her house just moments before they'd escaped it. It was a chilling memory, and it told her that something weird was going on, even if she didn't know what.

Eva turned and headed back to the door just as Frank entered carrying two polystyrene cups. They collided, and coffee sloshed over Frank's suit. 'Oh my God . . . sorry . . . *sorry* . . .' But she didn't stop to help him. She just wished he would go, so that she could change her own clothes. But it was clear he wasn't going to and she gave up on that idea. A few seconds later she was back out in the corridor and running back towards the lift.

The offices of Scotland Yard's Homicide Command Unit were on the first floor. Ordinarily they had just a skeleton staff during the night, but it was immediately clear to Eva, as she walked along the corridors, that at least one MIT was active. She counted about fifteen people in the first incident room she passed, all of them looking busy.

Eva stepped inside the room. It was ten metres square and its tinted-glass windows looked down on the Yard's main entrance. There was the constant noise of muted telephone rings, the tapping of keyboards, the chuntering of a photocopy machine. The room smelled of warm printers and coffee. Eva was a familiar enough face here, but nobody even acknowledged her arrival.

A woman approached from the far side of the room. She was wearing a two-piece suit and her grey hair was very short. For a moment, as the woman looked her shabby clothes up and down, Eva thought she was going to challenge her, but she swerved to Eva's left and pinned a photograph to a corkboard on the wall adjacent to the door. Eva looked at it and felt her skin prickle. It was an old photo, but it was clearly Joe.

She scanned the room. Frank had mentioned DCI Jacobson, head of one of the MITs. She knew him well – chubby, with brown hair, and always a bit crumpled. Jacobson was one of the few people in this place who didn't have time for the constant inter-departmental sniping. A good man. She couldn't make him out in the room. She swallowed hard, then followed the grey-haired woman back to her desk on the far side of the office.

'Yes?' The woman sounded impatient and didn't look up from her screen to talk to Eva. It was clear she felt her personal space was being invaded.

'Jacobson sent me,' Eva said, as briskly as she could. 'I need to cross-check visitors to Barfield over the last week.'

'First I've heard of it.'

Eva gave a half-smile and decided it was better not to volunteer anything. The woman sighed, but rummaged through a pile of papers on her desk until she found a plastic sleeve with a single data stick in it. Without looking at her, she handed it to Eva.

'Good. Thanks. I'll, er . . .' Eva jerked a thumb over her shoulder, stepping backwards, and smiled. It wasn't returned.

She walked as casually as possible back to the door, holding her breath, positive that she was going to be called back at any moment. But she wasn't. Out in the corridor again, she did her best not to run, looking for an empty room with a spare terminal. She found one three doors along, and within seconds she was sitting in front of the screen, plugging in the data stick.

The information was divided into folders, one for each day over the past two weeks. She opened a file marked '08_05_11', to be presented with a list of twenty thumbnail images. Her own photograph was third in the list. For a moment she considered deleting it, but she knew that would be stupid, and she hurried on.

The image she was looking for was two places from the bottom. She double-clicked on it, and a larger window appeared with the grainy but familiar face of a man of Middle Eastern appearance staring out at her. Dark skin. Hooked nose. And underneath the picture, a scan of his hand print, the time he checked in and the time he checked out.

His name: Sarmed Ashe.

Her heart was thumping. She closed the window on the screen and removed the data stick, then went to the door. She was about to step into the corridor when she saw the portly frame of DCI Jacobson walk past.

She cursed under her breath and moved to the side of the door, pressing her back against the wall. How long had it taken her to get here from the incident room? Fifteen seconds? She hadn't exactly been paying attention. She counted to twenty before taking another deep breath, opening the door and leaving the room.

There was no one in sight.

She walked briskly, but not so fast as to attract attention. As she passed the incident room her eyes darted through the interior window. Jacobson was talking to the woman with the short grey hair. Impossible to tell what she was saying. But easy to guess. Ten metres to the lift. She picked up her pace, feeling like she had half the Met following her. On reaching the lift she pressed the down button and waited.

Movement further down the corridor. The door to the incident room opened. Three seconds later the lift hissed open. Eva glanced to her right. Jacobson had emerged into the corridor and was staring in her direction. Was she paranoid, or did he look suspicious? She saw him mouthing the word 'Eva?' just as she stepped into the lift and slammed the button for the basement.

Safely inside, she found herself almost hyperventilating and felt trickles of sweat all over her body. This wasn't just a sacking offence, it was a prosecution offence. And all to help a man accused of murder?

The basement was the lair of the forensic teams. Like nearly everywhere else in the building, it was pretty much empty at this hour. She passed a pale-faced young man in his early twenties who barely seemed to notice her, but apart from that she met no one until she stepped into the badly lit room of the fingerprint department.

Two young men were on duty. Neither looked like he saw much daylight and only one looked up when Eva entered. Eva forced her face into an expression of confidence and marched up to him. 'DI Buckley,' she said. 'Can you run me a search?'

'ID?' the young man asked.

Eva casually handed over her ID, which the young man barely glanced at – and so he didn't see that her hand was trembling.

'What is it?' he asked.

Eva handed him the data stick. 'Biometric details of prison

visitors. There's a Sarmed Ashe on there. I want to cross-check him with the system.' The young man shrugged, as if to indicate that this was trivial for someone of his technical ability, and plugged the device into his terminal. Eva helped him navigate to the correct file. As the young man's fingers flew over the keyboard, she felt her heart hammering in her chest and her eyes kept flickering to the door. She expected Jacobson to step inside any second.

'Gotcha,' the young man said finally.

'What do you have?'

'Well . . .' said the fingerprint technician, relaxing a little, clearly enjoying his moment in the sun. 'You're lucky we've got him, to be honest. It's only because he had a break-in back in 2008. SOCOs dusted him off just to eliminate his prints from the crime scene. Clean as a whistle otherwise. But what did he say his name was?'

'Sarmed Ashe,' Eva breathed.

'Tch tch tch . . .' tutted the technician, nodding. 'Giving false ID to a prison officer. Naughty boy. 'Fraid that's not his real name.'

'What is?'

'He's *actually* called Hussein Al-Samara. Let's have a look. Iraqi born. Granted political asylum 9 November 2001 – that's, like, nearly two months to the day after 9/11, right?'

'Right,' Eva breathed.

'Naturalized 15 December 2006 . . . I suppose you want his address?'

Eva tried to keep her voice steady. 'Yes,' she said quietly. 'Print it out for me, would you?'

Ten minutes later, and clutching a single piece of paper, she was once more nodding at the security guy at ground-floor reception, before striding out of the Yard and wondering to herself whether she would ever set foot in that place again.

0700 hours.

Joe was wearing black jeans, a tight grey polo neck, a black woollen hat and a thick, checked lumberjack shirt. It had taken him two hours to find a charity shop where someone had left a black plastic bag of donated clothes in the doorway. These were the best-fitting, and warmest, items he could find. But anything was better than the dirty prison uniform that he had rolled into a bundle and chucked into a big metal catering dustbin at the back of an Indian restaurant on Tooting High Street. With one of the £50 notes he'd taken from Eva's place, he'd bought himself hot, sweet tea and two platefuls of shepherd's pie from an all-night café. It tasted disgusting – even the food in Barfield had been better than this – but he needed fuel and he wolfed it down. Just to get hot food inside him felt fantastic.

On the other side of the road was another all-night establishment. Posters in the window advertised the ability to wire money to any country in minutes, cheap phone calls to Nigeria and Delhi and internet access at £1 for twenty minutes. Three men – Turkish? he wondered – loitered by a counter, smoking cigarettes and drinking coffee from tiny cups. A fourth man, slightly older, stood behind it. They'd gone silent as Joe entered, and given him an unfriendly stare. He had just pointed at one of the computer screens, received a nod from the man behind the counter, and taken a seat. It took him five minutes to set up the Hotmail accounts using a false name and address. As soon as he was done, he'd walked up to the counter and handed over a fifty-pound note. The proprietor had taken it into a back room to get change while the three men moved over to a nearby table to continue their conversation in their own language, leaving their cigarette packets, keys and smartphones in plain view.

Joe's plan was executed almost as quickly as it was formulated. He had surreptitiously removed the smartphone from the middle pile as he leaned over it, depositing it in the left-hand pocket of his lumberjack shirt. Seconds later the man had reappeared with his change. Joe had grunted a word of thanks, left the shop and hurried down the road before his act was discovered. Once he had turned off the main road, he'd switched off the phone and removed the battery. A mobile, he knew, was as good as a tracking device. But if anyone was going to track him, it needed to be on *his* terms . . .

The first Tube to Waterloo had left Tooting Broadway at 5.53 a.m. He bought himself a tin of Tennent's Super from a local Spar, poured half of it away and sat at the end of the Northern Line carriage, head bowed, eyes half closed but still alert, the beer can that instantly marked him out as a wino to be avoided held lightly between his knees. As he'd hoped, the few bleary-eyed commuters on the carriage kept their distance and avoided eye contact. There are ways of being invisible, Joe understood. This was one.

Joe's carriage on the train from Waterloo to Epsom was almost empty. Few people travelled *out* of London at this hour. He stared through the window, watching the suburban gardens whizz past . . . allotments . . . high streets . . . , churches. So much normality. It felt alien to him. A copy of the *Metro* freesheet was on the floor by his feet. He picked it up and opened a page at random. He stared blankly at the drawing that took up half a page for a good five seconds before he realized what he was looking at: an artist's impression of the compound in Abbottabad, with images of crashed helicopters and arrows representing troop movements. In a sudden fit of anger he screwed the paper up and threw it back onto the floor. He figured that the world would suddenly be full of experts on what had happened that night.

He stepped out of the train at Epsom just as the Tannoy announced the arrival of the 08.32 to Waterloo. The platform was busy, but Joe's can of lager did the trick as the harried commuters walking in the opposite direction separated to let him pass. Minutes later he was walking south through the residential area of Epsom. He knew his route. He had walked it often enough with Caitlin and Conor. His father-in-law, or whatever you wanted to call him, lived alone in a quiet road ten minutes' walk from the station. But he knew something was wrong before he'd even walked for half that time.

These streets were always lined with parked cars, but they were seldom busy. This morning they were gridlocked. Drivers were performing tight three-point turns to get out of the solid, unmoving traffic, which only made matters worse. Several had got out of their cars and were looking ahead, trying to see the cause of the blockage.

Joe, though, realized what it was the moment he turned left into Mr O'Donnell's street.

There were no sirens, just the ominous blue and white flashing of four emergency vehicles – one ambulance, three police – stationed in the middle of the road. They were thirty metres from Joe's position. Midway between them and him was a police cordon, delineated by a strip of fluorescent tape and with three uniformed officers on duty. Ten metres from the cordon a four-man TV crew had set up a camera in the road and were standing beside it: two smoking, two drinking coffee, looking bored and clearly waiting for something newsworthy to happen.

The cordon, the camera crew, the blocked-off street: these were the cause of the traffic jam. They were also the cause of Joe's sudden nausea. He didn't even need to check that the emergency vehicles were positioned outside Caitlin's father's house.

It was all he could do to resist the urge simply to barge through the cordon. What the fuck had happened? Conor? Was he . . . ?

Suddenly his pulse was racing, his breath short. If he'd lost Conor, he'd lost everything. He ran towards the camera crew. Before he knew what had happened, the camera itself was lying smashed on the ground and he had grabbed one of the team by the front of his coat and was bellowing: '*What's happening here? What the fuck's going on?*'

He felt arms behind him – the rest of the crew were pulling him away. He made short work of them, jabbing one in the chest with the heel of his right hand, swiping another away with his arm like he was barely there. It didn't matter that they'd done nothing. Rage was burning inside him like he'd never known it.

From the edge of his vision, he was aware of two police officers – one male, one female – sprinting towards him from the cordon. The male officer was shouting something – in his confused state, he couldn't tell what – and the woman was talking into the radio attached to her uniform.

He stared at them for a second, breathless, teeth clenched.

And then he ran.

There was more shouting behind him. Someone was making chase. Joe hurtled round the corner of the street, running blindly but with all the speed he could muster. Sweat poured from him. His muscles burned. He didn't know where he was heading. He just had to get away, out of sight. He had no thought for himself, but only for Conor. He *had* to know what had happened. He *had* to speak to Eva. She would be able to find out . . .

He was in an alleyway behind a terrace of Victorian houses. He didn't know how he'd got there. It was quiet. A bold urban fox stared at him from ten metres away, but apart from that he was alone, standing by three green wheelie bins overflowing with stinking rubbish bags. He crouched down between two of them, making sure he was fully out of sight in case anyone should appear at either end of the alley. With trembling, fumbling hands he removed the stolen phone from his lumberjack shirt, replaced the battery and switched it on.

Ten seconds passed. The screen lit up with an animated Nokia logo. The service bars were half full, the data coverage good. He quickly opened the browser and directed it to the Hotmail homepage. After pulling out the scrap of paper with the email addresses he'd created, his calloused fingers tapped in the details on the touchscreen. In an instant he was staring at two emails in his inbox: one welcoming him to Hotmail, the other from the second address he had created. From Eva.

He tapped it and read the message that appeared: 'The visitor's name is Hussein Al-Samara. Address: Flat B, 23 Wimborne Road, Dagenham. There's a cafe directly opposite. I'm there now. E'.

Joe could feel the return of the anger that had just made him lose control. He didn't know who this Hussein Al-Samara was, but he knew he wanted to fuck the guy up. And if he knew anything – *anything* – about Conor . . .

Joe acted with sudden clarity. He had stolen this phone for a reason. If someone was searching for him – someone with resources – there was a chance they were monitoring access to his regular email account. If he accessed it from this phone, they could start tracing it. But it would be a moment's work to leave the handset under the seat of a bus and set his pursuers on a wild goose chase . . .

He didn't hesitate. Logging out of his new account, he typed in the username and password of his old one. Ten seconds passed while the connection was made. His inbox appeared.

There was a long list of unread emails. The usual shit: loan offers, porn sites and Viagra. Joe paid no attention to any of them. At the top of the list was an email from an address he did not recognize, but with a subject heading that he certainly did: 'Conor'.

He felt, as he lightly tapped the screen, that the world had slowed down. It seemed to take an age for the email to display. When it did, and he tapped on the link that formed its only contents, the delay was excruciating.

Ten seconds passed. Twenty. A YouTube video appeared on the phone's screen. No title. Number of views: 0.

Joe tapped the screen to play it. He saw dark, juddery camerawork. A time code read '06:03'. There were clunking noises, and then perhaps, very faintly, a whimpering sound.

A child's voice. Full of fear.

The camera swung round. There was a window. Beyond it, he thought he could make out the sea. The sky was growing light, but there was no sign of the rising sun. It continued to move. He saw a bed. On the wall behind it there was a picture of a sailing ship in stormy seas.

And, sitting on the bed, was his son.

Conor's face was beaten and bruised. There was a cut on his lower lip, and a daub of blood just below it. His eyes were raw and swollen. His hands were tied behind his back.

He tried to speak, but couldn't. All that came from his mouth was a weak, shuddering sound. But then he looked up, clearly paying attention to whoever was holding the video camera. Whatever sign that person made, it seemed to fill Conor with more horror.

Finally he spoke. Each word was an effort. He stuttered and stumbled, and it sounded more like weeping than speaking. The message, though, was sufficiently clear.

'Daddy . . . I don't know where I am . . . Mr . . . Mr Ashe . . . He killed granddad . . . He says he's going to kill me . . .'

The very second he had forced these feeble words from his terrified throat, the screen went black. The video was over.

With dread creeping through every cell of his body, Joe stared at the empty screen. And when he tried to replay the scene, he was unable. Instead of his beaten, terrorized son, he saw a brief message: a message that chilled him almost as much as what he had just seen.

'Video unavailable,' it said. 'The owner has removed this content.'

The full cup of coffee on the table in front of Eva was cold, the toast uneaten, the *Daily Mirror* unread. She had no stomach for either food or news.

She had chosen a seat by the front window. It looked directly onto the pavement and the busy street just off Dagenham Heathway. And on the other side of the road, the black door of number 23. Her eyes were stuck on it. If a lorry or a bus passed – which they did frequently – she had to suppress brief surges of panic. If the mysterious Hussein Al-Samara – or Mr Ashe, or whatever he wanted to call himself – came in or out of the premises, she needed to know about it. Joe would ask her what she had seen when – *if* – he arrived, and she wanted his approval. Given the events of the last twelve hours, there wasn't much else that seemed important.

She checked her watch: 09.48. Had Joe read her email? How long should she wait for him to arrive? All day? The café was full and the middle-aged Greek woman who had supplied her coffee and toast was eyeing her from behind the counter, obviously peeved that she was taking up a table that other customers might want.

Her eyes panned up to the first-floor window. Flat B. Was that Al-Samara's place? The wooden frame looked rotten, the pane was covered with a net curtain. A faint glow suggested that a light was on inside.

'You finished?'

Eva looked up. The woman from behind the counter was looking down at the uneaten food like it was a personal slight.

'Yeah . . .' she muttered. 'Thanks . . .' Her eyes wandered back to number 23. 'Um . . . maybe I'll have another . . .'

She'd seen movement in the first-floor window. The net curtain fluttered slightly. She thought maybe she'd seen a shadow passing it.

'. . . coffee,' she breathed. The woman cleared her table.

Eva's phone rang. She answered it immediately. 'Joe?' she said, before remembering that he didn't even have her number.

'DI Buckley?' A voice she half recognized.

'Who's this?' There was a tremor in her voice.

'Jason Riley, Scotland Yard.'

She didn't answer.

'You came to see me this morning? In the basement? It's about the fingerprint ID I gave you . . .'

'What about it?' she breathed.

'Well, I was just logging the query and something came up. There were two other male visitors on the day in question and their fingerprint records are all the same.'

'What do you mean?'

'Identical prints, all of them. Same bloke, this Hussein Al-Samara. Don't know how they did it, but it looks to me like someone's been tampering with the records. I'll need to refer this upwards, but I thought I'd just give you the nod—'

'*Shit!*'

Eva let the phone drop from her ear. The fingerprint technician's words were bad enough, but her view of the first-floor window of number 23 was even worse. The shadow had suddenly reappeared, but this time it had slammed against both the net curtain and the window pane, and a crack had suddenly appeared in the glass. 'Joe,' she whispered. 'Oh my God, *Joe – what are you doing?*'

She stood up immediately, pushing past the waitress.

'You haven't paid!' the woman shouted. Eva threw a note on the table without even checking what it was, before running out onto the street and straight across the busy road. Within seconds she was at the black door, pressing desperately, repeatedly on the buzzer for Flat B. It made no sound, but she pressed and pressed, thumping on the wooden door with her other hand.

Two minutes passed. Three. There was no response from Flat B. With a howl of frustration, Eva stepped back onto the pavement and cursed, before stepping up to the door once more and pressing the button for Flat A. It was answered within seconds.

'Police,' she bellowed into the intercom. 'Open up.'

There was a clicking sound. Eva pushed the door open and ¹ᵊd inside.

She found herself in a square lobby with grey ceramic floor tiles and on one side a row of pigeonholes for mail. There was a door to her left, which opened to reveal a frightened-looking old lady in a dressing gown and hairnet.

'Flat B?' Eva demanded.

'Upstairs . . .' The old lady nodded at a staircase with a wrought-iron banister. Eva ran towards it, but then stopped and looked back. 'Is there a rear entrance to these flats?'

The old lady nodded, but then frowned. 'Do you have any identification?'

Eva didn't answer. She ran to the old lady's door and pushed past her into the ground-floor flat. Ignoring the feeble shouts of protest, she ran along the dark hallway and into the tiny kitchen at the end, where a door looked out onto an alleyway from which an external iron staircase zigzagged up. She yanked the door open – a wailing sound reached her ears from above – and flew up the staircase to the first floor.

It was no surprise to see that the back door of Flat B was swinging open.

The bigger surprise was the baby, no more than three months old, lying in a Moses basket on the kitchen table, screaming its lungs out.

Eva ran past it, heading for the room at the front. She could hear more shouting from in there. Then she saw why.

There were three people in the room. One of them was a woman, short, dumpy, Middle Eastern-looking, wearing a tightly wrapped green headscarf. She was kneeling in the far-left corner of the room, just beyond a tatty sofa, her hands clutched in front of her, her face stained with tears, her eyes full of terror.

The second person was Joe. Eva could never have imagined that a familiar face could look so unfamiliar. His eyes were insane, his lips curled with anger. In his hand was the same scalpel with which he had threatened Eva.

The third person was another man, tall and thin, with dark

hair. Like the woman, he was on his knees, and he was sucking in deep breaths, two a second. Eva could not see his face because it was covered by his hands. What she *could* see, though, was the blood, seeping from behind his fingers.

'*Joe!*'

'Back off, Eva,' Joe growled, without even turning to look at her. He stepped forward, eating up the two metres that separated him and the man on his knees, then grabbed a clump of his dark hair with one hand and with the other placed the scalpel against his neck. '*You think I won't kill you?*' he hissed. '*I'll fucking enjoy it. The only way you've got any chance at all is to tell me!*' He yanked the man by his hair to his feet, and now he was shouting. '*Tell me! Where's my son?*'

'I . . . do . . . not . . . *know!*' the man groaned. As he spoke, his hands fell away from his face.

Eva gasped.

It was not the blood that shocked her, flowing from his nose like a torrent, nor the ugly welts that Joe had inflicted on both sides of the man's face with his fists. Nor was it his helpless expression of panic. It was something else.

'Joe,' she whispered.

'*Back off, I said!*' He yanked the man's head to one side and pressed the edge of blade against the soft flesh of his trembling neck.

'Joe, no . . .'

'You've got three seconds. One. Two . . .'

'Let him go! That's not the man I saw! We've got the wrong person! *That's not him!*'

And as she screamed at Joe, she ran forward and pulled him away, placing herself between her violent friend and the terrified, bleeding, messed-up man he was on the point of butchering.

SIXTEEN

CIA Headquarters, Langley, Virginia, USA. 0700 hours EST.
'Chocolate bourbon?'

Mason Delaney indicated a plate of biscuits on the coffee table. The man sitting at the other end of the comfortable sofa gave a barely perceptible shake of his head.

'You don't mind if I do?'

'Please . . .'

Delaney helped himself to a biscuit, placed it on the bone-china saucer that held his cup of tea, lifted the cup and took the tiniest of sips. Then he held the chocolate bourbon up in the air and examined it as if it were a precious stone. 'I became very fond of these when I was stationed in the UK,' he said. 'The British have given the world many things, but for me their greatest achievement will always be tea and biscuits.' To emphasize his point, he dunked the chocolate bourbon in his tea, before biting off a third of it and chewing it slowly and with emphasis. He did not take his eyes off his guest.

'I'm sure Her Majesty would be delighted to know that you approve.'

Delaney's guest had one of those British accents that ordinarily made him shiver with joy. So clipped, so restrained, so white. Now Delaney ignored the hint of diplomatically repressed sarcasm and leaned forward, his eyes sparkling behind his horn-rimmed glasses, his lips trembling with amusement. 'There are people in this very building who will try to tell you that the doughnut is a superior—'

'Mason, I wonder if we might move the subject on?'

Delaney smiled, dunked the remainder of his biscuit, and waited for his guest to continue.

'First, on behalf of the service I'd like to congratulate you on Operation Geronimo.'

'Come, Peter. MI6 played its part. Your people were very helpful.'

Peter Schlessinger, like Delaney himself, had no official title within the British Secret Service – at least none that Delaney was aware of. The Brit continued in a businesslike fashion: 'We have, of course, seen increased terrorist activity in the past few days. That's only to be expected. Our services are liaising, naturally, but I'm not sure how much of the day-to-day stuff reaches you.' Schlessinger bent down, picked up a leather briefcase, opened it and removed a sheaf of papers. 'Most of it's low-level, of course, but not all. Three men arrested at our East Midlands Airport, one of whom was trying to smuggle ammonium nitrate in a colostomy bag onto a flight to Newark.'

'Delightful,' Delaney murmured.

'We have three individual cells planning to plant explosive devices in the foundations of the Olympic Village in east London at some point during the next two months . . .'

'A year ahead of schedule,' Delaney observed. 'I didn't know they had it in them to be so well prepared.'

'Nobody wants another 9/11, Mason,' Schlessinger said, perhaps a little piously. 'We've had our people watching the site ever since the games were announced. A single watch battery could power a hidden detonator for several years. But that's by the by – all three cells are compromised. Frankly they won't be laying so much as a turd without us knowing about it.' Delaney's eyes widened in surprise at the director's language. 'There won't be another Munich – our combined intelligence is too good. We can guarantee the safety of any American athletes in 2012.'

Delaney returned his cup to the table, then sat back on the sofa and pressed his fingertips together. 'Do I sense the word "but" peeking over the hill, Peter?'

For a moment, Schlessinger didn't reply. He returned the papers to his briefcase and clicked it shut before replying to his American counterpart.

'Fifty per cent of our intelligence comes from sources outside the UK or the US, Mason. You don't need me to tell you that.'

Delaney inclined his head in acknowledgement.

'We will be withdrawing from Iraq in the next few months, and the President's rhetoric with regard to Afghanistan has not gone unnoticed.'

'Your point, Peter?'

'My point, Mason, is that the fewer people we have in the region, the more difficult *our* job of collecting information. Yours and mine. Does the President really believe that just because Osama bin Laden's at the bottom of the Indian Ocean with rocks in his shoes, the terror threat level is going to reduce?'

'We confiscated several hard drives—'

'Oh, come *on*, Mason. You know as well as I do that there are a hundred bin Laden replacements out there as we speak, just waiting for the chance to light up the sky. Don't tell me you disagree.'

A pause. Delaney removed his glasses, scrutinized the lenses from a distance, then replaced them.

'I do not disagree.'

'Then why . . . ?'

Delaney held up one chubby finger.

'I do not disagree, but this agency does not dictate American policy, no matter what some people would like to believe. We are a tool of the federal government, nothing more. In many ways, you British have more influence in this matter than the entire agency.'

Schlessinger looked confused.

'Let me explain, Peter. Some presidents establish their popularity by sending their soldiers to war. Others establish it by bringing them back home. Both approaches have their supporters among the little people.'

'The little people?'

'The public, Peter. The naive, uninformed public. If their opinion sways, then mark my words: the President's opinion will sway in a similar direction. Does the CIA have the ability to sway public opinion? Alas, no.'

There was a knock on the door. It opened immediately. Delaney looked up with sudden annoyance that fell away when he saw Scott Stroman. His assistant's handsome young face was serious, yet not without a gleam of triumph.

He turned back to Schlessinger. 'I do enjoy our little chats, Peter.'

Schlessinger looked confused. 'Mason, we have a lot to discuss. I've flown in especially to—'

'We'll do it again soon, no?'

The British man blinked, clearly angry, but then stood up. Delaney smiled blandly at him, but remain seated. 'So long, Peter,' he said in a sing-song voice, and his eyes followed his guest to the door.

Neither Delaney nor Stroman spoke until it was shut.

'Tell me, Scott,' Delaney demanded in a bored tone. 'What do the British put in their tea that makes them all such *fucking* idiots? They're so passive-aggressive you just want to give them a slap.' And when Stroman failed to respond, he asked quietly: 'You have something?'

The triumph in Stroman's face grew more pronounced. He stepped over to where Delaney was sitting and handed him a single sheet of paper. Delaney's eyes scanned it: a list of ten alphanumeric strings.

Flight numbers.

'How?' he asked quietly.

'Shampoo,' Stroman replied. 'They have people working in a factory in Delaware that supplies pretty much every drugstore in the country. Including outlets past security at JFK, LAX, you name it.'

Delaney smiled. 'Would you be so good, Scott, as to tell Herb Sagan that I would like a word in his exquisitely crafted ear?'

Stroman nodded. 'Anything else sir?'

'Yes. I'd like to speak to Ashkani. I want to thank him personally.'

Stroman nodded, but instead of turning and leaving the room, he lingered awkwardly.

'Come, Scott, we'll have time to play when this is over.' Delaney approached his assistant and brushed one finger against his perfectly formed right cheekbone. 'He is a greater patriot than you know,' he breathed.

Scott gave him one of those nervous, handsome smiles he so adored.

'Yes, sir,' he said, then left the room quietly.

Three thousand miles away, in a solitary house by the sea, an old lady was frowning. 'What in heaven's name *is* that noise, Dandelion?' Bethan Jones asked her cat. Dandelion seemed more interested in Jeremy Kyle and didn't respond.

It had started at about ten o'clock – two hours ago – the monotonous, regular knocking. It was coming from upstairs. She was used to the pipes banging in this old house – her Gethin had been able to fix it when he was alive, but there was no way she could tackle the plumbing at her time of life. She supposed she *could* call out a plumber to look at it, but from what she'd read in the papers they would probably be immigrants and she wouldn't even be able to understand them. No, she'd ask Mr Ashe to take a look. He wouldn't mind.

She wondered where he was and why he hadn't come in to say hello. She had heard him return in the early hours. She knew it had to be him, because Dandelion would have yowled and mewed and stuck her claws into the blankets of Bethan's bed if a stranger had entered the house before dawn, or indeed at any time. Besides, she had heard him moving around upstairs as she lay there dozing. He had been noisier than usual, but she couldn't complain: he was normally so quiet that you wouldn't know he was there. Such a nice man. So *thoughtful* . . .

Thump.

Thump.

Thump.

The sound was suddenly louder than before, and the old lady grew agitated. It didn't, on reflection, really *sound* like the pipes. 'Oh dear,' she muttered. 'What should we do, Dandelion? Go and look? Oh dear . . .'

She heaved herself up from the sofa. Dandelion jumped off her lap and gave her a reproachful miaow as she hit the floor. Bethan was too preoccupied with the stiffness in her joints to notice. Once she was on her feet, she fumbled for her stick and, leaning heavily on it, struggled to the door.

Thump.

Thump.

Thump.

It was even louder now. Did it sound like it was coming from Mr Ashe's room? Her hearing really wasn't what it once was . . .

Bethan didn't like using her stairlift. Oh, it was better than the alternative, but it made her rather giddy and at her age it could take the best part of a day to recover. With her frail, trembling hands, she strapped herself in securely, brought down the arms so that she had something solid to hold on to, and pressed the

254

button that would take her upstairs. The motor hummed noisily as the chair started its slow ascent.

Thump.

Thump.

Thump.

It was definitely coming from the room at the top of the stairs. 'Mr Ashe?' she called weakly. 'Mr Ashe, is everything all right?'

What on earth could it be?

The stairlift stopped. It was only halfway up. Bethan pressed the button again, but there was no movement. 'Oh dear . . .' She was getting agitated again. 'Oh . . .'

'Good morning, Mrs Jones,' said a quiet voice from the bottom of the stairs.

Bethan started, and looked down to her left.

'Oh, Mr Ashe,' she said, patting her chest lightly to demonstrate her relief that it was him. 'I didn't hear you. My hearing's not what it . . .' She looked from the bedroom door back down to her lodger.

Mr Ashe smiled, and continued to gaze up at her from the bottom of the stairs.

'There's a dreadful knocking sound, Mr Ashe. I didn't know what it was. I thought perhaps you were—'

'It's nothing, Mrs Jones. Come back downstairs. I'll deal with it.'

Bethan found herself frowning slightly. She glanced up at the door of Mr Ashe's room again. 'Of course,' she said finally. 'Thank you, you're so kind.'

Mr Ashe smiled again and, after he reset the power switch, the stairlift descended. Bethan unstrapped herself and accepted his arm as he helped her back into the sitting room. The knocking sound returned as they entered. 'Probably just the pipes, Mr Ashe,' she said. 'My Gethin used to see to all that, you know.'

Mr Ashe helped her onto the sofa. Dandelion jumped back onto her lap.

'I wonder, Mr Ashe, if you'd mind having a look?'

'Of course.'

He inclined his head towards her, then walked towards the door.

'Oh, Mr Ashe!'

'Yes, Mrs Jones?'

'It *is* good to have you back again. Isn't it, Dandelion?'

But Jeremy Kyle was in full flow, and yet again Dandelion failed to reply.

Mr Ashe checked that the sitting-room door was firmly closed behind him. As he crossed the musty hallway, he heard the sound again. He calmly climbed the stairs, inserted his key into the door of his bedroom, and opened it. Standing in the doorway, he observed the source of the knocking.

The boy was where he had left him: his body and legs tied to a ladder-back chair, his hands bound behind his back and with packing tape stuck over his mouth. The bruises on his face were substantially worse than when Mr Ashe had inflicted them – great purple welts, some of them weeping a colourless liquid, like tears. The chair was tied to the ancient yellow radiator on the far wall. At first his abductor couldn't work out how the boy was making this noise. He closed the door behind him and stepped into the room – past the single bed on the left with its patchwork quilt, past the round table bearing his laptop and satellite phone, along with piles of books and documents. Only when he was a few paces away from his prisoner did he see what had happened. The boy had managed to wriggle his left foot out of the rope that had previously bound his ankle. Now, knowing that it was his last chance, he started banging his free foot repeatedly and more rapidly on the floor.

Within twenty seconds Mr Ashe had silenced it, retying the

rope so tightly around the boy's ankle and the chair leg that he whimpered with the pain. Standing back, he examined the child's face. Although he could see the fear in his eyes, he felt a measure of respect that he had tried to raise the alarm. Maybe he was, after all, his father's son.

With a sudden swipe he slapped the back of his hand across the boy's face, making sure to hit an existing welt.

Pulling a chair up to the round table, he sat down and removed his leather-bound copy of the Koran from his coat pocket. He then rearranged some of the books on the table to access a small radio, boxy and bright orange, which he switched on. The radio emitted crackly white noise. He fully extended the aerial, then minutely adjusted the wheel on the side until the white noise subsided somewhat and a male voice became audible. It said a single word – 'Three' – before the white noise returned.

Mr Ashe laid the radio on his laptop and looked back at the boy. The petrified child was staring at him, shaking with fear and pain. Mr Ashe raised one finger to his lips, but otherwise remained expressionless.

Two minutes passed. The male voice returned to the radio.

'Fifty-five. Seven. Three.'

Mr Ashe picked up his Koran. He turned to page fifty-five, then carefully counted down seven lines before reading the third word. It was صَبْر – *sabr*. That made him smile. It meant 'patience'.

He opened the laptop, concentrating hard, deaf now to the white noise of the radio, and switched it on. He did the same to the satellite phone to which it was connected. Even if there had been ordinary internet connectivity in this out-of-the-way location, he would not have used it. The encrypted satellite connection was many times more secure, and without the decryption key, the online conversation he was about to have would be quite meaningless.

A window appeared on the screen, and at the top a blank text-entry box with a flashing black cursor. Below it, a virtual keypad displayed the Arabic alphabet. He used the trackpad to fill in the word رُبْص, then pressed 'enter'. The screen went black. And then, after ten seconds, a line of white text appeared at the top: '*Confirm UK strike to proceed?*'

Mr Ashe stared at the screen. Very slowly he looked over his left shoulder. The boy was watching him. Staring with what was perhaps a foolish lack of understanding. It didn't matter either way. He wouldn't have the opportunity to tell anybody.

'*Repeat: confirm UK strike to proceed?*'

The words appeared for a second time and he sensed his correspondent's impatience coming down the line. He turned his attention to the keyboard. Using his two forefingers, he typed slowly but deliberately: 'C . . . O . . . N . . . F . . . I . . . R . . . M . . . E . . . D'.

He pressed 'enter'. Two seconds later the screen went black again. The connection had been broken remotely.

It was the miaowing of a cat that warned him. Dandelion, on the other side of the door. He glanced up and saw the handle opening slowly. He was still calculating whether he could get to the door quickly enough, when it became academic anyway. It swung open. Dandelion was there. So was Mrs Jones.

She was leaning on her stick, and the stairlift was visible just behind her.

'Fifty-five. Seven. Three.'

Mr Ashe's eyes shot towards the radio and he silently berated himself for not having turned it off and so not hearing the stairlift ascend. He stood up, just as the boy, who was in full view of the old lady at the door, started to make desperate, inarticulate sounds from beneath the tape that covered his lips.

'Mr Ashe . . .' stammered Bethan. Her watery eyes darted between the boy and her lodger. 'I . . . I don't understand . . .'

Mr Ashe remained calm. There was, he knew, nothing to be gained from panicking. Ignoring the boy's helpless noises, he stepped towards the doorway, put his hands on Bethan's shoulders, and encouraged her to turn round.

'But Mr Ashe . . . that . . . that poor boy.'

'There is no boy, Mrs Jones. You're getting confused.'

He closed the door behind them.

'But I saw . . .'

'Sit down, Mrs Jones. I'm sure you'd like a nice cup of hot Ribena.'

'The knocking, Mr Ashe. Was that . . . ?' she asked as she eased herself onto the stairlift.

'You don't need to worry about the knocking any more, Mrs Jones. Let me help you down.'

He pressed the control and the stairlift started to descend, then he followed.

'Mr Ashe!' cried Bethan. 'I'm not strapped in. Mr Ashe! Please stop the chair.'

He did as he was asked.

The old lady was flustered. She looked back up at the open door of the bedroom, from which the boy's muted cries were still audible, but her hands were fumbling for the strap without which she clearly felt so nervous.

'Let me help you,' Mr Ashe said.

Perhaps it was something in his voice that startled her. She stared as though she was looking at him through new eyes. 'There *is* a boy in your room,' she whispered. 'You think I'm confused, but I'm not. I . . . I can still *hear* him.'

He bent down and seized her around the waist. She started to whimper and shake her head. She was tiresome, he thought to himself, but not a complete fool because she seemed to know what was coming.

Mr Ashe spoke very softly, his lips just a couple of inches from her ear. This time, however, his precise English had fallen away, to be replaced by the harsh, guttural accent of his native Arabic. 'You should never forget, old lady,' he whispered, cruelty dripping from his lips, 'to strap yourself in.'

He did it in one movement: a sudden, brutal tug that lifted her up from her seat and knocked her down the stairs. She made a feeble attempt to grab hold of him as she fell, but there was not enough strength in those frail, knotted hands. She tumbled backwards and slid to the bottom of the stairs, her decrepit spine sledging over the edges of the treads. There was a sickening crack as she hit the hallway floor and Mr Ashe could tell, from the thirty-degree angle at which her head was pointing from her body, that her neck had broken with the impact.

There was silence. Even the boy had stopped his pathetic noise. Perhaps he had guessed what had just happened. Perhaps he thought the same fate awaited him.

Mr Ashe left her body where it was. He didn't know how long it would be before anybody found it, but he did know how few visitors Mrs Jones had. She would probably be putrid and maggoty by the time she was discovered. But by then Mr Ashe would be long gone. His tasks would be complete. It was a relief to know that soon he would never have to visit this remote, disgusting house again. It would just be a fading memory to him, much as Mrs Jones, crooked and broken at the bottom of the stairs, was already.

'What do you mean, it's not there any more?'

'Which bit don't you understand? I watched it once, I tried to watch it a second time, it had been taken down.'

'Are you sure?' she said. 'I mean . . .'

'I know what you mean, Eva. You mean, was it really there in the first place? Did I dream it up? The answer's no.'

Joe was staring out of the grimy second-floor window of a tacky bed-and-breakfast place on Dagenham Heathway. An ambulance had screamed by three minutes earlier, and now two police cars, in quick succession, were heading towards Hussein Al-Samara's flat. Eva had protested at the idea of lying low so close to the terrified family of their now-defunct lead, but Joe had overruled her. The owners of places like this, with their damp-ridden walls and cash transactions, were unlikely to ask too many questions of their guests. Besides, Joe hadn't known where else to go.

There was a faint drizzle, but not enough to clear the pavements of pedestrians, or to encourage the busker, who had set up shop by the post office across the road and had been singing 'Yesterday', to pack up his guitar and go home. A bus trundled past with an advertisement for package holidays in Sharm el-Sheikh plastered to the side.

Eva, who was sitting on the edge of the lumpy double bed, looked terrible. Her mousy hair was tangled and greasy, her brown eyes sunken and shady, her lips cracked. Joe was well aware of the haunted expression with which she was looking at him. It wasn't just the violence he'd inflicted on Al-Samara, or the cold, ruthless way he'd stormed out of there without even a word of apology. It was more than that. He could tell she was wondering if the boy she thought she'd known so well when they were young really was a killer after all. He hadn't denied, when she confronted him, that he'd taken out the Arab in Barfield, but he'd refused to answer the questions that followed. How had he done it? Why had he done it? How many other men had he killed in his life? These were questions he would never willingly respond to, no matter who was asking. And in any case, he knew Eva wasn't equipped to deal with the answer.

'If they've got Conor,' she said, 'you *have* to go to the police.'

Joe threw her a dark look over his shoulder and went back to checking out the street below. Eva didn't pursue that line any further.

'How did he tamper with the fingerprint records?' she asked, her voice wavering.

Joe didn't answer, but the question had already occurred to him. Breaking into the prison service system was hard. Whoever he was dealing with had resources – the kind of resources that were hard to come by unless you worked with or for one of the authorities. He knew he'd be hearing from Ashe again. And, when that happened, he would do whatever it took to get Conor back and avenge Caitlin's murder. And if that meant adding another body to his unspoken tally of the dead, so be it.

'Maybe it's got nothing to do with what you saw?' Eva said.

'Maybe.'

'I mean, it's not so strange, is it? Two body bags? Perhaps they shot someone by mistake, and—'

'If they do,' Joe interrupted, 'they don't airlift them out unless they've been told to in advance.' He said it with a note of finality. The truth was, he didn't give a shit about compounds or body bags or US special forces. All he cared about was finding his son.

Eva took the hint. Almost half an hour passed in silence. There were no more sirens outside.

Then Joe turned to look at Eva. 'You don't have to stay with me,' he said.

She stared at him. 'I wish that was true,' she whispered, and she looked down at the brown carpet.

Joe nodded, more to himself than to her. 'I need to check my email again,' he said. 'Let's go.'

Eva stood up, attempted a smile, and made for the door.

'Eva?'

She looked back.

'Thank you,' he said.

She smiled awkwardly, and left the room.

If the owner of the B&B – a sweaty Greek Cypriot with a forest of hair sprouting from the top of his shirt – thought it was odd that they'd only stayed there an hour, he didn't let on. It was that kind of place. Once outside, Joe scanned the immediate vicinity. The busker was now singing 'Streets of London', but his voice was mostly drowned out by the busy traffic. Joe examined the man's face: late forties, greying beard. He didn't *think* anybody could be following him, but busking was a good cover and he mentally recorded that face in case he saw it again. He checked for police vehicles – nothing – then scanned left and right for any sign of surveillance. All he saw was mums with prams and old ladies with headscarves and shopping trolleys, and twenty metres to his right a group of three charity muggers accosting people as they passed.

'Let's go,' he breathed.

He took Eva by the hand. If anyone was looking for him personally, he would be more unobtrusive as one half of a couple. As they walked north up Dagenham Heathway he thought he sensed Eva squeezing his hand ever so slightly. He didn't return the gesture. He didn't want her to get the wrong idea.

The busker's voice faded away, to be replaced by the sound of a drunk couple arguing. The male, mid-twenties, pock-marked, ruddy face, the female hollow-cheeked and with a shaved head. Noted.

Fifty metres from the B&B, they passed a Currys. The shop was devoid of customers and three assistants were hanging around the till. Along the far wall was a bank of televisions, and the three aisles between that back wall and the entrance were filled with laptops and other electronics.

'In here,' Joe said. He let go of Eva's hand and headed for the laptop closest to the entrance.

It didn't take more than about ten seconds for one of the assistants to swoop – a young man with wispy facial hair that needed its first shave. 'You OK, boss?'

Joe jabbed a finger at the laptop. 'Listen, mate, do you mind if I have a quick go on this? I'm thinking of getting one.'

'Good deal on that one, boss. Ends today . . .'

'Is it online?'

'Course it is, boss.' He lingered.

'I'll give you a shout if I need anything, mate.'

The assistant took a couple of steps backwards. 'Course, boss. You just do . . . you know . . . whatever . . .'

But Joe was already navigating towards his Hotmail page. He logged on. He felt his heart stop. A new email was waiting for him. The world around him dissolved into a fog.

He clicked it open.

There was no link this time. No movie to watch, no images to horrify him. Just three sequences of numbers:

110511

0600

51.848612, −5.1223103

He stared at it, vaguely aware that Eva had joined him at the screen.

'What is it?' she whispered.

He didn't immediately answer.

'Joe, what *is* it?'

'Instructions,' he said quietly.

'I don't understand.'

He pointed at the first sequence. 'Tomorrow's date,' he said. 'May 11. Time, 0600 hours.'

'But what about the last numbers?'

'Coordinates,' he said. 'Latitude and longitude.'

'But . . . where?'

Joe navigated to Google Maps, but even as he did so, he was thinking out loud, remembering the details of the YouTube video that was no more. The sea, and the darkness of the sky despite the fact that it had been taken after sunrise. 'The west coast,' he said. 'Somewhere remote.' As he spoke, he tapped in the grid reference. Five seconds later he had zoomed in to a beach on the Pembrokeshire coast. The satellite image was indistinct.

'Joe . . .'

'That's where he is,' he murmured.

Eva tugged on his sleeve. 'Joe . . . *look!*'

He dragged his attention from the laptop. Eva was pointing at the TVs along the back wall. There were about twenty of them, of different sizes and quality, but they all showed the same image.

Him.

Joe's eyes flickered towards the three assistants. They had convened around the till again, and did not appear to have noticed what was on television. The image changed, to be replaced by a female news reporter standing outside the front gates of Barfield.

Calmly but quickly, Joe examined the map in front of him, scanning the surrounding area: the beach, a cliff behind, a single road leading there and a solitary house about a klick inland. His eyes narrowed as he examined that house.

'Joe . . .' Eva sounded desperate.

The nearest village: Thornbridge.

'*Joe!*'

He logged out of his account, then ushered her quickly out of the shop before any of the assistants tried to accost them. 'West Wales,' he said.

'But—'

'We *need* to get there.'

Eva stopped walking, and as Joe turned to look at her, she grabbed his hands and held them tightly. Fiercely. Joe glanced at her watch. Midday. He had eighteen hours. 'Listen to me, Joe,' she said. 'We *can't* do this alone. We've got to tell someone what's happening. We *need* to get help. I know people. I can speak to them . . .'

An old lady trundled along the pavement in an electric mobility vehicle. Her head turned as she passed. Had she recognized him? Or was it just that they were arguing?

'No,' he hissed.

'We *have* to.'

'Eva, even *you're* not sure this isn't in my head. Even *you're* wondering if I made it all up. Hey, I could have done. Abbottabad. Caitlin. The whole fucking thing. What if I really am out of my mind? What if I really am a psycho?'

Eva frowned and shook her head.

'You *know* me,' Joe insisted. 'But who the hell else could I go to that won't just shove me back in a cell and throw away the key?'

Eva had no answer. She just bit her bottom lip. 'What if it's a trap?'

'He killed my wife. He took my son,' Joe replied. Pulling himself away from her grasp, he continued walking along the pavement. He could feel her tearful eyes burning into his back. And he'd only gone ten metres when he heard her footsteps running along behind him, and felt her tugging at his sleeve once more.

'*But what if it's a trap?*' she repeated.

Joe gave her a hard stare. 'Of *course* it's a fucking trap,' he said. 'Come on, we've got a lot to do.'

SEVENTEEN

1300 hours.

There were easier ways than this to get your hands on a weapon, Joe thought to himself. There were contacts he could call. Favours he could pull in. But they involved showing his face. This, he decided, was the better option.

The tower block was the same grey colour as the sky. It was fifteen storeys high, and the side facing him had apartments two abreast, each with a balcony whose front was a dirty orange colour. A covered lobby jutted about five metres out from the block, and inside a bleak, dark, concrete-clad area led to stairs on the left and right.

Joe stood twenty metres from the entrance, on the edge of a small playground where three children clambered over a pyramid-shaped frame, while their mums sat on an adjacent bench, smoking, chatting and ignoring their kids. He was leaning against a lamppost beneath a sign indicating that this was an Alcohol Restricted Area. There was a car park between him and the entrance, about half full of clapped-out old vehicles, three of which had broken windows. A red mail van was just driving away. Joe had watched the postman hurry back to it having made his delivery, evidently keen to be somewhere else.

This was one of the high-rises that had been visible the previous night from their vantage point on the bandstand. He'd been born and brought up in this area. Lady Margaret Road was just a ten-minute walk in an easterly direction, and he had a suspicion that his mother, if she was still alive, lived in one of these blocks. But he wasn't here to visit family, and he hadn't chosen this particular block at random. He'd chosen it because it was, as it always had been, the shittiest, most run-down, god-forsaken spot in the whole of west London. If you weren't a waster or a junkie or a dealer when you first moved here, you would be pretty soon. No other type of person lived here. And even if he hadn't known the reputation of this block that the locals referred to as 'Heroin Heights', he'd have recognized the signs anyway: half the curtains drawn even though it was the middle of the day, several broken windows and all but three of the balconies stuffed full of debris – old mattresses, white goods, you name it. It was a real shithole, largely untouched by the police because they'd given up and it kept all the dregs in one place.

He had spotted the two kids immediately, and recognized them for what they were. One was black, one mixed race. Both were blinged up and wearing reversed baseball caps. They were standing on the north-eastern corner of the block, about ten metres from the entrance. Parked in front of them, two wheels on the pavement, was a black Range Rover with all the trimmings: tinted glass, alloys, the works. The driver's door, which was on the pavement side, was open and it was thumping out heavy gangster rap. There had to be sixty grand's worth of car there. Joe didn't get the impression these boys had saved up their paper-round money to buy it.

He continued to watch them from a distance. There was something about spending time in a war zone that made cunts like this all the more repellent. Ship them from Heroin Heights to the poppy fields of Helmand and they'd lose their attitude shortly before they lost their lives.

Five minutes passed. A thin woman with acne and piercings on her nose sidled up to them and handed the mixed-race kid what Joe assumed was a banknote. The dealer then turned his back on the woman, who shuffled off round the corner and out of sight. No doubt she'd be taking delivery of her purchase elsewhere.

Joe walked across the car park in the direction of the two dealers. They stared coolly at him as he approached. When he reached the Range Rover and slammed the door so the volume of the music faded by half, they stepped up, their faces instantly more aggressive. They were obviously used to people treating them with respect. Joe leaned nonchalantly against the car – it was vibrating with the music – and took in all the information he needed in a single glance. Apart from the colour of their skin, these two were identikit: baggy jeans revealing their boxer shorts, Puffa jackets, white trainers, chunky gold bracelets, maybe seventeen years of age. They stuck out their chins, but he saw the way their eyes flashed sideways at each other. They weren't quite as confident as they liked to make out. The mixed-race kid casually moved his right hand to his back pocket. Joe figured he had a knife. The black boy was digging his nails into his palm.

'Business good, lads?' Joe asked.

Neither of them answered. The mixed-race kid made a hawking sound in the back of his throat, then spat a mouthful of green phlegm in Joe's direction. It spattered against his trousers. Joe looked down at it. Then he looked at the kid.

'Fancy coming a bit closer to do that?' he said.

The kid snorted dismissively, his right hand still in his back pocket, but moving upwards slightly. His eyes darted towards his companion again.

He took two steps forward.

Then Joe made his move.

He was fully expecting the boy to pull the blade – a three-inch flick, small but no doubt sharp – so he was ready for it. As he stepped in the kid's direction, he grabbed the wrist of his raised knife arm. With a brutal yank, he twisted the kid's arm behind his back and forced it upwards until he heard bone splinter. The knife fell to the floor as the kid let out an agonizing scream and his friend scrambled towards the Range Rover. Joe blocked his way, shook his head and watched with satisfaction as both dealers – the injured boy clutching his arm behind his back, howling with pain and cursing – disappeared around the other side of the block in the same direction the junkie had headed. Spinning round, he opened the door of the car and removed the keys from the ignition. The ear-splitting music suddenly cut out. Joe slammed the door and clicked a button on the fob to lock the vehicle, before retrieving the knife from the ground and running over to the entrance of the block.

The lobby, which stank of piss and was littered with cigarette butts and beer cans, was deserted. The walls were plastered with graffiti, and on the left-hand side there was a broken lift, whose door kept trying to click closed, but to no avail. Joe positioned himself at the corner of the entrance. From here he could see the Range Rover twenty metres away, and he also had a clear view left and right of the road in front of the block.

Five minutes, he told himself. It wouldn't take a second longer.

The kids on the corner had been just that. Kids. They were neither old enough nor, underneath the bluster, streetwise enough to be in charge of their little operation. Joe knew how it worked. Stick the foot soldiers on the corners and let them do the dirty work. If the police came calling, they would have the incriminating merchandise or the money. But these enterprises had a hierarchy. Joe would have bet almost anything that the corner boys' boss man would already be on his way to defend his patch. And he wouldn't be doing that with a three-inch flick knife. He'd be altogether better prepared.

The lift clicked. Music from the flats above drifted down. Joe waited.

Three minutes passed. He heard it before he saw it: a screeching of car wheels and the roar of an engine. The vehicle that pulled up in front of the Range Rover was a BMW X5, also black, windows also tinted. And the man who emerged seconds later had murder in his eyes.

Sallow-faced and thin, he had short, bleached-blond hair and wide cheekbones. There was something Eastern European about his features. He had none of the hip-hop bling that the kids wore – just a slightly oversized tracksuit that had the effect of emphasizing his skinny frame. Joe noticed at once, however, that his right hand was tucked inside the zip of his tracksuit top. He might be skinny, but then he didn't have to rely on his strength to get what he wanted.

The man looked round, his eyes wary, clearly looking for whoever had dared to muscle in on his patch. Joe emerged from the shadows of the entrance and, the moment the newcomer observed him, made a clicking sound from the side of his mouth and winked. Then he stepped back into the shadows, his ambush prepared.

He could hear the man's footsteps approaching. They were swift and confident, the footsteps of somebody moving without fear. And Joe knew he was moving without fear because of whatever he had tucked inside his tracksuit. He held the flick knife lightly in his right hand, ready to attack the second he saw him enter the bleak lobby.

No words were spoken. There was nothing to be gained from delaying. The man was carrying a small handgun lazily by his side. Whether he meant to fire it or threaten with it didn't matter. He was armed, which meant he had to be put down. The instant Joe saw him come round the corner he attacked, swiping the knife across the width of his face. Joe felt the blade slice into the flesh at either corner of the man's mouth, and as he whipped it sideways there was a slight, spongy resistance as it cut into his tongue. The explosion of blood was sudden and shocking. It was accompanied by the clattering sound of the weapon falling to the concrete floor. The man threw his hands up to his face, but not before he had screamed loudly, a single word in a language

Joe didn't recognize. That was the worst thing he could have done. As he opened his mouth, the cuts on each corner ripped open like a seam splitting up the side of his face. The flow of blood doubled, and his hands were not nearly equal to the task of staunching it. He staggered back, his face a scarlet mess of horror.

Joe bent down to pick up his gun. It was a Smith & Wesson .38 snubnose – nothing to write home about but serviceable enough. It would fire a round, and that was the important thing. He opened the cylinder release to check it was loaded, then tucked the weapon into the front of his jeans and made sure it was hidden under his lumberjack shirt. Then, leaving his victim, who had sunk to his knees and had at least realized that keeping his mouth shut was a good idea, he walked back out into the open air. Nobody would be shedding a tear that a piece of shit like that had been cut up, and although Joe had hardly taken him on out of good citizenship, he couldn't help feeling grimly satisfied with what he'd just done. No doubt some other twat would grab this corner in the blink of an eye once word got out about what had happened, but that wasn't a reason not to sort the cunts out. You had to keep cutting the heads off the hydra even when they kept on growing back, otherwise the Regiment would have given up on the Taliban months ago.

The Regiment. He'd hardly thought about them since he'd been back in the UK. Had they heard what had happened? Was it being discussed in the squadron hangars of Hereford or ops centres of Bagram, Bastion and Kandahar? Were his mates ready to believe the worst of him? It wouldn't be the first time one of their number had gone bad.

The black corner boy had returned to his position, clearly expecting Joe to have been warned off by the moron with his .38. His eyes widened as he saw Joe emerge unscathed, and for the second time he scrambled out of sight. Joe dug the keys out of his pocket and opened the Range Rover. Should he risk taking it? He reckoned so. The people he was robbing were unlikely to go to the police and besides, they had nothing to link the vehicle to him. At the very worst it would be just another car crime to add to the stats.

As he turned the ignition, the music blared out again. He silenced it, then checked his rear and side mirrors. There was no sign of the man he'd just cut up. Over in the playground, the kids were still playing on the ropes, the mums still ignoring them with no inkling of what had just happened. He removed the handgun from his jeans and laid it carefully in the glove compartment before pulling away, his mind already working through the detailed logistics of his next move, and wondering if Eva had been successful.

'What is it, love? Birthday present for the fella? Into all this stuff, is he? Tell you what, we get them all in here.'

The military clothing store to which Joe had directed her, halfway between Mile End station and Stepney Green and just off the Mile End Road, was empty apart from her and the young man in his mid-twenties who broke off reading the *Sun* behind the counter. The wall behind him was plastered with pictures of short-haired, improbably good-looking men in camouflage gear and with paint smeared artfully on their faces. Eva was no expert, but she was sure they were more familiar with the catwalk than the battlefield.

'Two hundred and fifty, that one.' The young man indicated the helmet she was holding. 'Real McCoy, that. Kevlar, special forces issue. Here . . .' He turned his newspaper back a couple of pages to reveal a full-page spread with the headline '*Inside the top-secret unit that killed bin Laden*'. It accompanied a picture of a soldier in full military gear, each item labelled. The man jabbed a finger at the soldier's head. 'Same thing,' he said. 'Best there is. Full head and neck protection, so unless he's thinking of getting shot in the face . . .'

The man laughed at his own joke as Eva quietly put the helmet on the counter.

'Do you sell body armour?' she asked.

The shop assistant raised an eyebrow, then emerged from behind the counter and led her to an adjoining room, its walls lined with boots and berets. 'Not much call for it,' he said as he showed her a rail from which three chunky blue vests were hanging. 'Just the occasional war reporter, you know, but it's not the sort of thing you end up buying more than once. Anyway, that's why they're all blue. Identifies you as a journalist in a war zone. All good quality, though . . . Osprey Protective . . .' As he spoke, Eva saw his eyes wandering towards the small carrier bag she was carrying, from the top of which an Ordnance Survey map was peeking, the word 'Pembrokeshire' just visible. 'Course,' said the man, 'not much call for them in Welsh Wales, eh? Not unless your bloke's thinking of SAS selection.' He laughed again and, oblivious to Eva's discomfort, rapped his knuckles against one of the vests. 'Good thick ceramic plates . . . the dog's bollocks really, 'scuse my French. Got the elbow and shoulder pads to go with it too . . .'

Eva selected the largest of the three vests. She was surprised how heavy it was, but then she was only used to wearing a stab vest. 'Do you have side plates?' she asked, just as Joe had told her.

The young man looked surprised at the question. He shook his head. 'Like I say, not a lot of call . . .'

'Binoculars?'

'Sure.'

Eva paid with cash, withdrawn, at Joe's instruction, from a hole in the wall while she was still in Dagenham. If things went to shit, it wouldn't do her any good at all if her credit card records had shown her buying these items. But then things going to shit was something Eva didn't really want to contemplate. Had DCI Jacobson reported her little deception of that morning? Her absence from work must have been noted. Were people out looking for her? She was acting as if in a dream, against her better judgement, half of her wanting to run and hide, the other half knowing that she was too far gone for that. She just had to trust that Joe knew what he was doing.

'Hope it's what he wanted,' said the assistant as he handed over the goods.

'Yeah,' Eva murmured as she headed towards the exit. 'Me too.'

The boot of the Range Rover was up. Joe was checking the gear Eva had acquired as he stashed it away carefully.

'Joe,' Eva said. He continued working and didn't even look at her. '*Please* listen to me, I *know* what I'm talking about. If this vehicle is reported stolen, we . . . I mean the police . . . can track it. There's number-plate recognition on every major road.'

'Trust me,' Joe said. 'Nobody's going to report it missing. Did you get the optics?'

'The what?'

'Night-vision goggles.'

Eva shook her head. 'I drained my account, Joe. That was all I could—'

'Forget it. You got the important stuff.' He straightened up and looked round.

It was 6 p.m. The light was failing. Joe and Eva had parked at the crossroads of two residential roads in Wandsworth. A man wearing a suit and a woollen overcoat walked past, clearly intent on getting home. Two schoolkids walking their dog went by in the other direction. Joe slammed the rear door of the Range Rover shut and looked towards the crossroads. 'He lives alone? No girlfriend?'

'As far as I know.'

'Have you ever been in the flat?'

'Once,' Eva replied. Her skin flushed a little. 'We didn't . . .'

'There was no way of getting in through the back?'

Eva gave a helpless little shrug. 'It was dark, Joe. But no, I don't think so.'

'And he's definitely gone away?'

Eva nodded. 'He told me this morning. Spain, I think. Flew at midday. But I don't understand—'

'You're sure he has a bike?'

'Positive, but—'

'Wait here.'

Eva nodded, but as Joe stepped away from the car, she called after him. 'Frank's a nice guy. A friend of mine. Go easy on his place, OK?'

Joe found the motorcycle he was looking for easily enough, parked in the paved front area of number 63 and covered with a grey tarpaulin. Next to it, upturned on its side, was a bike trailer. Other than that, the front yard was empty, save for an old Pot Noodle carton that had blown in. A set of raised steps to his left led up to the ground- and first-floor flats, but the basement flat had a separate iron staircase. Once Joe had descended this, he was out of sight of the road in a gloomy, poky little entrance area. There was no light from the front window of the basement, and the curtains were shut. He knocked on the front door. It rattled slightly in its frame. Ill-fitting, Joe noted. Easier to barge down. After looking up to check he wasn't being overlooked, he took a step back, then rammed his shoulder against the door. He felt a little give. Ramming it for a second time, he heard the crack of a mortise lock splintering out of its cavity. A third barge and he was in.

He didn't enter straight away, but walked casually up the stairs to check nobody had been alerted by the noise. A woman walked past, white earphones plugged in, and didn't even seem to notice him.

The flat was tiny. There was a small kitchenette in one corner and crockery was upturned on the draining board. Clothes littered the floor. Eva's colleague Frank – was that what she'd said he was called? – was a messy bloke. At first Joe thought that might make it more difficult to locate his bike keys, but then he saw a leather jacket slung over the side of an armchair. He rummaged in the pockets and found a Yamaha key ring with two keys attached.

He stepped into the bedroom. It was even untidier. Eva had said that this bloke was about the same size as him, so Joe quickly scouted through clothes strewn over the floor and double bed. He selected a hooded top and, after poking around in a half-open drawer, a navy-blue snood. He hadn't been in the flat for more than ninety seconds before he was hurrying back up the steps, clutching the keys and the clothes.

Eva was sitting in the passenger seat of the Range Rover, chewing anxiously on her fingernails. 'Was he there?' she asked as Joe climbed in behind the wheel and started the engine.

He shook his head. 'I broke in. What is he, a boyfriend?'

'I told you, he's just a friend.' Eva said quickly.

They were pulling up outside the flat where the bike was parked when she spoke again. 'I still don't understand why we need Frank's bike. Can't we just use this thing?' She hit the dashboard of the Range Rover, frustration suddenly bursting out of her. She bit her lip and looked out of the passenger window. 'Can't you just let me call my colleagues? If they think Conor's been abducted, they'll be all over the place like a rash.'

'No!' Joe snapped, and instantly regretted it. Eva didn't have to be here, he reminded himself. She was risking as much as he was. Maybe more. But time was running out. He could explain once they were on the road. He jumped out of the Range Rover, ran up to the front of the house, pulled the bike trailer to the back of the stolen vehicle and attached it to the rear. After pulling off the grey tarp, he wheeled the bike onto the trailer. Once he had secured it, he got back in the Range Rover and eased out into the road, aware of the troubled stare Eva was giving him.

'Listen,' he said as he glanced in the rear-view mirror. 'I don't know who this Ashe guy is working for. Maybe it's Al-Qaeda, maybe the Americans. But we do know this: he doesn't care who he kills to get at me.' He paused. 'You didn't see Caitlin's body, Eva. You didn't see the look in her eyes . . .' He couldn't bring himself to say it, and he found himself breathing deeply just to calm his nerves. 'He *will* kill Conor if I don't stop him,' he continued after thirty seconds. 'If we call the police, they'll go in like a bull at a fucking gate and that's what'll happen.'

'You don't *know* that.'

'I won't risk it.' He breathed deeply to calm down. 'We have to think like him,' he said. 'Why has he chosen that precise location for the RV? I checked the satellite imagery when we were online. It's a remote beach with a high cliff behind it. *He* could hide anywhere; *I'll* be in plain sight. That's good for him and bad for us. But wherever he is now – right now – he has to transport Conor to the RV. That means moving him out into the open.' Joe felt his jaw clenching. 'I saw Conor's face on the video, Eva. It's bruised and cut. He was crying. Transporting a child in that state is dangerous. Our man won't want to move him far, so I think he's already close to the RV point, somewhere nobody else is likely to see them. The video I saw was taken in a house that faced west out to sea. The mapping I checked online showed a solitary house about a kilometre inland from the RV. So far as I can tell, there are no other dwellings for four klicks in any direction.'

'So what are you saying?' Eva asked in a small voice.

'That if he wants to lure me to that beach, he's holding Conor in that house. I'd bet anything on it. And I need to get there before they leave for the RV.' He glanced at the Range Rover's clock: 1820 hours. 'I think it will take us five to six hours to get to the coast,' he said. 'We'll be approaching at midnight. There's only one road leading to the house, and it slopes down towards it in full view. If I was him, I'd be watching that road. That's why we need the bike. The map shows a bridleway that circles the

278

house and approaches it from behind. It's a very long way round from where we can safely park this thing without being seen from the house – four or five miles – but the bike will cover it quickly. I can take it off road and approach from a direction he won't be expecting, then make the final approach by foot. That way I'll catch up with him before he has time to set up an ambush.'

Eva was quiet for a few minutes as Joe negotiated his way onto the South Circular.

'Joe,' she said at last, 'remember when your dad went to prison?'

He didn't answer.

'Nobody talked to you about it, but behind your back they hardly talked about anything else.'

'What are you trying to say?'

'You're in trouble. We both are. We can't run for ever. When they catch up with you, maybe – *maybe* – you can persuade them about Caitlin. *Maybe* you can persuade them that the guy you . . . the guy in prison . . . was self-defence. But can't you see what it *looks* like? You're leaving a trail of bodies everywhere you go.' She gave him a piercing look. 'You can't kill him, Joe,' she whispered. 'I won't *let* you.'

Joe felt his eyes flicker involuntarily to the glove compartment where his stolen weapon was stashed.

'Mr Ashe and I have a few things to discuss,' he said. 'That's all.'

He looked at the Range Rover's clock again. Less than twelve hours till the RV. He fixed his eyes on the road ahead, and drove.

EIGHTEEN

It was a largely silent journey. The Range Rover's satnav blinked monotonously as they ate up the M4. A full moon rose. Joe wondered how much light it would give him when they reached Pembrokeshire.

Around 1930 hours the traffic on the motorway suddenly slowed down. Glancing in the rear-view mirror, Joe saw a flashing blue light; seconds later there was a siren. He checked his speed – 65 mph – and pulled into the left-hand lane. Eva said nothing, but he could feel her tension. It was a relief when the car sped past. A minute later they crawled past the scene of an accident, with two ambulance crews and four police cars parked on the hard shoulder. Joe just kept a steady speed. 'They've got no reason to stop us,' he told Eva. She didn't reply.

At 2100 hours Joe turned on the radio and tuned into the news. He was the lead item. *'Following the escape of Sergeant Joseph Mansfield from Barfield Prison in London, the leader of the opposition has criticized the Coalition's "laissez-faire attitude to issues of public safety". Sergeant Mansfield, recently returned from Afghanistan, was being held in custody following the brutal murder of his partner. Police are advising that he is highly dangerous and possibly unstable, and that members of the public should not approach him under any circumstances . . .'*

It was Eva who turned off the radio. They continued in silence.

Joe used the last of the money he had taken from Eva's cash

box to buy petrol just beyond Reading and to pay the toll at the Severn Bridge. The further west they travelled, the more the traffic thinned out. But any speed a clear road might have offered them was cancelled out by the mist. It was barely noticeable at first, just a thin, wispy film in front of the windscreen. By 2200 hours, however, it felt as though they were surrounded, as though an army of ghosts was following them wherever they went. The mist swirled in the beam of the headlights, like a thick barrier.

A barrier between Joe and his son.

It was just gone 2300 hours when they entered Pembrokeshire. The roads became smaller. The red dot on the satnav approached the blue of the sea.

Joe looked at the time: 2330 hours. Six and a half hours till RV. Thirty metres ahead, the silhouette of an old church emerged from the mist, the clock face on its steeple glowing palely in the night like a second moon. Joe slowed down. The church was on their right. On the other side of the road was a small car park. He saw as he turned in that there were no other vehicles. It looked like the starting location for a country walk, but nobody was venturing out at this time of night and in this weather.

Nobody except Joe.

'You got the map?' he asked when he'd pulled over, positioned the car so that it was facing the exit again, and killed the lights.

Eva handed it over. Once he'd opened it out in front of him, it took Joe seconds to locate their position on the map with the interior light. They were two klicks, he estimated, from the house that was his destination. He studied the contour lines carefully. The road on which they were travelling was about to head uphill. Once they reached the brow, there was a direct line of sight from the house towards the road that led to it, in a westerly direction. Even if they travelled without the help of headlights, they would be completely visible to anybody watching them with the right kind of equipment: the warmth of the engine would burn brightly on any thermal-imaging equipment and NV capability would light them up like a fucking Christmas tree.

The bottom line was this: they could go no further in the Range Rover.

He turned to Eva. 'You'll be all right here?' he asked.

She looked around anxiously into the blanket of dark mist. Joe switched off the interior light. 'Keep it dark,' he said, 'otherwise you'll be blind. Keep the doors locked and the keys in the ignition. If anyone approaches you, head back the way we came. Don't worry about me.'

'What if you don't come back?'

'I will come back.'

'But what if you *don't*?'

Joe reached over her, opened up the glove compartment and removed the weapon. 'I will.'

Frank's bike was nothing special – a Yamaha TW, its tyres worn almost smooth by constant city driving – and it was certainly not designed to be driven offroad. He'd have to take it carefully to avoid a blowout, but he'd do that anyway: moving slowly, keeping the revs low in order to make as little noise as possible. Not easy, when he wanted to get to the house as fast as possible. To get to Conor. Ashe would definitely try to move him under cover of darkness. The question was, how long before the 0600 RV would he do it? Had Joe arrived in time?

He reversed the bike off its trailer, then examined the OS map again. He'd be heading north across a field for two klicks before coming to a bridleway that would take him through a forested area over the brow of the hill. From there, he hoped, he would be able to see the house – or not, according to the thickness of the fog. But he would need to follow the bridleway down the hill and three miles in a westerly direction, past the house and up to the clifftop by the coast, before heading south for a mile. The bridleway passed approximately half a mile to the west of the house – close enough for the bike's engine to be heard if the wind was in the wrong direction. He would decide whether to cover that final stretch on the bike or by foot when he was on the ground.

Eva had moved into the driver's seat. Her hands were resting on the steering wheel as if she was intending to drive away immediately. Joe gave her what he hoped was a reassuring nod. He heard the central locking click shut and started the Yamaha. It coughed unhealthily into life, but then he heard a sound from the Range Rover. He turned to see Eva opening the door again. 'Joe,' she said. 'I hope he's—'

'He's going to be fine,' Joe replied grimly. He had to believe that, otherwise nothing else mattered. With the bike's headlight switched off, he increased the throttle and moved away.

The field across which he needed to travel to reach the bridleway was located on the opposite side of the church. It meant manoeuvring the bike across a churchyard crowded with tombstones that seemed to jump out at him from the mist. Joe kept his attention fully fixed on the ground ahead. Within a couple of minutes, he came to the perimeter of the churchyard, where a metal gate, tied shut with a length of frayed rope, marked the edge of the field. Joe untied it, opened the gate and passed through. He left the rope untied: he might need to pass through this way again.

The ground was bumpy. Treacherous. It was beginning to freeze. Joe pushed the bike as hard as he dared, rebalancing himself every time it slipped. His visibility was no more than ten metres – the moon was little help. Beyond that, he was aware of bulky forms moving in the field. Cows, he presumed, or horses. The bike's low rumble kept them away.

It felt like it took longer than it should to cross the field and reach the bridleway, half his mind on Conor, the other half on the terrain. In reality it was probably no more than the ten minutes he had estimated. There was a second gate on the opposite edge of the field. Joe passed through it and headed up an equally bumpy track at a steep, 25 per cent gradient. Two minutes later he had travelled what he knew from his study of the map to be about a third of a mile – 500 metres or so – and emerged from the mist as he reached the top of the hill.

He dismounted before he reached the brow itself, laying the bike on its side and crawling up to his vantage point. The ground was hard and cold. From this location, looking west towards the shore, Joe could see that the mist, although thick, was patchy and low-lying. It appeared to glow in the yellow light of the hazy full moon, almost like snow. He couldn't make out where land met sea, but he could discern the lights of a ship out on the water. The rim of the hill on which he was standing ran north to south. He couldn't see the road he and Eva had been follow-ing, but his mental snapshot told him that it forked after about 100 metres. The right fork headed to the top of the cliff, the left fork to a lone house.

And it was this that he could just about make out now.

The house lay, he estimated, about three klicks to the south-west, at approximately ten o'clock from his current position. He used the binoculars to focus in on the house. The magnification was high, the field of view narrow. Normally that wouldn't be a problem, but tonight his hands were shaking. He had to concen-trate hard on making them still before he could get a proper look.

There were no lights on – not, at least, on the northern or eastern sides of the house. But then he remembered that the video he had watched had been shot in a room overlooking the sea. If, as he suspected, it had been taken in this house, that meant it was on the far western side, out of view from this pos-ition. He could see the front entrance, and tried to see if there were any vehicles parked outside. But the night was too dark and the binos too weak to make out that kind of detail. After thirty seconds the mist rolled in and obscured the whole of the ground floor from his view, leaving just the steep roof peeping out from above the white blanket.

He cursed under his breath. He'd been hoping for some indication that Conor was definitely there. His boy's face swam before his eyes, cut, bruised and terrified. With a pang, it hit him that his expression in the video was not so different from the one on his face when Joe stormed into his bedroom and tore his Xbox from the TV. He felt like throwing all this stealth out of the window and storming in a direct line down to the house to rip Conor from this bastard's clutches as soon as humanly possible. But his military training told him that would be the worst thing to do. He needed to approach unseen.

And he couldn't waste time. The mist would now be compromising the view of anyone watching from the house, so he took the opportunity to crest the hill and drop quickly to the west, keeping to the bridleway. Back on lower ground, the mist engulfed him again. He could see no landmarks, nothing with which to get his bearings. After ten minutes he estimated that he was directly north of the house, but his reckoning must have been off because two minutes later he had to brake as a sheer clifftop appeared with heart-stopping suddenness just five metres in front of him. He swung the bike round to the south and followed the bridleway along the clifftop, stopping after a couple of hundred metres to check the wind direction. It was onshore, blowing out to sea. He estimated that he could risk another 200 metres before ditching the bike and approaching on foot.

From there, it would be just half a klick cross-country to where Conor was surely being held.

He crawled along at less than 5 mph, to keep the noise of the bike's engine as low as possible. He could hear the sea crashing to his right, and a lone gull called somewhere in the darkness overhead.

To the left of the bridleway there was half-a-metre-high

bracken. Joe used it to hide the bike on its side. He ran east, away from the clifftop, along a mud path through the bracken and into an area of rough grassland. Fifty metres away, the house emerged from the mist.

No lights. Was his man sleeping? Joe doubted it.

His heart was thumping. He could hear his pulse as he advanced.

Halfway to the house there was a picket fence, but it was collapsing in places and Joe passed through a gap. He registered a tumbledown wooden shed five metres to his left, and a bleak concrete garage almost adjoining the right-hand wing of the house. Most of his attention, however, was on the two windows on the first floor. The curtains were open, but inside all was dark. Was Conor holed up in one of those rooms? Was that where his son was being held?

Joe removed the handgun from his shoulder bag. Then he approached the back door of the house, treading absolutely silently: toe first, then heel. He couldn't afford to make a single sound. A single stumble or broken twig.

Even his breathing was, despite his exertion, noiseless.

A sudden, clattering noise in front of him. Movement.

He froze, three metres from the door, his weapon at the ready. *What the hell was happening?*

Then he exhaled slowly. It was a cat, bursting through a flap at the bottom of the door. Its eyes glinted in the darkness as it stared directly at him. As Joe took another step forward, the cat turned tail and headed back into the house.

Joe glanced up to the first-floor window. No light. No movement. Nothing. The paint on the back door was gleaming in the moonlight. He moved quietly to the door, then slowly reached out his free hand and grasped the handle. He twisted it gently so as not to let it squeak or scrape.

It opened. Did that mean someone was here? Probably.

Inside it was even darker than out. Having silently shut the door behind him, he waited a moment for his eyes to grow accustomed to the lack of moonlight. It took him twenty seconds to realize he was in a small utility room that led into a kitchen. There was a strange smell, and it wasn't just the musty aroma of neglect. It was something else. A smell he recognized: sickeningly sweet. It grew stronger as he passed through the kitchen and along a narrow corridor that led to what was clearly the front hallway.

He had been expecting to see a body, so the sight of a crumpled human frame at the bottom of the steps was not a surprise. The cat was prowling around it. It miaowed, and that one sound seemed to echo around the house. Joe took a couple of steps closer. The strongest smell now was of shit: the corpse's bowels had loosened after death.

Don't let it be Conor, his mind was crying out. *Don't let it be Conor . . .*

He bent down in the darkness to examine the corpse's face.

It was an old lady. Her eyes were wide open, her expression terrified. A sticky, mucus-like substance had oozed from her nose and ears. Joe estimated that she had been dead for less than a day. Maybe she had accidentally fallen down the stairs. Or maybe – he noted that the stairlift was halfway up the staircase – she hadn't.

He stopped stock-still and listened. But there was nothing to listen to, other than silence.

Stepping over the body, he started to climb the stairs. His eyes were firmly fixed on the door at the top and to the left. It was slightly ajar.

The cat miaowed again. Joe froze. Had something disturbed it?

No sound.

He continued to climb.

At the top of the stairs he stopped. His finger was resting lightly on the trigger of his handgun. His breathing was shallow and silent. Slowly, he extended his right foot and gently kicked the door open.

By the misty moonlight shining through the windows, Joe immediately recognized the place. The video he had seen was burned on his memory. There, against the far wall, was the bed on which Conor had been sitting. On the wall behind it, a picture, its details obscured by the darkness, but Joe knew that if he looked more closely it would show a ship in a storm. His eyes panned round the room. There was a table in the middle, piled high with books. Boxes were piled up in corners and against the walls. The room was chaotic.

And it was clear nobody was at home.

Joe stepped over to the bed. Something had caught his eye. He bent down and picked it up off the blanket: a small, grey elephant, patched up and the worse for wear.

He flung the toy down on the ground, hissing with frustration. *There was nobody here*. Less than six hours till the RV that was only a couple of klicks away. Was it really likely that they'd already set out?

Joe raced through the rest of the house – two more bedrooms upstairs, a large sitting room and a fourth bedroom on the ground floor. He knew it was pointless. He knew the house was deserted apart from him, an old lady's body and a restless cat. Back in the room where Conor had been held he was almost careless enough to switch on the light. He stopped himself at the last second: if he could observe the place from afar, anybody could. And if Conor's abductor had even an inkling that events were not unfolding as he had planned, that could only be bad for the boy. He stalked round the room, seeking anything that might help him. It was only thanks to the moonlight streaking in through the window that he saw it.

The passport was in plain view, sitting atop one of the piles of books on the round table. On the front it had the words 'United States of America'. Joe examined the identification page. There was no mistaking the features of the man in the photograph. Joe had seen that face once before. Until now he had been unable to recall its features, but as it stared out of the passport at him, he was transported back to the visiting room at Barfield.

This was him. Mr Ashe.

But the name on the passport was Mahmood Ashkani.

Only two thoughts spun around Joe's head. Two simple statements of fact.

First: the Middle Eastern man who had abducted his son held an American passport.

And second, if he wanted to see Conor again, the only option open to him was to turn up at the RV tomorrow at 0600 hours. At which point, Mr Ashe, or Mahmood Ashkani, or whoever the fuck he *really* was, would undoubtedly try to kill him.

Eva was shivering with cold.

For ten minutes after Joe had left, she'd kept one hand on the key in the ignition. Now she was hugging herself to keep warm. More than once she found herself glancing at the door, checking that the central locking was on. She didn't know quite what she was scared of. But she was scared.

One seventeen. She was dazzled by the sight of a single headlight turning at high speed into the car park. She fumbled for the keys, one arm covering her eyes to block out the brightness, but then the light disappeared and she could just make out Joe, jumping off the bike and letting it fall to one side. A fist on the driver's window, and he was shouting: 'Open up!'

Eva had released the lock before she registered that Joe had returned alone. She twisted round as she heard Joe opening the rear door. His face was illuminated by the small internal light, and the look on it chilled her. 'What happened?' she asked. 'Where's Conor? Joe, what *happened*?'

When he didn't answer she opened the driver's door and ran round to the back of the vehicle. Joe had pulled out the body armour and was examining the Kevlar helmet. She grabbed his right arm but he shrugged her off.

'I was too late,' he spat. 'They've already left.'

'Are you sure it was the right place?'

He nodded. 'Conor was there.'

'So what are we going to do?'

'The only thing I can do,' Joe said. 'Turn up.' He started to pull on the body armour.

Eva peered nervously at him. 'Joe, you *can't*,' she said. 'He'll try to—'

'*What do you want me to do, Eva?*' he shouted. '*He's got my son!*'

'But—'

Joe put one hand to his forehead and paused for a moment, clearly trying to calm himself down after his outburst. Eva noticed that his hand was shaking, and she had to fight a sudden urge to put her arms round him.

'If I lose Conor,' Joe said, in a low voice that was on the verge of cracking, 'I lose everything. I'll have nothing left in the world.'

He wasn't even looking at Eva when he said it, so he could have had no idea of the effect the blunt truth of his words had on her.

'Wait,' she said.

He turned towards her.

She pointed at the body armour. 'How safe is it?'

'Depends on the round, distance, trajectory,' he said. 'He'll try to take me out from the clifftop, I reckon. It'll protect my vital organs, keep me alive to go after them. Probably.'

Eva nodded. She remembered how, when they were younger, Joe would do anything to keep her from harm. She remembered the look on his face when he told her that Conor had been abducted.

'Give it to me,' she said.

NINETEEN

0330 hours.

Mahmood Ashkani, aka Mr Ashe, aka any number of other names at different times and different places around the world, would be glad to get rid of the boy. Ashkani knew that he had a gift for terror. It was not surprising the boy should be scared. He had gone to very great lengths to ensure it. But to be encumbered by someone so silently helpless was wearisome. And his frail, child's mind was so damaged by what he had been exposed to that really he would be better off dead.

The grey light of dawn was still two hours away. The only light came from a street lamp ten metres to his right and it was further dimmed by the thick layer of condensation that covered the window of his grey Peugeot, parked in the car park at Thornbridge station. The first train would not leave here for another hour, so he knew the place would be deserted for as long as he needed it. The boy was in the back seat. Ashkani hadn't bothered to bind his hands. The child didn't seem to know where he was, or who he was. He just stared into space, never speaking, never moving.

Ashkani's left hand lightly touched the laptop that lay on the passenger seat. His fingertips brushed against the satellite phone resting on top of it, and against a 4GB data stick.

At 5.10 a.m. the headlights of a second car filled the rear-view mirror. It parked to the left of Ashkani. The driver exited and Ashkani gathered up the computer, phone and data stick so that the man could sit beside him. The newcomer looked not unlike Ashkani. He was a similar age and build, with black hair and dark skin. But he had a harsher, crueller face. The lack of lines around the side of his mouth did not make him look younger. It just made him look as though he seldom smiled.

'Do you really think he's coming?' The newcomer spoke in Arabic.

Ashkani sniffed, then replied in the same language: 'I killed his wife. I kidnapped his son.' Turning to look at the other man, he asked: 'Do you really think he's *not*?'

'I would have expected him to call the police.'

'I have eyes and ears among the police. He has spoken to nobody.'

This reassurance seemed to be good enough for the other man.

'You understand what you need to do?' asked Ashkani.

'It won't be a problem.'

Ashkani failed to stop a wave of annoyance entering his voice. 'If I knew it wasn't going to be a problem,' he said, 'I would not have insisted upon my best marksman. This man is good at staying alive. Do not underestimate him.'

'The reason I am your best marksman is because I underestimate nobody.' A pause. '*You* will be . . . ?'

'I will be where I need to be.'

'It is happening then? Today?'

Ashkani nodded almost imperceptibly. 'The British soldier and his son must not survive this morning. You would not wish to deny the Lion his final roar?' As he said this, he fiddled absentmindedly with the data stick.

The other man looked over his shoulder. His expression, when he looked at the boy, was one of contempt. 'Does he never speak?'

'Sometimes. When forced. He won't give you any trouble. He doesn't know what's going on.'

'Good. I will take him now.'

Ashkani nodded. 'Don't let him out of your sight.'

'I can't have him with me when I—'

'*Don't* let him out of your sight.'

'Whatever you say.'

Ashkani did not expect the boy to make any fuss when he was removed from the back seat and transferred to the other car, and he wasn't disappointed. The child said nothing. He still didn't even seem aware that anything was happening. Not that it mattered to Ashkani any more. He wound down the passenger window and looked out at the other man when he'd bundled the boy into the back of his car. 'I want to know when it is done,' he said.

The other man nodded, before climbing into the car, closing the door and driving off. Ashkani waited for five minutes, then he too drove from the station car park. Commuters would start arriving soon and besides, he had somewhere else to be.

Ashkani's marksman drove slowly, westwards towards the coast. He wanted to be there early and if he could set up his position when the light was still dim, so much the better. As he drove, he cursed the mist that seemed to cling to this country. He had not wanted to say so in front of Ashkani, but it made things a great deal more difficult. Still, he had done difficult jobs before, and he had never failed yet.

He looked in the mirror at the kid. There was something unnatural about him, the way his pale face simply gazed into the middle distance, the way his silence seemed to fill the whole car. He considered disobeying Ashkani, gagging the kid and leaving him in the boot. He thought better of it. Ashkani was not a good man to disobey. But the sooner this morning was over, the better.

The marksman had already decided that he would not park the car at the clifftop car park, but would drive it out of sight down an old dirt road about a kilometre from the coast. He and the boy would then walk to the firing point under cover of darkness. He had already chosen, too, the precise location from which he would take the shot. The beach itself was 500 metres wide and the part of the cliff that overlooked it was covered in vigorous bracken, almost a metre high and stretching back about 100 metres from the edge of the cliff. There were many channels in the bracken – made mostly by walkers and children playing hide and seek, he supposed – and that was to his advantage. It meant nobody could tell what path he had taken through it to the cliff's edge. And because the bracken extended all the way to the edge, he could overlook the beach and remain completely hidden, except for the barrel of his rifle peeking out, which nobody would be able to see in poor light and at a distance. Ordinarily he would have found some way to set up a ribbon on the beach to tell him which way the wind was blowing. On this occasion it was not necessary: the safety flag, there to indicate how safe or dangerous the sea was on a given day, would do the job for him.

Getting the boy out of the car was simple. Forcing him a kilometre cross-country was less so. He tripped and stumbled, falling helplessly to his knees on three occasions, and once flat on his face. Each time, the man pulled him up by his hair, thinking that the pain would make him stand more quickly. But the boy didn't even seem to feel it. He said nothing. He didn't complain, howl, or gasp. He just pushed himself slowly up and continued at his own pace.

It was four thirty by the time they reached the cliff's edge. He pushed the boy to lie down and kicked his knee when he didn't respond. But once he was down, prostrate on the cold ground, he didn't move. He just shivered. The man eyed him suspiciously for a moment. It was all very well for Ashkani to believe that the kid was beyond causing problems, but he preferred to be sure. From his rucksack he pulled a length of rope. He tied the boy's limp hands behind his back and bound his ankles together using the other end of the same piece. The boy didn't struggle or complain.

The marksman turned his attention to the other contents of his rucksack. First, a satellite phone, which he laid on the ground next to him. Then his sniper rifle – a Galil .308 with a full magazine of tuned, match-grade rounds – which was separated into five sections. He could have slotted them together blind-folded – indeed, he had practised doing so many times in the past – so the darkness was not an obstacle for him. In less than a minute the rifle was assembled, its magazine of five 7.62mm rounds firmly clicked into place. He unfolded a small bipod, placed it on the edge of the bracken, and rested the barrel of the rifle on it. Lying on his front behind the weapon, he closed his left eye and looked through the sight.

It was still dark and the mist was thick, yet he could just make out the individual waves crashing onto the beach. He estimated the distance between his firing point and the sand at about 350 metres. Close enough for a swift, clean kill.

He looked over his shoulder. The boy was still lying on the ground. Still shivering. Still silent. It crossed his mind that he should kill him now, but Ashkani had been quite clear: the boy would only cease to be useful once his father was dead. The marksman looked at his watch. Four fifty-six: that gave the kid just over an hour to live.

0558 hours.
The gulls that had flocked on the flat, sandy beach had predicted the arrival of dawn. Their chorus had lasted for a full half-hour. There hadn't been a particular moment when night had become morning. The sky had just grown almost imperceptibly lighter. The marksman lay very still, watching, waiting. There was a weak offshore wind. It blew the safety flag almost exactly in the marksman's direction. He checked the direction of the spray, to make sure it matched up with the wind direction further from

the ground. It did. He would wait until his target was positioned on a straight line between the rifle and the flag. It would make the shot more accurate because he would then not have to adjust for the altered trajectory of the round.

It was the gulls, too, that announced the arrival of the target. The marksman became aware of crowds of them flocking up from the sands at the northern end of the beach, shrouded by the mist and screeching loudly.

The figure came into view at 0600 hours exactly.

At first he was just a vague darkening of the mist 200 metres to the north, the shapeless form gradually developing a human frame as the gulls screeched and flew away from him. He was walking slowly, his head bowed, his hands stuck into the pockets of his hooded top. His frame was bulky – barrel-chested, almost – and although the hood he was wearing obscured his features, the marksman had the impression that his gait was slow and ponderous. Almost as if he knew he was walking to his death.

'*Do not underestimate him,*' Ashkani had said. The marksman didn't. He examined every facet of the man's movement. Something wasn't right. Why was he not looking around? If he was here to see his son, why was he not searching for him?

Perhaps he was not so impressive as Ashkani had predicted.

Or perhaps he thought that if he sacrificed himself, his son would be set free. A foolish thought, but the marksman knew that, at times of stress, a person's decision-making could lose clarity.

The figure continued to walk at a slow, steady pace. He was ten metres from the line of fire.

Five metres.

Three.

The marksman's fingers brushed the cold metal of the trigger.

Two metres.

One.

The target stopped.

He turned round, peered out to sea and stood there immobile. Some of the gulls he had disturbed had settled on the sand again, and he was surrounded by them. The marksman experienced a moment of doubt. If this man was here to find his son, why was he not looking around? But he put that thought from his mind – Ashkani's instructions had been very clear – and adjusted his line of fire by the fraction of a degree necessary to get the target in the centre of his sight. The edge of his body was slightly ill defined because of the mist, but he placed his crosshairs over the centre of the target's back: a location as deadly as the head, but broader and therefore easier to hit.

He heard a whimper from the boy: the first sound that had escaped his lips since the marksman had taken possession of him. It was almost as though he knew his father was about to die.

Which he was.

The marksman squeezed the trigger.

The retort of the rifle echoed over the vast expanse of sea and air. The gulls that had congregated on the sand flocked up into the sky with a single mind, and a sudden, frightened squawk.

And the target crumpled, instantly, to the ground.

The gunman watched the body. He didn't know why. Something told him he should. Its head was pointing out to sea, and as the waves swelled towards the beach, the water lapped against it. A seagull settled on the body, and then another. To them, the corpse was clearly as still and solid as a rock.

The marksman lowered his gun. His fingers felt for the satellite phone at his side and, for the first time since arriving at the firing point, he rose to his feet. He stood a metre from the edge of the cliff, looking out to sea. Without the aid of the sight on his rifle, the body on the beach was just an indistinct lump. Further out, he could see the grey outline of an oil tanker. The breeze was a little stiffer now, and it blew his black hair away from his face as he called a number, which rang only once before it was answered.

'Well?' came Ashkani's voice in Arabic.

'It's done.'

'Good. See to the boy and do not contact me again.'

'Wait!'

'What is it?'

A pause.

'*Allahu Akbar*,' said the marksman.

'*Allahu Akbar*,' Ashkani replied.

The line went dead.

The marksman stared at the digital display for a brief moment. He thought of Ashkani. Thought of what he was about to do. '*You would not wish to deny the Lion his final roar?*' he had said. No indeed. A picture rose in his mind: a thin, weak old man, wrapped in a blanket as he watched television in a shabby room in a compound far away in Pakistan. That was the image his killers wanted to present of the Sheikh al-Mujahid, but his last act would strike fear into the heart of the West.

Then he saw the briefest glint of something reflected in the screen.

He had no way of knowing what it was. No way of recognizing the checked lumberjack shirt or the expression of purest menace. And no way of defending himself as the figure marched relentlessly towards the edge of the cliff, his arm outstretched, a handgun in his fist as, having located the marksman, he strode close enough to ensure a single round from that weapon would serve its purpose.

The marksman closed his eyes. The flicker of a smile played across the corners of his lips. He had been beaten. He did not mind. He had always known that Paradise would come earlier to him than to others who did not fight the *jihad*.

He heard the gunshot from three metres behind, and felt the round enter the back of his neck and become lodged in the gristle at the front of his throat. He felt the sudden impact pushing him forward. He might not have toppled quite so soon if the heel of a shoe hadn't jabbed him hard in the small of his back. As it was, he experienced the sudden weightlessness of freefall less than a second after he had been shot. As he fell, the breeze that had blown his hair back from his face slammed his body against the side of the cliff and it was the impact of this that finally knocked the life from him. He was dead seconds before he crashed onto the rocks below.

Joe watched him fall.

The sound of the body's final impact did not reach him at the top of the cliffs. There was just the wind in his ears and the hissing of the waves against the sand. From the back pocket of his jeans, Joe pulled the American passport in the name of Mahmood Ashkani and threw it after its owner. By the time it had hit the ground, he was kneeling next to his son, untying the ropes that bound him and rolling him over onto his back.

'Conor?' he breathed.

The boy's face, pale and bruised, stared back blankly.

He checked Conor's vital signs. His pulse was weak, his breathing shallow. Every limb was trembling. There was a cut on his lip that looked like it had become infected. But it wasn't his physical state that made fear rise in the back of Joe's throat. It was his mental condition. It wasn't just that he didn't recognize his own father: he didn't seem to be aware of anything at all.

Joe scrambled the three metres back to the cliff's edge. His eyes narrowed as he saw the motionless form of Eva down below, wrapped in Kevlar and body armour and wearing the clothes Joe had stolen along with the bike.

She wasn't moving.

Joe quickly detached the sight from the dead man's sniper rifle and used it to zoom in on her. The tide was lapping around her head. Two seagulls had settled on her body. Although it was difficult at this distance to be sure, Joe thought he could make out a dark patch, about the size of his hand, on her hooded top. And he knew what that meant.

Icy dread crashed over him. He looked from his oldest friend to his son. Had he sacrificed one for the other?

He shoved the sight in his shoulder bag, quickly dismantled the sniper rifle, then picked Conor up from the floor as easily as if he was a rag doll. With his son lifted over his shoulder, he started to run through the bracken. There was a steep, rocky descent to the beach 150 metres to the north. He covered the ground in less than twenty seconds, even with Conor's extra weight, spurred on by adrenalin and a deep, horrible sense of foreboding.

He descended sideways, but otherwise with no thought for his own personal safety as he scrambled and slipped down to the beach, barely aware of the rain that had just started to fall. As he ran towards Eva, the sand felt like glue, dragging him back, holding him down . . .

And then he was just two metres from her, laying Conor gently on his back and kneeling down in the cold, salty water as he pressed his hand to the dark patch which had doubled in size . . . ripping the hood back from Eva's face to see it pale and waxy, her nose and half of her mouth submerged in the water. He scooped her up and moved her away from the water's edge, before pressing his fingers to her neck. Her skin was icy, but there was a pulse. She was still alive. Just.

Joe pulled the top over her head to reveal her torso clad in body armour, her shoulders and elbows wrapped in Kevlar pads. The blood was seeping from her left side, where the front armoured plate met its rear twin. He quickly undid the straps that held the two together. She was wearing a T-shirt underneath it, and this too was saturated with blood. Joe pulled it up to see the damage. An open wound. Massive blood loss. The rain was heavy now, but not heavy enough to wash away the blood. He quickly unstrapped the Kevlar helmet from Eva's head, ran to the sea and filled it with water. Back at her side, he poured the salty water over the wound. As the blood washed away, he saw a gash at the side of her abdomen about two inches long and found himself exhaling deeply with relief. It was a flesh wound, not an entry wound. The round must have ricocheted somehow and punctured the gap between the plates. Had the angle been only slightly different, she would have been dead.

But even this wound was dangerous. The blood was flowing again. Joe had to stem it. He grabbed the top – it was covered with salt and sand now, but he couldn't do anything about that. He ripped it along one of its seams and then wrapped it round Eva's abdomen, tying the sleeves in a tight knot so that the material pressed firmly against the wound. It was hardly ideal, but it was the best he could do.

Eva coughed. Seawater spilled from her mouth. Her eyes flickered open. At first he thought she couldn't see anything – her pupils expanded and contracted as she tried to focus. But then her vision seemed to clear. 'Joe?' she whispered.

'We've got to get you back to the house.' Joe's voice was breathless. 'You've lost a lot of blood . . .'

'Conor . . . ?'

'He's . . . OK. He's here. Eva, do you think you can walk?' He knew he couldn't safely carry them both, not in the state they were in.

Eva closed her eyes. With a great effort she nodded, then tried to push herself up onto her elbows, before sinking back into the sand.

Joe put his hands under her arms and helped her to a sitting position. Her face was creased with pain, but she gave no word of complaint. Moments later she had one arm around Joe's shoulder as he bent to pick up Conor, who was still lying, eyes open, on the sand, shivering but otherwise motionless.

It was still not fully light. The beach was deserted. His son over his shoulder, his oldest friend leaning heavily on his other side, Joe staggered slowly back towards the cliff. They needed shelter. They needed care. The nearest place was a kilometre from the clifftop. It was a deserted house where the body of an old woman lay rotting at the bottom of the stairs. A place where Joe was hopeful of finding something that might tell him more about the man he had just sent to his death.

It was not in Mahmood Ashkani's nature to smile often, but he did sometimes. It was a sign of how much Mansfield's continued refusal to die had unnerved him that confirmation of his death had lifted a weight from his shoulders.

He glanced at the passenger seat, at his laptop and satellite phone, and at the small data stick that looked so ordinary but whose contents would, within a few hours, have been viewed by half the people on the planet. Then he glanced at the dashboard clock. Seven thirteen. No need to increase his speed. He had plenty of time.

He arrived at his destination half an hour later. It was the bleak entrance to a deserted slate mine that had long since been abandoned. He parked his car behind a ten-metre-high pile of slag, quite confident that nobody would disturb him here. He had not chosen this place for that reason, however, but simply because it was the right place to be. He plugged his satellite phone into the side of his laptop before doing the same with the data stick.

Then he turned his eyes to the sky.

Not long, he thought to himself.

Not long now.

TWENTY

The White House, 0200 hours EST.

Herb Sagan did not like Mason Delaney. He didn't like the way he surrounded himself with pretty boys, or the way he so obviously felt superior to everyone. But he had to hand it to him. First bin Laden, now this. The President's Chief of Staff, Jed Wallace, who was sitting with Sagan and Delaney, clearly felt the same.

Wallace's face was white. 'How did you *get* this information, Mason?'

The glance that Sagan and Delaney shared was only momentary, but filled with meaning.

'Your predecessor was very fond of that question, Jed,' Delaney sighed.

'Mason, the President's going to—'

'The President, Jed, does not want to know where this information came from, believe me. It's a lot easier for him to *deny* all knowledge when he *has* no knowledge, wouldn't you say? And in approximately . . .' he looked at his watch '. . . eight hours' time, he'll be able to tell the nation that he has just foiled a plot to blow up five domestic and international flights in mid-air, and that on top of his recent PR success in Pakistan. I don't think right-minded people will be asking too many questions about where the information *came* from. Am I wrong?'

Wallace looked uncertain. 'You know what his manifesto was, Mason. An end to torture . . . extraordinary rendition . . .'

Delaney started to stand up. There was a new edge to his voice. 'Well, Jed, if the President would rather have a 9/11 of his very own . . .'

'For God's sake sit down, Mason,' Wallace snapped. Delaney gave a look of mild surprise at this display of authority, before settling back once more. Wallace turned to Sagan. 'Herb, run it past me one more time. If I'm going to wake him, I want to have my ducks in a row.'

Sagan nodded. He had notes in the bag by his feet, but having worked on this since breakfast time he didn't need them. 'We have evidence of a coordinated mid-air strike over American soil. Five flights in total. Projected death toll, just over 1000 people. Thanks to Mason's source, however, we have the precise flight numbers. We know which aircraft the terrorists are target-ing. Tampa to JFK, Boston to LAX, Orlando to Montreal, Philadelphia to Seattle, Cincinnati to Newark. They all depart between 0500 and 0505 hours, so they'll be in the air simultaneously.'

'And in time for the whole eastern seaboard to wake up to the news,' Mason murmured.

Sagan continued: 'There's a shampoo factory in Delaware. At midday yesterday we apprehended a US national who admitted receiving money from an unknown source in return for filling certain bottles of certain batches with the chemicals necessary to create binary explosives. The batches in question were ear-marked for drugstores beyond the security gates at Tampa, Boston, Orlando, Philly and Cincinnati. They left the factory two weeks ago and there's no way to trace them.'

Wallace's face was still pale. 'I'm assuming we need to ground all flights in and out of the US?'

Sagan and Delaney exchanged another glance.

'That won't be necessary, Jed,' said Sagan. 'We have the situ-ation under control . . .'

'How?' Wallace breathed.

'We're going to isolate the terrorists before they get on the planes. We're already coordinating with the Transportation Security Administration, Immigration and Customs Enforcement. And of course the Feds. We've planted air marshals among the passengers on each flight. We'll load them onto buses from the gates, but none of them will get within sniffing distance of an actual aircraft. Once we've quarantined the passengers, we'll search them. In a few hours' time we'll have a bunch of Al-Qaeda brains to pick. Without anything approaching coercion, naturally.' He gave Wallace a flat look.

There was a silence in the room.

'The President will need to give the final go-ahead for the strategy,' Sagan said.

'He'll want to know the potential risk to the other passengers.'

'I'm not going to sit here and tell you it's risk-free, Jed.'

Wallace nodded. 'Tampa, Boston, Orlando, Philadelphia, Cincinnati.' He repeated Sagan's list. 'You're sure that these five flights are the only ones that are being targeted?' He had directed the question towards Delaney, who affected a look of surprise at having been consulted.

'I'm ninety-three per cent sure,' he said. He smiled at Sagan. 'Herb does love his statistics.'

Wallace ignored the barb. 'I'll wake the President now,' he said. 'Wait here. I'll be back with an answer.'

He left the room. Sagan and Delaney sat silently, two enemies, joined by a common purpose.

'Ninety-three per cent, Mason?' Sagan asked.

Delaney raised an eyebrow. 'Maybe ninety-two.'

The two men went back to their wordless waiting.

Pembrokeshire, 0715 hours.
Under normal circumstances it would have taken no more than fifteen minutes for Joe to get from the beach to Ashkani's safe house. Carrying a traumatized Conor, and with Eva limping

along beside him, it took nearly an hour. By the time they approached the front door, which Joe had left unlocked, he had given up offering Eva words of encouragement to help her push through the barrier of pain and exhaustion. He could feel her body convulsing. She badly needed medical attention. So did Conor.

The hallway stank of the rotting corpse of the old woman. Eva showed no sign that she even knew what she was stepping over – her glazed eyes were as desensitized as Conor's. With difficulty, Joe manoeuvred the two of them up the stairs. It was with an overwhelming sense of relief that he turned left at the top, into the room where he had found Ashkani's passport. He didn't know why he wanted them to stay in this room – it was just a vague sense that Ashkani, whoever he was, had been a pro, and that there was a chance of finding medical supplies in here. Plus, of course, he wanted to strip the place down for information.

He helped Eva and Conor over to the bed on the far side of the room. Eva collapsed heavily onto its edge. Her lips had a bluish tinge. Her shaking hands clutched the wound on the side of her abdomen. Joe gently lowered Conor from his shoulder and sat his son next to her.

'You OK, champ?'

Conor's blank face looked around the room. For a few seconds he appeared not to know where he was, but then his eyes widened. He slipped off the bed, his head in his hands, and curled up into a little ball on the floor. No words escaped his throat, just a pathetic mixture of frightened sounds.

Joe knelt down and put his hands awkwardly on his son's shoulders. 'Hey champ,' he whispered. 'It's all right . . . he's gone . . . I'm here now . . .' His words had no effect. The boy remained huddled on the thin carpet.

Joe turned his attention to Eva. Her face was racked with pain and she winced as he removed the hooded top to look at the wound. It was a mess, no doubt about it. The skin where the bullet had clipped her was torn and the tissue beneath it was a bloody pulp. The heavy bleeding seemed to have stopped, but Eva was very weak and in great pain. He couldn't risk moving her any further.

'Ashkani?' she breathed. Her voice was fragile and cracked.

Joe looked around the room. 'You needn't worry about him.'

A pause. Speech was clearly a huge effort for Eva. 'Is he dead?'

'I shot him in the back of the head. That normally does the trick.'

Joe strode into the hallway and started checking out the other rooms on the first floor. The old lady's bedroom – a riot of floral wallpaper, floral bedding and a violet carpet – revealed nothing but clothes, photographs and a handful of old jewellery. The spare bedroom, with its two single beds, was similarly empty. His search of the bathroom, which didn't give the impression of having been used very often, despite the limescale stains around the edge of the roll-top bath and inside the sink, was more productive. In the mirrored cabinet above the sink he found a pile of large swabs, still in their sterile packaging, and a roll of bandage. He rushed back to Eva, ripped open the swabs and pressed them against her wound, before tying them into position with the bandage. Eva winced, but didn't cry out. Joe was grateful for that. 'You'll be OK,' he told her, and she nodded as though she believed him.

The cupboard in the corner was filled with grey suits – nothing in the pockets – as well as a couple of old coats that he assumed belonged to the dead woman at the bottom of the stairs. He pulled out the coats and took them over to Conor and Eva. Eva accepted the coat over the shoulders of her trembling frame. Conor was still on the floor. Joe lifted him up again and laid him on the bed where once more he curled foetus-like. He lay the coat over him to keep him warm.

'I'll be back in a minute,' he said, and hurried downstairs, stopping only to pull the old lady's body out of the hallway and into the front room. Conor was traumatized, that much was clear. The last thing he needed to see was dead bodies on the floor.

In the kitchen he looked for provisions. He found a cupboard full of cat food, a bottle of Ribena, the remains of a loaf of Hovis that was covered in a dusting of mould and, in the fridge, an unopened carton of milk. He filled two glasses with water, as both Eva and Conor needed rehydration, even if there was no food to give them. Back in the bedroom he managed to get some fluid into Eva, but Conor would not, or could not, move. Joe stood over him, and for the briefest moment he was back in JJ's house, lying next to Caitlin, shortly before their life had been ripped apart.

I'll be a dad, he was telling himself. *I've had enough of being a soldier . . .*

He snapped back to the present and looked around. This had been Ashkani's room. His safe house. It had all the hallmarks – remote, unexpected, easy to leave. He had no doubt that the bastard had been paying the old lady a fair whack to keep this room available for him whenever he needed it. Who did she think he was? A travelling salesman, maybe? Someone who just wanted a place to get away to? And why had she ended up dead at the bottom of the stairs? Had she started to suspect something?

His thoughts turned to Ashkani himself. He remembered the man's American passport. What did that mean? Whatever it meant, Joe needed to search this room. Find out everything he could about Mahmood Ashkani, if that really was his name. Find out who he was working for. And try to locate *anything* that might prove Joe's own innocence.

Underneath the wardrobe he found four shoe boxes. They contained nothing but shoes. On top of the wardrobe was an old leather suitcase. Empty. He swiped the pile of books off the table

– all in Arabic, they were meaningless to him, but he held each one upside down anyway, in case anything had been secreted between the pages. Nothing. And so he turned his attention to the cardboard boxes.

The room was littered with them – Joe counted fifteen in all. Three stood against the wall opposite the bed and window. He ripped them open. In the first he found nothing of interest – just old clothes, musty-smelling and crumpled. The second was more revealing. It contained a handgun – on examination he recognized it as a Glock 22 – along with a box of .40 S&W rounds. There was also money – not sterling, but a thick wad of Eritrean nakfa, bound together with a rubber band. Why did Ashkani have this currency? What were his links with Eritrea, that lawless land in East Africa that Joe knew was a sanctuary for AQ?

The third box contained the treasure.

The box itself was the smallest in the room – a 50cm cube. Its flaps were well sealed with packing tape, which meant that Joe had to rip through the cardboard to get inside. The first thing he pulled out was a newspaper: *The Times*. It took only a glance at the front page for Joe to see that it was the one that had his name, photo and crime plastered over the interior. He had no desire, or need, to read it again. In any case, he had already pulled out two DVDs in clear plastic cases. Each disc had been written on in black marker pen: the lettering was Arabic and Joe couldn't understand it. And at the bottom of the box was a single sheet of A4 paper, on which was written, in a neat hand, a column of ten alphanumeric strings, followed by a three-letter code, followed by four digits. Joe only had to cast his eyes down the column once before realizing what they were.

Flight numbers. Airport codes. Take-off times.

'Joe?'

Eva's voice was weaker than ever.

'Joe, I think we need to get to a hospital . . . Conor too . . .'

Joe nodded. She was right. He looked across the room at her, then back to the contents of the box. 'Give me two minutes,' he said.

Clutching the two DVDs, he hurried downstairs again, barely glancing at the old lady as he ran into her front room. The red standby light of her television was on. He opened the white-painted cabinet beneath it to find an ancient VHS machine and a DVD player, both covered in dust and clearly seldom used. He switched on the DVD player and inserted the first of the two discs. Moments later he was staring at a black and white image on the screen with a sick, knotted feeling in his stomach.

He recognized Lancing Way at once, and the black Discovery that had pulled up in front of his own house. And, of course, he recognized himself stepping out of the car on the day he had returned from Bagram, his scruffy black beard still intact, his North Face bag slung over his shoulder. He stared in shock at the screen, trying to work out where the image had been shot from. From the angle he deduced that a camera must have been hidden on the first floor of the house directly opposite his, where old Mr Thompson lived by himself. He watched himself knock on his own front door before disappearing inside.

The screen went black.

His hands were trembling as he ejected the disc, proof positive that he'd been under surveillance and that Ashkani had at least had access to it, even if he hadn't organized it. What would the second DVD show? He barely dared look. JJ's house? Caitlin? Was his murdered, brutalized partner about to appear before his eyes?

He started the disc and, with his heart thumping, stepped back to watch it.

He did not see himself. He did not see Caitlin.

He saw a dead man talking.

Thin, Middle Eastern, with a grey-streaked beard and wearing a simple, plain *dishdash* and a white headdress.

The nose was pronounced. The lips were slightly apart. The

forefinger of his right hand was held aloft, but he was looking down, as if reading from some text that was out of shot.

The last time Joe had seen this man, he'd been shrouded in a body bag, carried by two SEALs through a compound in Pakistan towards a waiting Black Hawk. Now he lived again on this television screen.

The footage was grainy and shaky – clearly taken on a hand-held camera, or even a mobile phone – but Osama bin Laden's voice was clear enough. He spoke in Arabic, calm and measured, but whoever had made this video had intended it for English-speakers, because at the bottom of the screen were some amateurish subtitles in gaudy white letters. Rage rising in his gut, Joe read the words as the voice of bin Laden filled that quiet, dark room:

'*People of America and Britain, I address my words to you all. I begin by telling you that, although your governments spend more money on wars against the people of Allah, who built the heavens and the earth in justice, than . . .*'

The screen crackled and blurred for a moment, then grew sharp again.

'*. . . once more we have shown that it is not within your power to stop the brave ones whose purpose is holy Jihad. It was on September 11 that nineteen young men were able to bring fire and death to America. And on May 11 we will have done it once more . . .*'

The sick feeling in Joe's stomach intensified. Suddenly only half his mind was on the screen. The other half was calculating today's date.

'*. . . the infidels will be brought from the skies in balls of flame . . . None of you are safe . . .*'

He'd got it wrong. *Surely* he'd got it wrong . . .

'*. . . know that His law is retaliation in kind. The killers will be killed . . . whoever obeys Him will enter the Garden, whoever disobeys Him will be refused . . . by the will of the Prophet my people can strike you down with ease . . .*'

311

The screen went blank. Joe continued to stare at it for a handful of seconds.

He *hadn't* got it wrong. The eleventh of May was today.

Joe was on his feet and hurtling up the stairs three at a time. As he burst into the bedroom he startled Eva. Conor was still motionless on the bed. Joe strode over to the cardboard box that had contained the DVDs and grabbed the A4 sheet again. He scanned down it: the first five flight numbers were adjacent to airport codes that he recognized: Heathrow, Gatwick, Stansted, Edinburgh, Belfast. The following five were American: Portland, San Diego, Minnesota, Detroit, Chicago.

He checked the flight times. All the UK flights were scheduled to leave at or around 1000 hours, the US flights any time between five and seven hours earlier local time, because of the time differences.

Ten planes. All in the air at the same time.

A video of bin Laden, clearly recorded before the raid in Pakistan, gloating about a fucking spectacular to take place today.

'What time is it?' Joe breathed still staring at the piece of paper in his shaking fist.

Eva didn't answer.

'*What's the fucking time?*' he yelled. He spun round, to see Eva's pale face looking warily at him. Conor had started to cry. Joe rushed over to the other side of the room, grabbed Eva's wrist and looked at her watch: 0744 hours. Two hours and sixteen minutes. Could he get to one of the airports on the list in that time? Not a fucking chance.

'Joe, what's wrong?'

He didn't answer. Not immediately. His mind was turning over. 'Where's your phone?' he said.

With obvious pain, Eva pushed herself to her feet and pulled her phone from her pocket. Joe grabbed it.

No service.

'*Fuck!*' he hissed.

'What is it?' Eva groaned. She'd collapsed back down onto the bed and was holding her wound. Joe found himself clutching his hair. Everything was spinning. He didn't know what to do . . . 'Joe, *what is it*?'

Words started to spill out of him. 'There's a terrorist plot. Ten planes, flight times 1000 hours UK time. They'll all be in the air at once. Ashkani's behind it.'

'How do you know?'

'I just know!' Joe roared.

Eva looked stricken. 'What about security? I mean, it's impossible, isn't it, to get explosives on-board a plane nowadays? All the checks . . . How are they *doing* it?'

Joe put a lid on his exploding temper. 'Could be anything,' he hissed. 'Maybe the fucking pilots are involved . . . or the baggage handlers. I don't know. If some fucker wants to blow themselves up . . .' He was pacing up and down, feeling like he was being ripped apart. He had to *do* something, warn someone. But who would listen to him? The whole fucking world thought he was unhinged and dangerous. An anonymous call would be ignored. He didn't know how the strike was going to happen, and he couldn't reach any of the airports in time.

And – he looked over his shoulder at Conor and Eva – he needed to be here.

'You have to go,' Eva said.

He blinked at her.

'I mean it, Joe. You have to go now.' She winced as she spoke, and clutched her side again. 'I'll be fine. I can look after Conor . . .'

'You're too weak.'

She stood up again. It was clearly an immense effort.

'Ten planes, Joe,' she whispered. 'How many lives is that? Hundreds? Thousands? How many more people are you going to let him kill?'

The question hung in the air between them. And Joe knew

she was right. He nodded and crossed to the other side of the room. The Glock was still in its box. Almost as a reflex, he clicked out the magazine, then loaded and locked it. 'You know how to use this thing?' he asked.

Eva nodded, but when she took the weapon from him, she held it tentatively, like an amateur.

'You won't need it,' Joe said. 'We're in a safe house. I don't think anybody except Ashkani knows about this place.' He looked over at Conor. 'Take care of him,' he said.

'What are you going to do?'

Joe narrowed his eyes. The answer to that question wasn't even clear in his own mind.

'Anonymous tip-offs are no good,' he said. 'They get hundreds a day, and without knowing how they're getting their explosives on-board . . .' He closed his eyes. 'I can't turn myself in – nobody will listen to me. And I can't get to any of those airports, which means I can't get anywhere near the target flights.'

Eva couldn't stop the panic rising in her face. 'But if you can't persuade anyone to ground these ten flights . . .' she breathed, 'what *can* you do?'

Joe opened his eyes again. A sudden calm had descended on him. Like in the old days, before an op. Everything was clear. He knew what he had to do.

'Joe?'

'Give me your watch.'

She obliged and he looked at it: 0746 hours. Two hours and fourteen minutes to go. Joe put the watch on his wrist and opened his shoulder bag. The Galil .308 was there, separated into its component parts. Lurking at the bottom was the ammo he had confiscated from the scene: the match-grade rounds that had been loaded into the weapon, but also a small box of HE incendiary rounds. Overkill – literally – for taking out an individual, but for what Joe had in mind . . .

'*Joe?*'

If he couldn't ground the planes in danger, there was only one other option open to him. To ground every plane – both sides of the Atlantic. Full stop.

'Don't let go of the gun. Keep an eye on Conor. I'll be back.'

Without another word, Joe raced from the room, down the stairs and out of the house. The motorbike was back with the Range Rover. They were parked two klicks away. If he pushed himself, he could cover the distance in five or six minutes. He sprinted, spurred on by the certain knowledge that if he failed, bin Laden's curtain call would be complete.

Hundreds of people would die.

Time was not on his side.

TWENTY-ONE

0800 hours.

The motorbike was still lying where Joe had left it after returning to Eva, on its side by the Range Rover in the small car park opposite the church. The helmet, lying next to the vehicle, was soaked with dew. Joe's muscles were burning as he hauled it up from its hiding place. His dirty clothes were drenched with sweat. Tightening the straps of the rucksack over his back, he pulled on the helmet, started the engine and screeched past the Range Rover into the road.

As Joe roared down the deserted lanes, the speedometer topped eighty even on sharp bends, which he hugged tightly. Hedgerows and fields were nothing but blurs in the corner of his eyes. There were still patches of early-morning mist compromising his visibility as he cut through them. All his attention was on the road ahead. The wind cut through him, sticking his sweat-soaked clothes to his clammy skin, and before long he was very cold. He knew he should stop and move around. He vaguely tried to remember when he had last eaten. All he could do, though, was drive, and drive as hard and as fast as the bike would go.

The jagged form of the Galil in his rucksack dug into his back. It was comforting. Although he knew that if he was pulled over, the presence of such a weapon would be enough to get him arrested, at least he had the tool he needed to deal with the police. Because his word wouldn't be enough to ground so much as a paper dart. Disgraced and discredited, he was going to have to be rather more persuasive. And there weren't many things more persuasive than an incendiary .308.

The miles disappeared. Ten. Twenty. Thirty. The small, winding roads grew wider and straighter. There was more traffic now. Time check: 0832. He pulled out to overtake a trundling Eddie Stobart lorry and immediately his eyes and ears were filled with the sound of another truck thundering towards him from the opposite direction, twenty metres and closing, its horn blaring. Joe yanked the bike back over to the left, just in time. The truck powered past him, the slipstream knocking him slightly off balance. He pulled out again. This time the road was clear. Opening the throttle, he overtook Eddie Stobart, passing under an overhead sign as he did so. Cardiff: seventy-five miles.

He did a quick calculation. A hundred and twenty-five miles to go. He hunkered down to reduce wind resistance and increase speed.

0900 hours.

It was cold in the house, but that wasn't the only reason Eva shivered. The pain was getting worse. The wound in her side was too sore to touch, and though she wanted to take a look, the idea of removing Joe's hastily applied dressing was more than she could bear. If only she could stop herself shaking as she sat on the edge of the bed, the handgun gripped tight in her fist. She didn't know why she was still trembling. She and Conor were alone, weren't they?

She looked at the door. It was open just a couple of inches. Fighting the pain, she eased herself up and moved towards it, stepping round the Arabic books that Joe had swept onto the floor.

She stopped suddenly.

The door was opening.

Shaking even more, Eva raised the gun. A cat miaowed, then

appeared in the doorway. Eva dropped her hand in relief, hissed the cat away, then lurched to the door. She closed it and turned the key. It wouldn't help much, but she felt safer.

With her back to the door, she surveyed the room. It was chaotic. Not so much a bedroom, she thought, as a storeroom.

Her eyes fell on Conor. He hadn't moved since Joe had left. How long had it been? Half an hour? An hour? She limped back to the bed and perched by the boy's small, motionless body.

She found herself grinding her teeth. Complex, conflicting thoughts troubled her. She realized she'd been avoiding looking at Conor. Joe's little boy. Caitlin's little boy. She realized, in a moment of honesty, that she was jealous. Eva had never thought of herself as the maternal type, but maybe that was just her way of protecting herself. Whatever the truth, the kid needed her help.

'Conor?' she whispered. 'Conor, sweetheart, are you OK?'

No answer. She stroked his lower leg gently.

She winced suddenly as a stabbing pain seared out from her wound. She clenched her teeth again as she mastered it. Then, very gently, she pulled the coat to cover the boy properly. He was still hugging himself, and although he wasn't moving, his eyes were wide open, staring without expression. Did he know where he was, or who he was with? Eva thought not. She could see Joe in him – something in the eyes – and she remembered him when he was Conor's age. Quiet and serious, but stockier, less frail. But then he'd never had to go through what Conor had gone through. She stroked his calf again. He was so thin. There was barely any flesh on him. Had Ashkani given him anything to eat? She doubted it. Why would he, when he wanted to keep him compliant in the hours leading up to his death?

'Are you hungry, sweetheart?'

No response.

Eva chewed on her lower lip. 'I'm going to go downstairs, find you something to eat.'

Silence.

Descending the stairs, clutching the banister so hard that her knuckles went white, was among the most painful things she'd ever done and by the time she reached the ground floor she was gasping in agony. Even though it was fully light outside, it was gloomy in this shabby hallway, and just as gloomy in the kitchen. All the cupboard doors were open – Eva vaguely remembered that Joe had come downstairs to fetch water – but there was no food. Just mouldy bread and tins of Whiskas, and they hadn't been reduced to that yet.

A noise at the front door. She stopped dead.

Her pulse thudded in her ears. But there was no other sound. She crept out of the kitchen, doing all she could to ignore the stabbing pains in her side, holding her breath, clutching the gun.

The hallway was undisturbed, the door shut. She took another few paces.

There were letters lying on the doormat. They hadn't been there before. With a surge of hope, she struggled to the door, fumbled desperately with the latch and opened it. A red mail van was pulling back onto the road – thirty metres away.

Help.

Eva stumbled outside and waved her hands in the air. She tried to shout, but lacked the strength for more than a feeble croak.

'Don't go . . .' she whispered. '*Please don't . . .*'

But moments later the van was gone. All was silent, and they were alone again.

It was everything she could do to stop despair from overcoming her. She wanted to hammer her fists against the cold stone walls of the house. *Think of Conor*, she told herself. *He needs you.* She stepped back inside, closed the door and hobbled up the stairs again.

The boy hadn't moved. She had to do something for him. She couldn't just sit here, getting weaker and weaker and worrying

319

about whether Joe had managed to raise the alarm. The wild look in his eyes as he left had lingered with her. She pushed from her mind the idea that he wasn't in control.

Joe had said this was Ashkani's safe house. Surely he would have food here – something the boy could eat. She stared helplessly at the boxes on the floor. There were so many of them. Where to start?

The largest boxes were the two to the right of the wardrobe. They were sealed with so much packing tape that it took her two or three minutes just to open the first one. It was only half full with toiletries: shaving gel, razors, toothbrushes, everything Ashkani might need to take care of himself. The second box was filled with a bewildering array of medicines, most of them with long names Eva did not recognize. She emptied both of them onto the floor, hoping to find something to eat hidden among the bottles and boxes. There was nothing. She spotted a box of codeine and swallowed a couple of tablets. She didn't know if it would do any good for the splintering pain in her side, but it couldn't harm her.

Which box to try next?

It was a smaller one that caught her eye. The bizarre thought came to her that it looked like the box in her attic that was full of baubles for the Christmas tree she decorated every year. She limped over to it, knelt on the floor and started picking at the packing tape with her broken nails. As she tore off the tape, the top layer of cardboard came with it.

When she saw what was inside, she held her breath.

The box was brimful of ammunition. Eva had received very little firearms training, but she recognized the magazines full of rounds and the neat little packs of plastic explosive. There were wires and battery packs and even four small canisters that looked like grenades. Sitting on top of all this equipment, however, was something that perplexed her.

It was a small tray, about eight inches by four, wrapped in a cardboard sleeve that was emblazoned with the British Airways logo. Eva picked it up. It was heavier than she expected for an airline meal, but that was what it must be – food. She noticed that, despite not being chilled, it had no smell. Eva stared at it, barely daring to slide the tray out of its paper sleeve. What would Ashkani be doing with an airline meal in a remote safe house?

Her mouth was dry, her limbs heavy. She removed the sleeve. The food tray had a foil lid, crimped around the edges, though it was clear that even if the tray had once been factory sealed, someone had opened it. She pulled the foil off.

She almost dropped it with shock.

The tray was divided into compartments: one for the main meal, one for dessert, another for cheese. None of them contained food. The two larger compartments had been filled with a substance resembling bright orange plasticine. Each had a small metal probe attached to a red wire that snaked into the third compartment, where two AA batteries were nestled in a battery pack.

Eva swallowed hard, then laid the tray gently back on top of the ammunition.

She stared at it.

Then she looked up at Conor, who was still lying on his side.

She heard Joe's voice: '*Maybe the fucking pilots are involved . . . or the baggage handlers . . .*'

Or the catering staff.

'*If some fucker wants to blow themselves up . . .*'

Unless you know how they're going to do it. And suddenly, Eva realized, she did.

0915 hours.

The wind on the Second Severn Crossing buffeted Joe. But he neither reduced his speed, nor looked left or right at the mist-shrouded expanse of the estuary around him. If the police stopped him, it would be a fucking disaster. But if he slowed down it would be disastrous too. He had no choice but to push on at full throttle.

The moment he'd cleared the estuary, he turned off the M4 and headed south. Time check: 0926. Thirty-four minutes to go. His fuel level was low. *Fuck!* There was no time stop. He screamed past an Asda van and was rewarded with a deafening klaxon and, he saw in his side mirror, a wanker sign from the driver.

A sign overhead: Bristol International Airport, ten miles.

At his current speed that would take between seven and eight minutes.

He looked up. A helicopter had appeared in the sky. He knew its shape: an Agusta A109, the aircraft on constant standby at Hereford. Joe estimated that it was two miles ahead. Was it the Regiment? Some other agency?

Could he have been spotted?

He pushed away the thought and sped on.

Eva switched on her phone. She didn't really expect to get a signal, but she moved closer to the window, holding the handset up against the pane, hoping she might just pick up one in this remote place.

Nothing.

'Conor,' she whispered, doing everything she could to keep her panic under control. 'Conor, you *have* to listen to me.' She gently shook his shoulder. He just stared into space. Then he blinked, but nothing more.

'I have to leave you here, sweetheart . . . you'll be OK. Just . . . just wait for me to come back. I'll be quick, I promise . . .'

If he understood what she was telling him, he gave no sign of it. Eva rearranged the coat over him once more – she didn't know what else to do. She limped towards the door, gave a final look over her shoulder, then closed it behind her and struggled down the stairs and outside.

It was cold. She should have put on the old woman's coat but she didn't dare return for it. She stared at the screen of her phone. Ten past nine: fifty minutes to find a signal and somehow raise the alarm. She'd barely struggled twenty metres, past the boundary fence and onto the road, before the piercing agony of her wound made tears streak down her cheeks. She fixed her eyes on the phone, muttering prayers under her breath that the service bars would spring into view.

She couldn't think about the pain. All she could think about was the little tray packed with explosive, her mind full of images of metal trolleys being pushed down the aisles of airplanes in flight, and of hunks of metal plummeting from the sky. She limped and winced, and occasionally groaned. But she kept on walking, as fast as she could.

0430 hours EST.

The departures lounge at Tampa International Airport was not busy. At this time of the morning there were only two kinds of passengers: professionals, whose jobs dictated they should book themselves onto the 'red-eyes' in order to make their meetings in distant parts of the country, and those whose circumstances dictated that they take advantage of the cheaper fares of these early-morning flights.

For these passengers there were only a handful of distractions. A single coffee shop was open, and it was here that some forty bleary-eyed travellers had congregated, trying to perk themselves up with shots of espresso. Opposite, a clothes store selling gaudy swimming shorts and tropical shirts already had Katy Perry booming from its ceiling despite the early hour. It was brightly lit and staffed by a young woman with three nose piercings, but was otherwise empty. The neighbouring drugstore was quieter, and only fractionally busier. A middle-aged businessman was buying toothpaste and roll-on deodorant. Behind him, a short, rather dumpy young woman with Middle Eastern looks carried a wire basket containing mouthwash, sanitary pads and two bottles of shampoo.

She paid for her items using cash, stowed them in her plain brown shoulder bag, then stepped out onto the concourse and looked up at the departures board. Her eyes scanned down the list of flights until she found hers. Flight number: AA346. Destination: New York JFK. Time: 0500. Gate: 24. Status: boarding in twenty-five minutes.

There was a line of ten plastic yellow chairs in the middle of the concourse facing the coffee shop. She took a seat here and placed her shoulder bag next to her, waiting patiently for her flight to be called. Her eyes caught those of an older man sitting at the edge of the coffee shop's seating area. He had a bottle of mineral water in front of him, but he wasn't drinking it. He broke their gaze as soon as it connected. Ten seconds later a voice came over the Tannoy: 'This is an announcement for all passengers travelling to New York JFK on flight number AA346. The gate for this flight has changed owing to a technical difficulty. Please now proceed to Gate 3, where your flight will shortly be boarding. All passengers for flight AA346 to New York, please proceed now to Gate 3, where your flight will shortly be boarding.'

The woman looked up at the departure board. Sure enough, the gate number had changed. She glanced over at the man who had just dragged his gaze from her. He too was staring at the board.

She stood up and slung her bag over her shoulder. The man picked up the briefcase at his feet and went to join the crowd of people that were starting to cross the concourse, following the signs for Gate 3.

0930 hours.

Terminal 5 at Heathrow was a great deal busier than Tampa International. It was later here, and the passengers were swarming – scanning their passports at the self-service check-in desks, greeting and saying farewell to loved ones. The air rang with echoing announcements – security warnings and final calls. 'Passengers for flight BA729 for Dublin are requested to make their way to Gate 12, where boarding will shortly commence.'

The 186 people who, having heard the announcement, started to filter out of the shops and restaurants and seating areas in the direction of Gate 12, made no impression on the thousands of other passengers milling around, waiting for their own flights. Why would they? They were not out of the ordinary. Just normal men, women and children. Preparing to take an uneventful flight.

Unaware anything might be wrong.

0935 hours.

Joe skirted south along the western edge of Bristol International Airport. Somehow he needed to gain access to the airfield.

He was off the main road now, speeding along a deserted lane. Every 100 metres or so there was a little cluster of red-brick houses, long since left empty because they were so close to the airport. Beyond the houses he saw glimpses of overgrown gardens and tumbledown sheds. Then fifty metres of wasteland. And then the wire fence, easily five metres high and topped with razor wire, that marked the airport's boundary.

Unscalable. But not impenetrable.

Joe stopped by one of the empty houses. The front garden was a jungle and the windows were boarded up. There was, however, a cracked tarmac driveway leading to the back of the house. He dismounted and let the bike fall. He was clearly alongside the runway now, because he could see and hear an EasyJet flight rising in a straight line into the air, about 200 metres to his east. The roar of its engine thundered across the sky. A hundred metres beyond it he could see the Agusta circling. To have a chopper in the airspace around a commercial runway was unusual. That it appeared to have followed a route similar to his own was suspicious. They were looking for someone.

He ran five metres along the cracked tarmac and into the back garden, crashing through metre-high grass and thistles to a dilapidated shed at the end. The door came off in his hands as he pulled. Inside it was filled with cobwebs and old paint pots. There was a mouldering deckchair and three dusty demijohns. Then Joe spotted a pair of rusty secateurs. He grabbed them and scaled the wooden fence at the end of the garden, before sprinting across the wasteland between the house and the airfield's boundary.

The EasyJet plane that he had seen taking off was a speck in the distance to the south. By the time, half a minute later, that Joe had reached the fence, a second aircraft, with a logo he didn't recognize, had taken its place. Not that he was paying much attention to it. The secateurs in his right hand were stiff and blunt and it was with difficulty that he cut through the reinforced wire of the airfield's perimeter fence. He'd made twelve incisions before he had created a hole large enough to stuff through the bag containing the sniper rifle, and then himself. The jagged wire cut through his clothes and into his arms.

Time check: 0939. The Agusta was still hovering 300 metres away on the far side of the airport.

As far as he could see in front of him, there was a open expanse of airfield. If the guys in the Agusta had eyes out for him, there was nowhere he could hide from them. He had two or three minutes before they spotted him. If that.

He had to focus on just one thing. A diversion. Big enough to put the shits up every air-traffic controller from Bristol to Bangalore. And he had less than twenty minutes to do it.

0440 hours EST.

The waiting area for Gate 3 at Tampa International's departures lounge was filling up. Two smiling air hostesses stood at the entrance, inserting the boarding cards of each of the passengers and checking that their features matched the image that appeared on the screen in front of them, before ushering them through with a cheery 'Good morning'. The grunts they received in return were, in general, not friendly. The passengers for flight AA346 were tired from rising early, and not pleased with the long walk to this gate in an isolated part of the airport. It didn't stop the two hostesses from sounding chirpy.

When a plain-looking young man wearing a University of Miami sweatshirt and carrying a bright orange shoulder bag handed over his card, there was nothing to give the two young ladies any indication that he was not a student. But then an FBI air marshal who was scanning the assembled passengers for suspicious-looking personnel noticed the way he was avoiding eye contact with his five colleagues who had already passed through.

A bland voice from the Tannoy: 'This is the final call for flight AA346 to New York. Will any remaining passengers please proceed directly to Gate 3, where your aircraft is ready to board.'

Five minutes later a middle-aged man with a grey beard and wearing an airport uniform approached the hostesses. 'All passengers accounted for?' he asked them.

They nodded, and when the man took hold of the microphone that they themselves would normally use to address the passengers, the two hostesses exchanged a glance. This was unusual. But they were practised at looking unflustered, and their faces registered no surprise when he spoke. 'Excuse me, folks, if I could have your attention. As you know, we've encountered a few technical difficulties with our gate system. We've arranged for some buses to take you directly from your gate to the aircraft. If I could ask all passengers sitting in rows A to G to make their way to the first bus, we'll have you all boarded and in the air in no time at all.'

He released the button on the microphone and turned to the hostesses. 'Emergency code Alpha Twelve,' he breathed. 'We'll take it from here.'

The two young women looked startled. One of them glanced

over her shoulder. Standing in the stark white corridor twenty metres distant from the gate, she saw two broad-shouldered men. They were wearing holiday gear and carrying shoulder bags. But they didn't approach the gate. They didn't move at all. They stood there, human barriers, waiting for anyone who felt the sudden need to run from the gate.

0940 hours.
Eva fell.

She cried out as her phone dropped to the ground, and although she barely felt the strength to stand up, her hand shot out to check it wasn't damaged. The screen was still intact. But there was still no signal.

Mustering all her energy, she got to her feet again. The bandage around her waist was soaked with blood – the wound was suppurating again. She put it from her mind. The road was heading uphill to a rise thirty metres away. Her teeth grinding, her jaw set, she limped on.

0945 hours.
Joe ran north, keeping close to the perimeter fence. Airport security was always tight, but whether anyone had eyes on the right place at the right time was impossible to predict. Joe just had to keep to his plan, and that meant following the runway up towards the taxiing area, and from there in the direction of the terminal building.

A hundred metres passed. Two hundred. The Agusta was still circling in the sky above the far side of the runway, about a half klick from his position. He counted three aircraft queuing for the runway and a fourth accelerating down it. He could see the terminal now, a quarter klick to the north-east. He stopped and crouched down low in a patch of long grass, before removing the telescopic sight from the bag and using it to scan the intervening ground. There were a number of vehicles: passenger buses, forklifts for the luggage and small trucks that refuelled the aircraft, their sides emblazoned with green BP logos. Three of the fuel trucks were parked in a line, 100 metres to the east and adjacent to a steel hut. Two men, dressed in blue overalls and with ID tags clipped to their chests, were standing and talking between the hut and the fuel vehicles. One of them had a cigarette behind his ear, unlit while he was in the vicinity of the aviation fuel. Panning south he saw two airport security vans 300 metres away on the other side of the airport; as he moved the sight upwards, he got a closer look at the Agusta. There were no distinguishing marks to indicate whom it contained.

Joe stowed the sight away, making calculations that were second nature to him. How quickly could he get to the steel hut, and could he do it without being seen? Twenty seconds max, he reckoned. As for remaining unseen? No chance. The two men by the fuel trucks were looking in his direction, and it wasn't like he had time to wait for them to wander off for a slash.

Stealth wasn't an option. The only tools available to him were speed, and when he got there, brute force.

He felt for the handgun he'd taken from the drug dealer what seemed like days ago but was only the previous afternoon, then pushed himself to his feet and started to run.

Joe ate up the first fifty metres in less than ten seconds, and as he reached that halfway point he thought he might be getting away with it. The two airport workers were just staring at him stupidly, their feet glued to the ground.

But with forty metres to go, the two men had turned and were going into the hut. They had definitely seen him. Joe forced himself to move even faster. After another ten seconds he had burst through the door of the hut, weapon in hand. The place stank greasily of aviation fuel. One of the men had a telephone to his ear, the other was just standing in the middle of the hut, frozen with fear.

'*Get on the fucking floor!*' Joe roared, aiming his pistol first at one man, then the other. '*On the fucking floor, now!*'

Both men dropped to the ground.

There was no time to restrain them. Joe had to put them out of action, and fast. He turned the gun round to hold it by its barrel, then slammed the grip down on the back of each man's head, knocking them out cold.

Joe straightened up. He could hear the tinny, urgent sound of a man's voice from the telephone handset. He ignored it as he slipped his bag from his shoulder and took out the components of the sniper rifle. He fitted these together, each section clunking solidly into its neighbour until, fifteen seconds later, the weapon was ready to use. He pulled out the ammunition and loaded up, then looked once more around the hut. A steel cabinet standing against one wall, lockable but open, contained six keys hanging on hooks. Joe grabbed them all. The rest of the hut was a jumble of tools, jerrycans, greasy rags – everything needed to keep the fuel trucks on the road. Stashed in one corner were five handheld air-traffic-control beacons, each a couple of feet in length. Joe grabbed one and, beacon in one hand, sniper rifle in the other, ran back outside.

He knew he had less than a minute – the alarm had been raised by a phone call – and although the Agusta was still circling, it would be heading in his direction any moment. Joe sprinted towards one of the fuel trucks. A dial on the back indicated that it was three quarters full. He ran round to the cab, laid his rifle on the tarmac and jumped up into the driver's seat, pulling the keys from his pocket one by one and trying them in the ignition. The engine started on his fifth attempt. Joe pressed his foot on the brake, then knocked the automatic gearbox into drive.

The sound of sirens reached him. He blocked them from his mind as, foot still awkwardly pressed on the brake, he manoeuvred himself into a position half in, half out of the cab, clutching the beacon and preparing to jam it against the accelerator.

A hundred metres away, a plane was turning onto the runway, and the Agusta was suddenly changing course.

Heading in his direction.

He pressed the beacon against the accelerator and released the break. The truck slid forward. With a sharp jab, he forced the opposite end of the beacon against the front of the driver's seat and let go.

The truck continued to move.

Joe jumped out.

As he ran back to the sniper rifle, the air was filled with a riot of noise: the sirens were getting louder, the engines of the aircraft were rising in pitch as it prepared for take-off, the rush of the Agusta's rotors was getting nearer. Joe flung himself on the ground, grabbed the rifle and took up the firing position.

The fuel truck was accelerating towards the plane that had stopped at the end of the runway in advance of take-off. It was twenty metres away – then thirty – heading at right angles towards the runway. Joe was right in the zone. There was no longer any panic or fear. Just a ruthless, clear-headed determination. He had to turn this truck into a moving fireball. It was his only chance of seeding panic in the international air-traffic control network. His only chance of keeping flights on the ground.

He fired a single shot into the truck's massive fuel tank. He didn't expect an explosion at first, even with this HEI round. Aviation fuel was not as flammable as regular petrol, and even that was difficult to explode without a bit of help. Unless he got oxygen into the tank, the plan was fucked.

The Agusta was directly over the moving truck. He heard a strident voice coming from a loudspeaker. '*Stand away from your weapon! Stand away from your weapon!*'

The truck had swerved. It was heading towards the aircraft

standing at the end of the runway. Joe fired a second round. He saw it impacting, but there was no explosion.

The Agusta was touching down, just fifteen metres to his right. He had one more chance. One more shot.

He fired.

An immense explosion was followed by a massive fireball of orange flame and black smoke. The blast knocked the fuel truck onto its side and boomed out over all the other noises. The ground shook. The heat radiated towards Joe's face – a harsh burning that he felt singe his hair and skin. Immediately he rolled away from the rifle, flinging his hands up to his head. The noise all around was deafening – from the Agusta's rotors, the burning truck, the sirens on two airport security vehicles as they roared up and came to a halt just metres from where he was lying.

In seconds he was surrounded. Five flak-jacketed armed police with MP5s dug into their shoulders, the barrels pointing directly at Joe, each of them screaming instructions at him: *'Don't move! Keep your hands on your head!'* Two more officers arrived. They rolled Joe onto his belly and jerked his hands behind his back. He felt cold metal against his wrists as they cuffed him.

He started to shout. *'Listen to me! You've got to listen to me! Ground all flights!'*

But the only response was rough hands pulling him to his feet. 'We know who you are! Get into the fucking chopper now . . .'

'Listen to me! Listen!'

But nobody listened. They just shoved him, stumbling, through the downdraft of the helicopter and into its body. The MP5 barrels didn't deviate. The shouting didn't stop.

'There's going to be an attack! I know which planes! I know which fucking planes!'

'Shut him up!' roared a voice.

Joe felt a boot in his stomach knock the wind from his lungs. He tried to shout again, to tell them, but it was no good. Now he couldn't even speak.

The chopper was already lifting off.

He'd failed.

It was five minutes to ten.

TWENTY-TWO

0455 hours EST.

At Tampa International there were no signs that any of the passengers for flight number AA346 knew there was anything wrong. They had filed from the gate and into the waiting buses without comment. If any of them thought it unusual that the airport had laid on three buses and that each person had a seat, rather than being packed into one vehicle as was the norm, they didn't mention it. And since they were all looking out of the side windows at the lights twinkling in the early-morning darkness, they did not notice that the buses moved nose to tail, just a couple of metres apart.

The convoy trundled in a straight line north from the gate. Those passengers on the right-hand side of the buses saw, approximately thirty metres to their right, a vast aircraft hangar, 200 metres long, ninety wide, fifteen high. Its steel doors were closed and they remained so until, in perfect synchronization, all three buses turned ninety degrees clockwise.

They accelerated. The hangar doors slid open. Inside each bus, two men stood up. They all wore sports jackets which they unzipped to reveal blue flak jackets with 'FBI' emblazoned on the front. 'Federal officers,' they yelled. 'Stay in your seats and put your hands on your heads. *Stay in your seats and put your hands on your heads!*'

Confusion. Anxious, alarmed faces. Sitting in the back row of the bus that had been at the head of the convoy and which was now on the left as they sped, three abreast, towards the hangar, a woman who looked Middle Eastern slowly put her hands on her head. Her bag was nestled firmly on her lap. Her eyes flickered down towards it, and then in the direction of an FBI officer who had drawn a Glock 22 and was still yelling.

They were inside the hangar within seconds, screeching to a halt approximately twenty metres from the entrance. The hangar was very brightly lit, thanks to a series of floodlights along both of the longer sides. And there were a lot of people: a sixteen-man FBI SWAT team, each packing an M4 with racks, torches and laser markers, as well as Glock 22s identical to those carried by their colleagues in the buses and loaded with hard-hitting, high-calibre .40 S&W rounds. There was a dog unit – eight German shepherds, harnessed and waiting calmly despite the sudden activity. The SWAT team immediately formed a circle round the parked buses. In a second layer beyond them, fifteen members of the Transportation Security Authority and ten members of Immigration Customs Enforcement – all of them armed, though their weapons were not on show. Between the fronts of the buses and the back wall of the hangar was an X-ray machine, manned by another four members of the TSA.

The doors of the buses hissed open; the on-board FBI sleepers started shouting at the passengers to file out. The passengers were throwing wild looks around, murmuring to their neighbours, but the FBI personnel did nothing to soothe their nerves. Two members of the SWAT team boarded each bus, screaming ferociously: '*Keep your hands on your head! Leave your hand luggage on the seats . . .*'

They passed through the buses, hauling passengers to their feet, many eyes widening as they saw the SWAT team's personal weapons. The travellers were herded towards the central doors, and as they filed out, stumbling, into the hangar, they were met by the sight of more weapons, the sound of more barked instructions. The children – there were five in all – were crying; some of the adults looked like they wanted to. The Middle Eastern woman was expressionless. She glanced over at the man whose eyes she had met by the coffee shop – he had been on the second bus – and again he broke away from her gaze as they were rounded up with all the others and made to stand against the back wall with their hands still on their heads.

The buses were empty now, apart from passengers' bags. Five TSA personnel boarded each one to start examining the hand luggage, carefully carrying each piece towards the X-ray machine. Along the back wall, a rotund, flabby-jawed man lowered his hands with a disgruntled: 'What the hell's going on anyway?' Three SWAT team members stepped towards him, screaming at him to return his hands to his head while three red dots from their laser markers danced across his chest like fireflies. His ruddy skin turned pale; he raised his arms. And any murmuring from the other passengers instantly died away as the security personnel started passing their luggage through the X-ray machine.

A trickle of sweat dripped down the side of Mason Delaney's face.

He was sitting once more at the long, narrow table in the White House Situation Room. There were no photographers. The President was absent. There was just him, Scott Stroman, Herb Sagan and four of Sagan's little people. General Sagan had two fingers to his ear and was listening to updates over a headset.

'We have an all-clear from Tampa,' he said. 'All passengers isolated, no incidents.'

A thirty-second silence. Delaney wiped away the sweat with a silk handkerchief.

'Boston, Orlando, Philly, all clear,' Sagan stated.

'Cincinnati?' Delaney breathed.

The general held up one finger.

'That's an all-clear from Cincinnati,' he stated, before

removing the headset, leaning back in his chair and exhaling explosively. 'Gentlemen,' he announced. 'That's a wrap.'

Unnoticed by anyone else in the room, Delaney and Stroman exchanged a look. It would have meant nothing to anybody else, but the two CIA men knew it was not a wrap at all. The morning's activity hadn't ended.

It was only just beginning.

'Ladies and gentlemen, welcome aboard flight BA729 from London to Dublin. We'll be underway in a couple of minutes' time, just as soon as we get the nod from air-traffic control. In the meantime, please make sure your luggage is safely stowed in the overhead lockers or beneath the seat in front of you. Our cabin crew will shortly be taking you through some of the safety features of this Boeing 737. Please do pay attention, as these may differ from other aircraft you've travelled on . . .'

Flight BA729 was full, but nobody seemed to paying any attention to the captain's clipped tones. They were all too busy sending last-minute text messages, or trying to stuff their coats into the overhead compartments as the heavily made-up hostesses filed up and down the aisle, checking seatbelts and handing out colouring packs to the children on the flight. An air steward and a stewardess remained at the back in the service area, replenishing the drinks trolley that they would be pushing through the cabin just as soon as they were airborne. Then they would hand out the airline meals that had just been loaded onto the aircraft by a friendly young man with a wispy blond beard that failed to hide the pockmarks on his face.

The steward noticed that a Middle Eastern gentleman in an aisle seat in the back row looked unwell. Perspiration was dripping down his face, and he seemed to be muttering something to himself. The steward put a slightly overfamiliar hand on his shoulder and bent down over him.

'Are you OK, sir?'

The man didn't meet the steward's eyes. He just nodded silently.

'Nervous flyer?'

'I'm fine,' said the man. He looked at his watch. Two minutes to ten. He closed his eyes and continued his muttering.

Eva's world was spinning. She didn't know what time it was, nor how long she had been away from the house. All she knew was that the Range Rover was in reach, ten metres away, still parked opposite the church. But she was in such agony that it could have been ten miles.

She stumbled into the car park and fell against the vehicle, gasping for breath and retching. It took a full thirty seconds for her shaking hands to align the key with the lock. Scrambling inside, she turned on her mobile phone and put it on the dashboard.

No signal.

She started the engine. As she turned the steering wheel, she cried out, and she was sobbing as she pulled out into the road and started to drive eastwards, away from the coast. In her distress she veered to left and right.

She checked the phone again. Still no signal.

She drove a mile, her speed increasing. A mile and a half. A white Bedford van – the first vehicle she'd seen – sped past in the opposite direction, the aggressive sound of its horn fading into the distance behind her.

Suddenly she slammed her foot on the brake.

A single bar had appeared on the phone's screen. Eva grabbed the phone with one trembling hand and scrolled through her address book. Names appeared in front of her and, with fear surging through her gut, she realized that she'd been so focused on getting to an area where she could get a signal that she hadn't even thought about who she was going to call.

Three minutes to ten. Panicking, she scrolled through her contacts again.

'Jacobson, John, DCI', she read.

The image flashed into her head of Jacobson staring at her as she slipped into the lift having stolen the Barfield files back at the office. The last thing he'd be expecting was a call from her. Perhaps that was to her advantage. Perhaps he would take her seriously.

She called him. After four rings voicemail cut in, scratchy and crackly. The signal was terrible. 'This is Jacobson, leave a—'

Eva hung up and called again. She could tell from the number of rings that Jacobson had manually declined the call. The third time she tried, however, he answered it. 'Who's calling?' he demanded.

Eva's voice didn't sound like her. 'It's me . . .' she rasped. 'Eva . . .'

'Hello? Can you hear me? Who's this?'

'Eva Buckley!' she shouted as loud as she could. The line was still poor. 'You have to listen to me! There's going to be a ter- rorist attack . . . ten planes . . . five in the UK . . . five in the US . . . explosives in the food trays . . . they'll be in the air any second now . . . you need to find Joe Mansfield . . . he has the flight numbers . . .'

Silence.

Eva looked at the mobile's screen. It was blank. No battery.

'*No!*' she yelled, and in a fit of frustration she hurled the phone against the windscreen. It clattered down into the foot- well, but Eva didn't see it. She was looking at the clock. Ten precisely.

She was too late.

0500 EST.

The hangar at Tampa International was almost silent. The pas- sengers were still held at gunpoint. Two of them had been removed from the others. They were a short, dumpy Middle Eastern woman and a taller man, also of Arabic extraction. Two members of the SWAT team had brought them over to the other side of the parked buses and forced them onto the ground with their hands on the backs of their heads. Their two items of hand luggage were next to each other on a trestle table, behind which a studious-looking young woman wearing a white coat and latex gloves was examining four identical bottles of shampoo.

She picked one of them up, opened it rather nervously, and squirted a small puddle onto a petri dish. It was green, thick and viscous. A look of suspicion crossed the woman's face. She dabbed the substance with a strip of litmus paper, which she held up to the light. She sniffed the petri dish and then, working quickly, checked samples from the other three bottles. When she was done, she looked up at a waiting member of the TSA.

'I'll need to do more tests,' she said, 'but . . .'

She hesitated.

'Binary explosives?' the TSA man asked.

The young woman looked back at the petri dishes. 'No. I think it's . . .'

'What?'

'. . . just shampoo.'

Pressed to the floor of the Agusta, MP5s pointing at him and the vibrations of the aircraft juddering through him, Joe couldn't tell in which direction they were travelling. A voice above him – one of the ARU – was barking into his headset: 'Roger that, we have him apprehended . . . heavily armed, sir . . . firing on a moving fuel truck.'

'*You have to listen to me!*' Joe roared again, and was rewarded with a boot in the ribs. He barely felt it. All his attention was on the voice.

'I don't recommend uncuffing him, sir . . . the guy's . . . a threat to the safety of the aircraft . . .' And then, in shocked tones, as though someone had just torn a few strips off him: 'Yes, sir . . .'

Joe was pulled to his knees, and he felt the cuffs being unlocked. A quick glance at the position of the sun told him they were heading north, but he had no more chance to get his bearings before one of the ARU thrust a headset at him. '*Put it on – now!*'

Joe did as he was told.

'Who am I talking to?' he demanded.

'*This is GCHQ. Give me the flight numbers, now!*'

There was no time to think about this sudden change of heart, or even how they knew he had the intelligence. Joe just ripped the handwritten A4 sheet from his pocket and started screaming the flight numbers down the line: '*Bravo Alpha Seven Two Niner, Echo Zulu Three Eight Six, Lima Tango Two Two Three . . .*'

Flight BA729 from Heathrow to Dublin was gaining speed down the runway. The cabin crew were strapped in, and all phones and electrical equipment had been switched off. The man in the back row continued to sweat and to mutter silently to himself as the G-force pressed him back into his seat. The aircraft shuddered; the engines screamed. Any second now they would be airborne.

But then the sound of the engines changed. There was a murmuring in the cabin. The plane was slowing down.

The man at the back had stopped muttering and was now looking sharply around. Just behind him, by the catering trolleys, the air steward who had checked he was OK was looking at one of his colleagues. This was clearly unexpected.

The conversation in the cabin was louder now, but the engines were quieter. Above both noises came the distant sound of sirens, growing nearer. The man in the back row looked left, across his two neighbours, and out of the window. He saw two police cars, an ambulance and an unmarked white van screaming across the airfield.

'Ladies and gentlemen.' The captain's voice was not panicked, but he was clearly being very careful to sound calm. 'There's nothing to worry about, just a minor technical issue . . .'

But the passengers weren't fooled. They too had seen the emergency vehicles. And as the aircraft ground to a complete halt, they saw the flak-jacketed, armed police burst out of the unmarked white van. Someone screamed. At least half the passengers ripped off their seatbelts and got to their feet.

The captain's voice came over the Tannoy again: 'Cabin crew, engage the emergency chutes. Ladies and gentlemen, please stand clear of the aisle to allow . . .'

Nobody was listening. Passengers were already rushing towards the emergency exits, even though they hadn't been opened yet. From the rear of the plane two members of the cabin crew tried to push themselves down towards the centre, passing the sweating Middle Eastern man and his two neighbours, who had got to their feet and were trying to squeeze past him. The man angled his legs to the right, allowing them into the aisle to follow in the wake of the cabin crew.

And only then, as the other passengers scrambled for the exits, and the blue neon of the emergency vehicles flashed in through the windows of the aircraft, did the man remove his mobile phone from his pocket. His hands were shaking, his brow a sea of sweat. He felt detached from the noise and hysteria of the rest of the cabin as the emergency chutes opened. He felt at peace. He looked over his right shoulder. From here he could see, in the cabin crew's service area, the metal food trolley. It was no more than three metres away.

He switched on the phone. It took thirty seconds to power up.

Half the passengers had alighted now. The man could hear harsh voices shouting instructions somewhere outside and although he could not make out what they were saying, he knew he didn't have much time.

The cabin was almost empty now. The harsh voices grew

more distinct. He could understand them: 'Get away from the aircraft! *Get away from the aircraft!*'

He activated Bluetooth. The phone started to search for nearby devices.

He was muttering again. This time his words were not silent, but formed the dull drone of a whispered prayer. The harsh voices were closer. They were in the cabin and were shouting not at the passengers who had, he estimated, all disembarked, but at each other: 'Rows A to F, clear! Rows M to S, clear!'

His prayer continued. Still seated, he couldn't see the new-comers, but he could sense one of them drawing closer. They would shoot him on sight, of course. Sweat trickled down the back of his neck as he stared at his phone.

New device found.

He sensed the approaching man stop. How far away was he? Five metres? A little more?

Device connected.

Had the newcomer seen the man still sitting in his seat? Had he worked out something was wrong?

He had only to press a button now, and his phone would detonate the Semtex stashed in the meals on the food trolley.

Then the man heard the newcomer's voice. '*Evacuate the air-craft! Evacuate! Now!*'

The time had come. He would take at least one person with him.

He closed his eyes, raised his face to heaven, and pressed the button on his phone.

Mason Delaney prided himself on his ability to read a man's face. But he didn't need much skill to realize that something was going wrong. One look at General Sagan's expression was enough for that. The man's leathery skin had turned several shades paler; his brow was furrowed.

'What is it, Herb?' Delaney asked quietly. And then: '*What is it?*'

'I'm getting word from Tampa,' Sagan breathed.

Delaney closed his eyes. 'What?'

'They've located the bottles.'

Delaney could feel his fat neck pressing against his tight collar. 'And?'

But Sagan was holding up one finger, listening intently to his headset. 'Boston, Orlando, Cincinnati, Philly . . . same goddamn story.'

Suddenly Delaney was on his feet, clutching the edge of the table. His mouth hardly moved as he spoke. 'What story, Herb?'

The general stared at him. 'They've isolated all the passengers, they've located the bottles and they've done preliminary tests on the contents.' He blinked. 'Shampoo,' he said. 'They all contain shampoo.'

Delaney felt as if the blood was draining from his veins.

'What do you mean?'

'What the hell do you think I mean, Mason? Goddamn it, I thought you said your information was—'

But at that moment the door swung open. Scott Stroman appeared. He was out of breath and his eyes were slightly wild. He looked awkwardly over at Sagan, then at his boss. 'Sir, we've just had word from the Federal Aviation Administration.'

'What? *What?*'

'All US and UK flights grounded, sir. There's been an explosion at Heathrow, but the British were pre-warned.' He looked over at Sagan again, before taking another deep breath. 'They were also pre-warned about five strikes on US soil, sir.'

Delaney fell back into his seat. A chill wind was blowing through the room. 'They had the same information as us?'

But Stroman was shaking his head. 'We've been misled, sir. The explosives . . .'

'Where?' Delaney whispered.

'Semtex, sir. In the in-flight meals.'

Sagan was looking between them, his expression somewhere

344

between confusion and suspicion. 'What the hell's going on, Mason?' he demanded, a dangerous edge to his voice.

But Delaney didn't answer. Not immediately. For a full ten seconds he sat stunned.

Then he stood up and walked over to Stroman. When he finally spoke, it was in a low hiss that only his white-faced assistant could hear.

'Find him,' he said.

'Sir?' Stroman asked.

'Find Ashkani! Now!'

TWENTY-THREE

Mahmood Ashkani was staring at the sky, awaiting the moment when Flight BA729 from London to Dublin entered his line of sight.

His laptop was open on the car seat beside him, its sat-phone connection to the internet established. He had chosen his viewing point with precision. At 1013 hours the British Airways flight would be in this airspace. And at that moment he would see it fall from the heavens. Only when he had verified, with his own eyes, that the strike had been successful, would he upload the footage to YouTube. No doubt it would be taken down within minutes, but that would be ample time for bin Laden's taunt to go viral across the world.

Eight minutes past ten. He thought of Delaney. His handler, the man he had been playing like a finely tuned instrument, would know by now that something was wrong. And when the planes started dropping from American airspace as well as British, he would finally understand the extent of Ashkani's deception. He wished he could see Delaney's pasty face when he realized what he'd done.

Eleven minutes past. He thought of Joe Mansfield. He thought of how desperate Delaney had been to eliminate him and how much effort he, Ashkani, had put into the job. Mansfield could have ruined everything.

Twelve minutes past.

The sky overhead was clear. He took a pair of wire-rimmed spectacles from his jacket and put them on.

Thirteen minutes past. There was nothing in the sky except a flock of seagulls heading for the coast.

Ashkani breathed deeply, trying to keep a lid on his sudden unease. Perhaps there had been a delay.

Two minutes went by. Three. The sky remained empty of aircraft.

Ashkani glanced down at his laptop. It was all ready. He simply needed to press a button. But he could not do it. Not until he was sure . . .

He opened a new Firefox window and, typing meticulously with his two forefingers, navigated to Heathrow's departures page. And as his eyes fell upon the list of flights, his slow, careful breathing suddenly became irregular. Each flight on the page was followed by a single word.

'Cancelled'.

Ashkani stared at the page, and back at the sky. Then, in a sudden burst of anger, he ripped the phone from the laptop and hurled it to the floor by the empty seat. He stared at himself in the rear-view mirror for thirty seconds, his mind full of the explosions he could not see, trying to straighten his head and formulate a new strategy.

He was exposed. His cover was blown. By now Delaney would know that he had been double-crossing him, and Ashkani had nothing to show for it. But that didn't change what he had to do right now: disappear. Quickly. Completely.

But first he had to cover his tracks. His mind wandered. He saw an isolated house and the dead body of an old woman at the bottom of the stairs. He saw a room filled with incriminating evidence.

He started the engine, performed a three-point turn, and began driving back the way he had come.

Both Eva's body and mind were numb.

She had watched the clock tick relentlessly past ten.

Ten past.

Twenty past.

She couldn't move. She could barely think. Her gunshot wound was terrible, but the state of her head, filled with images of burning aircraft and screaming children, was worse. She had no other thoughts.

Her body temperature dropped. Coloured blotches appeared in front of her eyes. She was vaguely aware of the clock. Ten twenty-eight.

Conor.

The thought was like a shot of adrenalin. She had forgotten him. Eva shook her head clear of the mist that was clouding her thoughts, and winced as a burning sensation shot through her trunk. Her breath had caused condensation on the inside of the windscreen and to lean forward and wipe it off with her sleeve was so painful that she gasped.

And she gasped a second time when she saw a grey Peugeot speed by in the opposite direction. The car passed in a flash. But she'd had enough time to see the face of the man at the wheel: the hooked nose, the dark skin and hair, even the slight hunch in his shoulders.

The same man she had seen just days before in Barfield, and whose photograph had since stared out of computer screens and been burned into her brain.

But he was dead. Joe had shot him. *Hadn't he?*

Within seconds Eva was swinging the Range Rover round, ignoring the stress the movement placed on her side. Ahead there was a bend to the right, and the Peugeot was out of view. She stamped on the accelerator and the car screamed through the automatic gears as she gripped the steering wheel and peered through the windscreen still half obscured by moisture.

Three minutes later she was speeding past the car park where they had stopped the previous night and surging over the brow of the hill. The sea appeared, about two kilometres in the distance, and between the top of the hill and the coast, about 250 metres inland, was the solitary house. Eva didn't slow down. As the vehicle jolted over the hill she felt another hot jab of pain in her side, but she also saw, maybe a mile along the road that snaked out ahead, the Peugeot. It had taken a left at a fork in the road. There was no doubt about it: it was heading for the house.

Eva trod down hard, her face set in an expression of fierce concentration. A minute or two later the house was just thirty metres ahead. She barely slowed down as she entered the driveway, and came to a noisy, skidding halt a car's length from the front door.

Silence.

The Peugeot was parked five metres to her right, at an angle that suggested its driver had also come to an abrupt stop. Sweating now, Eva fumbled for the handgun Joe had left her with, quietly opened the door and stepped outside.

There was no sign of Ashkani. She found herself gripping the weapon hard, resting it on her left forearm, which was raised in front of her. She felt faint, and worried that she would pass out any moment. She couldn't prevent her footsteps crunching a little on the gravel as she covered the three metres to the door. It was ajar – just an inch – so she prodded it gently with her right foot, keeping her weapon raised.

The entrance hall was murky and quiet. No sign of anyone. It looked just as it had when she had left. She listened hard – no sound – and as she stepped inside she quickly checked left and right that there was nobody waiting to jump her.

Nothing.

Lightly pushing the door shut behind her, she crept across the hallway to the bottom of the stairs. Her weapon was pointing upwards now. The door of the bedroom where she had left Conor was wide open. Was that how she'd left it? She couldn't remember.

The treads creaked as she ascended – each pace sent a tremor through her. By the time she reached the top of the stairs she was gulping for air.

She paused, gritting her teeth. Then she inhaled deeply several times and lunged into the room.

It was empty.

'Oh my God,' she breathed. '*Conor . . .*'

She limped across the room to the bed where he had been lying. The indentation of his little body was still there, and the coat that had covered him was lying over the open box in which she had found the airline meal tray. But there was no sign of Conor.

She turned.

Otherwise the room was just as she had left it: full of boxes, the books still lying on the floor. She blinked. There was something on the table that hadn't been there before. She took a step towards it; her eyes lingered on a plain black laptop and, lying squared up on top of it, a small, leather-bound book. On the cover it said: 'Holy Koran'.

A sound from the corner of the room sent a jolt through her veins. Instinctively she pointed her gun at the wardrobe. It was open just a fraction. Hadn't it been open wide when she left?

She edged round the table, her weapon still primed, and, treading lightly, covered the three metres between herself and the cupboard. Taking a deep, slow breath, she eased the wardrobe door open with the gun barrel.

Pale, frightened eyes looked up at her.

Conor was crouched in one corner, his knees pulled up to his chest.

There was a mirror on the inside of the wardrobe door. Eva caught a glimpse of her face. It was corpse-white. She tried to smile at the little boy; to pretend that she was not as scared as him. She held out her free hand and took one of his. It felt surprisingly warm.

'Let's go, sweetheart,' she breathed. 'Don't be scared . . . let's go.'

Conor climbed out of the wardrobe, his little hand clutching Eva's. The timber frame groaned, but then all was silent as he stood next to her and looked up for reassurance. Eva gave him another weak smile, then led him to the bedroom door.

She stopped and listened.

Silence.

They couldn't walk down the stairs two abreast, because the stairlift took up too much space. Eva went first, walking down into the dim hallway, her right hand in front of her clutching the gun, her left hand behind holding Conor's. The stairs creaked, but once they reached the bottom, everything was deathly quiet once again.

Eva bent down so that her lips were inches from Conor's ear. 'My car's out the front, sweetheart,' she said. 'It's the black one. As soon as we're outside, we'll run straight for it. Do you understand?'

Conor was staring at the door.

'Do you understand, Conor?'

He nodded.

Eva straightened up and they started to cross the hallway.

A noise behind them. Eva spun round and peered through the gloom.

Nothing.

She could feel Conor squeezing her hand a little harder as they covered the remaining three or four metres to the door.

'Ready?' she mouthed silently.

Conor nodded.

She opened the door.

And screamed.

He was there. Standing in the doorway, his shoulders bent, his head slightly bowed, strands of black hair straggling over his menacing eyes. Ashkani moved with sickening speed, grabbing her wrist and slamming it against the frame with such force that the gun flew from her grasp as she pushed Conor back towards the stairs.

He let go of her wrist and quickly bent down to pick up the

weapon. Eva seized her chance to run. Conor was already racing back up the stairs. Eva limped after him, arriving at the bottom step just as Conor reached the top and disappeared into the bedroom again.

She didn't have to look over her shoulder to see Ashkani coming after her. She could sense his approach and expected any moment to either hear gunfire or feel the chill of a hand on her shoulder. Pounding up the stairs, she ignored the stabs of agony that streaked through her side, and tried not to let the sound of his footsteps behind her freeze her muscles into inaction.

At the top of the stairs she glanced back. He was just five steps behind her, and he was smiling. Eva hurled herself into the bedroom and slammed the door shut. Her shaking fingers felt for the key in the lock; just as she attempted to turn it, she saw the doorknob twist. She threw herself against the thick wooden door and wrenched the key to lock it.

Conor was back on the bed, huddled up against the window. Eva limped to the nearest cardboard box and dragged it with difficulty against the door, not sure that it would make any difference.

A sudden thump felt like it went right through her. The door rattled. She froze.

Another thump. The door rattled again.

And a third.

As she ran to get another cardboard box she flinched at the sound of a fourth strike against the door. She dragged the box up against the first, then stood back.

The thumping had stopped. She felt a moment of relief that quickly morphed into more panic. She could hear footsteps descending the stairs. Staring at the door, ice in her veins, she tried to work out what exactly Ashkani was doing.

He was prepared. A safe house wasn't safe unless, when you left it, you could easily remove all traces of your existence.

Having descended the stairs two steps at a time, he hurried through the kitchen at the rear of the house and out the back door. Mrs Jones's garden, which faced the sea, was neglected. On occasion he had tended it as part of his strategy to keep the foolish old woman compliant, but over the months that he had used this house as a base, he'd also been careful to take advantage of the prefab concrete garage at the side. How well he knew from Mrs Jones that 'her' Gethin had erected this ugly thing with his bare hands, and one look inside was enough to confirm that the old woman had barely ventured into it in the years since her husband's death. It was thick with dust and spiders' webs; most of the floorspace was taken up by an ancient green Morris Minor with flat tyres, and along the far wall were four large, red metal cans. He seized one and shook it. It gave off the thick, greasy stench of petrol.

The cans were all full, and with some difficulty he carried two at once. He went back into the house with them, leaving one in the hallway and taking the second through to the front room where Mrs Jones's body lay mouldering. He undid the cap and sprinkled the petrol first over her body, then over the sofa and surrounding carpet, before heading to the tall windows and dousing the base of the curtains and the carpet beneath them. Back in the hallway, he looked up: the door upstairs was still shut. Having seen the terror on that woman's face, he knew it would remain shut. Smiling to himself, he carried the second can halfway up the stairs, opened it and allowed the petrol to gush over the threadbare carpet and trickle down into the hallway.

Having brought in the third and fourth cans, he placed them in the middle of the hallway, uncapped them both and knocked them over in the direction of the stairs. Petrol coughed out, and the floor in the hallway became a puddle. Ashkani returned to the fuel-sodden front room, taking care not to tread in the soaked areas. Mrs Jones's electric heater sat in the fireplace. He unplugged it and carried it back into the hallway.

He looked up again. Still no sound from the bedroom. The woman and child clearly had no idea what was about to happen.

By the front door there was an old, yellowed double wall socket. Ashkani plugged in the electric heater and ensured that both bars were on. They soon turned orange. He stepped swiftly outside. It would not take more than thirty seconds, he figured, for the petrol fumes to ignite. Hurrying to the Peugeot, he climbed in and started the engine.

Ashkani was five metres from the road when the explosion happened. It was loud and brutal enough to give the car a jolt as it moved away; he looked in the mirror just in time to see a flash of orange and black from the doorway he had purposefully left open to ensure a flow of oxygen.

By the time he was ten seconds away from the house, he could see smoke billowing from the windows; from the brow of the hill two kilometres away, he could still make out flickers of orange as flames licked up the building's exterior.

And as the house disappeared from view, he found himself thinking deeply – so deeply that he failed to notice, high above him, a black Agusta, flying in the opposite direction, towards the coast.

He was thinking not of the woman and child who were even now suffocating and burning to death; nor even of how his plan had been frustrated; but of the Lion. The Director. The Sheikh al-Mujahid. He was thinking about a thin old man who had once been great, no doubt, but whose time was over and whose head had been filled with incorrect intelligence the better to confound the Americans.

The Americans.

He thought of Delaney, and wondered just what his people would be doing with bin Laden right now.

* * *

354

'There!' Joe bellowed. '*There!*'

'Roger that.' The pilot's voice was unflappable. But the sight of smoke billowing from the isolated house was like a knife in Joe's guts. '*Get down there!*'

The armed unit that had apprehended him at Bristol Airport could not have looked less sure of themselves. Twenty minutes ago this man had been public enemy number one. A communication from GCHQ and another from MI5 and their instructions had been turned on their head: take him where he tells you. He'd roared a grid reference number at the pilot, who had immediately diverted the Agusta and headed north-west.

The chopper started to lose height and, now that they were no more than twenty metres above ground, the extent of the inferno became clearer. The house and gardens were covered in a shimmering heat haze and shrouded in black smoke. Joe scanned the surrounding area, desperately looking for the figures of a woman and a young boy, but he saw nothing. And the sight of the black Range Rover, parked in front of the house, was enough to make dread seep into his marrow.

Thirty metres east of the house, they touched down. The chopper had barely hit the grass before Joe jumped out and, hunched against the downdraft, raced towards it. The front of the house was engulfed in flames – the front door had fallen forward and flames were licking around the frame. It looked like the entrance to hell. The crackling of the fire was deafening and the heat was immense – by the time he was ten metres away he had to place one hand in front of his face to protect it. He could hear voices behind him – 'Get back from the house . . . it's not safe!' – but he ignored them and skirted round to the left side, looking up to find the window of the bedroom where he'd left Conor and Eva. It was open, but the interior was obscured by a film of smoke.

The heat was not quite so intense here as it was at the front of the house. He managed to get within five metres of the wall, then screamed at the top of his voice: '*The window! Get to the window!*'

He saw nothing but smoke wafting from the opening.

'*Conor! Eva! It's me!*'

Panic surged through him. He couldn't bear it . . . he couldn't bear to lose them . . .

'*The window!*' he shouted. '*Get to the—*'

He stopped.

The outline of a child's face appeared in the smoke.

'*Conor, I'm here!*' Joe roared. '*Jump – I'll catch you. Don't be scared, champ, I'm here!*'

There was a devastating crash from somewhere inside the house. The sound impacted through Joe like a bullet. He looked over his shoulder. Three members of the armed unit had joined him, but they were standing a good ten metres further back. Joe looked up to the window again. 'Conor!' he screamed. '*Conor!*'

But the boy wasn't there. The face had disappeared.

Smoke billowed into the bedroom through the gap between the door and its frame. It hurt Conor's eyes and made it difficult to breathe. The nice lady had moved the boxes away and stuffed clothes from the wardrobe along the bottom, where the gap was largest, but it was seeping through the material and filling the room. She was on her knees by the bed, bent double and coughing her guts out. Together they had tried to fold the mattress in half and squeeze it through the window to give them something to jump onto, but she was in pain and it was too heavy for them. He had tried to get her to the window, where she could breathe more easily, but she couldn't move and he couldn't lift her.

Conor coughed. It hurt, and it felt like he was choking and unable to breathe as his throat and mouth filled with warm phlegm. But he struggled into the centre of the room, where the smoke was thickest. Because the laptop was there, and the black book he had seen the man use. They were important. His dad would need them.

After everything that had happened, he wanted his dad to be pleased with him.

Carrying the two items, he clambered over the bed towards the window. He was still coughing and retching, but he could hardly hear the sound he was making because the fire in the rest of the house was so fierce.

Conor could hear his dad shouting. There was no way he could shout back – his throat and eyes were too full of smoke – so he didn't even try. He just balanced the contents of his arms on the window ledge, then pushed them over, as if he was posting a letter.

'Conor – jump!'

Conor knew his dad would catch him if he did. But he didn't want to leave the nice lady here. He didn't know who she was, but she had come back to help him and he wanted to help her too. That was what his mum would have expected, and his dad. He retreated back into the room, feeling his way to the end of the bed and down onto the floor where she had collapsed and was now choking. He pulled at her arm and tried to say, 'Come on,' but he just started coughing even more. Maybe if he pulled his T-shirt over his nose, he thought, that would help. As he did so, he gulped down a mouthful of air that was slightly less thick with smoke. The coughing eased for a moment.

'Dad's here!' His mouth formed the words, but no sound came from his dry throat. 'He says we should jump!'

The lady didn't move. Not at first. But Conor continued to tug her arm, and after ten seconds she rose from her crouching position. She turned, and peered through the smoke at him. Her face was black, with wet streaks around her eyes, beneath her nose and around her mouth.

'Dad's here!' He tried to say it again. He was kneeling now.

The lady's eyes lingered on his lips and he thought that perhaps what he'd said had made her feel a bit better.

That look didn't last long.

The sudden creaking sound was louder even than the roar of the flames. Conor had seen a programme on TV once all about earthquakes and how they could make whole houses move and tumble into rubble. It was like that now. The floor suddenly seemed to slant. At the far side of the room a gap appeared between the wall and the floor. Beyond it he could see flames.

The lady grabbed hold of him. Together they tried to push themselves to their feet. But there was another great creaking, cracking sound as the floor gave way. The two of them collapsed with it, holding each other tight as they fell into a cloud of smoke, dust and flames.

Joe's throat was raw from shouting. He had heard the noise, and now he saw an ominous crack along the exterior wall, at the height of the first floor and extending along its entire width. It could only have been caused by a collapse of the ceiling joists.

The laptop was on the ground in front of him, broken and smashed. Next to it, a leather-bound book, face down and open, its pages crumpled. Joe grabbed them and ran round to the front of the house, where he dropped them again. He could hear the scream of fire engines not far off, but he knew he couldn't wait for them, and he ignored the shouts from the ARU.

He was five metres from the main door and the heat was almost unbearable. But he didn't stop. With his head bowed and his right forearm covering his eyes, he strode forward, vaguely aware that someone had tried to pull him back – he'd shrugged them off without even looking back.

Joe burst through the burning doorframe and into the oven of a house.

He crouched low, almost crawling, because he knew that the floor of a burning building could be at least 100 degrees less hot than the ceiling, and the toxic CO_2 levels much lower. The closer he kept to the floor, the longer he had. Even so, the heat was overpowering. It hurt just to breathe – like pumping fire into his nostrils – and it was all he could do to keep his eyes open. The staircase had completely collapsed and there was a great hole in the ceiling that seemed to be dripping flames. The wall two metres to his left was a crumbled mound of smouldering rubble; he could see through it to what remained of the bedroom on the first floor – the burning wardrobe, boxes ablaze. But a section of the floor had collapsed into the room below, and it was here that he saw the sight that ripped his heart out.

He could see a mattress, seven metres away to his left, upended against the exterior wall and burning; smouldering cardboard boxes that had also fallen through the floor were bursting into flame. And he could see, through the poisonous smoke, a small boy lying on the ground. To Conor's right, through a screen of flames, a second figure was pushing itself up to its knees.

Joe didn't have time to think, only to force himself further into the oven, through the smoke towards his son. He wanted to crawl more quickly, but the hot air pushed him back. His clothes, his hair, everything scalded, as though he too would ignite any moment. He shouted his boy's name, but the shout was only in his head because his lips were clamped shut.

It took ten seconds to reach him; ten seconds that felt like an hour. Conor's eyes were open and he was coughing. He was alive, so Joe turned to Eva.

They had not fallen in the same place. She was five metres away, but it might as well have been five miles. Two burning rafters had fallen in front of her and the wall of flame that burst from them had closed her into a corner. She was kneeling, and Joe could see her face through the flames and the heat haze. Half her hair had already been singed away, revealing her scalp; what remained had curled with the heat. The skin on her face and neck was blistering. She clearly wanted to break through the flames, but the heat was holding her back.

Half of Joe wanted to run – not for himself, but to get Conor out of there. The other half told him he couldn't. Eva needed him. If he could just break through that barrier of flame, grab her and pull her back. He had to try – she would die if he didn't.

Joe was steeling himself to burst through the wall of flame when he saw her lips move. No sound came from them, and he wouldn't have heard anything over the roar of the blaze even if it had. But he could understand the exaggerated form of her mouth, carefully shaping two single words, her lips continuing to blister gruesomely even as she did so.

'*Ashkani*,' she mouthed. '*Alive*.'

A great groan from the old house told him another section of ceiling was falling. Burning timber thundered down on Eva. Joe roared her name, but even as he did so he had to fall back to protect himself and Conor from the collapsing building. He caught a glimpse of a solid wooden joist cracking against Eva's head and her body bursting into flames as she dropped. He shouted again, and tried to step forward, but it was useless. He knew he couldn't save her. He could only save his son.

Joe was still shouting as he ran from the inferno – ten metres, fifteen metres – before falling to the ground, exhausted, with Conor. He was aware of fire engines and neon; of men barking instructions and a bustle of activity; of Conor, groaning weakly on the ground next to him.

Ricky. Caitlin. And now Eva.

Joe barely realized he was curled on the ground. He didn't notice four members of the ARU, their expressions full of shock at the insane howling of this grizzled, battered figure. They approached him with care, preparing to secure him if necessary. He did not notice how Conor, alive against the odds, pushed himself feebly to his feet and, unnoticed by the men going about their emergency work, staggered to where a damaged laptop and a leather-bound book were lying on the grass. He did not notice how the roof of the house suddenly caved in, thrusting smoke and rubble ten metres up into the air and all around.

The only fire he was aware of now was the fire in his soul. A furnace of hatred, fuelled by images of the dead, and by two words.

'*Ashkani. Alive.*'

TWENTY-FOUR

London. The following day, 1100 hours GMT.

It was most unusual for Mason Delaney not to have slept on a transatlantic flight. But these were most unusual times. His bow tie was not tied with quite its regular precision, and a smear on his horn-rimmed glasses went unwiped. He sat in the rear seat of a black Daimler that swept away from Terminal 5. The windows were dark and a glass screen separated the front of the vehicle from the back. Delaney's chauffeur glanced repeatedly in the rear-view mirror, but he was sufficiently discreet not to speak into the intercom.

They had just slipped onto the A4 when Delaney's phone rang. He answered it immediately.

'It's me, sir. Scott.'

Delaney didn't reply. His eyes did not light up as they normally did when he heard the voice of his young assistant. He looked out of his window. It was raining as if there was no air outside, just pounding sheets of water. A black London cab was overtaking them. Beyond that, an enormous airport hotel slid past.

'Something's come up, sir.'

'It'll have to wait, Scott,' Delaney said, his voice distracted. 'I'm expected at Thames House in—'

'It's Ashkani, sir. We've heard from him.'

Silence. Delaney blinked.

'You're sure?'

'His encryption is good, sir. We've been broadcasting the access codes, just in case. He's requesting a meeting. I can have him apprehended—'

'*What?*' Delaney hissed.

'Sir?'

'You want him *talking*, you *fuckwit?*'

A pause. 'No, sir,' Stroman replied, chastened.

'Where is he?'

'West London, sir. Uh, Hounslow. He communicated a grid reference. I can send it through to your driver.'

But Delaney was only half listening. 'Send it through,' he said. He was looking out of the window again. The rain was coming down even harder. 'The soldier,' he said. 'Mansfield. You know where he is?'

'Secure hospital, sir. Our guys are working on it. Sir? *Sir?*'

Delaney had moved the handset away from his ear. Stroman's voice sounded distant. He disconnected the line, stared into the middle distance for a moment, then knocked on the glass screen.

'Mr Delaney?' the driver's voice came over the intercom.

'We're re-routing?'

'It's just coming through now, sir.'

Delaney sat back in his leather seat and did what he could to clear his mind. Perhaps, he reflected, Ashkani did not realize Delaney was on to him. He pulled his attaché case onto his lap and slipped a gloved hand inside to pull out a small, snubnose handgun, which, with half an eye on the driver, he surreptitiously placed in his coat pocket.

The rain did not let up for the whole journey. When the Daimler pulled over forty-five minutes later, its windscreen wipers were barely up to the job. Delaney removed the handkerchief from his breast pocket and wiped his misted-up window. They had parked in a small road that ran alongside a children's playground. On the other side of the playground he could just make out a bandstand and, beyond that, parkland that disappeared into the rainy haze. He squinted. The whole area was deserted, with the exception of the swings in the playground. Despite the rain, there was a boy on one of them, swinging back and forth, wrapped in a navy blue raincoat.

Back and forth.

Back and forth.

Where was Ashkani? Hiding, until Delaney showed himself?

'Umbrella, Mr Delaney, sir?'

Delaney nodded, unable to take his eyes off this child playing alone in the pouring rain. Moments later his driver had opened the passenger door and was standing holding a large black umbrella. Delaney climbed out. 'Stay in the car,' he instructed. The driver nodded and hurried back behind the wheel while Delaney crossed the twenty metres between the Daimler and the bandstand, one hand in his pocket, clutching the gun. The lower halves of his trousers were sodden by the time he reached it, and he was already shivering with the cold. Water was leaking from the bandstand's neglected roof in several places. Delaney closed the umbrella and stood at one edge, away from the leaks, his eyes still fixed on the child in the rain.

Back and forth it swung.

Back and forth.

Where was Ashkani?

Something made him turn. He looked back towards the Daimler and once more squinted through the rain. The front door was open. The driver was no longer behind the wheel. He was sprawled on the sidewalk, face down, motionless, the rain beating onto his back.

Delaney found himself holding his breath. He turned back to the child. He looked one way, then the other. The chauffeur flashed in front of his eyes, then the child. Then the chauffeur, then the child turned to look at him and . . .

He had appeared as if from nowhere, ten metres away, perhaps from some ornamental shrubs between the Daimler and the bandstand. He was a giant of a man, with broad shoulders, a hooded top and a bowed head, charging forward. Even through the rain-haze, Delaney could make out the mad fury in his eyes. Stumbling backwards in the face of that oncoming rage, it was everything Delaney could do to stop himself falling as he tried to pull the gun from his pocket.

Too late.

The sudden violence with which the man launched himself at Delaney shook him to his core. He felt like he had been hit by an unstoppable force. It threw him back three metres, to form a heap on the ground, where dirty rainwater sluiced over his glasses and down his front. Although blinded by the water, he had managed to keep hold of his umbrella, and he held this up now, point outwards, in a feeble attempt to defend himself as he meanwhile tried again to remove his weapon. The umbrella, though, was swiftly ripped from his hands; seconds later he felt it brutally whack the right side of his face. His glasses clattered away from him and he groped in the direction they'd fallen, pulling out his gun as he did so; but just then he felt that being kicked away. It rattled across the decking as his attacker lifted him by the scruff of his neck and back to his feet, then pushed him hard against the back wall of the bandstand.

A face dominated his vision, five inches away from Delaney's own. He recognized the features and they were not Ashkani's. He had seen them, barely two weeks ago, enlarged on a screen in the basement of CIA headquarters. What he didn't recognize was the mania in this man's expression. Delaney had never seen such hatred.

'You,' he whispered.

'Yeah,' said Sergeant Joe Mansfield. 'Me.'

'But you're . . . you're supposed to be in a secure hospital.'

'I guess it wasn't that secure,' Mansfield growled.

'I have backup personnel,' Delaney wheezed. 'They'll be here any—'

His feeble ploy degenerated into a howl of pain as Mansfield headbutted his nose. Delaney heard the bone crack and collapse half a second before he felt it. When Mansfield stood back again, he had Delaney's blood dripping down between his eyes, but that was nothing to the torrent that flowed from the CIA man's nostrils, over his bow tie and down the front of his shirt.

'What's your name?'

'S . . . S . . . Stroman . . .' Delaney lied, but then he shrieked again as Mansfield smashed his forehead once more against the already shattered nose, intensifying the pain. Out of the corner of his compromised vision, he was bizarrely aware of the kid still swinging in the playground, but before he knew it, he was squealing his own name: 'Delaney . . . Mason Delaney . . . *Please don't hit me again . . .*'

Another brutal shove and Delaney was back on the floor, his fierce-eyed, menacing attacker looking over him.

'Talk,' Mansfield said.

'I . . . I don't know what you want me to—'

The blow Mansfield gave Delaney's ribs cracked a few. The American wheezed and spluttered as the air, and not a little blood-flecked saliva, escaped his mouth.

The monster was kneeling now. 'Why,' he hissed, 'has your man been trying to kill me?'

'My man?'

Suddenly Mansfield was holding something in front of Delaney's face. A smoke-damaged, leather-bound book. A Koran. *Ashkani's* Koran. His cipher. '*You* sent the message to meet here?' the CIA man croaked. 'How?'

'My son.'

Delaney glanced myopically over his shoulder towards the swings where he could still see a blurred movement. 'Your man used the codes in front of my son. Bad mistake.'

Mansfield had something else in his hands now. A gun. He pressed the barrel into the soft flesh of Delaney's cheek. 'They want me for two murders, Delaney. You really think a third will make any difference?'

'The raid,' Delaney squealed. 'Abbottabad. You saw—'

'*What* did I see? Two body bags – you killed bin Laden and who else?'

'*Killed* bin Laden?' Delaney hissed. 'You've got it all wrong. Why would I want to *kill* him?' He coughed again, and more bloody spittle dribbled from the side of his mouth. 'Why would I want a bullet in the brain of the person with more information on Al-Qaeda than anyone else?'

The barrel of the gun dug deeper into his face. His eyes widened with the sudden fear that this lunatic was going to shoot him; instead, he heard him talk, under his breath, sounding as though something had just clicked. 'A decoy corpse,' Mansfield breathed. 'A lookalike. Gun wounds already inflicted. The SEALs brought it in with them, took bin Laden alive, and photographed the decoy . . .'

'Very smart,' Delaney wheezed. 'Smarter than our President, at least.'

'You removed the corpse in one bag and bin Laden, still alive, in another . . .'

Delaney, despite everything, gave a sickly little laugh.

'How many people know?'

The American tried to answer, but succumbed to another fit of coughing. His attacker kneed him in his already broken ribs. 'The SEALs,' Delaney spat. 'And a handful of people close to me.'

'And Ashkani?'

'Of course Ashkani! It was Ashkani who told us where bin Laden was in the first place.'

A pause. The monster looked like he was absorbing this information.

'Where is he now?'

'I don't know.'

His attacker didn't hesitate. In a single, swift move, he grabbed the little finger of Delaney's right hand and yanked it back so that it cracked noisily. Delaney screamed again, and the noise echoed off the roof of the bandstand.

'You've got nine fingers left before I start on the bigger bones,' Mansfield said once the shriek had withered to a whimper. 'Where's Ashkani?'

'I swear, I don't . . . You must see I thought he was here . . .'

Mansfield cracked back the ring finger as easily as flicking a light switch.

Delaney was sobbing now, trying desperately to talk, but struggling to get the words out through the pain. 'I swear . . . *I swear I don't know . . . I would tell you . . . he's been playing me all this time . . .*'

Mansfield had narrowed his eyes. 'What do you mean?'

'I thought he was my man . . . I thought he was arranging things for me . . .'

'What things?'

Delaney closed his eyes again.

'The planes,' Mansfield breathed. 'He was doing that for you?'

The American slowly shook his head.

'What the hell? Why do you want to blow up British planes?'

Delaney coughed again, and struggled to get his breath. 'Ashkani tipped me off,' he continued, even more weakly than before. 'He told me Al-Qaeda were planning a strike. Five planes in the UK, five in the US. Bin Laden's swansong. The UK planes were Ashkani's personal responsibility. He said he didn't know which US flights were to be targeted. Only bin Laden had that information . . .' The words faded away on his lips; the world seemed to spin and it was hard for him to keep his thoughts in line. After a few seconds, though, he felt Mansfield clutching a third finger and he managed to spit out some more words in a choked, throttled voice. 'I told him to go through with the UK attacks . . . and we would get the remaining intelligence from bin Laden . . .'

'Why? *Why?*'

'To keep you on side, of course. The British. To keep you in the Middle East. To make you put pressure on our administration to do the same. Americans don't have the stomach for any more body bags. But the little people . . .' he coughed again '. . . the little people don't understand how many more body bags there'll be if we *don't* have a presence there . . .'

He started to spit pathetically. The blood that was still oozing from his nose had flooded over his fat upper lip and into his mouth, sticky and metallic.

'You said Ashkani was playing you?' said Mansfield.

Delaney managed a weak nod, another almost-laugh. 'I should have guessed . . . a feeble old man sitting in a compound in Pakistan . . . Ashkani had it all set up . . . make us raid the wrong aircraft and when we were looking the other way . . .'

Everything was spinning again. He stopped talking. Mansfield had withdrawn the gun and was getting to his feet. Delaney looked up, glad that this animal, who seemed to revel in the infliction of pain, was moving away from him. He was still holding his gun, but now Delaney saw he had something else in his other hand: a digital voice recorder. There was a faint click as he switched it off.

'The CIA will claim responsibility for the death of my partner,' Mansfield said. 'You'll inform the British authorities that the raghead I did in Barfield attacked me on your orders. Fail to do that, or if anything happens to me or my son, this tape will be on every fucking website in the world. '

'Along with the sound of you coercing me,' Delaney noted.

'You think people will give a shit about that?'

Delaney didn't.

He summoned every ounce of energy he could and pushed himself up into a sitting position. Mansfield was staring at him with utter contempt, but he could deal with that. Insane though he obviously was, the son of a bitch clearly didn't intend to kill him.

It was still raining hard. The kid was still swinging. 'That boy,' Delaney spat. 'What is he? Simple?' He touched his good hand to his broken, swollen nose and winced before examining the blood on his fingertips. He peered around for his glasses, and thought he could see them at the edge of the bandstand. He started towards them, but immediately found his way blocked by a pair of large, booted feet. He looked up to see Mansfield staring at him with more loathing than he'd ever seen. The laugh that had been threatening to erupt through the pain, broke out. 'Your kid, is he retarded?'

It felt good to insult his tormentor, and as he did so, a thought struck him. Mansfield *couldn't* kill him. He needed Delaney alive, his get-out-of-jail card. The thought made him laugh even more; somehow it even took the edge off the pain in his hand, face and ribs. Carefully nursing his broken fingers, he stood up.

'You're just one of the little people, Mansfield,' he spat. 'You don't see the bigger picture . . .'

Delaney knew in an instant that he'd gone too far.

Within seconds Mansfield had thrown him off the bandstand. He landed with a brutal thump on the tarmac surrounding it, the rain hammering down on him. In a moment of panic he looked around, hoping to see someone – anyone – who might be able to help. But there was nobody. Just an unconscious driver and a small boy still swinging in the rain.

And Sergeant Joe Mansfield.

His face was contorted. His right arm – clutching the handgun – was outstretched. He was striding off the bandstand . . . towards Delaney . . . he was standing above him . . .

'You need me!' Delaney hissed. 'You'll never see the light of *fucking* day without me . . .'

Mansfield didn't even flinch.

'You won't do it,' the CIA man whispered. 'Not in front of your boy . . . How much *more* fucked-up do you want him to be?'

No movement.

'I can help you find Ashkani.'

Was there a sudden spark of interest in his eyes?

'Think of my resources . . . I can track him down in hours . . . I'll tell you where he is . . .'

Delaney was nodding enthusiastically.

But why hadn't Mansfield lowered his gun?

They stood there in the rain. From the playground, Delaney could hear the regular squeaking of the swing.

'You *need* me,' he whispered again.

'But I'm just one of the little people,' Mansfield said, and he fired.

The driver stirred. The back of his head throbbed. He was wet through.

He pushed himself groggily to his feet, trying to work out what he was doing here, a crumpled heap in the teeming rain. He saw the bandstand and the playground. The strange child was no longer swinging. Mr Delaney was no longer taking shelter.

He walked nervously in the direction of the bandstand, clutching the welt on the back of his head. Once he reached it, he stopped in the centre of the decking and spun round.

He stopped.

A figure was lying on the ground three metres away. Perfectly still.

His hand fell, and he walked on.

He stopped a metre from the body, and now his hand was over his mouth.

Mr Delaney was identifiable only by his bow tie. His face was a mess, with five very distinct bullet wounds. He was clearly freshly dead because blood was still oozing from the flesh, and the rain was washing it away to reveal the full devastation of the impact. The shattered bone. The brain matter, clearly visible through the damaged forehead.

The driver staggered backwards. And as he looked up he thought he saw something. Two figures, perhaps fifty metres away, disappearing into the rain-haze. A grey man, one arm around the shoulders of the boy from the swing.

A moment later they were gone. The driver didn't dare chase them. He ran back to his car, grabbed his phone with trembling hands, and called for help.

TWENTY-FIVE

An old, thin man shivered in the dark. He was naked, and had been for days. He did not know for sure where he was, but he assumed it must be America. Nowhere else could he be treated to such satanic torture.

He was underground. He knew that because, having arrived in this place by helicopter, he had been forced down a flight of stairs and had not ascended since. There were two rooms down here: the cell in which he now sat, with its ice-cold concrete walls and the overpowering stench of rancid, mouldering human waste from where he had been forced to defecate and urinate in one corner; and the other room, which he had learned truly to fear, and where they had taken him when he first arrived.

It looked rather like a hospital room. There was a bed in the centre with a rack of machines beside it to monitor vital signs. Steel cabinets along the walls contained an enormous variety of chemicals to be injected and implements with which to inflict pain in precise, measured quantities. They had stripped him naked the moment he arrived and strapped him to that bed. Then they had shaved him. Not just his head and beard, but also his pubic hair, the hair around his anus, the hair on his chest, his arms, his legs. He was bald and humiliated by the time they threw him in the cell. Now the hair had started to grow back, sharp and stubbly. If they needed a patch of truly bald skin for one of their tortures, it was their habit to rip the stubble away using a wax patch – the sort of thing Western whores used upon their intimate areas.

And the tortures. Such tortures.

He had thought he would think of Allah and withstand them. And at first he had. He had always known there was a possibility of such a fate awaiting him, and he was prepared for it, or so he believed. But these Americans had a gift for cruelty he could never have imagined. Now his body had been cut and punctured in a hundred places; they had injected him with compounds that set his veins on fire, and others that turned them to ice. They had driven needles into the roof of his mouth and through the centre of his joints, and cracked his bones with clinical precision. They had used electricity. They had beaten and crushed his genitals.

They had kept him awake with loud music. They had locked him in his cell for twenty hours between tortures, and then only for twenty minutes, so he never knew when it was going to come. They had shown him pictures: mutilated corpses, Western pornography, blasphemous images of the Prophet.

They had starved him, then laughingly offered him only pork to eat. They had offered him cool water when he was thirsty, only to snatch it away when it was near his lips. They had thrown him into that unclean corner of the cell where he was forced to relieve himself so that for days now his skin had been covered in stinking dried excrement and his captors were forced to approach him wearing latex gloves and surgical masks.

But worse than all this, they had kept him alive: daily antibiotic injections, a saline drip that hydrated him but did not relieve his constant thirst. The same doctor was always on hand, there to ensure that he always remained the right side of consciousness. The right side of the death he would have welcomed.

To start with, they did not even ask him any questions. He understood why. They wanted to break him first. When, eventually, they did – two days in, perhaps, maybe three – they seemed only to focus on questions to which they knew the answer. If he responded correctly, he was given a sip of water.

If incorrectly, a swift, brutal punishment. He became grateful for the former and fearful of the latter.

They tried to confuse him with their questioning, pretending he had given answers he had not given. They had burst into his cell when he was on the verge of sleep, screaming questions at him, demanding answers. They had injected him with substances that made him drowsy and confused, eager to be compliant, reluctant to fight. It was during one of these periods that a new face had appeared: the well-fed, fattened face of a man in horn-rimmed glasses and wearing a neat little bow tie. He had stood over the bed, looking down with interest as the room swam, but he had not appeared again.

He had been wrong to think he could withstand it. They had broken him completely. He had told them everything. He had given them names; described places. He could not think how they knew about the plane attacks, but he told them about those, too. His final act ruined. Anything to stop the torment.

Anything for the death these Americans were denying him. Their final act of revenge for the glorious eleventh.

The door to his cell opened. A figure stood in the doorway, silhouetted by the light behind him. The sound of the door opening always made him jump. He jumped now, then trembled even more violently as the figure stood there in silence. What fresh hell did they have for him now? They had bled him dry. He had no more to give them.

The figure spoke. 'Time for your burial at sea, you piece of shit,' he said.

Burial at sea? His English was not good, but even when he had worked out what the silhouette had said, he didn't under-stand it. *Burial at sea?*

But then his eyes widened. There was movement in the doorway. A flash of red caught his eye and he saw it was coming from some-thing the silhouette was holding. He looked down at his naked, bony chest. A tiny red dot of light flickered over his heart.

He could not smile, but that didn't mean he wasn't glad.

The three bullets, fired in quick, ruthless succession, did not kill him instantly. There was a brief moment, as he fell to his side and blood spewed from his ulcerated mouth, for him to rejoice.

He was to be welcomed into Paradise.

His struggle was complete.

Joe had crossed four borders in seventy-two hours. A cross-Channel ferry train to Marseilles and from there to Alicante. Another boat to Oran, Algeria. Only when he was in Africa, where technology was less advanced and a few banknotes could buy him his way out of any difficulty, did he feel in any way confident showing his passport at an airport. Even so, boarding a flight to Asmara International Airport in Eritrea had been tense.

Not as tense, though, as landing. If their presence had been logged, they could expect a welcoming party the moment they touched down. Joe knew this, which was why, as they flew over the parched continent, he had said everything to Conor that he wanted to say. That he was proud of him. That he was sorry. That from this moment on there wouldn't be a single day that he wasn't there for him. He hadn't told him all there was to tell – that could wait until he was old enough and well enough to understand. In any case, all that was over. At least it would be soon.

Conor hadn't responded. Not in words. He hadn't spoken since the fire. He had stared out of the aircraft window, as totally silent as he'd been since the fire. But Joe knew, by the squeeze of his son's hand, that he understood. That it was OK between them. Or as OK as it could ever be without Caitlin.

Conor was clutching his hand again now, nervously, as they queued in the bleak, sweaty terminal, the only white faces here, both of them bruised and scarred. The instant he'd walked into the building, Joe had checked for security cameras. There were none that he could see, but he kept his head bowed anyway, and pulled his son's baseball cap a little further over his eyes. They walked towards the immigration queue, ignoring the armed guards.

The queue was short, but slow. A single booth, with a dark-eyed official scrutinizing every passport thoroughly. There were only ten passengers ahead of them, but it was still fifteen minutes before he and Conor approached the booth. He handed their passports over silently, squeezing Conor's hand a little harder as he did so.

The immigration official started on the boy's passport, examining every page, looking back and forth from the document to its owner. Joe looked straight ahead, past the two guards standing five metres beyond him, AK-47s strapped to their bodies, towards the shop fifteen metres beyond them advertising duty-free goods and 'Gift Articles'.

The official spoke. 'Mr Conor?' he asked, in a dead, unenthusiastic voice. He looked at Conor, one eyebrow raised. Conor looked back.

'He won't answer you,' Joe said quietly.

The man looked unimpressed. He placed Conor's passport on the counter in front of him before turning his attention to Joe's. Opening it, he immediately found the five 100-nakfa notes Joe had slipped inside. He removed them without shame, placed them in a breast pocket of his uniform and continued examining the passport as if nothing had happened.

After thirty seconds he spoke again, his voice slow and ponderous. 'Are you coming to Eritrea on business,' he asked, 'or pleasure?'

Joe looked at him, but it was not the official's face that he saw.

He saw Caitlin, her eyes pleading in the moments before she had died.

He saw Eva and the knife twisted further. Poor Eva, who had risked everything for him and expected so little in return. He saw her sitting by him at the bandstand. Lying motionless on the beach. Staring through the fire, half her hair burned away, seconds before the flames had consumed her.

And he saw the face of a man of Middle Eastern extraction, with a hooked nose, stooped shoulders and black hair streaked with grey, responsible for the death of these two innocent women. The women that, each in a different way, Joe loved. In Joe's imagination the Middle Eastern man was struck dumb with terror as he, Joe, held a .38 snubnose to his forehead. The weapon that would kill him just as soon as Joe had tracked him down.

Joe blinked. The customs official was waiting for a reply.

'A bit of both,' he said.

GLOSSARY

AQ: Al-Qaeda

ARU: armed response unit

CO: commanding officer

DEVGRU: United States Special Warfare Development Group (SEAL Team 6)

DOD: US Department of Defense

EST: Eastern Standard Time

HE: high-explosive

HEI: high-explosive incendiary

HESCO: flat-packed containers filled with dirt or sand to create a protective barrier

ICOM: intelligence communication

IED: improvised explosive device

JPC: jumpable plate carrier

klick: kilometre

L Detachment: a territorial unit attached to 22 SAS, under the command of E Squadron

LZ: landing zone

MIT: murder investigation team

MRAP: mine-resistant ambush-protected vehicle

MRE: meal, ready to eat

OC: officer commanding

PIRA: Provisional IRA

plate hanger: armoured operations (ops) vest

PTSD: post-traumatic stress disorder

REME: Royal Electrical and Mechanical Engineers
RTU: order to return to unit
RV: rendezvous
SOCO: scene of crime officer
SOP: standard operating procedure
SUV: sport utility vehicle
UAV: unmanned aerial vehicle

For a first glimpse of the latest *Chris Ryan Extreme* book, *Night Strike*, turn the page and jump straight into the action.

ONE

His name was Hauser and he moved down the corridor as fast as his bad right leg allowed. The metal toolbox he carried was heavy and exaggerated his limp. He paused in front of the last door on the right. A yellow sign on the door read 'WARNING! AUTHORIZED PERSONNEL ONLY'. He fished a key chain from his paint-flecked trousers and skimmed through the keys until he found the right one. His hand was trembling. He looked across his right shoulder at the bank of lifts ten metres back down the corridor. Satisfied the coast was clear, he inserted the key in the lock and twisted it. There was a sequence of clicks as the pins inside jangled up and down, and then a satisfying *clack* as the lock was released.

Hauser stepped inside the room. It was a four-metre-square jungle of filing cabinets, cardboard boxes and industrial shelves with a tall, dark-panelled window overlooking the street below. Hauser hobbled over to the window. An electric pain shot up his leg with every step, like someone had taped broken glass to his shins. He stopped in front of the window and dumped a roll of black tarpaulin he'd been carrying under his left arm. Then he set the toolbox down next to the tarp and scanned the scene outside. He was on the fourth floor of an office block adjacent to the Lanesborough Hotel at Hyde Park Corner. The current tenants were some kind of marketing agency who, he knew, were badly behind with their rent. They'd have to relocate soon.

Shame. From that height Hauser had quite a view. The pavements were packed with commuters and tourists flocking in and out of Hyde Park Corner Tube station. Further in the distance lay the bleached green ribbon of the park itself.

Yep. It was quite a view. Especially if you wanted to shoot somebody.

Hauser was wearing a tearaway paper suit that had been vacuum-packed. The overalls came with a hood. He also wore a pair of surgical gloves. The suit and gloves would both prevent his DNA from contaminating the scene, as well as protecting his body from residue such as gunpowder. Now Hauser knelt down. Slowly, because any sudden movement sent fierce volts of pain up his right leg, he prised open the toolbox. It was rusty and stiff and he had to force the damn thing apart with both hands. Finally the cantilever trays separated. There were three trays on either side of the central compartment. Each one was filled with tools. Hauser ran his fingers over them. There was a rubber-headed hammer, tacks, putty, bolt cutters, a pair of suction pads, a large ring of different-sized hexagonal keys and a spirit level.

There were two more objects in the bottom of the main compartment of the toolbox. One was a diamond cutter. The other was a featureless black tube ten inches long and three and a half inches wide. Made of carbon fibre, it weighed just 300 grams, no more than a tennis racquet. Hauser removed the tube. There was a latch on the underside. Hauser flipped this and a pistol grip flipped out, transforming the tube into a short-barrelled rifle.

Hauser cocked the bolt. The whole operation had taken four seconds. Four seconds to set up a selective-fire rifle effective up to 300 metres.

Hauser set the rifle down and took the diamond cutter from the toolbox. Moving with speed now, he ran the cutter around the edges of the window until he had cut out a rectangle of glass as big as a forty-inch TV. Then he took out the suction pads and, with one in either hand, pressed them to the sides of the cut-out sheet. The glass came loose easily. Hauser laid this down on the floor with the suction pads still attached. Then he took the black tarp, hammer and tacks and pinned one end of the material to the ceiling, allowing the rest to drape down over the opening. Seen from the street below, the tarp would give the appearance of reflective glass. If anyone looked up at the window, they wouldn't see shit.

Going down on one knee, Hauser tucked the stock tight into the Y-spot where his shoulder met his chest. His index finger rested on the trigger, then he applied a little pressure. He went through the drill he had practised thousands of times before.

Breathe in. Breathe out.

Keep the target in focus.

Firm shoulder. Left hand supporting the right.

The woman in his sights meant nothing to him. She'd simply been the first person he targeted. She was sitting on a bench and eating a sandwich. The optics were so precise that Hauser could identify the brand. Pret a Manger.

He pulled the trigger.

She was eating a sandwich one second and clutching her guts the next.

The subsonic .22 long-rifle rimfire round tore a hole in her stomach big enough to accommodate your middle finger.

And he went for the stomach with the next seven targets too. Unlike head shots, gut shots didn't kill people, and Hauser had been specifically told not to kill. Only maim. He kicked out the rounds in quick succession. Two seconds between each. With each shot the muzzle *phtt-ed* and the barrel jerked.

The bodies dropped.

The crowd was confused by the first two shots. The built-in suppressor guaranteed that the shots didn't sound like the thunderous *ca-rack* of a bullet. But when the third target fell they all knew something terrifying was happening. Panic spread and everyone ran for cover.

Twenty-four seconds. That's how long it had taken Hauser to leave eight civilians sprawled on the pavement soaked in their own blood and pawing at their wounds. The victims were strangely silent. No one else dared approach them. Any sane person would wait for a clear sign that the shooting had stopped.

Hauser stepped back from the window. He was confident no one had seen him. The suppressor had phased out more than 90 per cent of the sound, making it difficult for anyone to clearly understand that they were gunshots, let alone pinpoint their origin. A breeze kicked up. The tarp fluttered. Hauser quickly folded up the weapon and stashed it in the toolbox. He removed the overalls and stuffed them into the toolbox. The overalls he would dispose of shortly, in a nearby public toilet, courtesy of a lit match and some wetted toilet paper to cover and disable the smoke detector. He left the room.

Police sirens in the distance. And now screams from the crowd, as if the sirens had given them permission.

TWO

He downed it in three long gulps that had the barmaid shaking her head and the three gnarled alcoholics at the other end of the bar nodding welcome to the newest member of their club. Joe Gardner polished off his London Pride and tipped the foamy glass at the barmaid.

'Another,' he said.

The barmaid snatched his empty glass and stood it under the pump. Golden beer flowed out of the nozzle and settled into a dark-bronze column. She cut him a thick head and dumped the glass in front of him.

'Cheers, Kate.' Gardner raised his glass in a toast but she had already turned her back. 'But you're forgetting one thing.'

Kate sighed. 'What's that?'

'Your phone number.'

'The only thing you'll get from me is a slap.' A disgusted expression was plastered over the right side of the girl's face. Gardner doubted her left side was any more pleasant. 'That's your last pint till you settle your tab.'

'Give us a break,' Gardner grunted, rooting around in his jeans pocket for imaginary change.

Then a voice to his left said, 'This one's on me.'

At the edge of his vision Gardner glimpsed a red-knuckled hand slipping the barmaid a pair of crisp twenty-quid notes. She eyed the queen's head suspiciously before accepting it.

'Thanks. This'll about cover it.'

'My pleasure,' the voice said. 'After all, we've got to look after our own.'

The voice was hoarse and the man's breath wafted across Gardner's face and violated his nostrils. It was the smoky, medicinal smell of cheap whisky.

'Didn't I see you on the telly once?'

Gardner didn't turn around.

'Yeah,' the voice went on. 'You're that bloke from the Regiment. The one who was at Parliament Square. You were the big hero of the day.'

The voice swigged his whisky. Ice clinked against the glass.

'You look like a bag of bollocks, mate,' said the voice. 'What the fuck happened?'

Gardner took a sip of his pint. Said nothing.

'No, wait. I can guess what happened. I mean, fucking look at you. You're a joke. You're a right fucking cunt.'

Gardner stood his beer on the bar. Kate was nowhere to be seen. Then he slowly turned to face his new best friend.

'That's right. A complete and utter cunt.'

He looked as ugly as he sounded. Red cheeks hung like sandbags beneath a pair of drill-hole eyes set in a head topped off with a buzzcut. He was a couple of hundred pounds or thereabouts, half of it muscle and the rest fat that had been muscle in a previous life. The glass in front of him was half-full of whisky and ice. The glazed expression in his eyes told Gardner the drink had not been the guy's first of the night, or even his tenth.

'I'm not looking for trouble,' Gardner said quietly.

'But you found it anyway. You know, there's nothing more tragic than a washed-up old Blade.' The man pulled a face at the prismatic bottom of the tumbler. 'Know what? Someone should just put you out of your fucking misery now.'

Gardner attempted to focus on the guy and saw two of him. Sixteen pints of Pride and a few shots off the top shelf will do that to a man. Rain lightly drum-tapped on the pub windows. The guy leaned in close to Gardner and whispered into his left ear.

'Me, I'm from 3 Para. Real fucking soldier. Real fucking man.' He winked at the barmaid. 'Ain't that right, Kate?' She smiled back flirtatiously. Then the guy turned back to Gardner. 'Now do me a favour and fuck off.'

A shit-eating grin was his parting gift.

Gardner swiftly drank up. Made for the door.

Outside in the deserted car park the rain was lashing down in slanted ice sheets. Gardner zipped up his nylon windcheater to insulate himself against the cold and wet. The Rose in June pub was set on the outskirts of Hereford and the low rent was probably the only reason it hadn't shut down. Gardner made his way down the backstreets, snaking towards the Regiment's headquarters. He navigated round the housing estate that used to be the site of the old Regiment camp on Stirling Lane. Now it was all council-owned. The rain picked up, spattering the empty street that edged the estate. Gardner couldn't see more than two or three metres in front of him. A ruthless wind whipped through the street and pricked his skin. Gardner closed his eyes. He heard voices, subdued beneath the bass line of the rain.

When he opened his eyes a fist was colliding with his face.

THREE

The fist struck Gardner hard and sudden, like a jet engine back-firing. He fell backwards, banging his head against the kerb. A sharp pain speared the base of his skull and it took a moment to wrench himself together. You're lying on your back. Your cheek is on fire from a fucking punch. And Para is towering over you.

Para's hands were at his side and curled into kettlebells. He hocked up phlegm and spat at Gardner. The gob arced through the rain like a discus and landed with a plop on his neck.

'Get up, prick.' Para's voice was barely audible above the hammering rain.

Gardner wiped away the spittle with the back of his hand.

'I said, get the fuck up.'

Gardner noticed two guys with Para, one at either shoulder. The guy on the left was shaven-headed with dull black eyes and the kind of hulking frame that you only get from injecting dodgy Bulgarian 'roids. He wore a grey hoodie and dark combats. Gardner noticed he was clutching a battery-operated planer. The guy on Para's right stood six-five. A reflective yellow jacket hung like a tent from his scrawny frame. He smiled and revealed a line of coffee-brown teeth. He was holding a sledgehammer. Raindrops were cascading off the tip of its black head.

'Call yourself a Blade,' Para said. 'You're just a washed-up cunt.'

Hoodie and Black Teeth laughed like Para was Ricky Gervais back when he was funny.

Gardner began scraping himself off the pavement. The rain hissed. The guys were crowding around him now. He swayed uneasily on his feet.

Black Teeth was gripping the sledgehammer with both hands. He stood with his feet apart in a golf-swing posture and raised the hammer above his right shoulder. Gardner knew he should be ducking out of the way but the booze had made him woozy. Dumbly he watched as the hammer swung down at him.

Straight into his solar plexus. Thud!

A million different pains fired in the wall of his chest. He heard something snap in there. Heard it, then felt it. His ribcage screamed. He dropped to his knees and sucked in air. The valley of his chest exploded. He looked up and saw Black Teeth standing triumphantly over him.

'What a joke,' he said.

Black Teeth went to swipe again but Hoodie came between them, wanted a piece of the action for himself. He'd fired up the planer and was aiming it at Gardner's temple. Gardner managed to climb to his knees. He didn't have the energy to stand on two feet, but he wasn't going to lie down and leave himself defenceless. First rule of combat, he reminded himself: always try to stay on your toes. The planer buzzed angrily. Gardner was alert now, his body flooded with endorphins and adrenalin. In a blur he quickly sidestepped to the left and out of the path of the planer. Momentum carried Hoodie forwards, his forearm brushing Gardner's face, the planer chopping the air.

Then Gardner unclenched his left hand and thrust the open palm into Hoodie's chest. Winded the cunt. Hoodie yelped as he dropped to the ground. The planer flew out of his hands and Gardner reached for it, but Black Teeth was on top of him and bringing the sledgehammer in a downward arc again. Gardner feinted, dropping his shoulder and leaving Black Teeth swiping at nothing. Out of the corner of his eye Gardner spied Para fishing something out of his jacket. Gardner folded his fingers in tightly and jabbed his knuckles at Black Teeth's throat. He could feel the bone denting the soft cartilage rings of the guy's trachea. The sledgehammer rang as it hit the deck.

Para had a knife in his hands now. Gardner recognized the distinctive fine tip of a Gerber Compact.

'Fuck it, you cunt,' said Para. 'Come on then.'

Para lunged at Gardner, angling the Gerber at his neck. Gardner shunted his right hand across and jerked his head in the same direction, pushing the blade away. Then he launched an uppercut at Para's face. His face was a stew of blood and bone.

Gardner moved in for the kill. He grabbed the planer and lamped it against the side of Para's face. Para groaned as he fumbled blindly for the Gerber.

Too late.

Gardner yanked Para's right arm. He pinned his right knee against the guy's elbow, trapping his forearm in place. Then he depressed the button to start the planer. The tool whirred above the incessant rain as he slid it along the surface of Para's forearm. The blade tore off strips of flesh. A pinkish–red slush spewed out of the side of the device. Gardner drove the planer further up Para's arm. His scream turned into something animal. The skin below was totally shredded, a gooey mess of veins coiled around whitish bone. It didn't look like an arm any longer. More like something a pack of Staffies had feasted on.

Pleased with his work, Gardner eased off the button and ditched the planer. It clattered to the ground, sputtered, whined and died.

The rain was now a murmur.

'My arm,' Para said. 'My fucking arm!'

'I see you again, next time it's your face.' Gardner's voice was as sharp as cut glass. 'Are we fucking clear?'

Gardner didn't wait for an answer. He gave his back to the

three fucked-up pricks and walked down the road, past the construction site. He had reached a crossroads in his life. Lately he'd been getting into a lot of scraps. And deep down he was afraid of admitting to himself that fighting was all he was good for. The problem was, he was no longer an operator. His injury had reduced him to cleaning rifles and hauling HESCO blocks around Hereford, and the suit did not fit a fucking inch.

He was a couple of hundred metres from the site when his mobile sparked up. A shitty old Nokia. Gardner could afford an iPhone 4, but only in his dreams. The number on the screen wasn't one he recognized. An 0207 number. London. He tapped the answer key.

'Is that Mr Joseph Gardner?'

The voice was female and corporate. The kind of tone that belonged in airport announcements. Pressing the phone closer to his ear, Gardner said, 'Who's this?'

'Nancy Rayner here. I'm calling from Talisman International.'

Gardner rubbed his temples, trying to clear the fog of booze behind his eyeballs. The name sounded vaguely familiar.

'The security consultancy?' the woman went on. 'You submitted a job application . . . let me see . . .' Gardner heard the shuffle of papers '. . . two weeks ago.'

Her words jolted his mind. Fucking yes. He did recall applying for a job. He also recalled thinking he had next to no hope of getting it. Talisman were one of the new boys on the security circuit. He'd not heard anything, and figured it was the same better-luck-elsewhere story.

'We'd like to invite you for an interview.'

Gardner fell silent.

'Mr Gardner?'

'Yes?'

'How does tomorrow sound? One o'clock at our offices?'

It sounded better than good. It was fucking great.

He said simply, 'OK.'

'Excellent. So we'll see you tomorrow at one.'

Click.

Gardner was left listening to dead air. Suddenly the drunken mist behind his eyes was lifting. He tucked the mobile away, dug his hands into his jacket pockets and quickened his pace.

Maybe he wouldn't be hauling gravel around Hereford for the rest of his miserable life.